# HE NEVER FORGOT

BY
ANNE FRASER

# THE LONE WOLF'S
# CRAVING

BY
TINA BECKETT

D1343926

MILLS
BOON

# MEN OF HONOUR

### Ex-army docs…finding love back home!

Gorgeous, brave and brooding, these ex-soldiers
and army medics are back on Civvy Street.
After everything they've seen, adjusting to life outside
the war zone can be just as painful as the memories.
But saving lives is what these men do best, and they
always rise to the challenge. Their hearts, however,
are on lockdown…until they meet the only women
to break past their soldier's defences…

### THE WIFE HE NEVER FORGOT
#### by Anne Fraser

### THE LONE WOLF'S CRAVING
#### by Tina Beckett

# THE WIFE
# HE NEVER FORGOT

BY
ANNE FRASER

First published in Great Britain 2013
by Mills & Boon, an imprint of Harlequin (UK) Limited.
Harlequin (UK) Limited, Eton House, 18-24 Paradise Road,
Richmond, Surrey TW9 1SR

© Anne Fraser 2013

ISBN: 978 0 263 89911 5

Harlequin (UK) policy is to use papers that are natural, renewable and recyclable products and made from wood grown in sustainable forests. The logging and manufacturing process conform to the legal environmental regulations of the country of origin.

Printed and bound in Spain
by Blackprint CPI, Barcelona

**Dear Reader**

I have long been fascinated with the role men and women (particularly women) have played in war, wondering how I would have coped with the fear and horror.

A couple of years ago I heard a doctor speaking about his time in Iraq, when he accompanied soldiers on patrol, and found his talk riveting. A few months later I watched a documentary series about the men and women who care for the wounded at Camp Bastion, the main British military base in Afghanistan. One episode in particular, in which a nurse had to accompany the doctor into a firing zone in order to rescue a badly injured man, had me thinking. What kind of men and women would risk their lives in order to save the life of another?

So when my editor asked me if I wanted to write the first book in a military duo with a fellow author, the wonderful Tina Beckett, I leaped at the chance and *Men of Honour* was born.

Dr Nick Casey is an army doctor who feels responsible for the men and women under his care. Tiggy is a nurse in Afghanistan for a short tour. When they first meet, sparks fly.

But when Nick can't stay away from Afghanistan it seems their love isn't enough to keep them together.

I hope I have successfully conveyed the reality of a medic's life in a war situation while keeping Nick and Tiggy's love story at the forefront.

I would love to know what you think. You can find me on Facebook at www.facebook.com/AnneFraserAuthor or on my blog at http://annefraserauthor.wordpress.com

Best wishes

*Anne*

**Anne Fraser** was born in Scotland, but brought up in South Africa. After she left school she returned to the birthplace of her parents, the remote Western Islands of Scotland. She left there to train as a nurse, before going on to university to study English Literature. After the birth of her first child she and her doctor husband travelled the world, working in rural Africa, Australia and Northern Canada. Anne still works in the health sector. To relax, she enjoys spending time with her family, reading, walking and travelling.

**Recent titles by Anne Fraser:**

CINDERELLA OF HARLEY STREET
HER MOTHERHOOD WISH**
THE FIREBRAND WHO UNLOCKED HIS HEART
MISTLETOE, MIDWIFE…MIRACLE BABY
DOCTOR ON THE RED CARPET
THE PLAYBOY OF HARLEY STREET
THE DOCTOR AND THE DEBUTANTE
DAREDEVIL, DOCTOR…DAD!†
MIRACLE: MARRIAGE REUNITED
SPANISH DOCTOR, PREGNANT MIDWIFE*

***The Most Precious Bundle of All*
†*St Piran's Hospital*
**The Brides of Penhally Bay*

**These books are also available in eBook format
from www.millsandboon.co.uk**

Dedication:

To my wonderful, encouraging and patient editor,
Megan Haslam

## PROLOGUE

NICK HAD BEEN leaning against the wall of their temporary shelter, checking his rifle and thinking of nothing much, when all hell broke loose.

As the part of the troop that had remained behind exploded into action, he retrieved his Kevlar helmet and peered over the wall of the sangar.

'Keep your head down, sir!' one of the men shouted as he rushed past and took up his firing position immediately in front of Nick.

Nick did as he suggested, just as a bullet whizzed over the top of his head and landed in the wall behind him in an explosion of dust.

It was supposed to be a routine patrol where his platoon would join up with the Americans to decide how far north they should go before setting up a base.

'Man down!' The anguished cry came over the radio.

Nick glanced around. They'd arrived thirty minutes ago and there had only been time to set up a small receiving space in the overhang of the rock that they were using as the temporary forward operating base.

Adrenaline tore through him. This was what he'd trained for. He had to ignore what was going on below and concentrate on any casualties.

But damn, if he needed a medevac for any of them,

it was going to be difficult. He would worry about that later. Right now he had to focus on the present.

The first casualty to be brought back to the relative safety of the sangar was the medic. Luckily, he had no more than a bullet graze to his arm and someone had already applied a temporary dressing.

'I need to get back out there, sir,' he yelled. 'It's only a graze.'

'It might be only a graze but it's going to keep you out of action for a few days,' Nick responded firmly.

Quickly he examined the wound. The bullet had passed through the flesh of the medic's upper arm. Right now there was little Nick could do except clean it again and rebandage it. When they got him back to camp he would do a more thorough job. Perhaps, with a bit of luck, they'd get out of this with only this one casualty.

But it wasn't to be. The sound of gunfire increased, as did the noise on the radio.

'Five men pinned down—Americans among them,' Captain Forsythe muttered. 'They're holing up in one of the empty houses. My men can't get to them.'

'Injuries?' Nick asked.

The captain nodded. 'At least one down. That's all I know.'

Nick risked another glance over the wall. Beneath him, about fifty metres away, was the deserted village the soldiers had been searching.

Nick picked up his bag and headed for the wall.

'Where the hell do you think you're going?' Captain Forsythe snapped.

Nick barely glanced at him. 'There's a man out there.

If he's not dead, he's badly injured. I'm a doctor—and a soldier. Where the hell do you think I'm going?'

Nick, accompanied by several of the soldiers, zigzagged his way towards the house and the wounded soldier.

He had his own rifle slung over his shoulder. As part of the platoon he was obliged to carry a weapon but was only required to use it in self-defence. Whether he would was not a question he chose to ask himself.

As bullets spat into the ground he concentrated on one thing and one thing only: getting to the injured man, hopefully in one piece.

He leapt over a low wall and into the deserted house, conscious of two of the men from his own company following close behind him while the remainder of the soldiers continued to lay down covering fire.

The casualty was an American. Not that it mattered. His job was to treat the injured regardless of nationality, and that included the enemy.

The soldier was conscious but bleeding from a nasty wound to his shoulder. As Nick set about putting up a drip he asked one of the soldiers to call for a medevac.

'You'll be lucky, sir,' Private Johnston muttered. 'Don't know how the 'copter can land with all this going on.'

'Just let them know we're going to need them whenever they can make it, Private, ' Nick said. 'Hold onto the drip for me while I dress his wound.'

A shadow fell across the door as another American appeared at the doorway.

'Have you got Brad?' he demanded. 'Is he all right?'

'For God's sake, get down!' Nick yelled. Was the American crazy?

Just then there was an explosion that robbed Nick of his breath. He was flung backwards as debris rained through the narrow doorway.

It took him a few moments to catch his breath. He was lying on his back with something heavy on top of him. He spat dust from his mouth.

'Johnston!'

'Over here, sir. I'm all right.'

'Our patient?'

'He's okay too. But don't think I can say the same about the other one.'

Nick became aware that the weight pinning him down was the young American who only seconds before had been standing at the door. His body had probably shielded him and the others.

'Help me here, Johnston.' Gently he rolled the soldier from on top of him, feeling the sticky wetness of blood. Poor sod hadn't stood a chance.

But as he sat up he became aware that the soldier was conscious.

'My leg,' he groaned.

Smoke clouded their small shelter and Nick used a torch to examine the young American. Blood was spurting from his groin, soaking into the dirt floor.

'What's your name, soldier?' he asked.

'Luke.'

'Okay, Luke. Stay still while I have a look at your leg.'

But the blood pumping from Luke's groin told Nick everything he needed to know. Shrapnel had pierced his femoral artery and the boy—because that was all he was—was bleeding to death in front of him. His

pulse was thready and his skin had taken on the damp
sheen of shock.

'Is it bad?' the wounded soldier asked.

The lad needed to be in hospital. He probably had
twenty minutes at the most.

Not long enough, then.

Damn it.

Another explosion rent the air and it sounded as if
the gunfire was getting closer.

'We need to get the hell out of here,' Johnston said.

Nick jammed his fist into the hole in the young soldier's leg. 'He can't be moved.'

'Go!' Luke's voice was faint. 'You gotta leave me.
I'm not going to make it.' Every word was coming with
increasing difficulty.

He would almost certainly bleed to death before they
got him back to the sangar and Nick couldn't leave him
here on his own—even if he knew there was almost no
chance of saving his life. Nick made up his mind.

'Johnston, get two men to take the other man back
to the sangar. Tell them to let Captain Forsythe know I
need the medevac. Now!'

'I'll stay with you.'

'No. Get the hell out of here. This man and I will
be fine.'

'But, sir!'

Nick cursed. 'That's an order, Johnston.'

The soldier hesitated. 'I'll be back for you as soon
as I can.'

As Nick turned his attention again to the wounded
American he was only dimly aware of Johnston and
another soldier taking Brad, the other casualty, from
the room.

'Get out of here,' Luke murmured. 'Save yourself. I don't want someone to die because of me.'

'I'm not going anywhere, son.' Nick cut the soldier's combat trousers away, struggling to see the wound for the blood. He did the same with his jacket and shirt. He needed to make sure Luke wasn't bleeding anywhere else. *Look beyond the obvious* was the mantra for an A and E surgeon. It was the ignored and uninvestigated that often killed.

As he worked he noted that Luke had an eagle tattooed on his right biceps. That wasn't unusual—for a soldier *not* to have a tattoo would have been noteworthy—but the soldier also had a scar that ran diagonally across his chest. This was no aftermath of surgery.

However, Nick had no time to wonder about past wounds. He inserted the venflon into a vein and, mercifully, Luke lost consciousness. Now he could get fluids into him, but he had to stop the bleeding. It was the only way to save the boy's life. Pressure wouldn't be enough. He would have to find the artery and clamp it—a procedure that was tricky enough in the luxury of a fully equipped theatre and with the help of experienced staff. But here? Almost no chance.

Nevertheless, he had to try. Even if he managed to stop him from bleeding to death, it was likely that Luke would lose his leg. But better a limb than his life.

The impact of the shrapnel had blown part of Luke's trousers into the wound, obscuring Nick's view even further. He took the clamp from his bag and took a deep breath as he tried to find the bleeder. It was almost impossible in the dim light of the house, without the blood and pieces of uniform further obscuring his view.

Working more by instinct than anything else, Nick

clamped down on what he hoped was the right place. To his relief, almost immediately the blood stopped pumping from the wound.

Nick sat back on his haunches and wiped the sweat from his eyes with the back of his sleeve.

He'd stopped the bleeding, but if there was to be a hope in hell of saving Luke's life, he needed to get him back to the hospital at the camp.

He became aware that the gunfire was more sporadic now and in the distance he could hear the powerful blades of a Chinook.

There was still a chance.

# CHAPTER ONE

*A year later*

IT WAS HOT. Forty degrees Celsius and it was only just after six in the morning. The dust was everywhere, swirling around like dirty talcum powder coating the inside of her mouth and settling on every inch of her exposed skin.

Tiggy swigged from the water in her bottle, which was already turning tepid in the heat, brushed a damp curl from her forehead and sighed. The shower she'd had ten minutes before had been a complete waste of time.

She bent her head against a sudden dust ball. Everything was the same dun colour: the tents; her uniform; the Jeeps—there were even dust-coloured tanks parked along the high walls surrounding the compound. Tiggy didn't know if that made her feel better or worse.

She must have been crazy to come. Although back in the UK they had been thoroughly briefed as to what to expect—down to practising what medical emergencies they might encounter in a mock-up of a building with soldiers acting the part of casualties—nothing had really prepared her for the reality of living in a war zone. And nothing had prepared her for the sheer terror she felt.

Coming in to land last night on the Hercules, the pilot had dimmed the cabin lights in case they attracted enemy fire. When his words had come over the intercom, Tiggy had almost lost it.

Enemy fire? She hadn't signed up for that. She'd signed up to be looking after soldiers miles away from danger in a camp protected by soldiers.

She'd squeezed her eyes shut, not even able to force them open when she'd felt someone sit next to her. She had become aware of a faint scent of citrus.

'You can open your eyes, you know.' The laughter in his voice bugged her.

She'd opened one eye and squinted. In the dim light of the cabin all she had been able to make out had been a powerful frame in uniform and the flash of even, white teeth.

Whoever it was had been studying her frankly in return.

'For all you know, I'm having a nap,' she'd said through clenched teeth.

'I've never seen anyone nap while holding on to their seat so tight their knuckles were white.'

'God!' She gave up all pretence. 'What if they hit the plane? I'm scared to death of flying as it is.'

'Hey, relax. It will be okay. The pilots have done it scores of times and no one has shot them down yet. They just say what they do to make all the newbies cra— Apologies, ma'am. To scare the newbies.'

She hadn't been sure she'd entirely believed him, but she had felt a little better.

'How much longer until we're on the ground?'

'Another twenty minutes or so.'

'Twenty bloody minutes!' she groaned.

'Why don't you tell me all about yourself? It'll help distract you.' He held out a hand. 'I'm Nick, one of the army doctors. You?'

'Tiggy. Casualty nurse.'

'Then we'll be working together,' he said with a sideways grin. 'You with anyone? Married? Engaged?'

This was not exactly the sort of route Tiggy wanted to go down. Men didn't exactly queue up at her door. Might have been something to do with the fact that her brothers appeared to think it was their duty to guard her honour as if she were some early-twentieth-century maiden, or it might—and this was more likely—have to do with the fact that she wasn't particularly pretty or vivacious.

'No. You?'

'God, no!' He laughed.

The sound of sniggering came from the seats behind them.

'Major Casey married?' A soldier leant over the top of her seat. 'You have got to be kidding. The major barely stays with a woman long enough to—'

'That's enough, Corporal.' The words were quietly spoken but stopped the soldier from finishing his sentence.

Stay with a woman long enough to what?

The plane lurched to the right and Tiggy yelped.

'You have a strong grip for such a little thing,' Nick drawled.

She hadn't realised that she'd grabbed his hand, but when she tried to pull away he curled his fingers around hers.

It was easier to leave her hand where it was. Especially when it felt so reassuring—or would have if it

weren't for the millions of little sparks, enough to ig-
nite the whole plane, shooting up the side of her arm.

Adrenaline made you over-sensitive, didn't it?

'So, tell me, what made you come out here?' Nick
asked.

Anyone would have thought they were on a day trip
to the seaside.

'Brothers. One in Engineers, the other an Apache
pilot. Thought I'd better come and check up on them.'

'I'm surprised they let you come out.'

'Let me? You mean you think I should have asked
their permission?' Actually, if they had known she was
planning to head out after them to a war zone, she had
no doubt they would have stopped her—forcibly if necessary.

They might all be adults now, but her two brothers
continued to protect their little sister as they had all
their lives. Although they liked to spoil her, there were
disadvantages to having older brothers.

'If I had a sister I wouldn't let her come out here,'
Nick continued. 'No way. Women have no place in a
war.'

Even if that was almost exactly what her family
thought, Tiggy wasn't prepared to let it pass. 'Oh, for
goodness' sake! This is the twenty-first century.'

'Doesn't matter. Women should be safe.'

'Barefoot, pregnant and in the kitchen? Please!' She
had only just got started on putting him right when the
plane lurched once more. She yelped again.

The I-told-you-so look he gave her was enough to
make her decide that even if the plane went into a spiral
she'd rather die than let him hear her scream.

Die? God, don't let her mind go there.

She took a deep breath. 'Just because I'm a little frightened of flying, it doesn't mean I shouldn't have come here.' She lifted her chin and stared at him. 'I'll be fine once we're on the ground.' At least her voice sounded reasonably steady.

He laughed. 'Good on you. Now, why don't you tell me about those brothers of yours?'

When the plane touched down with a skipping bounce, Tiggy was surprised. Despite her terror, the last twenty minutes or so had flown past. She realised that she'd told Nick about her brothers, her parents, every place her father had been posted and even the family's pet dog, Hannibal.

God, she'd been babbling so much Nick knew almost everything about her life. On the other hand, she knew nothing about him. Probably because she hadn't let him get a word in edgeways.

Her companion returned her hand—she hadn't even realised she was still holding onto it—and eased out of his seat.

He touched his cap in a mock salute. 'See you around, Lieutenant.'

Tired and disoriented, Tiggy had only a vague recollection of being shown to her quarters by a friendly nurse in army uniform who had greeted her sleepily, shown her to her bunk and then, with a yawn, excused herself with a 'Catch you at breakfast'.

Even if the bed had been comfortable, Tiggy doubted she would have slept anyway. The adrenaline that was still making her heart hammer would have kept her awake even if she'd had a feather mattress to sleep on. And as for the heat! She couldn't remember being as hot during the day as she had been last night. Plus she was sure her foot had been chomped to bits by some horrible insect through the night.

How the hell was she going to manage six weeks of this? She'd have to. She doubted if the British Army would put on a special plane to fly her back out.

She straightened the collar of her uniform and took a deep breath. *Courage, girl*, she told herself. *You can do this.*

The mess tent was a hive of activity and noise as soldiers and medics helped themselves to breakfast. Tiggy looked around, unsure of what the correct protocol was. She didn't want to make more of an idiot of herself than she'd done on the flight. She tried to swallow past the lump in her throat. She had never felt so lonely, or so out of her depth.

A familiar smell drifted on the air. Coffee! That would make it better. She'd never be able to force solid food down her constricted throat but she'd kill for a cup of coffee. Wrong choice of words. She felt the tension in her limbs ease as a bubble of nervous laughter rose to the surface.

Someone came from behind and touched her on the elbow, and Tiggy jumped.

'You look lost.' It was Sue, the nurse from last night who'd showed her to her accommodation. Sue lowered her voice 'And absolutely terrified. Don't worry, we all felt the same way when we first arrived. In a day or two everything will seem as familiar as the good old NHS.'

Tiggy managed a smile. 'I doubt that.'

'You'll see, I'm never wrong.' Sue pressed a mug of coffee into her hands. 'Get that down you. You'll feel better. If you want breakfast, help yourself from over there.' She nodded in the direction of a counter where cheerful men in army fatigues were piling plates high with what looked like a full English breakfast. 'But I'd stay away from the scrambled eggs. They're powdered. Yuck.'

Tiggy shook her head. 'I think I'll give breakfast a miss, thanks all the same.'

Sue smiled. 'Can't say I blame you. But you'll get used to the food in the same way you'll get used to everything else. Finish your coffee and I'll take you across to the hospital and show you around. We've fifteen minutes before rounds.'

Tiggy took a grateful swig of coffee and almost spat it out. It was the worst she had ever tasted. And if Sue thought the eggs were bad… She gave herself a mental shake. Where was her usual optimism? Okay, the food might be rubbish, but she was always meaning to go on a diet—so what better way to give it a kick start? And if the coffee was hot, she would get used to that too.

Her mood improved further when she saw the hospital. Divided into separate sections, it had two well-equipped theatres, a resus area as well as a couple of wards and three intensive-care beds.

Looking at the facilities, she felt reassured. She could almost forget she was in the desert on the edge of a war zone—until the low rumble of an explosion made the building shudder. When no one else even flinched, she forced herself to concentrate on what Sue was saying

'You'll have been briefed before you came out, but it's different once you actually come here. I'm a full-time army nurse and this is my third tour. Don't worry, we're perfectly safe here. The hospital has never come under attack and even if it did, we're well protected.

We nurses all take turns working between Resus, ITU and the wards. Your background is casualty, if I'm not mistaken?'

Tiggy nodded. 'Eight years in a busy city-centre A and E. I've seen most things.'

Sue smiled wryly. 'But not, I'm afraid, anything like you'll see here. And it's not just the soldiers, we get civilians too. Anyone who needs us, we patch 'em up before sending them on. The soldiers go to a military hospital in Germany or the UK; civilians we transfer to their local hospital.'

Tiggy's head was beginning to reel. Not for the first time, she wondered if she'd cope. What if one of her brothers was brought in? But then, that was why she was here. Even if, pray God, they didn't get injured, she would be able to help someone else's brother.

Sue paused in front of an open door. Inside, a group of men and women sat around joking and drinking tea and coffee.

'That's the team,' Sue said, 'a mixture of lifers, like me, and volunteers.'

Tiggy's eyes were immediately drawn to a man sitting in the centre of the group. Nick. He was laughing at something someone had said. Then he looked up and caught her eye. He pursed his lips in a soundless whistle and let his eyes roam over her body before dropping one eyelid in a wink. Whether it was the weather or something else, Tiggy felt heat race across her skin. In the dim light of the descending plane last night, she hadn't noticed just how gorgeous he was with his toffee-coloured eyes, weatherbeaten face and high sharp cheekbones.

There was something about him that was sending

warning signals to Tiggy's overheated brain. Danger and excitement radiated from him—along with a casual self-assurance, as if he was used to women gawping at him and almost expected it.

She tore her eyes away. Men like him were so out of her league. And even if he wasn't, he wasn't her type. When she fell in love it would be with a decent, steady, one-hundred-per-cent monogamous man. The only type who asked her out. Not that she had managed to fall for one of those, come to think of it.

Sue tapped her on the arm and grinned at her. 'Major Nick Casey—our very own playboy doctor.' She dropped her voice. 'Let me give you a word of warning. He eats woman like you for breakfast. If you want to survive with your heart intact, keep away from him. Trust me.' Her lips twitched. 'I've known Nick for a while and picked up the pieces of his conquests' broken hearts too often to count.' Sue's grin widened. 'Thankfully I'm married and immune to his charms.'

Nick stood and held out a chair, indicating with a tilt of his head that Tiggy should take it. Acutely conscious of his eyes on her, every step of the dozen or so required felt like a mile.

'Everyone, this is our latest, crazy volunteer, Lieutenant Tiggy Williams—otherwise known as Casualty Nurse Extraordinaire,' Sue introduced her with a flourish.

Tiggy knew she would no more get used to being called 'Lieutenant' than she would get used to the army revolver she had in her possession. It was beyond her why they had issued her with one. There wasn't the remotest chance of her ever firing it. She was more likely to shoot herself in the foot.

'Good to have you with us.' Nick grinned at her. His accent, like Sue's, was an unusual mixture of Irish and Scottish.

Her heart did a crazy pirouette and it took all her willpower not to whimper. She managed a cool smile— at least, she hoped it was a cool smile and not a grimace—in his direction before turning to hear the names of the folk with whom she'd be working closely over the coming months.

Apart from the surgeons, there were nurses, radiographers, physios and several other professionals all involved in making sure casualties had access to the best care. The names were too many for Tiggy to remember, but she felt reassured by the warmth of her colleagues' welcome.

'If you need anything, let us know,' an older nurse called Pat said. 'There's hardly any of us women so we have to stick together. Don't mind this lot, I keep them in order.'

Nick detached himself from the desk he'd been leaning on and loped towards Tiggy. Everyone was too busy catching up with one another to notice him bending his head and whispering in her ear.

'You recovered from the flight to hell yet?' His warm breath fanned her neck causing goose-bumps to spring up alarmingly all over her body. She much preferred it when he was way over on the other side of the room.

'Completely.'

'Good. You may have to go out in the 'copter sometimes, though, on a retrieval. You do know that?'

Although Tiggy had heard it might be a possibility that she'd be asked to accompany the medical emergency response team, she hoped to hell it wouldn't happen. If last night's flight had been scary, how much worse would it be going into an actual hot zone? She lifted her chin. 'If I'm needed, of course I'll go. I'm here to do my bit, the same as everyone else.'

'Good girl.' He straightened and once again Tiggy was aware of his eyes sweeping over her body.

'Hey, do you play poker?' one of the male nurses asked. 'I need someone new to take some money from. With the exception of Nick here, no one else will play with me any more.'

As everyone laughed, Nick turned towards them. 'Time for ward rounds. Let's go.'

They all started to troop away, leaving Tiggy feeling like a spare part. Nick fell back and touched her elbow. 'What's up, Red?'

If there was one thing Tiggy didn't like it was being teased about her hair. She had put up with twenty-six years of it from her brothers and she was damned if she would put up with it from him.

'The name's Tiggy,' she said through clenched teeth.

As Nick's grin widened, dimples appeared on either side of his mouth and her overactive heart skipped another beat. Why did he have to be so damned sexy?

'You'll find out everyone here has a nickname,' he drawled, and ruffled the hair on top of her head. 'Come on, follow me.'

Had he actually done that? Ruffled her hair? Like she was his kid sister?

She raised her hand to her curls in a vain attempt to restore some order. She had cut her hair into its current pixie style hoping it would make it more manageable, but the heat of the desert had its own ideas and she knew her fringe was curling.

She nibbled her lip. Why the hell was she fretting about how she looked? Just because she'd be working with a hunk it was no reason to be fretting about a curling fringe. And hunk or not, he clearly thought he was God's gift to women and, by the looks of it, probably tried it on with every new arrival. On the other hand, what did she have to worry about? Someone like him was bound to go after tall blondes with sylph-like figures—not curvy redheads with freckles.

She stared after his retreating back. Why, then, did the realisation give her no pleasure?

There were four patients between the two wards. In the first were three soldiers who, Sue explained, were in for observation and rehydration after a nasty bout of gastroenteritis. 'We don't keep the injured men here for long. We patch them up, operate if we have to, then we pack them off to the Queen Elizabeth in Birmingham as soon as they're stable. You'll find that nursing here is a mixture of frenzied activity followed by hours of boredom.'

Sue introduced her to the patients while Nick read their notes. After he'd ordered more tests he spent a few minutes chatting with them, teasing them a little for shirking. Then they moved to the next ward.

Its only occupant was a little Afghan girl with masses of dark curls and round brown eyes who was sitting up in bed looking lost and scared. Her body, from her forehead to the top of her pyjama bottoms, was covered in red angry welts and her right arm was heavily bandaged.

'This is Hadiya,' Sue said with a smile at the little girl. 'She knocked over the family's paraffin heater a few days ago and sustained severe burns to her face, neck, chest and arm. We managed to save the arm, but she's going to require extensive reconstructive surgery if she's to regain full use of it.'

Nick said something in Pashto and the little girl giggled. All at once some of the fear left her eyes and she looked up at Nick with adoration.

'The surgeons had to remove a great deal of tissue from her hand and arm,' Sue continued, 'but she needs grafts.'

'The problem is,' Nick said slowly, 'we can't do it for her. Now she's stabilised she has to go to a local hospital and it's highly unlikely she'll get the surgery she needs there.'

'Why can't we do it here?' Tiggy asked.

'Because this is a military hospital and the reality is, if we make an exception for one civilian, how do we say no to others? Our resources would soon be overwhelmed. As difficult as it is, we have to transfer noncombative cases once they have stabilised.'

'But that's not right!'

Nick raised an eyebrow. 'What would you have us do?'

'I don't know! Something.'

He eyed her thoughtfully. 'I haven't given up on her if that's what you're thinking. In the meantime, however, we have other patients to see.'

# CHAPTER TWO

HOW ANYONE COULD expect her to run around the perimeter of the camp in this heat while carrying a rucksack that weighed more than her own body weight, Tiggy couldn't imagine. It wasn't as if she was ever going to go out on patrol. That was left to the regular army doctors and the medics.

Although it was only just after six, the sun was already beating down and making her skin sizzle. She gasped for breath. If they didn't let her stop soon she was going to have a heart attack.

'Okay. Drop to the ground and give me twenty pressups,' the sadistic sergeant shouted. Twenty! She doubted she could manage more than five. If that.

She didn't so much drop to her knees as collapse in a heap.

She had just finished her fourth press-up and was lying face down with her forehead resting on her hands when someone grabbed the back of her trousers and lifted her six inches off the ground.

'I believe you have a few more to go,' a familiar voice said. She didn't have to turn her head to know it was Nick, and that he was laughing.

She tried to wriggle out of his grasp but it was no use. The grip he had on the waistband of her trousers was such that she couldn't even turn far enough to see his face. 'Let me go,' she hissed.

'The sergeant isn't going to let up until you finish.'

As she was bobbed up and down she turned her head to the side. Sure enough, everyone else had finished and were all, including the traitorous Sue, sitting back on their haunches, taking long swigs from their water bottles and watching the scene with evident glee.

'Sixteen, seventeen,' Nick called out, and to Tiggy's added chagrin he was joined by several voices.

'Eighteen!'

Was this nightmare ever going to end? She took her mind off what was happening by imagining what she would do to Nick when she got the chance. Diuretics in his coffee? No, this needed something worse.

'Nineteen! Twenty!' He let her go so unexpectedly she sprawled face down in the dust. She staggered to her feet and furiously patted the dust from her front.

Nick held out his water bottle. 'You might need a drink.'

'If you ever—and I mean ever—do that to me again,' she snarled, 'I'll...'

He folded his arms and raised an eyebrow. 'Do what?'

She drew herself up to her full height and pushed away the water bottle. She wouldn't give him the satisfaction. 'Try it again, and you'll see.' God! Was that the best she could manage?

Then, unbearably conscious of everyone's eyes on her, she stalked away with as much dignity as she could muster.

Later, after she rinsed as much of the sand from her hair as she could in the dribble that passed for a shower, she went to report for duty, pausing only to pick up a banana from the mess.

She was still livid with Nick. Okay, so she might have poured out her life story—or at least the first half of it—to him while they had been on the plane, but that was no reason for him to treat her like an annoying kid sister. Hell, she was twenty-six.

And she didn't want Nick to treat her like a kid sister.

The thought brought her up short. Damn, she was no better than the rest of Nick's admirers. But she had one card up her sleeve. At least *she* knew he couldn't be taken seriously. Her brother Charlie had been just like Nick. He too had thought he was God's gift to women, having had a seemingly endless series of short-term girlfriends until he'd met and married Alice. Her other brother, Alan, was still working his way through the female population of the UK.

To her dismay, Nick was standing outside the main tent when she arrived, almost as if he'd been waiting for her. He had a cup of coffee in his hand.

'Recovered?' he asked.

'Very amusing. You've had your fun, now why don't you go…' she waved her hands vaguely in the direction of the camp '…and do some weightlifting or something?'

Dark eyes studied her and a small smile played on his lips. 'Don't be mad,' he said softly.

'I don't get mad. I get even.'

She groaned inwardly. Couldn't she have thought of a retort that was a little less clichéd? She was becoming more inarticulate by the minute. At least it was better than blushing.

'Look,' she said, 'I know you're a major and I'm only a lieutenant, but I won't be made a fool of.'

That was better! Now she was showing some backbone.

He lost the smile, although there was still a suspicious glint in his eyes. 'You're right.' He raised his hand to his head in a mock salute. 'I apologise. Unreservedly.'

Flustered by his unexpected apology, she looked at her watch. Seven-thirty. 'Don't you have work to do?'

He tossed the dregs of his coffee onto the ground. 'Actually, I don't. I've finished rounds and it's all quiet.' He eyed her speculatively. 'Don't suppose you play poker?'

'As a matter of fact, I do. However, unlike you, *I* have work to do.' She swept past him, aware that he was following her. Every hair on her body stood to attention.

'What about tomorrow? When you're finished for the day? Come over to the bar—the NCOs', that is. It has, let's just say, a more relaxed atmosphere there.'

Why was he so interested in what she did in her spare time? Why couldn't he just leave her alone? If he wanted someone to amuse him there were bound to be plenty of others happy to fill that role. However, a plan was forming in her mind. She turned around and smiled. 'Sure. Why not? Let's say six.'

Determined never to have a repeat of the fiasco with the press-ups, Tiggy decided to run around the camp perimeter every morning before breakfast. Despite the humiliation of having hundreds of men calling out encouragement as she wheezed and puffed her way around the track, she gritted her teeth and kept telling herself that she could do it. Anything was better than yesterday's embarrassment of having Nick's hands on the waistband of her trousers when he'd helped her complete her press-ups.

But once again, damn the man, he appeared like the devil from hell beside her. He shortened his strides to keep pace with her.

'Hello, Red. Turned over a new leaf, have you?'

'If you call me Red again,' she wheezed, 'so help me, I won't be responsible for my actions.'

A slow smile crossed his face. He held up his hands with his fingers crossed. 'I promise never to call you Red again. If I do, you can have all my poker matches and that's a promise.'

She hid a smile. She hadn't known she could smile and run at the same time. He turned round so that he was running backwards. He was shirtless and his combat trousers were so low on his hips she couldn't help but notice his six-pack. She averted her eyes, pretending an interest in a passing Jeep.

'How many circuits?' he asked.

'This is my last.' She wasn't about to tell him it was also her first. One circuit was torture enough and she was determined to wait until she got to the safety of her quarters before she collapsed.

'I'm impressed.' His toffee-coloured eyes crinkled at the corners.

'Don't you have lives to save or something?' She indicated the hospital tent with her arm.

'Not right at the moment.' Even running backwards, he managed to look her up and down. 'I saw you come out for your run and the thought struck me that I might have to save yours. Looks like exercise hasn't exactly been high on your agenda until now.'

Was he implying she looked like a couch potato?

'Although you clearly do something to keep in shape,' he added.

*Oh, please.* Despite everything, the look of frank admiration in his eyes made her heart skip a beat.

*Come on, Tiggy. Get a grip. This man is out of bounds and even if he wasn't, he is so not your type.*

But it was as if her mouth had a mind of its own. 'Been watching me, huh?' A stitch had started somewhere below her ribs and the last word came out more as a cry of anguish than the casual reference she'd meant it to be. How long could one kilometre be? It could be the damned end of the world as far as she was concerned.

She gasped for air, trying to ignore the increasing pain in her side.

His eyes flickered over her and he frowned. 'You all right?'

'Never been better—or at least I will be when you leave…me…alone…' She managed another couple of strides and then had to stop. She bent over, clutching her knees, as a wave of pain slammed into her. Dear God, was she having a heart attack?

Before she knew it she was being lifted over his shoulder.

'Put me down,' she yelled into his back—a back that she couldn't help noticing, even from her upside-down position, was ridged with muscle.

'I will as soon as I find some shade. Don't you know better than to exercise in this heat? Are you crazy, woman? You should have started earlier, or there's a decent air-conditioned gym on the other side of the camp that's better suited for someone who's not used to exercise.'

There was a gym? An air-conditioned gym? Why on earth had no one told her? Why hadn't she asked?

Then she was inside her tent and he was laying her on the bed. Sue rushed over, concern furrowing her brow. 'What happened? Is she okay? Tiggy, speak to me.'

'I'm fine. Just need some water.' Sue held a bottle to her lips and she gulped thirstily.

'What have you been doing to the poor girl, Nick?' Sue demanded.

'Hey, don't blame me. I was just an innocent by-stander.'

'Come off it! You've never been innocent or a by-stander in your life!'

Nick laughed. 'Make sure she cools down before she goes on duty.' He leaned over and ruffled her hair. 'Stick to the gym in future.'

Later that afternoon, Tiggy studied the cards in her hand and suppressed a smile. Although every muscle ached, including some she hadn't known she had, her mood was improving.

She tossed a matchstick onto those already on the table. 'I'll raise you ten.'

Nick lifted an eyebrow. He counted out some match-sticks from his pile and added them to hers. They'd no casualties that day and Tiggy had spent most of her day with Hadiya, re-dressing her burns and being taught some words of Pashto by the little girl and her giggling mother. When the patients had all been seen to they'd set up a temporary poker table, at Nick's suggestion, in an empty cubicle. Some of the nurses and technicians had started off playing, too, but after two hours Nick and Tiggy were the only ones left in the game.

The rest of the team was either watching them play, flicking through magazines or answering the occasional call from the patients.

Nick wasn't to know, of course, that she played most nights with her father and her brothers whenever they were at home.

'Twenty and I'll see you.'

Nick leaned back in his chair and grinned. He placed his hand face up on the table. 'A flush! Beat that!'

Tiggy pretended to look dismayed, studying his cards as if she couldn't quite believe her bad luck. Then she allowed herself a small smile before laying hers down. 'Think my four aces beats your flush.'

Nick laughed. 'Beaten by a girl! Who would have thought? You have some poker face there, Red.'

She glared at him but before she could say anything he smiled and corrected himself. 'Apologies. Not Red, Tiggy.'

She blushed. She wished she managed her poker face as well in her private life.

At that moment the siren sounded.

'Two men down and possibly civilian injuries forty klicks away,' Sue interpreted the cackle from the radio. 'They're requesting a rapid medical response team to go in and bring them out.'

Nick had stood and was shrugging himself into his flak jacket. 'I need a nurse—any volunteers?'

'I'll go,' Tiggy said.

'No way,' Nick replied tersely. 'Anyone else?'

Irritated and relieved in equal measure, Tiggy glared at him. He didn't even seem to notice.

There was a show of hands and Nick picked an older man. 'Okay, Scotty, you're with me. The rest of you prepare to receive the casualties. I'll let you know what to expect as soon as I've made an assessment. Those who aren't needed and haven't donated recently, please give blood—just in case. Sue, turf out anyone from the wards who doesn't absolutely have to be there.' He grabbed his helmet and strode out of the room.

Instantaneously, everyone exploded into action. Sue, remembering Tiggy was there, propelled her towards the resus room. 'We need to make sure we have everything ready. At this stage we don't know what to expect or how much blood we'll need. What group are you?'

'O positive.'

'Perfect. One of the medics will get you started on a line.'

'Can't I help prepare for the casualties?'

Sue hesitated. 'We need your blood more than we need you right now. Don't worry, you'll get your fair share of action before your time here is up. In the meantime, watch and learn.'

When Sue was satisfied everything was ready for the incoming casualties, she came to check up on Tiggy.

She eyed the bag of blood. 'Another ten minutes max.'

While she'd been waiting for the bag to fill with her blood, Tiggy had been thinking about the little Afghan girl. She hoped Nick hadn't included her in his instructions to clear the ward.

'What about Hadiya?' she asked Sue. 'We're not going to discharge her too?'

Sue shook her head. 'Nick wants to keep her in for a bit.'

'But are we really going to send her away without further surgery?'

'It can't be helped.'

'Surely Nick can make an exception?'

Sue sighed. 'Believe me, if he could he would. And I haven't given up hope that he won't. If anyone can make a miracle happen, it's Nick. Now, I'd better get on. You just relax.'

Tiggy had finished giving blood, although Sue had insisted that she stay lying down afterwards. Frustrated, she watched as everyone double-checked that everything was ready. The radio crackled again and the staff paused to listen.

'We have two soldiers with shrapnel wounds. One has an injury to his left arm, the other abdominal wounds.' Nick's voice was calm over the roar of the helicopter's engines. 'ETA five minutes.'

The surgeon in charge of receiving the casualties turned to his team. 'It sounds as if we'll need both theatres. Everyone to your stations.'

Tiggy eased herself up from the gurney and grabbed a leftover biscuit from the coffee table where everyone had been sitting. Although she still wasn't hungry, she knew she had to eat something. She was damned if she was going to stand by while everyone else around her worked, and fainting wouldn't endear her to anyone. Slipping into the changing room, she found a clean pair of scrubs and changed quickly. Her throat was still dry but she knew it wasn't from dust this time.

Before she could find Sue, the doors burst open and Nick entered, along with a couple of soldiers pushing a trolley. Nick was kneeling on top of his patient, doing chest compressions.

'He stopped breathing in the 'copter, but CPR has

been given continuously. We've given him two units of red cells and two litres of colloid en route. We need to get him to Theatre stat.'

Willing hands stepped forward and rushed the patient through to Resus. Moments later, Scotty and more soldiers burst through the swing doors with the other stretcher.

'This man has shrapnel wounds to his arm,' Scotty called out. 'I've applied a temporary dressing and started a drip. Vital signs all okay.'

The injury to the second soldier's hand was such that for a moment Tiggy couldn't move.

As he too was wheeled into Resus, her training kicked in. She grabbed a pair of scissors and started cutting away the soldier's uniform, only vaguely aware of the staff crowded around the other patient, shouting orders.

Sue wheeled the portable X-ray over to Tiggy's patient. There was another flurry of activity as the soldier with the abdominal wound was taken into Theatre.

Nick crossed over to them, peeling off his gloves. Tiggy handed him a fresh pair. The soldier's vitals were getting worse. His blood pressure was dropping and his pulse becoming increasingly rapid and weak.

'We need to get his arm off. It's the only way to stop the bleeding,' the orthopaedic surgeon said, examining the wound.

'Let's try and stop the bleeding first, shall we?' Nick said quietly. 'The hand might not be salvageable, but we might be able to save his lower arm.'

'You have five minutes,' the orthopod said. 'After that, he's going to Theatre.'

They did everything they could to stop the bleeding,

pumping the soldier with blood, but when Nick, along with the other surgeon, looked at the X-ray of the soldier's injury, he sighed, his eyes bleak. 'The damage is too bad,' he said. 'You're right, Simon. Amputation is the only way to go.'

Before she could help herself, a small cry escaped from Tiggy's lips. 'Are you sure? Isn't there anything we can do?'

Nick and Sue were already preparing the casualty for Theatre. 'If there was, we would do it,' Nick said tightly.

Tiggy swallowed hard. The boy was so young. But she knew Nick was right. The X-ray was there for them all to see, and Nick had already taken a chance by not sending the lad to Theatre straight away.

Nick looked at Tiggy and if she had any doubts as to how much he'd hoped to save the soldier's arm they vanished when she saw the anguish in his eyes. 'I promised these boys we would get them home and that's what we're going to do. I'll assist, Simon.'

Moments later, the resus room was empty.

Much later, when Dave, the soldier whose arm had been amputated, was settled on the ward, Tiggy escaped outside. She tried to control the tremors that kept running through her body.

'You okay?' Nick's voice came from behind her.

'No. Yes. I will be.' She took another deep breath. 'He's so young to lose an arm.'

'He'll learn to live without it.'

She whirled around. 'How can you say that? You don't have the remotest idea what it will be like for him.'

Nick's expression didn't change. 'No, you're right. I don't. If I lost my arm or the use of any of my limbs, I don't know what I'd do. But at least he's alive. At least he won't be going home in a body bag. Not like his colleague.'

They had been unable to save the other casualty. They all felt his loss as if he'd been their brother, their husband. When Nick had told them, his expression hadn't changed, and Tiggy wondered if she'd imagined his anguish earlier.

'How can you be so...' she sought for the right word '...unaffected?'

'Because they need me to be professional. They need us *all* to be professional.' Nick's voice was flat.

Tiggy slumped against the wall and wiped a hand across her perspiring brow. He was right, of course he was. If he could have saved the soldier's arm, he would have. Wishing otherwise wouldn't help anyone, least of all Dave.

She thought about her brothers. God help them all if either didn't make it. She couldn't even begin to imagine how her own mother would react. She loved her children with a tiger-like ferocity. Without warning, tears sprang to her eyes and she blinked furiously. She just couldn't help herself. It was too awful.

'Hey, Tiggy. Don't do that. Dave will be okay.' It was the first time outside work she'd seen him look serious. 'We make it our job to get these boys back home alive, and mostly we do.' His eyes darkened. 'God, don't you think I hate not being able to send that boy home in one piece?'

'It's not just him—or the man who died. It's all of them. They're so young. And my brothers—they're out there, too.'

'There will be another team doing the same for them if they ever need help.'

Tiggy dabbed at her eyes with a tissue. 'I can't bear to think of them hurt.'

Nick reached out a hand and touched her shoulder. 'Most soldiers make it home, Tiggy,' he said. 'You have to hold on to that.'

She nodded, not trusting herself to speak.

He took her by the arm and steered her across the dusty strip of land in front of the hospital. 'Let's walk.'

'I'm not sure I can after this morning,' she said. Nevertheless, she allowed him to lead her across to the far side of the camp. A gentle breeze stirred the dust of the camp, cooling the intense night air. Above them a thousand stars studded the crystal clear sky. How could a place so beautiful hold so much heartache? When they reached a flat rock, Nick indicated with a nod of his head that they should sit. For a while they remained silent. Eventually Nick turned to her and grinned.

'So, Tiggy, the last I recall we were up to when you were thirteen. Why don't you tell me the rest?'

Later that week Tiggy was sitting outside her tent, drinking coffee with Sue. Across the camp men, most stripped to their combat trousers, were playing football or working out. Thankfully there had been no more life-threatening injuries to deal with. Dave had been transferred to the military hospital in Birmingham.

As a bare-chested soldier jogged past them, Sue grinned.

'You see? It's not all bad out here. Where else would you get the chance to ogle so many fit guys?'

'I can almost see the testosterone,' Tiggy admitted.

Her eyes drifted over to Nick, who was pulling himself up on a bar suspended between two walls. He too was stripped to his combat trousers and the muscles in his naked back bunched every time he raised himself. Some soldiers sat in a circle, counting off every time he pulled himself up.

Sue followed the line of her gaze. 'As I said, forget him. He might be a hero but he's a woman's worst nightmare. As soon as he gets the girl he's been chasing, he loses interest. There's hardly a female on the camp—or off it for that matter—who hasn't had her heart broken by him.'

'You don't have to worry on that score. Nick might be a fine doctor, but his type has never appealed to me.'

Sue groaned. 'Don't say that! If he sees you're not interested, that will only make him worse.'

'I doubt I'm any more his type than he is mine, so you can rest easy.'

Sue eyed her speculatively. 'I would say you're just his type.' She drained her coffee mug.

Something Sue had said was niggling at the back of Tiggy's mind. 'Hey, before you go, what do you mean about Nick being a hero?'

Sue hesitated before sitting back down. 'Well, I guess I should tell you, although I'm surprised you haven't heard the story already.' Sue looked across at Nick. 'It was last year. Nick was out on an op with the men. They were making sure that a deserted village wasn't being used as a base for insurgents. It was a joint op with the Americans.

'Anyway, they got to the place—they call it a sangar—where they were going to base themselves for the couple of weeks they expected the mission to last when fighting broke out. To cut a long story short, Nick left the safety of the sangar and, despite being fired on, ran to the aid of an injured man who had been dragged into one of the houses.'

'Good God!' Tiggy glanced across at Nick with new respect. So he wasn't just a playboy? Of course she already knew he was a great doctor but this latest revelation was making her assess him all over again.

Sue half smiled. 'That wasn't the end of it, though. While he was treating the American, one of his fellow soldiers came looking for him and took shrapnel to his upper thigh—straight into his femoral artery.'

Tiggy knew what that meant. The soldier wouldn't have stood a chance so far away from a proper medical facility.

'Poor sod.'

Sue rolled her empty mug between her hands. 'That's just it. He made it. And all because of Nick. Incredibly, Nick managed, while under fire and with the enemy practically at the door, to clamp off the artery. Thankfully he'd called in the medevac 'copter and God knows how but they managed to land close enough to get Nick and the injured man on board. Nick kept him alive until they made it back to camp. You can imagine how slim the soldier's chances of survival were—never mind keeping his leg—but Nick refused to give up. Somehow, he and the rest of the team were able to save the soldier's life and also salvage his leg.

'Since that day he's become a bit of a hero around here—and, believe me, there are no shortage of heroes in a place like this—as well as a talisman. The men believe that as long as Nick is with them, or as long as he's here on camp, they'll be all right. Sometimes I think they've invested him with supernatural powers.'

Perhaps that went some way to explaining Nick's arrogance, the air of total confidence surrounding him like an aura. She only hoped to hell there would be someone like him around if ever her brothers needed help.

'I had no idea,' Tiggy said softly.

'It's not something he goes around telling people.' Sue glanced at her watch. 'Time to get to bed.' When she looked back at Tiggy, her eyes were bleak. 'He might be a hero to the men but I think it's also a burden. Nick isn't a miracle-worker. He's human. I sometimes wonder if he hasn't started to believe his own legend.'

'And what's that?' Tiggy asked, rising too.

'Believing he's indestructible. And that as long as he's here, he can save everyone who has a chance.'

Tiggy's eyes strayed back to Nick. He had finished showing off and had picked up a towel and was wiping the sweat from his chest. Some six-pack, Tiggy thought distractedly. At that moment he looked up, and catching her staring at him, winked.

Tiggy blushed.

'Oh, dear,' Sue said. She picked up her mug again. 'Don't tell me I didn't warn you. See you at six.'

# CHAPTER THREE

*Nine years later*

TIGGY RAN DOWN the hospital corridor with her heart in her mouth. A woman pushing an elderly man in a wheelchair flattened herself against the wall to make room for her to pass while a doctor, talking into her mobile phone, looked at her with sympathy.

Had a corridor ever seemed so long? Would she make it in time? What if his condition had deteriorated while she'd been on her way? What if he died before she had a chance to see him? A sob caught in her throat.

She skidded to a halt in front of the triage desk. Damn, damn, damn, there was a queue. She spun around, wondering whether she should risk slipping into Resus uninvited, but just then a doctor spotted her and came over.

'Mrs Casey?' he asked. 'I'm Dr Luke Blackman. It was me who called you.' She had already guessed that as soon as he'd started to speak. She recognised his voice straight away.

Today had started like any other day. She'd been off duty when the phone had rung. At first the American accent on the other end of the line had thrown her.

Then, when the male voice had identified himself as a doctor from the Royal London, her first panicked thought had been that something had happened to Alan, who was still flying Apaches in Afghanistan. But it was Nick he was calling about. Nick had been brought into the hospital with a head wound and was asking for her.

Without waiting to hear any more, she'd dropped the phone and bolted for her car.

She searched Dr Blackman's face, trying to read his expression for clues, but his calm exterior gave nothing away. 'Why don't we go into the relatives' room? It will give us some privacy.'

She felt sick. People were usually invited into the relatives' room so they could be given bad news.

'Just tell me.' Her lips were so numb she could barely articulate the words. 'Is he dead?'

'Dead?' Dr Blackman's mouth relaxed into a smile. 'No the lieutenant colonel is very much alive. He was drifting in and out of consciousness for a while but he's going to be just fine.'

Relief buckled her knees. Still, she had to see Nick for herself.

'Take me to him,' she said.

'I think we should talk first.'

Tiggy straightened to her full five feet five. Whatever Dr Blackman had to tell her could wait. 'Please, Doctor, I need to see him. Now.'

The doctor clearly realised she was in no mood to be thwarted. 'Very well. If you'll follow me?'

Nick was lying on his bed, as still and as white as a corpse. His head was bandaged and there was a dark bruise on his left cheekbone only partly hidden by the stubble of his unshaven face.

But it was still Nick. Her husband. The man she hadn't seen for six years.

Nick's head was filled with images. Bombs were exploding, helicopter blades whirled incessantly, scattering dust everywhere. There was blood, so much blood, and soldiers and civilians running in panic. Then someone was sticking something into his arm.

Slowly the nightmare scenes began to fade and a strange sense of calm filled him as Tiggy's face appeared before him; her blue eyes were wide, her red hair a sharp contrast to the paleness of her skin. The vision shifted and he was holding her, kissing her——she was in his bed, in his arms, laughing up at him, giggling at something he'd said.

He liked it when he dreamt of her.

'I'm here, Nick,' he heard her saying in that quiet, determined way she had. 'Everything's going to be all right.' Her voice was like cool rain on a hot night. Even in his nightmares the memory of her voice, her touch, always soothed him. It was when he was awake that the memory of her tormented him.

'Can you hear me, Nick?' a different voice said. An American, by the sound of him.

'Come on, Nick. You need to open your eyes.' It was Tiggy speaking again. Much better. He far preferred her voice to the American's. But he was damned if he was going to wake up. The dream was so much better.

'Nick, for God's sake, say something!'

If he hadn't known he was dreaming, he would have sworn it was Tiggy. But that was impossible. Tiggy was lost to him. Well and truly lost, as he was damn well going to tell that nagging voice.

He shifted slightly, trying to force his limbs to move. God, his body was aching. It was as if he'd been driven over by a Humvee. But he hadn't been run over by a military vehicle or anything else. He hadn't been in Afghanistan. He'd been in London. Other fragmented memories flooded back. The last thing he remembered was that he had been walking down a street. Which one he couldn't for the life of him recall. A man had been on the ground. Someone had been kicking him. He'd moved in to stop the fight. He'd taken a blow to his stomach, but not before he'd landed one of his own. After that? Nothing. Except an exploding pain in his head.

Using every ounce of willpower he could muster, he reluctantly opened his eyes.

He had to be still dreaming. Tiggy was bending over him, her beautiful eyes awash with tears. It couldn't be her. Not after all this time, and not after what he'd put her through. He closed his eyes again. Now, if only he could get back to the dream where she was lying in his arms, laughing up at him. He didn't like Tiggy being sad.

But damn. He was awake now. He opened one eye. The image of Tiggy was still there. He closed his eyes and opened them again. No, it was no hallucination. No dream. It was her.

'What the hell are you doing here?' he growled.

Tiggy reeled as if she'd been slapped. But what had she expected? That Nick would be pleased to see her? Considering the way they'd parted, it was as likely as a snowstorm in the desert. Yet when he'd first opened his eyes she could have sworn it had been hunger—and pleasure—she'd read in their brown depths. She had been wrong.

At least he wasn't dead. In fact, as Dr Blackman had said, he was very much alive.

She looked at Dr Blackman and raised her eyebrows.

'Lieutenant Colonel—Nick—this is your wife. You were asking for her. I found her details on your records and called her.'

'Not possible. Not married.'

Tiggy's throat tightened. Now she knew he was in one piece, she felt all her old anger resurface. She turned to the bemused-looking doctor.

'I should tell you that Nick and I are separated, and have been for six years.' Six long years, where every day at first had been a fight to get through it without him. And now, just when she'd thought he was out of her head and her heart, here he was, and, even unshaven and with his bruised cheek he still made her pulse leap.

God damn it.

Nick's hand snaked out from under the sheets and grabbed Dr Blackman by the arm. 'Who the hell gave you the right to call my ex-wife?'

It was on the tip of her tongue to point out that whatever he said, or wanted to believe, she wasn't actually his *ex*-wife. Although she'd always intended to, she'd never quite got around to signing the divorce papers. And neither had he. Clearly he hadn't removed her as his next of kin either.

'You were asking for a Tiggy when you came in. It was the same name listed on your record as next of kin. Of course we contacted her,' Dr Blackman replied, looking baffled.

Tiggy couldn't blame him. His patient had been calling out for a woman who was listed as his wife, yet the patient obviously couldn't bear the sight of her.

'I don't care if her name is up somewhere in lights. Get her the hell out of here.'

Tiggy's throat tightened. 'Don't worry, Nick, you don't have to ask me twice. I'm going.'

She turned on her heel and headed for the door.

She heard Dr Blackman tell Nick he'd be back to see him shortly then the doctor was by her side.

'Mrs Casey, don't take his reaction too much to heart. The head injury is probably making him confused and irritable. I wouldn't put too much store in what he's saying now.'

She smiled tightly. 'Trust me, he's not confused. He knows exactly what he's saying. I shouldn't have come.' She glanced over towards the exit. She needed to get out of there.

'Look, I can see you're upset. Come into the staffroom. We can talk there.'

'Really, I don't think that's a good idea. Find someone else.' Her mouth twisted. 'I'm sure Nick has some woman in his life you should call. Why don't you ask him?'

'Please, Mrs Casey. It won't take long.'

Tiggy hesitated before nodding. Of course she couldn't leave. Not without knowing for certain he wasn't in any danger.

The thought almost made her laugh out loud. For years she'd been terrified something would happen to

Nick in Afghanistan, and he'd had to come back to the UK for her worst fears to come true.

'What happened?' she asked when they were both seated.

'He was brought into A and E a few hours ago. There was a bit of a...' Dr Blackman looked as if he was struggling to find the right words '...er...scuffle. At the moment my main concern is with the injury to his head. I've scheduled him for a scan.' He leaned forward, his eyes curious. 'We'll know more once we have the results of all his tests.'

'What was he doing in a fight anyway?' she asked. Nick had always been impulsive and his behaviour had become increasingly erratic towards the end of their marriage, but a fight in the street? That didn't fit with what she knew of Nick. Had he been drinking? In the past he'd hardly touched alcohol. But a person could change in six years. If she wanted any evidence of that, all she had to do was remember how much he'd changed in the three years they had been married.

Dr Blackman looked at her and smiled. 'I understand that LC Casey was breaking up a fight. Some thugs had a young man on the ground and were kicking him. LC Casey intervened.' His smile grew wider. 'He always was a hero.'

'You know Nick, Dr Blackman?'

'Please, call me Luke. Not really. We met ten years ago. I was with the forces back then. I've never forgotten him.'

She half smiled. Nick wasn't exactly forgettable. She of all people knew that.

Luke's pager bleeped and he paused to look at it. 'I'm

sorry, I have to go. I'll contact you again when we have the results of the scan.'

As he rose, she stumbled to her feet and held out her hand, swallowing the hard lump in her throat. 'Thanks for calling me. Take good care of him.'

Nick gritted his teeth and, as instructed, squeezed Dr Blackman's hand as hard as he could.

Damn the doctor for contacting Tiggy. But he couldn't really blame him. He should have removed her as his next of kin years ago. The problem was there hadn't been anyone else to put down. But was that the only reason? Or was it that he hadn't been able to bring himself to sever his last ties with her, no matter how much he knew it was the right thing to do?

'You don't recognise me, do you?' The doctor took out his ophthalmoscope. 'I'm going to look in your eyes.'

'Should I?' Nick muttered. Why had Tiggy come anyway? Knowing her, it would be out of some misplaced sense of duty. He didn't want, or need, her sympathy.

'We met ten years ago. In Afghanistan. You saved my life.' Dr Blackman shone his light in Nick's left eye. 'I was a soldier with the US Army back then.'

Immediately Nick was transported back to the deserted house and the soldier with the pumping femoral artery. He'd thought there was something familiar about the A and E doctor, but it hadn't crossed his mind that he was the same man he'd treated all those years ago.

'Good God! What are you doing here?'

The American straightened and flicked through Nick's notes. 'Didn't think I would end up a doctor?'

He grinned. 'It's down to you that I am. Coming face to face with death is enough to make any man re-evaluate where he's going with his life.'

Nick remembered the scars on his chest, the tattoo. Not a man he would have ever expected to find in a hospital, let alone treating him.

'I owe it to you. Back then, well, let's just say I was set on a course to hell. As soon as I recovered I left the army and went to medical school. I'm here on an exchange fellowship.'

They had more in common than Luke could possibly know.

'How's the leg?' Nick asked.

'It's good. I limp a little when I'm tired, but apart from that…' Luke closed the case notes and studied Nick thoughtfully. 'I'm sure you're aware that you have some left-sided weakness. I see you had an injury to your spine a few years ago and that there was some shrapnel that the surgeons decided it was safer not to remove. I think we should do an MR scan.'

Nick shook his head. 'I don't think so.' The weakness was barely noticeable and certainly wasn't hindering his ability to do his job. But once people started poking around, who knew what would happen?

Luke folded his arms and returned his stare steadily. 'Lieutenant Colonel Casey, I want to thank you for saving my life and my leg. I always regretted that I never got a chance back then. But the best way I can thank you is by looking after you the best way I can.'

Nick raised himself on his elbows. 'If you really want to thank me, Doctor, get me the hell out of here.'

# CHAPTER FOUR

THAT NIGHT TIGGY barely slept. It had been a shock seeing Nick in the hospital looking so helpless. He'd always been so alive—so vital. How could he have risked his life to save someone he didn't know? But that was Nick all over. He had always done whatever he needed to do to save the lives of his men—and damn the consequences. And wasn't that part of the reason she had fallen in love with him in the first place?

The day she'd realised she was falling in love with Nick was forever imprinted in her memory.

Back then there had still been a truce of sorts between the locals and the army and they hadn't been very busy. At least, not since the two badly injured soldiers had been brought in. In the weeks that had followed most of the patients they'd treated had been locals presenting themselves at the clinic with the same sort of injuries Tiggy had experienced in her A and E department: burns; broken bones; car accidents; as well as the usual bugs and infections. Every now and again there would be a shout and injured soldiers would be brought in requiring the staff's full attention, but in between there had been plenty of time off to socialise.

To her surprise, Nick had kept seeking her out, although she had gone out of her way to avoid him. Then one day the team had been called out to a medevac case.

Nick was already putting on his flak jacket when Tiggy, early for her shift, arrived in the department.

'Where's Sue?' he asked.

'Still in the shower. Why?'

'Damn. The night staff are busy in Theatre or in the wards and I need a nurse to come on a retrieval. There's been some trouble in one of the villages. There might be multiple casualties.'

'I'll come.'

Nick shook his head. 'You're not regular army.'

'But I am a nurse.'

When Nick hesitated, Tiggy continued, 'The night shift are due to go off duty when they finish, and the day shift aren't on yet. However, I'm here, qualified and ready to go.'

'Going out to retrieve patients isn't part of your remit. I don't have time to argue, Tiggy.'

'In that case, don't.'

She picked up the nurse's bag and her flak jacket.

Nick frowned and glanced around as if he could conjure up a nurse out of thin air. Anyone but her. But not even he could do the impossible.

'Okay. But *don't* even *think* of getting off the 'copter. Understood?'

'Aye, aye, sir.' She grinned and saluted him.

But as reality sank in—she'd be going in a helicopter, for God's sake, and flying into a hot zone—her excitement was replaced with nauseating adrenaline. Luckily, before terror gripped her completely, she found herself in the back of the Chinook alongside Nick. He picked up a pair of noise defenders and, pushing her curls under her Kevlar helmet, placed them on her ears.

'We'll speak through the mike from now on. Only talk when you have something to say.'

Tiggy had been in a Chinook during training so she knew that the helicopter was fitted out like a mini casualty unit with everything they needed to keep a soldier alive until they got him back to base.

However, in training there hadn't been soldiers armed with machine guns hanging out the doors. She shuddered.

When they took off, the helicopter's nose pointed sharply downwards and for one horrified moment Tiggy thought it was going to plummet to the ground. She squeezed her eyes shut.

'You okay?' Nick's disembodied voice came through her earpiece.

She opened her eyes slowly and managed a nod.

He studied her. 'You're terrified of flying, yet you volunteered to come?'

'Not going to let it get the better of me,' she replied through gritted teeth.

He grinned and touched his helmet in a mock salute. He covered the mike with his hand and bent towards her. 'You're something else, you know that? You have some guts.'

'I'm bloody terrified,' she yelled back.

'Hey, don't you know that doing something when you're scared is the true test of bravery?'

He was right. She might be scared out of her wits but she was there. The realisation calmed her and somehow the flight wasn't so terrifying after that. Ten minutes later they were touching down.

'Stay here,' Nick said again, before leaping out of the helicopter and following the soldiers in a crouched position as they ran towards what once must have been a house and was now a pile of rubble.

After what seemed like hours but could only have been minutes, the soldiers returned with the casualty.

As the stretcher was lifted on board, Nick jumped in and the helicopter rose steeply and headed off back in the direction from which they'd come.

But the injured man wasn't a soldier. It was a young Afghan, who was bleeding from a head wound.

She hooked him up to the monitor and glanced at Nick.

'Head injury, Glasgow coma scale of seven,' she said quietly. 'Not good.'

'Where to, Major?' The pilot's voice came through the headphones. 'I'm assuming the local hospital?'

'No. Head for base,' Nick replied.

'Is that an order, sir?' the pilot said. 'You are aware that's contrary to standing instructions?' Tiggy knew it was standard practice to take civilian casualties to the local hospital, but they were badly equipped and understaffed. This boy needed the expertise and resources he'd only get back at the camp.

'I know what the damn standing orders are,' Nick said tersely, 'but this man will die unless he's treated by us. While I'm on board, where we go is my decision.'

Tiggy sucked in a breath. Nick could be in deep trouble for disobeying orders.

He looked up and caught her eye. Unbelievably, he winked. 'Never have been one for doing what I'm told.' He grinned. 'Now, Nurse, let's do what we have to do to keep this man alive.'

And it was then, at that precise moment, that Tiggy knew. She was falling in love with Major Nick Casey.

# CHAPTER FIVE

THANKFULLY, PAEDIATRIC A and E was quiet, with no more than a few colds and sniffles and the odd sprained or broken limb. For once, Tiggy worked on autopilot and somehow managed to get through her shift. She was just about to leave when one of the nurses held out the phone.

'Call for you. It's a Dr Blackman from the Royal London.'

Tiggy's heart froze. Had Nick relapsed? It was always possible after a head injury.

Her hands were shaking so badly she could hardly hold the phone.

'Mrs Casey,' Luke said, 'don't worry, the LC is not in any immediate danger, but I think it would be a good idea if we talked. He'd probably have my head if he knew I was contacting you again but, in my opinion, Nick is going to need all the help he can get.'

Tiggy closed her eyes. It was on the tip of her tongue to tell Dr Blackman to go to hell and take Nick with him. But of course she couldn't.

'I'll be there as soon as I can.'

Thirty minutes later she was sitting opposite Luke, trying to focus on what he was saying. Something about an operation…

'But Nick's okay?'

'Yes and no. He's up in the surgical ward. When we did the MR scan we discovered an old injury.'

'What kind of injury?'

'Two years ago, the LC was in a convoy when an IED exploded under the truck in front of him. He and his men managed to get out of their truck and the LC was going towards the injured men when the insurgents, who'd been waiting in a ditch by the side of the road, opened fire.'

Tiggy's mouth was so dry it felt as if her tongue was stuck to its roof. Was Nick determined to kill himself one way or another? 'What happened to him?'

'He took some shrapnel. He was wearing his Kevlar vest, otherwise he'd be dead for sure.'

'Oh, God!' Her heart catapulted at the thought of Nick being injured and her not even knowing.

'He was in Intensive Care for two weeks. But luckily, like most men in the army, he's as strong as an ox. Regular soldiers are so fit that if they survive the initial assault to their bodies they heal remarkably quickly. The LC seemed to make a full recovery.'

'Seemed? I'm afraid I don't understand.'

'There was a piece of shrapnel close to his spinal cord. To remove it could have caused paralysis. Where it was, it wasn't doing any harm, so the operating surgeons decided on balance to leave it.'

She shook her head. 'But why am I here? I think Nick has made it perfectly clear he doesn't want me involved in his care so I'm afraid you're going to have to spell it out.'

'The piece of shrapnel the surgeons left has moved. When he was in A and E we put him through the usual battery of neurological exams. Although he tried to hide it, we picked up some weakness in his left side. After we applied a little verbal pressure…' Luke frowned and Tiggy guessed it had to have been more than a little pressure '…the LC admitted that he started having headaches and some left-sided weakness a couple of months ago. I persuaded him to go for a scan. He was pretty reluctant, but eventually he agreed after I threatened to call the GMC if he didn't.'

Tiggy almost smiled. Nothing had changed. Nick had always been a law unto himself. 'So you're wondering whether to operate?'

'That's what I'm recommending, but he won't listen to me.' He sighed heavily. 'I thought you might be able to persuade him. I know I'm going out on a limb here, but I owe the LC big time. He saved my life, you know.'

Tiggy leaned forward. 'Tell me.'

'Ten years ago, I was a soldier in the US army. We were doing a joint manoeuvre with the British. Out of the blue everything went to hell. One of my buddies was hit. We were pinned down behind some walls and Brad was in one of the deserted houses. We knew he'd been hit, but nobody could get to him. We never leave a man down, so I thought I would fetch him.'

The smile he gave was fleeting and Tiggy knew there was a lot more he wasn't saying. 'LC Casey—he was Major Casey back then—was the platoon doctor with the Brits. I didn't know it, but he was already there with Brad.'

All at once, it came to Tiggy.

'You were the American with the bleeding femoral artery.'

'You know about that?'

'Not from Nick. He never spoke about it but he couldn't stop the story passing into camp folklore. I still don't see how I can help. Nick never listened to me in the past so I doubt he's going to start now. Besides, you saw how he was yesterday. He couldn't have made it clearer that he doesn't want me involved.'

Luke placed his elbows on his knees and leaned closer. 'I also heard the way he was calling for you when he was barely conscious. In my experience, nobody calls out for someone like that if they mean nothing.'

Nick calling for her didn't make sense. Apart from sending her the divorce papers to sign, Nick hadn't tried to contact her in six years. He'd walked away from her, and their marriage, as if she'd meant nothing.

'You have to try,' Luke continued. 'If we don't remove that shrapnel he could become completely paralysed. Worst-case scenario, he could die.'

Tiggy jumped to her feet and started pacing. Didn't Luke know what he was asking was a waste of time? She was the last person Nick would listen to.

'Does he know you've contacted me again?'

'No.' Luke's lips twitched. 'In fact, he told me if I did, he would make sure I never worked again. Or words to that effect.'

'Then I don't know what I can do. I wish I could help. But apart from yesterday I haven't seen my husband for six years.'

'Please, Mrs Casey. Give it a try at least.'

Tiggy sighed. Her insides felt like a washing machine. Of course she had to give it a try. Whatever had happened between Nick and herself, she couldn't sit back and do nothing.

She got to her feet. 'What are we waiting for?'

* * *

She picked him out straight away. He was playing cards with a group of men in the centre of the ward and his height meant that even sitting down he towered above the other men. She wondered if the game they were playing was poker. If it was, no doubt Nick would be fleecing his fellow patients.

As if he felt her presence, he looked up.

They'd removed the bandage from his head and now that he was up and no longer attached to monitors, she could get a proper look at him.

His hair was longer than when she'd last seen him and he had more lines than she remembered. Two deep grooves bracketed his mouth.

But it was his eyes that made her catch her breath. They were empty, almost entirely devoid of emotion. Whatever Luke said, whatever she'd imagined, Nick felt nothing for her, not any more.

A lump of ice took up residence in her chest.

Nick said a few words to his fellow card-players, stood up and started towards them. Although he was trying to hide it, he couldn't quite disguise his limp.

'What the hell are you doing back here?' he growled, glaring at her.

So her intuition had been right. Yesterday hadn't been an aberration. He didn't want to see her.

It took every ounce of her willpower not to back away from his fury. God only knew how, but she managed to keep her voice even. 'Hello to you too, Nick.'

He turned cold eyes on Luke. 'Did you contact her? Because I remember explicitly telling you that I refused to give my permission. I could have you up in front of the GMC for this.'

'I see a blow to the head hasn't changed you,' Tiggy said mildly, although her heart was beating like a drum against her ribs.

'I want you to leave,' Nick said flatly. Had this man ever looked at her as if she were the most precious thing in the world? 'In case you've forgotten, we're no longer married.'

'Actually, Nick, in case you've forgotten, we *are* still married. And I'm still your next of kin.'

His mouth settled into the hard, stubborn line she had come to know so well. 'It doesn't matter what it says on a piece of paper I'm able to make my own decisions.'

'Why don't we all sit down?' Luke said, apparently oblivious to the tension that fizzed between them.

Looking capable of picking Tiggy up and carrying her outside himself, Nick reluctantly led the way across to his bed. When Tiggy went to help him, he shrugged her away.

'I'm afraid, Lieutenant Colonel,' Luke said, 'we're not convinced that you can make rational decisions. If you were, you'd see that an operation is essential.'

Nick turned the full force of his fury on Luke. 'I'd like a word with *my wife*,' he ground out, emphasising the last two words with heavy sarcasm.

Luke glanced from Nick to Tiggy as if he too wasn't sure of what Nick would do if left to his own devices. Then he shook his head. 'Sure. I have patients I want to look in on. I'll be back in a while.'

Nick waited until Luke was out of hearing. 'As I said, Tiggy, I don't want you here. My health is not your concern.'

Tiggy folded her arms. 'That's tough. I'm not going anywhere. God, Nick, why didn't you tell me you'd been badly injured? You were in Intensive Care and you didn't even let me know!'

But was she really surprised? Two years after they'd married Nick had stopped talking to her about the important stuff.

'What difference would it have made? Our marriage was—is—over.'

'I'm not likely to forget that,' she retorted. 'Look, Nick, I'm here now. Can't we at least be civil to each other?'

He glared at her but she refused to look away. Suddenly the grim line of his mouth softened and when he smiled she caught a glimpse of the Nick she had first known and her insides melted. 'Sorry. Of course.' He dragged a hand across the stubble on his cheek. 'Forgive me.'

As he turned away to take something from his locker, she studied him more carefully. He may have changed, but he still made her catch her breath. She still remembered the feel of him, remembered every inch of his body, the hard muscles of his abdomen, his long legs and powerful thighs, the feel of his fingertips on her skin, the planes of his face under hers. She bit back a groan and closed her eyes.

Six years, and he still made her pulse race. Six years since she'd seen him and one glance was enough for her to know she'd never got him out of her head. She should get the hell away from him—simply walk out the door. Not just walk—run as fast as her legs could carry her.

'Okay, now we've caught up, thanks for the visit.' Nick shifted in his seat. Clearly his leg was causing him some discomfort.

'It's started,' she said softly, 'hasn't it? The paralysis Luke was talking about. Oh, Nick…' He'd been a triathlete in the past and had always been so fit. She knew how much he'd hate not being in peak physical condition.

His eyes were cool. 'It's a little stiff, that's all. Comes from getting in a fight, I guess.'

'And as for fighting in the street, what were you thinking? They could have had knives. God, you could have been killed.'

Nick shrugged. 'Nothing else I could do.'

'You could have called the police. It's what any sane person would have done.'

Nick shook his head. 'And waited ten minutes for them to arrive? I could hardly stand around doing nothing while they kicked a man to death. Surely even you can see that?'

Of course she did. The Nick she knew would never have stood back. Not even if the men had been armed to the teeth with guns as well as knives.

'Still playing the hero, then?' she said.

Wasn't his hero status part of his attraction? Why, even when she knew she was getting in too deep, she couldn't resist him? She closed her eyes, remembering the day she'd realised she was in love with him and that he had felt something for her too…

The time in the camp had passed quickly. When she hadn't been working she played poker with Nick and some of the others, using one of the resus beds as a table. In the evenings the staff who were off duty got together for drinks in the bar—although while it was called a bar, in camp only soft drinks had been served. Other nights there were plays, sometimes even concerts.

A group of army medics had brought their instruments with them and often in the evenings she and Sue, along with the other nurses and doctors, would sit around and listen to them play.

Nick had invariably been there. The man had known more about her than anyone, apart from her own family. He'd seemed to *adopt* her as an honorary kid sister. Sometimes she would catch him looking at her and her heart would thump and she would have difficulty breathing. Despite everything she'd told herself, her reaction to him had been anything but that of a sister.

If Nick had been hauled over the coals for disobeying orders the day she'd accompanied him on the retrieval, she never found out. What she did know was that their young Afghan patient, who turned out to be only seventeen, went on to make a full recovery. Something that was unlikely to have happened in his local hospital.

And soon after that she discovered that Nick had arranged for Hadiya, the child with burns, to be flown to the UK, with her family, *for treatment*.

Everything she learned about him just made her fall for him a little deeper every day.

She'd been at the camp for four weeks when, after a late night listening to the band, she looked up to find him standing behind her.

He held out his hand. 'Come with me, Tiggy.'

She thought her heart would stop. Almost in a trance, she took his hand and allowed him to lead her away from the group and into the darkness.

'Where are we going?' she whispered.

'Somewhere away from prying eyes.'

Her heart pounding, she let him lead her to a quiet

place behind one of the accommodation blocks. Suddenly he pulled her against him and kissed her.

His kiss was everything she'd imagined and more. And, God help her, she had been fantasizing about how it would feel to be in his arms. She'd been kissed before but likening Nick's kiss to her previous experiences was like comparing a single star to the Milky Way.

His mouth was hard and demanding, in a way that reminded her that he'd kissed a hundred women before her.

One hand was on her hip, pulling her close, the other was in her hair. His lean, muscular body felt just as good as she'd anticipated, and her very bones seemed to melt.

When he let her go she found it so difficult to breathe she thought she would hyperventilate.

'Do you know, I've wanted to do that since the first time I saw you?' he asked.

'You have?' she squeaked. *Oh, God*, couldn't she at least pretend to be more used to being kissed like that?

His eyes locked on hers. 'I don't know how I've managed to keep my hands off you until now.'

As he bent his head to kiss her again she came to her senses. Nick wouldn't be satisfied with just kisses. And she was damned if she would be his plaything. She placed her hands against his chest. She loved the feel of his muscles under her fingertips, which wasn't helping her resolve.

'Don't, Nick,' she managed.

'Why not? I know you liked me kissing you.' When he reached for her again, she stepped away.

'I'm not one of your conquests, Nick.' She lifted her chin. 'I have my pride.'

To her disbelief, he threw back his head and laughed.

'Tiggy, if you were just that, don't you think I would have made my move before now? Do you have any idea how difficult it's been for me to keep my hands off you, knowing that if I made my move too soon I'd scare you away?'

He'd been thinking of her, just as she'd been thinking of him? Warmth curled in her belly. Perhaps everyone was wrong about Nick...

Perhaps even Sue was wrong about Nick...

She sighed. Sue wouldn't have warned her off if she hadn't been sure *he* couldn't be trusted.

'Don't make fun of me, Nick. I'm not good at these kinds of games.'

His smile disappeared. 'Make fun of you? Don't you have any idea what you do to me, woman? I kept away from you not just because I didn't want to frighten you off but because of what you were doing to my head. No one has done this to me before.'

She wished she could believe him. If only wishes were horses, or whatever the expression was. But she wasn't so naive that she didn't know Nick was the kind of man to take whatever he wanted and to hell with the consequences.

'In that case,' she retorted, 'you're going to have to work hard to convince me that's true. In the meantime, I'm going to bed.' And as his eyes glinted in the moonlight, she added. 'Alone. Goodnight, Nick.'

'Time for your medication, Nick.'

Tiggy was brought back to the present as a nurse with a perky smile appeared by the bedside.

Nick held out his hand and, taking the small plastic cup from the nurse's hands, tossed the tablets down his throat.

The nurse eyed Tiggy then looked back at Nick. 'I see we have visitors today.' Her glance at Tiggy wasn't exactly friendly.

'This is Tiggy. She's just leaving.'

Tiggy ignored him. Although every cell in her body was screaming at her to run, she knew she wasn't going anywhere. Not until Nick had promised to at least consider the operation. After that he was on his own, and they could go back to acting like strangers instead of two people who had once loved each other more than she'd thought possible.

'I hope Dr Casey hasn't been giving you too hard a time,' Tiggy said to the nurse with a smile. 'He can be a little grouchy.'

The nurse giggled and blushed. 'No, not at all…'

Whatever else was wrong with Nick, it wasn't his flirting skills.

Jealousy ripped through her, stealing her breath. How many women had he slept with since they'd separated? There were bound to have been several. It had been years after all.

Not that it was any concern of hers. Not any more.

All of a sudden she'd had enough. Her head felt as if it was about to explode. She had to get out of there.

She bent over Nick and took the plastic cup from his hands. She thought about kissing him on the cheek, but at the last moment decided against it. Knowing Nick, he would consider it a sign of possession.

'I'll be back this evening,' she said. 'We'll talk more then.'

Nick waited until the nurse had disappeared before

shaking his head. 'Don't come back, Tiggy. Can't you get it into your head? You and I are nothing to each other any more. Haven't been for years. In fact, tomorrow I intend to call my lawyer and restart the divorce proceedings.'

Tiggy sucked in a breath. 'Very well,' she replied, glad her voice wasn't wobbling the way her heart was. 'You do that. But in the meantime I'm your next of kin. I'm coming back tonight. You can choose to ignore me if you want but, whether you like it or not, I am coming back.'

Nick watched Tiggy leave.

She was still beautiful. Thinner perhaps, and her hair was longer, but she still made his gut tighten.

He clenched his jaw. He still hated himself for the way he'd hurt her. Why had he married her in the first place? He should have known that he and Tiggy were never going to have a happy ever after.

But, God, he'd been in love. So much he'd thought it could work. If anyone could save his soul, he'd told himself, Tiggy could.

He'd been wrong. His soul wasn't salvageable. At least, not by someone like Tiggy. He'd tried to make her happy and in the first year of their marriage it had seemed he'd succeeded. He'd hated being away from her, but then... He shook his head. Being with her had become the thing that had torn him apart. So he'd done the only thing he could. The only honourable thing, even if it had been three years too late: he'd left her, knowing it was the only way that she would find the happiness she deserved.

She had moved on with her life so she had to be here

out of a sense of duty or, even worse, pity. The thought made him cringe. He didn't need or want her pity.

He wanted her to look at him the way she used to.

Why was he thinking that way? That was the road to hell for both of them.

So now, more than ever, he needed to convince her to forget about him. Even though seeing her again was doing something to him he hadn't felt for a long, long time.

A nurse stopped by his bed and pulled the screens. 'Time for your nap, Nick.'

Time for his nap? Did she think he was a child? Hell. He needed to get out of here.

# CHAPTER SIX

As soon as Tiggy got home she changed into her running gear and, despite the rain soaking the earth, decided to go for a ten-mile run. She needed to exhaust herself if she wanted to stop thinking about Nick. Not for the first time she wondered what would have happened if she'd listened to Sue and kept well away from him. Of course, that would have been easier if she hadn't fallen in love with him, and if he hadn't convinced her that he loved her too.

After the night they'd kissed, Nick had continued to seek her out. And despite resolving every day not to have anything to do with him, she'd go with him, though walking or playing cards or even working out together had been pretty much as far as it had gone. Inevitably word had got around the camp about her and Nick.

One evening, as she was getting ready for bed, Sue had come to sit on the edge of her bed.

'Do you know what you're doing, Tiggy?' she asked.

The sun and dust was playing hell with her light skin. Tiggy finished rubbing moisturiser onto her neck before answering. 'What do you mean?'

'Come on, Tiggy. I've seen the way you look at each other. I've never seen him so bowled over by someone,

but that's not to say it will last. Your tour will come to
an end soon, you'll be going home, and he'll be staying here.' She took Tiggy's hand. 'I don't want you to
get hurt. Nick will move on to someone else. Maybe
not straight away, but eventually. That's the way he is.'

Tiggy gave up trying to pretend she didn't know
what Sue was talking about. Of course she'd wondered
the same thing.

She sat down next to her new friend. 'I can't help
it. I know I should stay away from him, but I can't. I
love him, Sue, and, as crazy as it sounds, I know I'll
never stop.'

'Oh, Tiggy, I'm *not* saying he doesn't care about you.
How could he not? It's just that it never lasts with Nick.
I wish I could say it would be different with you…'

'Perhaps this time you'll be wrong.'

Sue looked at her for a long moment. She shook her
head. 'Perhaps you're right. I hope so, for your sake.
He's got to settle down some time, so why not with you?
But take care, Tiggy. Please.'

Sue's words stayed with Tiggy. Her friend was right.
Nick would tire of her sooner or later—it was inevitable. If he was attracted to her now, it was because she
hadn't succumbed to him completely and because she
wouldn't be around for much longer. As soon as she left
he would move on to the next woman who intrigued
him. So by the time the following evening came around
she'd decided to finish it—whatever 'it' was. She sent
a message saying that she couldn't meet him at their
usual place. She wasn't really surprised when he came
looking for her.

'What's up, Tiggy?' He stepped into her tent without
giving her a chance to reply. 'You okay?' He placed one

hand on her forehead and the other on her wrist. Typical Nick to think the only reason she wasn't meeting him was because she was ill. And she did feel ill. Not physically, but ill at the thought that this would be the last time she felt his touch.

She jumped to her feet and moved away from him. It was so easy when she was away from him to tell herself that she could live without him, but now, with his presence filling her tent, his eyes warm with concern, she couldn't imagine a life without him.

She kept her back towards him, knowing that if she looked at him she'd be undone.

'It's over, Nick,' she said quietly.

His laugh was incredulous. 'Over?' He came to stand behind her and wrapped his arms around her waist. 'You're kidding, right?'

'I have never been more serious.'

He pulled her around until she was forced to face him. He lifted his thumb, tracing the curve of her mouth. She shivered and closed her eyes.

'I'm sorry, but I can't do this, Nick,' she whispered.

He frowned. 'Do what?'

'I can't be with you and pretend that it means nothing. I'll be going back home in a week but you'll be staying here.' She forced a smile. 'Don't even try to pretend that there won't be others after I've left.'

He dropped his hands and studied her for a long moment. 'What are you saying?'

'I'm saying that it's over. Time for us both to move on.'

'Hell, Tiggy. What do you want from me?'

What did she want from him? She sighed inwardly. Nothing much. Only his heart and soul, for him to care about her the way she cared about him, and not for a few days or weeks but forever. Nothing else would do. She loved him, but she didn't want the leftover bits of him. She wanted it all. She raised her chin and told him.

But if she'd expected him to look at her with horror and run for the hills she was mistaken. Instead, a slow smile crossed his face. 'Typical Tiggy. Always have to tell it like it is. I think that's why I've fallen in love with you.'

His smile disappeared and a look of bafflement crossed his face. 'Did I just say I loved you? Hell, Tiggy.' He grinned. 'I don't know what it is about you, but I can't get you out of my head. I love you, you idiot. I admit it's come as a bit of surprise to me too. But I love you. God knows why, as you're the prickliest, most infuriating woman I've ever known.'

'And you're easy?' Tiggy snapped back. 'Personally I have never met a more arrogant, over-confident man who thinks that he deserves nothing but worship, who thinks that the world revolves around him, who thinks that all women should fall at his feet. God knows why I let myself fall in love with you. I must be a bigger idiot than I thought.'

They stared at each other for a moment. Then suddenly she was in his arms.

Tiggy was back at the hospital at six. She paused in the doorway. Nick was at the table again, still playing cards. When he looked over at her, for a moment she thought she saw pleasure in his brown eyes and the hint of a smile on his full mouth, but almost immediately his expression hardened and she knew she'd been mistaken.

He threw his cards on the table and excused himself.

She could tell that it took every ounce of willpower for him not to limp as he came towards her.

'I thought I told you not to come back,' he ground out through clenched teeth.

'And I told you I was coming back whether you wanted me to or not. You see, Nick, even if you were in a position to give me orders, which you aren't, I'm no better at obeying them than you are.'

When he eyed her speculatively for a long moment she could almost see the wheels turning in his head. 'In that case, if you're so determined to act the part of a wife, I want you to tell the harridan of a ward sister that I'm coming home with you.'

Home. One simple word could still tear a hole in her heart. It hadn't been a home since he'd left. She should have put the house on the market, but couldn't bear to, not even when she knew without a shadow of a doubt that Nick wouldn't be coming back.

But that was not to say she wanted Nick within a mile of the house she considered hers. He had to be kidding if he thought it was even a remote possibility. It was one thing seeing him in hospital, but to have him back in the home they'd once shared? No, she didn't think she could do that.

'There is no reason why I have to be here,' he continued. 'Even if I decide to go ahead with the operation, I don't have to be in hospital until the day before the procedure. In the meantime, they won't sign me out unless I have somewhere to go and someone…' he raised his eyebrow, '…and I quote, who is "willing and able to look after you and ensure that you won't do anything you shouldn't".'

So she'd been right about the flare of hope in his eyes she'd seen earlier, only it hadn't been for her.

'We are, as you keep reminding me, still married and the house is still in both our names.'

He was right. But he'd long ago given up the right to live there.

He lowered his voice. 'I don't intend to actually come home with you, of course, but I need you to say I am.'

'You want me to lie for you?' she asked, finding her voice at last.

'Don't make me beg, Tiggy. But if I don't get out of here, I won't be responsible for my actions. You know how I hate being cooped up.'

Tiggy's breath came out on a sigh. She had no doubt that Nick would abscond from the hospital if she didn't agree.

'Look, I'll go to a hotel and even promise to take it easy. Just tell them that you're taking me home.'

She didn't want him in their—her—home. She wanted him out of her life again. She wanted… Her head was beginning to throb. She didn't know what she wanted. Actually, come to think of it, she wanted to poke her finger in Nick's wound and twist. She wanted to hit him with her fists, she wanted to let him stew here in hospital where she hoped he'd be bloody miserable.

She sighed again.

'I'm not lying for you. If I tell them you're coming home with me, then that's what's going to happen.'

He paused and studied her through narrowed eyes.

'Isn't there the small matter of your partner? Won't he object?'

Partner? What was he on about? 'What on earth do you mean?'

'I saw you. With two little girls. You were taking them out of the car.'

'You were in London?' she asked incredulously.

'I came to see you. That's when I saw you with them.'

'You came to see me? Why?'

'I wanted to make sure you were okay. As soon as I saw that you were, I left. I didn't think the father of your children would appreciate a visit from your ex.'

'The father of my children?' Then it dawned on her. She couldn't help it, she had to laugh. If only Nick knew that apart from a few awful attempts at dating she'd remained on her own in the years since he'd left. 'Nick, the children you saw me with are my nieces—Charlie's twins. I have them to stay on a regular basis.'

'The children are your brother's?' Something flashed in his eyes before the old hooded expression she remembered so well was back. 'I assumed they were yours. I know you always wanted children.'

Yes, she had. But didn't the idiot know that she wanted *his* children and not just anyone's?

The first time she'd brought up the subject they'd been married for a year. They'd been lying, limbs entangled, in their bed in the warm afterglow of lovemaking. She'd had her head on his chest as he'd run his fingers through her hair. He had been due to go back to Afghanistan the next morning and the thought of being without him again had been tearing her apart.

'I'm thinking of stopping the Pill,' she'd said.

His hand had stilled.

'What's the rush?'

She wriggled around so she could see his face. 'No rush. I'm just thinking long term. It's better to be prepared for pregnancy. You know, stop the Pill six months in advance, start taking folic acid, that sort of thing.'

He tossed the blanket aside and got out of bed. Even after all these years she remembered exactly what she'd been thinking—actually, not so much thinking as feeling—a lethargic longing to have him back in bed beside her. She'd certainly had no inkling of what was to come.

'I don't want children.' His back was towards her.

'I don't mean right now.' Her laugh had sounded shaky even to her own ears.

He turned to her and smiled. 'Good.'

'But I do want them some time, Nick. I know we've never spoken about it, but I always assumed you wanted them, too.'

He sank back onto the bed and wrapped her in his arms, burying his face in her hair. 'You're all I want, all I need, Tigs.'

She'd knelt and placed her hands on either side of his face. She could never get enough of looking at him. She could never get enough of him. That was part of the reason she wanted his child. Children would make them complete.

'And you're everything I ever wanted.' She smiled. 'And everything I didn't even know I wanted. But to have a baby…'

He'd kissed her and immediately she wanted him again.

'You haven't stopped taking the Pill, have you?' he whispered into her hair.

'Of course not!'

'Then wait until I get back from Afghanistan and we'll talk about it again. In the meantime, we only have a short time before I have to leave and I know how I want to spend it.'

And as he buried his face in her hair, the subject had been forgotten. If only she had realised then...

Nick was looking at her, waiting for her to say something.

'You can have the spare room. I'll have to clear the twins' stuff out and evict the cats. They won't be best pleased, but it won't be for long.'

'You have cats?'

'Two.'

'And no new man?'

'No,' she admitted, but couldn't resist adding, 'At least, not living with me.'

Once more something shifted in his eyes, but once again it was gone in an instant. 'I'll be out of your hair within a week.' He gave her a quirky smile that sent shock waves down her spine. 'Now that that's settled, could you tell the nurses while I get dressed?'

# CHAPTER SEVEN.

'IT'S CHANGED,' NICK said, looking around the sitting room.

'Hardly surprising in six years,' Tiggy responded dryly. 'I've redecorated. And without your stuff...' The sentence hung in the air. 'Why don't you sit down?' she added. God, this was going to be so much more difficult than she'd imagined. It felt weird treating Nick like a stranger in the home they'd once shared.

Tiggy frowned at his solitary small bag. Nick always travelled light but this was ridiculous. 'Where's the rest of your stuff?'

'In storage.'

'In storage? After six years?'

'Don't need much.'

'But you must be staying somewhere?'

'I have a rented flat near the hospital in Birmingham. I considered buying but...' He shrugged.

She wasn't really surprised. Part of the problem when they'd been married had been Nick's refusal to put down roots. His reluctance to have children only the first sign that he couldn't cope with domestic life—at least, not with her.

'I'll put your bag in the spare room then I'll make us something to eat. Chicken stir-fry okay?'

'Sure.' He got to his feet. 'Let me help.'

For a moment she felt a smile cross her lips. Nick had been hopeless in the kitchen, but that hadn't stopped him from coming up behind her whenever she'd been cooking and distracting her by nibbling her ear lobe… The images came thick and fast: her stirring a pot, Nick standing behind her, his hands on her hips as he nibbled her neck, her turning in his arms to return his kiss— whatever was cooking on the stove burning but neither of them caring. Nick lifting her onto the kitchen counter, sweeping away the makings of the dinner with his hand, hiking up her dress, his hands under her bottom, his thumbs on her inner thighs. No wonder so many of the meals she'd cooked had ended up uneaten.

Sex had never been the problem. Whenever Nick had come home on leave they'd rarely made it to the bed, at least not until much, much later. He had barely come through the front door before he'd been kicking it closed and pulling off her clothes, kissing her, pinning her against the wall, his lips hard and demanding, snaking a path from her mouth, down her breasts and across her abdomen.

She'd matched him step for step; her hands on his waist, unbuckling his belt with fingers that had shaken with the urgency of her need for him. She'd never thought she could be so wild when it came to sex, but with Nick it had been hard to be anything but.

Good God, was the kitchen always so warm? She shook her head in an attempt to clear it. With memories like that, how the hell was she going to get through the next few days?

Somehow.

She chased the last of the images away and lost the

smile. She would *not* remember that. She had to remember why they'd broken up, the stuff that had torn them apart.

'No. Stay where you are. I'll manage.'

His mouth tightened. 'For God's sake, Tiggy, I'm not an invalid. I'm perfectly able to help.'

'I wasn't making a reference to your physical health, Nick, I was simply remembering how useless you were in the kitchen. Last time I checked, you could barely make toast. Unless that's changed?'

When he smiled lazily, her bones turned to liquid. 'Hey, if you remember, I can do a mean dissection on a chicken or a carrot.'

She bit her lip. The sooner Nick was out of her life the better.

In contrast to her fevered memories, dinner was an awkward, stilted affair; more like those at the end of their marriage than the beginning of it.

'Tell me about the operation they're proposing, Nick. From what Luke told me, you don't really have a choice.'

Nick leaned back in his chair, tipping it up on its rear legs just as he always had.

'I took some shrapnel two years ago. I was out on a rescue that didn't go according to plan.'

She noticed he didn't say what the rescue had involved and she knew better than to ask. Besides, Luke had already told her most of it.

'Luckily I was wearing my Kevlar jacket, but a piece of exploding shrapnel found its way into the base of my neck. I was knocked out but when they X-rayed my spine they decided it was too risky to operate.

'And now?'

'It's moved. I always knew it was a risk. They think it's better out than in.'

'And you? What do you think? Surely having the operation is a no-brainer?'

'You would think, huh? Unfortunately, they're going to have to cut away some tissue that's grown over the shrapnel and they can't be certain what will happen when they do. It's possible, even likely, that the bit that's left is lying close to the nerves emerging from the spine and they might sever them if they try to remove it.

'On the other hand, if they leave the shrapnel where it is, it might not get any worse—or at least not for years. Either way, I might have to leave the military.' His eyes were bleak. The army was everything to Nick. More than she could ever be.

Even though he'd hurt her more than she could bear, a part of her longed to reach out to him, to comfort him. Instead, she clasped her hands together tightly.

'Luke told me you saved his life.' It was all she could think of to say to change the subject.

Nick shook his head irritably. 'It was what we are all trained to do, Tiggy. Something you never seemed to understand.'

'Only because you stopped talking about it.'

Silence fell. Then he leaned forward and placed his elbows on the table. 'Anyway, enough about me. I want to know about you.'

'What do you want to know?'

'Are you happy?'

Tiggy started clearing their plates. Happy? Her life was full and she was reasonably content but there was still a deep, dark void that nothing could fill. 'Let's not go there, Nick.'

'You were better off without me,' he added so quietly that she'd almost not heard him.

She whirled around. 'Don't put the break-up on me. You left me long before you walked out that door.'

'Oh? If I remember correctly, it was you who left me.'

'Only because I didn't know what else to do to make you…' Tiggy struggled to get her breathing under control.

'Make me what?' he asked quietly.

'I came back the next morning but you'd gone. In the end you were the one who gave up on us.'

'It was for the best, Tiggy.'

'It wasn't for you to decide that on your own.' She took a deep breath and when she was sure she could speak calmly, she continued. 'What's the point in raking up the past? I actually do have a good life, Nick. I run the A and E department, I have friends, my family, my nieces—'

'Your cats.' He picked up Spike and rubbed his head. 'I can see you have a life. A good, safe life. Isn't that what you always wanted?'

No, it bloody well wasn't, and he knew that. She wanted to shout at him, to rage and throw the plate she was holding at him. But what was the point?

'Pudding?' she asked instead.

The next morning, Nick was up and at the table by the time Tiggy stumbled bleary-eyed into the kitchen.

'Coffee?' he asked, holding up the pot.

She nodded and took the chair opposite him, noticing that they'd both instinctively taken the same places at the table they'd done during their marriage. It could have been six years ago. Except that they had been two different people then. It was these small domestic details that threatened to undo her.

'No run this morning?' She could have bitten her lip the moment she'd said the words.

Amusement gleamed in his eyes. 'Not unless I want to give the neighbours some fun at the sight of a man with a limp jogging.'

'Sorry, Nick. Of course.'

'But I do intend to go for a walk.'

'Do you want me to come with you? Just in case?'

He raised a sardonic eyebrow. 'In case?'

'You know. In case you need help.'

His chair scraped back. 'How many times do I have to say I don't need mothering?'

Tiggy stiffened. He couldn't have chosen words that would have hurt her more.

The next time she had brought up the subject of babies, Nick's reaction was even more dismissive. 'I don't know if I'm cut out to be a father.'

'Of course you are. You're loving, kind…patient… You'd make a brilliant dad.'

They were in a restaurant, celebrating their anniversary and the fact that Nick was home again. For a whole three weeks this time.

Nick waited until the waiter had poured them some more wine, before leaning over the table and taking her hand. 'Can't you be happy with what we have, Tiggy?' he asked.

'I am. But a baby! Now, that would make everything perfect.'

He sat back in his chair, his eyes guarded. Tiggy had noticed that increasingly, when he returned from a tour, it took him days to get back to the teasing, happy-go-lucky man she'd married.

'I don't want a child of mine growing up without a father.'

His words chilled her to the bone. Lately Nick had been refusing to talk about what was happening in Afghanistan, saying he wanted to forget about it while he was on leave—a natural response perhaps. However, she knew from the news that the fighting was getting more intense and the knowledge filled her with dread.

'Like you did?' she asked quietly. Nick had told her not long after they'd met that his father had died when he had been ten. When she'd tried to probe deeper, he'd distracted her by kissing her until she hadn't been able to think straight. Since then she'd asked him many times about his family, but it had become clear it was one more topic to add to a growing list that was off limits.

'It's nothing to do with my childhood.'

'Then why? Talk to me, Nick. Please.' They both knew she wasn't just talking about his childhood. If only she could get him to open up to her, perhaps everything would be all right. 'Tell me what's going on in Afghanistan at the moment.'

His expression remained shuttered. 'There is nothing to say. Nothing I want to say. Believe me, you're better off not knowing.'

'Don't treat me like a child. I read the news, I watch TV. Part of me doesn't want to see it or hear about it, but I can't help it. You're out there so I need to know.'

He smiled sadly. 'I'm safe, Tiggy. I don't go out on patrol any more.'

She knew that. She also knew Nick had been told that he was too valuable to risk close to the fighting as his experience was of more value back at Camp Bastion. He'd tried to protest and argue that he was needed out on FOBs with his men. It had been the first argument he'd lost. Not even Nick had been able to defy orders on a permanent basis. After that, Tiggy had begun to notice he'd stopped talking to her about his life on the base.

'You'll be leaving the army soon and there isn't an A and E department in the country that wouldn't be glad to have someone of your expertise.' Nick had spent two three-month stints at the Royal London passing on his knowledge of emergency medicine to the doctors there. It had been the happiest time, for her, of their married life. Nick however, had been impatient to rejoin his regiment. That had hurt, even though she'd tried to understand his reasons.

'Surely we can have a baby when you're settled back here?' she continued. The thought of their baby had made her smile. 'He or she will be just like you…'

Nick frowned. 'Can we leave this conversation to another time?'

'When? We've been married for almost three years. Can't we at least agree that they're part of our future?' Despite the warmth of the restaurant, she felt chilled. 'Do you even want children, Nick?'

He sighed and looked away into the distance. 'One day, perhaps.' He fiddled with his glass, his eyes softening. 'Come on, Tigs, let's not argue. Not tonight.' He reached across the table and ran his thumb up the inside of her arm. Desire for him pooled in her belly. Even after three years one look, one touch was all it took. They would talk about having children again when he'd finished with Afghanistan. She smiled. 'What are we waiting for? Let's go home.'

\* \* \*

While Nick tapped away on his laptop, she fed the cats, cleared away the breakfast table, scrubbed the kitchen floor and put on a load of laundry.

Her frantic activity couldn't keep him out of her head. She should have let him rot in that hospital ward. What had she been thinking? She'd just about got over him and now she was letting him back into her life. Her nice, safe, contented, albeit grey and boring life.

Life had been so exciting with Nick. But the excitement had brought more pain than she'd ever thought possible. Six years it had taken her to get over him. Six long years.

Yet he still set her nerve endings on fire.

She thumped the washing machine to make it go on—she really needed to get it fixed someday—and stomped up to her room.

She dressed in jeans and a long-sleeved T-shirt and pulled her recalcitrant curls into a ponytail.

Now she felt more able to deal with him. She'd been at a disadvantage earlier in her Snoopy pyjamas. At least now she looked more like the grown-up, mature, sensible woman she was. She added a touch of lipstick and some foundation just for good measure, before stomping her way back down the stairs.

He still made her feel like a teenager. Damn the man.

A short while after they'd had lunch Nick went out for his walk. Unable to settle down to her computer, Tiggy tackled some more housework, tightened the loose wire on the washing machine and cleaned the windows till they shone. When he wasn't back by early evening she began to worry. Perhaps something had happened to him. He might have had a seizure—it was perfectly possible for someone with his kind of injury. Or maybe he'd fallen?

The roast in the oven was in danger of drying out and her anxiety was increasing with every minute that ticked slowly by. To hell with this! She'd rather risk his wrath by going out to look for him than sit here and do nothing. She'd just turned off the cooker and was picking up her jacket when she heard a knock on the door.

Her heart pinged around her chest. Was this someone calling to tell her he'd collapsed and she needed to come to the hospital straight away?

But when she opened the door it was to find Nick, holding a bunch of flowers, with a sheepish grin on his face.

'No key,' he said. 'Bought some flowers to say sorry. I remembered tulips were your favourite. Took me a while to track them down.'

His smile melted her insides. That had always been the problem; she could never stay mad at him for long. But what was she thinking? He was a no-good, cold, self-centred man who had broken her heart and not even cared.

She grabbed the flowers from him and stepped aside to let him in. As he brushed past her she smelled alcohol on his breath.

'You've been drinking!' She was shocked. Nick never drank.

'So I have.' He grinned at her. 'Feels pretty good.'

'Are you out of your mind?'

He looked at her from the corners of his eyes. 'Perhaps.'

He took a few steps, his limp more evident than ever, before sinking into one of the armchairs.

Tiggy shoved the flowers into a vase and turned to face him. 'Do you really think that, given your current medical condition, it's wise to be drinking?'

'I'm pretty sure it's not wise. But when did I ever follow the path of reason?'

When indeed? 'I think you should go and lie down,' she said frostily.

He grinned again. This time it was nothing short of a leer. 'Great idea.' He struggled to his feet and swayed. Tiggy reached him before he fell. He threw his arm across her shoulder as she struggled to hold him up. Nick was over six feet tall and well built.

'You coming?' he asked. Then without warning he sank back onto the chair, pulling her with him. Somehow, she wasn't quite sure how, she landed on his lap.

She practically inhaled him as his arms tightened around her.

'God, you're still so beautiful,' he said roughly. 'Do you know how long it's been?'

For a split second she was tempted to stay where she was. It felt so good, so right to be back in his arms.

Thankfully she came to her senses. She pushed away from him and leaped to her feet. 'If it's sex you're wanting, Nick, I'm sure there's plenty out there who'll be happy to oblige. Any more of this and I'm taking you back to the hospital.'

'You wouldn't deny a dying man his last wish?' He reached out for her again but she avoided his grip.

Hands on hips, she raged at him. 'Of all the idiotic things to say. You think I feel sorry for you? Let me tell you, I've never felt less sorry for anyone in my life.'

Still blazing, she picked up a blanket from the back of the couch and flung it at him.

'Go to sleep, Nick. I'll see you in the morning.' And without giving him a chance to reply she flicked the sitting-room lights out and marched off to bed.

## CHAPTER EIGHT

IT WAS A very sorry-looking Nick that she found in the kitchen the next morning, slumped over the table with his head in his hands, an empty pot of coffee in front of him.

'God, I know now why I never drink.'

Barely glancing in his direction, Tiggy opened the blinds. Sunshine streamed in.

Nick opened one eye then quickly closed it again. 'Do you have to shine a torch in my eyes? Do you have no pity?'

'Not much, no.' She put on a fresh pot of coffee and sat down at the other side of the table.

'How much did you have?'

'No idea. I stopped counting after the third—or was it the fourth?—pint.'

She went to the fridge, poured a glass of orange juice and shook some painkillers into her hand. She plonked them down on the table.

Nick winced. 'Could you do that a little more gently?'

He swallowed the tablets down with the orange juice then opened both eyes. 'I didn't behave very well, huh?'

'You behaved like an idiot, but I guess a *dying man* is allowed some leeway.'

He winced again. 'I did say that, didn't I?' He groaned. 'Can we forget about last night? I'm guessing, since I woke up on the chair, that my words didn't win a place in your bed.'

Tiggy had to laugh. 'It wasn't one of your best chat-up lines, Nick, no.'

'What was my best, Tiggy? Do you remember?'

'Unfortunately I remember too much—the good the bad and the plain hurtful.'

Nick studied her for a long moment through dark, sombre eyes then raked a hand through his hair. 'This was a bad idea. I'll check into a hotel,' he said quietly.

Regardless of how difficult it was having him there, she couldn't turn him out. Surely they could manage a couple of days together? She swallowed. 'There's no need for you to do that. We—our marriage—are all in the past. You can stay here…as long as you promise me, no more drinking.'

His mouth tipped up at the corners and the darkness left his eyes. 'I promise. Now, how about I attempt to make us some scrambled eggs?'

The rest of the day passed as if they were an old married couple. Nick read the papers while Tiggy caught up on a report she had to do for work. Often she'd catch him looking at her with a puzzled expression.

Later that night, unwilling to break the harmony but knowing she had to, she waited until after dinner to raise the subject of his operation.

'Have you decided what to do?' she asked.

He glanced up from his laptop. 'About what?'

'The operation, of course.'

'Oh, that. Yes.'

'And I don't suppose you're going to share with me what that decision is?'

'I'm going to have it, of course. It's the only logical decision. If I do nothing, the shrapnel will keep moving. At least with the operation I won't have the sword of Damocles hanging over my head forever.'

How could he sound so calm, as if it was a stranger they were talking about? But then, that was Nick—the Nick of their last year of marriage. Closed off, unwilling to discuss anything, not even when it was clear to both of them that their marriage had been crumbling. Although she'd tried desperately to find him again, to keep their love alive, she hadn't been able to reach him.

After their anniversary dinner, everything had seemed to get worse. Whenever he'd been home on leave he'd prowl around the house like a caged tiger or go for runs without her that had lasted for hours. Then he'd started going away on his own for days at a time. Mountain climbing—or so he'd said.

She'd tried everything. Invited friends around for dinner, stopped inviting friends around for dinner, booked them romantic weekends away in the country, arranged walks, parties—everything she could think of to make life exciting for him, hoping that he'd forget about Afghanistan.

None of it worked. If anything, whatever she did seemed to push him further away. In the end she stopped trying to reach him, hoping that when he left the army the old Nick would return and everything would be as it had been in the beginning.

Then, as he became increasingly tense and withdrawn, she began to wonder if Nick was having an affair. It would explain his silence, his lack of engagement with her when he was at home. It would also go some way to explain why he kept putting off the decision to have a child.

But she couldn't believe that Nick would do that to her. He was impatient, difficult, but deceitful? No. She would have staked her life on his loyalty. Did he still love her? Sometimes she was certain of it. Other times, when he was in Afghanistan and she so alone in their bed that seemed far too big without him, she wondered if he was only staying with her because he believed it was the right thing to do.

They still made love. Their incessant need for each other had never disappeared, but she knew that somewhere in the darkest part of his mind he was lost to her.

She would never hold on to him if he didn't love her anymore. She would rather lose him than have him stay for all the wrong reasons—even if the thought of losing him felt like having her heart ripped from her body. She couldn't go on living with him not knowing if he still cared. She couldn't go on living with him and not knowing.

She met him at the airport and he lifted her and hugged her so tightly he almost squeezed the breath from her body.

'God, it's so good to see you,' he whispered into her hair. 'Sometimes the thought of being without you…'

He didn't finish the sentence and on the drive back home he was preoccupied, only half listening to her chatter on.

But she'd become accustomed to that and she still hoped she was wrong about everything. Perhaps when he was out of the army for good, the Nick she'd known would come back to her. Perhaps the best thing to do was wait?

One thing that hadn't changed was their need for each other. With the dark winter nights closing in, Nick lit a fire after they'd made love and they lay together, still naked, wrapped in each other's arms, watching the flames cast shadows on the ceiling.

'How was this tour?' she asked eventually.

'Same as always.'

She sat up and hugged her knees to her chest. 'Come on, Nick, you can do better than that.'

He placed his hands behind his head. 'It was grim. Is that what you want to hear? We lost two boys and sent another half-dozen home without limbs.'

Tiggy sucked in a breath. 'I heard some of it on the news. I'm so sorry. But what about the ones you saved?'

'It's not enough just to save them.'

'You're not God, Nick. You can't let every case tear you apart. Thank goodness you'll be out of it soon.'

He looked away. 'There's something I need to tell you. I've signed on for another tour.'

Tiggy stared at him in disbelief. 'You what?'

'I know I said I wasn't going to, Tigs, and I promise after the time's up I'll leave. I'll do anything, go anywhere. We can even have the family you want.'

'The family I want? You talk as if having a family is a favour to me—some sort of compensation. That you agreeing to have a child is going to make it all right that you signed up again when we agreed you wouldn't.'

'Tiggy…' He reached for her but she jumped up and out of his reach. In the past she'd always let their love-making heal the wounds between them. But no more. Couldn't he see what was happening to their marriage?

'The men need me,' he said softly.

'Please don't try and make me feel guilty for wanting my husband back. Because you've been gone for a long time, Nick. And not just when you've been in Afghanistan. I need you, Nick. What about me? I'm your wife. I don't even know why you married me.'

'I married you because I love you. I never thought it would be this hard.'

'Life with me is hard? Oh, Nick.' Her chest was tight. Feeling dead inside, she walked upstairs, quickly got dressed and threw some clothes into an overnight case. When she came back downstairs Nick was staring into the fire. He didn't even seem to notice that she was holding a bag.

'I'm going to my mother's,' she said. 'While I'm gone I want you to think about what you want. Me or the army. It's your choice.' She couldn't even cry. If he'd taken her in his arms then, if he'd done anything to convince her otherwise, she would have stayed. But when he made no move, he gave her no choice.

'Goodbye, Nick,' she said. Then she stepped out into the cold night air.

And until the day at the hospital she hadn't seen him again.

Nick was looking at her. She realised she hadn't replied. 'I think you're making the right decision,' she said.

'Good.' He turned back to his computer screen.

Are you frightened? she wanted to ask. She almost laughed out loud. Nick frightened? Not in this lifetime. No, the only thing that scared him was commitment and the thought of being tied down.

He glanced over at her. 'If I don't make it, as you're still my wife, you'll get everything.'

Good God—as if she cared a jot about that! What did he take her for? 'I don't need anything from you. I can manage fine. I've managed perfectly well on my own for the last six years.'

He narrowed his eyes. 'When you wouldn't take maintenance, I put it all in a deposit account. It's there when you need it.'

Tiggy gritted her teeth.

'I have no intention of taking your money, Nick. And you are going to be fine. I won't, I repeat won't, have this conversation again. Now, if you'll excuse me, I'm going to bed.'

The next morning, Nick made himself coffee, feeling worse than he'd done the previous day. What the hell was he doing here? He'd barely slept at all. He kept seeing the pain in Tiggy's eyes when they'd talked last night. Was it possible she still cared? In that case, to come here, to the home they'd once shared, had been madness.

Even after all these years she still did something to his insides no woman before or since had.

Why hadn't she signed the divorce papers? She deserved to find happiness with someone else instead of an emotionally bankrupt, potentially soon to be ex-army doctor, who couldn't give her what she wanted.

Permanence. A family. A future.

He should never have married her, but he hadn't been able to help himself. He'd fallen for her before he'd known what was happening and had allowed himself to believe that she could save his soul and fill the emptiness inside him.

It was only later that he'd realised he didn't have a soul to save.

Where was she anyway? In their too-short married life, she'd always been up early, accompanying him on his runs. He smiled at the memory. Over the years she'd taken up running with a vengeance until she'd almost been able to keep up with him. Her determination was one of things he'd loved most about her—that and her soft heart.

One of the cats jumped into his lap and lay there purring, stretching its paws in ecstasy. Nick had never expected to find Tiggy still living in their home, surrounded by cats instead of babies.

The door swung open and he heard her deep breathing before he saw her. When she came into the kitchen his heart kicked. God, she looked good in a cropped top that exposed her flat stomach and tiny shorts that emphasised her long, slender legs.

She glanced at him coolly. 'Coffee on the go?'

'Can I pour you some?'

She shook her head, opening the fridge and taking out some orange juice. She held it towards him with a raise of one eyebrow and when he shook his head she poured some into a tall glass.

'You still run, then?' he asked. 'Hell, that was a stupid question.'

A small smile tugged at her lips before quickly disappearing. 'I'd hardly mow the lawn dressed like this.' She turned her cool blue eyes on the cat. 'He bothering you?'

'No. He's fine. I never thought of you as a cat lover.'

'Seems there was quite a bit we didn't know about one another,' she said shortly. Then she sighed and sat down at the table. 'Sorry. I promised myself I wasn't going to bitch about the past.'

'I wouldn't blame you if you did.' Silence hung between them. Nick shifted in his chair. 'You never met anyone else?' He had to know.

Something flashed in her eyes before she regarded him steadily. 'Now, why would you think that?' Her smile was tight. 'What did you think, Nick? That I sit at home night after night with only my cats for company, content to let life pass me by?'

It didn't matter that he'd told himself over the years that she would meet someone else and it would be for the best. The thought of her in someone else's arms turned his stomach.

She studied him over the rim of her glass. 'As a matter of fact, I am going out tonight. I'm sure you'll cope on your own for a few hours.'

Jealousy wound like a snake in his guts. 'Of course.' What else could he say? Even if he wanted to bar the door.

She finished her juice and got up from the table. 'Now, if you'll excuse me, I have things to do. She waved vaguely in the direction of the kitchen. 'You know where to find everything.'

As she stalked out without a backward glance, Nick knew for certain that even if she'd stopped loving him, his feelings for her were far from dead. He groaned. He should never have come here, but he'd been unable to stop himself from stealing this bit of time with her. He was a selfish bastard. If he had been no good for her back then, he was less so now.

Now, why had she lied about going out? Just because Nick had implied that she didn't have a life was no reason to make up a date that didn't exist. Over the last few years friends had always been trying to set her up with someone. But no matter how much she told herself that the banker or teacher or whoever it was she faced across a dining-room table was perfectly nice, good looking and decent company, they never matched up to Nick. Not for a single second.

In the end she'd put her foot down with her friends. No more dates, she'd told them. She would rather, in fact, chew off her arm than waste another moment of her life listening to someone in whom, when all was said and done, she wasn't remotely interested.

None of that helped with tonight's predicament. Sally was out of town, Lucy just had another baby and it was too short notice to call any of her other friends. Besides, what would they say when they learned that Nick was staying with her?

They'd tell her she was out of her mind—and they'd be right.

She showered and tried to settle down at her desk to work. She hadn't been lying when she'd said she had work to do. But, acutely aware of Nick's footsteps and the occasional opening and closing of a door, she couldn't concentrate.

Once he popped his head round her door and asked if she wanted anything from the shop as he was going to stretch his legs.

'You might want to get something for your evening meal,' she said. 'Remember I'm going out.'

'For dinner?' he asked with a lift of his brow.

'Yes. Not that it's any business of yours but I have a date.'

She thought she saw something flash in his eyes but almost immediately he resumed his deadpan expression. 'Good for you,' he said.

Crap.

* * *

That evening, she dressed as if she were really going on a date. She chose a jade silk dress she'd decided was too short once she'd tried it on again at home but had never got around to returning, and scrunched her hair into ringlets, letting it fall free down her back. She left her legs bare and slipped on a pair of high heels.

She applied more make-up than usual—a dark metallic shadow the beautician in the high-street store had promised would bring out the colour of her eyes and a red lipstick that somehow, instead of clashing with her hair, gave her confidence.

While she was getting ready she wondered where she could actually go. She'd have to be away for at least three hours to make a date seem convincing. She tried not to think about why she was going ahead with a charade that was childish as well as pointless.

One thing she did know was that she couldn't back out now. Either she'd have to admit to making up the date or she'd have to pretend a last-minute cancellation. Neither option appealed to her. The first because she didn't want Nick questioning her reasons for fibbing, the second because she didn't want to him think, even for a moment, that her imaginary date had cancelled. The humiliation of Nick thinking she'd been stood up was too much to even contemplate.

She almost changed her mind at that point. What did it matter what he thought? He wasn't part of her life any more. He would have the operation, recover and be on his way. She would never see him again.

So why didn't the knowledge cheer her up?

She added mascara for good measure and clipped on

a diamond and jade bracelet. If she was going to do a Mata Hari she may as well go the whole hog.

Taking a deep breath and plastering an expectant smile on her face, she sashayed downstairs.

But to her chagrin, when she reached the sitting room, it was to find Nick fast asleep on the sofa.

She stood over him. Even in the semi-darkness she could see he was frowning in his sleep. What demons tormented him?

Her heart stumbled. What had happened to the Nick she'd fallen in love with? Where had the irrepressible, fun-loving man disappeared to?

A lock of hair had fallen over his brow. That too was different. In the past he'd always worn his hair cropped short. Unable to resist the urge, she bent over him and gently smoothed the errant lock of hair from his face.

His eyes snapped open and his hand wrapped around her wrist like a spring. The coldness in his gaze shocked her.

'What the hell?' he said. Still holding her wrist, he sat up. 'Don't you know better than to sneak up on a man when he's asleep?'

'Come on, Nick,' she said, trying to pull her hand away. But he held it in his vice-like grip. 'Don't you think you're overreacting?'

'You wouldn't say that if you spent nights sleeping with your weapon next to you, waiting for the next attack, not knowing when it would come or what you were going to have to deal with when it did.'

'I'm sorry,' she said softly. 'I didn't think.'

He sighed and finally let her hand go. It was painful where he'd grabbed her and she rubbed it absent-mindedly.

His eyes softened. 'Did I hurt you? Let me see.'

He took her hand more gently this time and turned it over. Red marks, almost as if she'd been handcuffed, had appeared.

'It's okay,' she said. 'Really.' The touch of his fingertips burned her skin worse than his grip had and her heart started to pound.

The pad of his thumb ran circles over the inside of her arm and her pulse upped another notch. He was bound to feel it racing. She snatched her hand away again and hid it behind her back.

She sat down on the sofa next to him.

'Tell me,' she said. 'Tell me what it was like. Help me to understand.'

He laughed harshly. 'Some things are better not spoken about.'

And that, of course, had been the problem. He'd refused to talk about it when they had still been together, even when he'd cried out in his sleep and she'd woken to find him entangled in their sheets and covered in sweat. If he wouldn't speak to her then, what made her think he'd talk to her now?

'Anyway,' he said, 'I thought you had a date.'

Oops. She'd forgotten.

His eyes travelled over her. He whistled. 'Lucky man. But don't you think that dress is a little short?'

She stood, all the old exasperation returning. 'No. And may I remind you, Nick, you're not my father.'

'As if I need any reminding.'

She tucked her hair behind her ears and picked up her bag. 'I have my mobile phone if you need me.' As soon as the words were out of her mouth she could have bitten her lip. If Nick noticed the irony he said nothing.

'Unlikely,' he said shortly. 'I'm going to watch football and make myself a sandwich. After that I'll probably go to bed.'

Tiggy swallowed her disappointment. Couldn't he even look marginally put out that she was going on a date with another man?

And *apparent* was the key word, she reminded herself. She still hadn't decided how she was going to kill enough time to prevent him thinking she'd been dumped. The library? No, that closed at eight. A coffee shop or restaurant? No, that was too sad. A movie, then. It was all that was left.

She smiled as coolly as she could and walked out the door.

In the cinema she couldn't focus on the film. All she could think about was Nick. Why had he come back into her life now? And like this? It was torture sharing the house with him again.

But surely she could cope with a few more days? She would be at work during the day, and could perhaps find an excuse to go out in the evening.

No. She was being ridiculous. It wasn't as if she could pretend to have a date every night. And besides, after six years surely she could manage to be around Nick for a little longer? She'd be polite, distant, cool. He would never know how much he'd hurt her.

She took another handful of tasteless popcorn and chewed morosely. The couple on the screen were kissing, her hands snaking around his neck, him kissing her as if he wanted to devour her… Tiggy knew only too well how that had felt. Couldn't she have found a different film? Something with no love scenes, for example? But, then, didn't every film have at least a small love story?

She glanced around. Everyone was with someone, except her. Most couples were holding hands as they stared at the screen; some were with children.

Families. She sighed again. Wherever she went, she was surrounded by children. This hadn't been one of her better ideas.

Her thoughts returned relentlessly to Nick. What if the operation went wrong? What if he was left paralysed, brain damaged—or worse? For someone as vital, as physically and mentally active as Nick, death would be preferable. She reached into her bag for her mobile, surreptitiously switching it on. What if he'd become unwell? What if he'd had a seizure and was lying on the floor, calling for help?

What if he was dead?

Of course he wasn't. If his life were in any immediate danger they would never have let him leave the hospital. But then again he'd forced the issue and they'd only reluctantly agreed because Luke had told them she was an A and E nurse.

She could call him. One little phone call to see if he was okay. If he answered she could hang up without speaking, but at least she'd know he was fine.

She crept along the row of cinema-goers, whispering her apologies as she went and slipped out into the foyer.

One phone call. He'd answer and then she could go back to her film. That would seem perfectly reasonable. Of course she wouldn't hang up—that would be childish and cowardly. Anyway, he'd probably phone the number back and then she'd have to explain herself.

She closed her eyes and sighed. Why was she behaving like a schoolgirl anyway? All this pretending to be out on a date so that her ex-husband, her *very* ex-husband, wouldn't realise that there was no one in her life was ridiculous.

Not that she was going to admit the truth. That would be too humiliating. He didn't have to know she'd never so much as had a second date with a man since they'd separated, never mind another relationship. So when Nick answered the phone she would simply say she was checking on him while her companion was in the bathroom. That was perfectly reasonable, *mature* behaviour.

When he didn't answer her landline she tapped in the number of his mobile. She let it ring until it went to voicemail, thought of leaving a message and decided against it.

A few minutes later she tried again. No reply. She tried another four times, waiting for several minutes between each call, her anxiety rising by the second.

Why wasn't he answering?

Her head filled with images of Nick lying helpless on the floor and she made up her mind. What had she been thinking? What was this whole fiasco about? Even if Nick was perfectly well and watching his game, not even noticing, never mind caring that she wasn't there, he could be dead in a few days and she was sitting in a half-empty cinema because of her pride?

She rushed outside, jumping impatiently from foot to foot as taxi after taxi sailed past.

Eventually she managed to hail one, squirming with frustration every time they stopped at a red light.

Finally she was home. She shoved some money into the driver's hand. Her own hands were trembling so badly she dropped her keys before she was finally able to get the right one into the lock and let herself inside.

The house was in darkness. God, oh, God, she was right. He was lying somewhere, unconscious and unable to call for help. Her heart in her mouth, she opened the door of her sitting room.

Nick was sitting on the sofa, his long legs propped up on the stool in front of him, a beer in one hand, watching rugby. He must have showered in the time she'd been away as his hair was damp and he was shirtless. She averted her eyes from the sight of his muscled chest.

He glanced her way in mild surprise and immediately returned his attention to the TV screen.

'Have a good time?' he asked mildly.

So he'd noticed she'd gone—even if he hadn't noticed she was back remarkably early for someone who was supposed to be on a dinner date.

All of a sudden, for some reason, the sight of him infuriated her. It was hard to believe that only minutes before she'd been imagining his death with a bleeding heart.

She stalked over and removed the beer from his hand. 'I thought we agreed that this isn't good for you.'

'It's non-alcoholic beer.' He smiled, reaching for it. 'When did you get so bossy? I don't remember bossy.' His eyes glinted. 'I remember assertive—particularly when it came to sex—but not bossy.'

Her breath caught in her throat.

'That was then,' she retorted. 'A long, long time ago.'

He switched off the TV. He'd lost some weight, she thought distractedly, his jeans were lying low on his hips. Her eyes followed the dark hair that started just below his navel and finished… She shook her head. Don't go there.

He glanced at his watch and frowned. 'Aren't you home a bit early for someone on a date? Did he stand you up?'

'Of course not!' It wasn't a lie. If someone didn't exist, he couldn't stand anyone up. But maybe next time she could borrow a real-life man, perhaps Lucy's husband. God, she was off in her fantasy world again. 'I'm home early because I was worried about you. Didn't you hear the phone ring? Why didn't you answer?'

'I didn't think I should answer your landline.'

Tiggy gritted her teeth. 'I also called your mobile. Several times.'

'You called me? In the middle of a date?' He felt in his pockets and shrugged. 'Must have left it in my room.'

She felt like such an idiot. His eyes creased at the corners as realisation dawned. 'You abandoned your date? Because you were worried about me?'

'You're my responsibility,' she replied. 'I shouldn't have left you alone.'

He narrowed his eyes. 'I am not your—or anyone else's—responsibility.' He sprang to his feet so that he was towering over her. 'I never have been and never will be. A piece of shrapnel doesn't make me anyone's responsibility.' He glared down at her before turning on his heel. He stalked out of the room, returning seconds later with his phone. 'You called me eight times? Good God, Tiggy, your date must have the patience of a saint.'

His mouth turned up at the corners and his eyes glinted. 'Did you tell him it was your husband you were

phoning? Did you tell him that your husband was staying with you? In the home we once shared?'

That was the trouble with lies—once you started
with them you wrapped yourself up in them like a ball
of string.

She shrugged, trying to look casual. 'He's a grown
man. He knows it's been over for years.'

Something flickered across his face. Disbelief. Pos-
sessiveness? Amusement? She couldn't tell. All she
knew was that her heart was racing. Suddenly his eyes
softened. 'I'm glad you're back,' he said. He picked
up a lock of her hair and twirled it in his fingers. 'I
missed you.'

Now her heart was galloping like a runaway horse.
Was he talking about just now? Or the last six years?
Her body swayed towards him as if it had a mind of
its own and before she knew what she was doing she'd
raised her face, wanting, needing to feel his mouth on
hers.

But to her mortification he turned away.

'Go to bed, Tiggy,' he said harshly, 'before I do
something we'll both regret.'

# CHAPTER NINE

THE NEXT DAY Tiggy used her lunch-break to go up to the children's ward. Jo Green had been admitted to A and E two weeks earlier with meningococcal sepsis. Sadly her parents hadn't recognised how ill their daughter was until the rash had appeared on Jo's arms and legs. By the time the ambulance had brought her in, she had been unconscious and had needed to be put on life support. The medical team had done everything they could, pushing IV antibiotics and fluids, and the girl had survived.

However, two days later her legs had developed gangrene and Jo had had to have both her legs amputated above the knee. Tiggy had popped up to see her and the parents several times before. In A and E, when you held a child's life in your hands, strong bonds often developed between the nurses and the parents. She and the Greens had been no different.

Mr and Mrs Green were, as usual, by their daughter's bedside. Jo was staring up at the ceiling, just as she'd done ever since she'd discovered her legs had been amputated.

'How are you today, Jo?' Tiggy asked softly.

Jo's eyes flicked towards Tiggy. 'I want them to go.'

'Who?'

'Those two. The ones who call themselves my parents but who let this happen to me.'

Jo's mother, Colleen, winced. 'Darling, we had no choice.' Her face was pale. It was clear she hadn't been sleeping. 'Don't you think I would have given my life to save yours?'

'Whatever.'

'Now, Jo,' her father said. He appeared to be in no better condition than his wife. 'Your mum is telling the truth.'

Colleen looked at Tiggy with anguished eyes. 'If only we'd taken her to the doctor sooner.'

'Yes,' Jo snarled. 'And if only you hadn't told them they could take my legs.'

'Sweetheart, we had no choice. You would have died if we hadn't agreed to the operation.'

'I'd be better off dead,' Jo said flatly. 'What sort of life do you think I'm going to have now? Who in their right mind is going to want to go out with a girl who doesn't have any legs? Who is going to want to be with someone who is no use to anyone? Who can't even go to the bathroom without help?'

'Can't you talk to her?' Colleen whispered to Tiggy.

Tiggy sat down on the bed. 'I know it's horrible now, but I promise you, you will have a life. In time you'll learn to walk again. You'll be able to do most of the things if not all the things you could do before.'

'Walk on wooden legs? You have to be kidding me.'

'They won't be wooden, darling. Remember that nice lady came up to show you what they'd be like?' Colleen pleaded.

'Oh, Mum. You're such a…' Jo bit down on her lip and blinked furiously.

Tiggy squeezed the teenager's hand. 'I'll come and see you tomorrow,' she said.

'Don't bother. What could you—what can any of you—know what it's like to be me? You have no idea.'

Colleen walked Tiggy to the door. 'What are we going to do? She just lies there. The physios can't do anything with her except some passive exercises. They say she needs to get out of bed and moving, but she won't even try to sit up. She won't eat. It's as if she hates us.'

'It's natural for her to feel angry and blame you,' Tiggy said, 'but give her time.'

'She was a runner, you know. Up for selection for the national training squad for the next Olympics. It was her life.'

'The same strength that made her a possibility for the squad will stand her in good stead when she's ready to accept what's happened to her.'

'And I'm afraid that that same strength of character will keep her from accepting what's happened. I know my daughter, Tiggy. Nothing you or I could say will make a difference. Unless she believes that she has a life worth living, I just don't know what she'll do.'

When Tiggy got home that evening she was still thinking about Jo.

Nick was in the kitchen, studying a recipe book and glancing at a chicken as if it was about to leap off the kitchen counter and attack him. He was wielding a knife like it was a scalpel.

'I thought I would make dinner,' he said, 'but I'm having a bit of a problem. How the hell do I make chicken stock?' But then he must have seen her face as he laid the knife on the counter and pulled out a chair for her.

'Sit down.'

She opened her mouth to speak but he shook his head. He reached into the fridge and poured a glass of wine and waited until she'd taken a sip. 'Now, tell me what's wrong?'

'How do you know something's wrong?'

'Because I've seen that shell-shocked look on nurses' and medics' faces too often not to recognise it. Did something happen at work? Did you have a bad case?'

It was a relief to have someone to talk to who knew what it was like. 'She came to us last week, Jo, I mean. She's fifteen, waiting for her GCSE results, a world-class runner, one of life's gifted and blessed children. At least, she was.'

Nick said nothing, just waited quietly for her to continue.

'She was diagnosed with bacterial meningitis. We didn't need to have the results of her lumbar puncture to know. It was evident from the rash straight away. Her parents thought she had flu and was feeling particularly bad because she'd been training so much. Anyway, by the time they recognised that she was seriously ill and called an ambulance Jo was already beginning to drift away. She lost consciousness on the way to hospital. We did everything we could. The works. But as you know, at that stage it was just a fight to save her life. And we did.

'She was transferred to ITU and I went up most days to see her. I was the nurse who liaised with the family. You know what it's like. They turn to you as if you are the only thing between them and this awful chasm. It's like a battle and you and they have joined forces.'

'I know,' Nick said.

'Anyway, two days after she was admitted to ITU she developed gangrene. There was nothing anyone could do except amputate. Both legs. Above the knee. She's only fifteen.'

Nick came to stand behind her and squeezed her shoulders. She let her head fall back against him.

'There's so much they can do now,' he said softly. 'They've—we've—had so much experience with amputees.'

'She's just a teenager, Nick. She thinks her life is over. She won't even get out of bed let alone start her proper physio. Her parents are beside themselves. They don't know how to get through to her. No one knows how to get through to her.'

Nick was quiet for so long she started to wonder if in his head he'd gone back to Afghanistan. Suddenly she was horrified. Of course talking about Jo must bring back memories for him.

'I think I know what we can do.' He leaned over her and picked up his mobile from the kitchen table. 'Leave this to me,' he said. Suddenly he smiled. 'In the meantime, could you see what you can do with that bloody chicken?'

He wouldn't say what he was up to, but the next morning he insisted on coming with her to the hospital. He was looking particularly pleased with himself. In fact, he was looking more relaxed than she had seen him since they'd met again.

This Nick reminded her of the one she'd fallen in love with.

Oops, she told herself. Don't go there. One swallow does not a summer make.

'If you have some bright idea about marching up to see Jo and telling her to pull herself together as there are many people in worse positions, forget it.'

He slid his eyes in her direction. 'Do you think I'm that insensitive—or clueless?'

'Then tell me what you're up to.'

'Nope, no can do. You'll have to wait.' He reached over and tweaked her nose. 'You always were a curious woman.'

'Did you just tweak my nose?' she spluttered.

He just laughed. 'God, I've missed you.'

She didn't know what to say to that so she didn't say anything. But she couldn't stop the warm glow that spread from her toes right up to the middle of her chest.

She shook her head. No. Definitely no. No way. Not in a million years. As soon as it was decent she was kicking him out of her house and back out of her life.

When Tiggy pulled into the car park, Nick almost leaped out of the car. His eyes searched until they came to rest on a beautiful blonde standing by the entrance. When his face broke into a wide smile, an unpleasant sensation gathered in the pit of Tiggy's stomach. Not jealousy—of course not—only an unpleasant feeling.

The woman smiled back and raised her hand. She came running over to them and flung her arms around Nick's neck.

Tiggy wanted to slap her. And Nick.

'Hey, Hazel, it's good to see you.'

'You too, boss. It's been far too long.'

'Hazel, this is Tiggy. Tiggy, Corporal Hazel Gray—

one of the best army medics I ever had the pleasure of working with.'

None of that made Tiggy want to slap her any less. However, she made herself smile as she held out her hand. She was still puzzled. Why was Nick meeting her here?

'How's that husband of yours?' Nick said as he hooked Hazel's elbow in his and started to walk towards the main entrance.

She had a husband! Tiggy's breath came out in a whoosh; she hadn't realised she'd been holding it. They were walking ahead of her and Hazel was saying something to Nick that made him laugh. The jealousy she felt this time was different. They were so easy with one another, easy in a way she couldn't remember ever being with Nick. Life with him had been exciting, fun—at least at first—but easy? No. Not that. Especially towards the end.

Feeling a little like an unwelcome guest at a party, she followed them. Hazel was tall and slim, but there was something in the way she walked that wasn't quite right. She was rolling slightly as she walked. It was almost indiscernible and if Tiggy hadn't been behind them she would never have noticed.

'Which way to Jo's ward?' Nick asked once they were inside the hospital.

'I think you should tell me what's going on.'

Hazel frowned. 'You mean you haven't told her?'

'No. I wanted to see if she noticed. And you didn't, did you, Tiggy?'

Tiggy was beginning to see where this was going. But it wasn't something she felt comfortable about asking.

'Hazel is a double amputee,' Nick said.

If they hadn't told her, Tiggy wouldn't have believed it.

Hazel's eyes dimmed, but just for a moment. 'I was the medic with the boys when the man in front of me stood on an IED. He didn't make it, and I was in a bad way. Nick was part of the rapid response team. He kept me alive.' Nick gave a dismissive shake of his head. 'You know you did,' Hazel said with a soft smile. 'Anyway, he told me about the girl with the double amputations. He thought it would be a good idea for me to speak to her. I do a lot of that now I'm no longer in the army.'

They stopped walking as Hazel continued.

'When I lost my legs, I thought my life was over. I hated Nick for saving me. My husband Davie and I were engaged at the time, but I didn't even want to see him. I certainly had no intention of going through with the marriage. All I wanted to do was curl up in a ball and die. After the surgery I was flown to the military hospital in Birmingham. I was still a mess—emotionally and physically. I thought of myself as literally only half a person then.

'But the others—the other patients, amputees—wouldn't let me give up. They pushed me and tormented me until I was determined to damn well show them I could—and would—walk again. Months later, Davie came back to visit. I still couldn't bear him to see me but he begged.' Her eyes softened. 'It was Nick who persuaded me in the end.' She glanced over at Nick and Tiggy followed her gaze. He was leaning against the wall, his eyes half-closed so she couldn't read his expression. 'Nick told me that if I didn't say goodbye properly to Davie, if I didn't tell him I couldn't be with him face to face, I would regret it for the rest of my life.'

Still Nick said nothing but a hard lump was forming in Tiggy's throat. Had he ever thought of how they'd never really said goodbye? Had he regretted the way things had ended between them?

'I gave in. And as soon as I saw Davie walking towards me, I knew. If he still wanted me in his life, I would never send him away again. I told him that the years would be hard, that I couldn't promise I wouldn't get depressed or angry, but if he was prepared to put up with all of that, if he could truly accept me, this new, broken me, I would do everything in my power to make him happy.'

Tiggy's chest was so tight she was finding it hard to breathe.

'What did he say?'

A smile lit Hazel's face. 'He said he loved me. Whole or not, he would never stop loving me, that being without me had been hell on earth. Then I guess we cried a lot.' Her smile grew wider. 'We have a daughter now. She's two. And I'm in training for the Paralympics. I dream sometimes that I'm whole again, but to be honest I couldn't be happier.'

Tiggy blinked the tears away. Had she been in Hazel's situation, would she have had a fraction of her courage?

'This is who I am now. I tour the country speaking to amputees, especially young amputees. I train, I have my daughter and I have my husband. I wouldn't trade any of it to get my legs back.'

Tiggy smiled. 'I think you're just the person Jo needs to chat to. Come on, let's find her parents and introduce you.'

* * *

Half an hour later Hazel was sitting on the chair next to Jo's bed talking softly. Jo was still staring up at the ceiling but Tiggy knew from the way her head was cocked that she was listening. It wouldn't happen overnight, there were bound to be ups and downs, but she knew that Jo was out of danger. This remarkable, courageous young woman would see to it.

Jo's parents were waiting by the door with Nick. They held out their hands to Tiggy. 'We don't know how to thank you. Where did you find Hazel?'

Tiggy looked directly at Nick, ignoring the warning shake of his head. 'It's not me you have to thank, it's Dr Casey here.'

Tiggy had to leave Hazel with the family to go to A and E to start her shift. She walked Nick to the front entrance and held out her car keys. She couldn't trust herself to speak.

He ignored her proffered hand. His eyes were dark. 'No, thanks. I think I'll walk.'

She didn't say all the things she wanted to, like 'Are you sure you'll be all right?' or 'Thank you' or 'Take care'. Nick was who he was. A grown man with the right to make his own decisions, however much she didn't agree with, or understand, them.

She nodded and before she realised what she was going to do she stood on tiptoe and kissed him full on the mouth.

# CHAPTER TEN

LATER THAT NIGHT Tiggy lay in bed, wondering if she was going completely crazy.

Hadn't she spent the last six years trying to forget him? Yet here she was longing for him with every damn cell in her body. How sad, pathetic and weak was that?

The wind whispered in the trees outside and she shivered. She got up to close the window and that's when she heard it. A cry, a shout?

It was coming from Nick's room.

She was in his room, kneeling by his bed, before she had time to think.

His naked limbs were tangled in the sheets and he was thrashing wildly, the sweat running down his forehead. She'd witnessed his nightmares before but never like this. Had she been right to worry all along? Was this a sign of the shrapnel moving in his spine? And, if so, could his uncontrolled movements shift the shrapnel and do more damage?

She placed a hand against his damp forehead and pushed the hair from his eyes. 'Shh, Nick. It's me, Tiggy. Everything's all right.'

She tried to press him gently back down onto the mattress but, still in the throes of his nightmare, he pushed her away. 'No! Go! You have to get away!'

Unable to bear seeing him like this, she lay down next to him and wrapped her arms around his waist. 'Wake up, Nick. You're safe now.'

His eyelids flickered. 'Tiggy?' He buried his face in her neck. 'You're really here?'

'Yes, it's me. You've been having a bad dream. But that's all it is, a bad dream.'

When his eyes opened his pupils were large and unfocussed. Her heart banged against her ribs. Was it just a nightmare or was there something else going on?

'Talk to me, Nick. Are you all right?'

'Tiggy,' he groaned, his voice thick, and as he gazed at her, his eyes regained focus and he whispered again. 'My Tiggy.'

Relieved that whatever was tormenting him was receding, she laid her head on his chest. The heat of his body burned through the thin material of her camisole. Despite her terror for him, she was aware of every hard muscle against her. 'Yes. It's me,' she said again. 'I'm here.'

His hands moved in her hair. 'I was dreaming… You were hurt. I was trying to save you… I couldn't get to you.'

'Shh,' she soothed. 'I'm safe. I'm here and I'm safe. You were having a nightmare. Go back to sleep now.'

His hands dropped to the curve of her waist, resting for a moment before moving on as if he needed to convince himself she was really beside him.

His touch sent shock waves of heat through her and, as she felt the familiar torturous ache of desire, she fought the urge to turn and press her body into his.

Tentatively his hand moved under her camisole and when she made no attempt to stop him he moved upwards to her breasts. Her nipples hardened under his exploring fingers and she moaned softly. His breathing was as ragged as hers as he pulled her against him. 'God, Tiggy, you're so beautiful.'

Her treacherous body melted into his. She knew, of course she knew, that she should unwrap his arms from around her and walk away, but she could no more do that than fly to the moon. Every fibre of her body ached for him. But more than that she wanted to comfort him, ease his mental anguish. He was facing a future where he could be paralysed, if he survived.

Immediately, she pushed the thought away. She mustn't think like that.

But one night. What could one last night hurt?

'Are you sure, Tiggy?' he murmured into her hair. 'Because if you don't stop me now...'

She arched her body into his and lifted her face. 'I'm sure,' she whispered. If he rejected her now she didn't know if she could bear it.

He brought his lips down and kissed her as if he was drowning and she was his salvation. She kissed him back, inhaling the familiar scent of him, soap and spice, revelling in the taste of him, the hardness of his lips.

His hands slipped further down her back until he was cupping her bottom. Apart from her camisole she was only wearing panties, and using his thumbs he quickly divested her of those.

As his weight shifted on the bed and he rose over her, a shaft of moonlight settled on his scars. She put a hand to his chest. 'Wait, Nick.'

With a groan of dismay he jerked away from her and sank back on the bed. But she bent over him removing the arm he'd flung across his eyes. 'Your injury. We need to be careful. Take it gently.'

He looked at her, his expression fathomless. Black diamonds, she thought as she covered his body with her own. 'Stay still. Let me.'

As they moved together in a slow and gentle dance, it was everything she remembered and more. Every time he tried to take control she would stop him with a kiss until he was content to match her careful rhythm. After they climaxed, crying out in unison, she sank into him and he held her, stroking her hair until she fell asleep.

The next morning Tiggy crept out of bed, careful not to wake Nick. She'd be driving him to the hospital later for his pre-op assessment, and after last night she wanted him to get as much rest as possible.

As she made some coffee she hummed. She blushed every time she thought about the passion they'd shared. It was as if they'd never been apart from each other. No, that was wrong, it was just like when they'd first started sleeping together. That same desperate need, the same instinctive understanding of what each other's bodies craved…that same mind-blowing release.

Maybe they could get back together, maybe they could put the past behind them, and once Nick had re-covered from his operation…start all over again? This time she would make him talk to her. Perhaps, in a few months, discuss having a baby.

Whoa! She was getting way ahead of herself. Nothing, essentially, had really changed.

She placed two mugs on a tray while she waited for the coffee to percolate.

It wouldn't be easy. Nick might have mellowed but

he was still the challenging, complicated man he'd always been. She wouldn't love him the way she did if he wasn't.

She still loved him.

Of course she did.

She'd never, not even for a single second, stopped. She'd been mad at him, almost hated him at times, but she'd never stopped loving him.

And she never would. She was bound to Nick for all her life. No question. Child or no child, life-threatening condition or not, he was the missing part of her soul. Was there some way they could find their way back to each other again?

She picked up the tray and walked to his room. The bed was empty and Nick, dressed once more in his jeans, was looking out of the window. She couldn't help the thrill of desire that ran up her spine when her eyes came to rest at the small dent at the base of his spine. Only hours before she'd been kissing him just there, knowing it always drove him crazy. And she had every intention of doing it again.

'Nick?' she said. 'I thought I'd bring you coffee in bed, but I see—'

Before she could finish, he'd spun around, his expression so remote it stopped the words in her throat.

'What's wrong? Why are you looking at me like that?' she managed at last.

He raked a hand through his hair. 'Last night. It was a mistake. I'm sorry. I took advantage. It won't happen again.'

Her pulse was beating in her temple as she placed the tray on the bedside table. 'You didn't take advantage, Nick. I wanted to just as much as you did.'

He groaned. 'Tiggy, don't say any more. You did what any caring woman would do. You gave comfort when it was needed.'

'That's hogwash, Nick. You can't possibly think I slept with you because I thought you might die. I have no doubt that you're going to be fine—just fine.' That wasn't exactly true, but she wasn't about to admit it.

'Then it was just one night? You don't expect…? You're not thinking that we might get back together again? Because that's not going to happen.'

It was as if the bottom was falling out of her world. Of course, that's exactly what she'd been thinking.

'Why not?' she said. 'When this is all over perhaps we could…'

He laughed, a cold, mirthless sound, his eyes empty, bottomless pools. 'I couldn't do marriage six years ago, Tigs. What makes you think anything's changed?'

Her hands were shaking and she laced her fingers together in case he noticed. 'I see,' she said quietly, unbearably aware of the tremor in her voice.

'I still care about you, Tiggy, you know that. And you're still the sexiest woman I have ever known, but that's it. If I let you believe otherwise I'd be a bigger swine than I already am.'

Red rage swept through her. Of all the patronising things to say! She had been such an idiot to think, even for a second, that they had a chance. 'Of course you haven't changed, Nick. Sex is all that matters to you. That and the admiration of your troops. You're still the selfish, self-centred man I married. You only care about satisfying your own needs. Well, let me tell you, I've changed. Last night was…was just meaningless sex.'

She knew she was lashing out to hide her own pain

but she didn't care. She searched around for something else to say, knowing but uncaring that she wanted to hurt him the way he'd hurt her.

'You're not a man who does relationships, you think I don't know that? It's the men out there who use up all your sympathy, all your heart. It's not their fault that there's nothing left for the rest of us.'

Her throat was so tight with the need to cry she could hardly swallow. 'Here's your coffee. I hope you choke on it.' And with that last, remarkably mature comment she stalked out of the room.

Nick had to stop himself from going after her. He'd hurt her, hurt her badly, and she was the last person in the world who deserved it.

What had he been thinking when he'd made love to her last night? The truth was he hadn't been thinking, not with his head anyway. When he'd woken from whatever nightmare had had him in its grip this time and had found her bending over him, her silky curls a whisper on his chest, the smell of the honey and jasmine of her perfume, his reaction had been immediate. And uncontrollable.

He'd dreamt of holding her so many times it had been impossible to push her away. So selfishly, his mind filled with his need for her, he'd accepted what she'd so innocently offered, without thinking about the consequences.

But when he'd woken up to find her gone, the sheet where her body had lain still warm from her skin, the scent of her still on his fingers, filling his senses, cold rational thought had returned. Too late perhaps, but it had come anyway.

He would give anything to be with Tiggy again. And it would be so different this time—but, hell, he couldn't. He had nothing to offer her. He had even less to offer than when he'd left her six years ago. In a few days' time he could be paralysed—or dead.

He cursed under his breath. She was right. He'd behaved in the worst possible way. He was a selfish bastard. But not selfish enough that he would tie her to a man who might end up having to be cared for. He'd done the wrong thing by agreeing to come home with her, but he could do the right thing now. He had to leave her to get on with her life. Without him.

Even if the thought of that ripped him in two.


Tiggy dried her eyes, resenting the fact they were still red. She had stayed in the shower for almost an hour. Every time she thought she had herself together, she'd start sobbing again. It was almost as if she was finally grieving for Nick.

Now she knew she'd always been waiting for him to see sense and come back to her. Now she knew with absolute certainty that it wasn't going to happen.

She sniffed loudly and pressed a cold cloth to her red-rimmed eyes. She was damned if she was going to let him see how much he'd hurt her. It was some while before she was ready to leave the bathroom. She'd promised to drive Nick to the hospital and that's what she'd do.

It didn't matter what he said, she was still his wife and she would be with him, at least until after the surgery. After that—supposing he came through—he was on his own. And if he didn't? She wouldn't think about that now. She was barely managing to cope with her thoughts as it was. She would face it if and when it had to be faced, and not a moment before.

When she was dressed she went to tell Nick it was time to leave, but he wasn't in his room or the sitting room.

Then she noticed the note on the table.

She picked it up. As she read it, her heart disintegrated.

*Dear Tiggy,*
*I've taken a taxi to hospital.*
*I think it's best if we don't see each other again.*
*I'm sorry about last night. Sorry for all the pain*
*I've caused you. If I could change the past, or who*
*I am, to make you happy, I would.*
*But I can't.*
*Take care.*
*Nick.*

Tiggy stared at the letter before crumpling it into a ball. Where did Nick get off telling her what she could and couldn't do? And in a note!

She deserved more than that.

She was done with him treating her like she didn't have a mind of her own.

Cold fury was rapidly taking over. Who the hell did he think he was? What gave him the right to waltz in and out of her life when it suited him?

If he thought she was going to accept a note as a goodbye, he had another think coming. And she planned to tell him so.

But first there was someone she needed to talk to.

# CHAPTER ELEVEN.

'WHY DIDN'T YOU tell me this before?'

Tiggy's mum slid a cup of tea in front of her.

'Because...I thought you'd disapprove,' Tiggy admitted. 'I know you're angry with Nick. I didn't know how to tell you he was back.'

Her mother pushed a lock of hair from Tiggy's face before sitting down opposite her.

As always, when Tiggy was in trouble she found herself turning to her mum. It didn't matter that she was thirty-six and should be able to work out her own problems. Somehow everything felt clearer once she'd talked it over with her mother.

'It doesn't matter what I think. And, for the record, I'm not angry with Nick. It takes two to make, or break, a marriage.'

Her words had Tiggy sitting bolt upright. 'You can't possibly think that the break-up was anything to do with me,' she spluttered. 'No way. He was the one who put an end to it.'

Her mother raised an eyebrow and Tiggy's cheeks reddened. Whose side was her mother on?

'Well, I may have left, but I always meant to go back. I mean I did, the next day. But he'd gone. He didn't even try to get me back. God, Mum, he didn't even wait a day before he was off.'

'But the fact is you did leave first.'

Tiggy jumped to her feet. 'I can't believe you're saying that!'

'For heaven's sake, Tiggy, sit down. I'm not saying that you were to blame for the break-up, but I'm not saying he was either. All I am saying is it takes two. You were always stubborn. And I always thought there was more to Nick than met the eye. That man is hiding something.'

'You never said!'

'It wasn't my place. You were his wife. It was for the two of you to work things out.'

'What do you mean, hiding something?' It was so close to what Tiggy had suspected that her heart sank. 'You mean like an affair?'

Her mother shot her a look of disbelief. 'No, of course not that. You couldn't have known your husband as well as you think you did if you believed that for one moment. Nick may be a complicated man but he's an honest one. It was clear to everyone who saw you two together that the man worshipped the ground you walked on.'

Tiggy sat back down at the table. 'Worshipped the ground I walked on? Really, Mum? Then how do you explain why he shut me out all the time? And…' her voice hitched '…never came back to me? If he really cared for me, why didn't he fight for our marriage? I loved him so much.'

'It seems to me, darling girl, that perhaps Nick isn't the man you wanted him to be. Perhaps he wasn't right for you. Not if you wanted him to be something he couldn't be.'

'You are so wrong. I didn't want Nick to change. I loved him and all that he was.'

But despite her protestations a horrible little thought was snaking its way inside her head. Could her mother be right? Had she been at least partly at fault? Had she given up too soon?

'Do you still love him?' her mother asked.

He had broken her heart and was still breaking it, so there was only one answer.

'Yes. I'll never stop loving him.'

Her mother sighed. 'What are you going to do now?'

'Nothing. What can I do? He doesn't want me in his life. He told me so this morning.'

Her mother reached out a hand across the table. 'You hear what he's *saying*, but what is he *feeling*? Do you really know for sure?'

'How can I know? He doesn't talk to me!'

'Then the question, surely, is why not? Has he ever said he doesn't love you any more?'

'No…'

'Is it possible you gave up on him too soon and not the other way around?'

Tiggy stood up. 'All I know is that I won't let him treat me as if I don't matter.'

Her mother arched an eyebrow. 'Well, then, isn't it time you told him so?'

# CHAPTER TWELVE

NICK GLANCED UP to find Tiggy bearing down on him like some sort of avenging angel. He could tell from the set of her mouth that she was seriously hacked off. He groaned. He should have known she would do what she wanted to do regardless of how much he tried to prevent her.

He looked around for an escape route but Tiggy was between him and the only way out of the ward. Besides, he was confined to bed. He'd been given his pre-med a few minutes earlier and was already feeling groggy.

'So,' she said, her eyes glinting dangerously, 'at least you turned up for your op.'

'Of course I did,' he said. 'Once I make a decision I stick to it.'

'Why didn't you let me know where you were last night?'

'I was in a hotel. I thought it best.' He'd walked away from her because he'd believed it was the right thing to do. Even if it had taken every ounce of his willpower. The thought that he'd never see her again had torn him apart, and only the knowledge that he'd been doing the right thing had stopped him from turning up on her doorstep and taking her back into his arms.

'Well, I'm here to tell you something.' She wagged

a finger at him. 'Don't you ever decide what's best for me. *I* make that decision.'

Her words made him smile. All he'd ever wanted to do was protect Tiggy. But she was right. She had coped, more than coped, in the years they'd been apart. He'd clearly underestimated her. Then—and now.

'I'm not finished yet, so you can lose the smile. When you're discharged from the hospital, you're coming home with me.' She held up a hand as if to ward off his protests. 'No arguing. As you pointed out, the house still half belongs to you.' She dropped her voice. 'We meant something to each other once, Nick. As you say, that's in the past, but I'm still your wife. For better or worse. You can go as soon as you're on your feet. I won't…' He was getting increasingly woozy but were those tears in her eyes? 'I won't hold you back from leaving, I promise, but until then you're my responsibility. Get it?' She leaned over the bed and kissed him on the lips. 'Get through this, Nick. Do whatever you have to, but get through this.'

A short while later Nick was wheeled down to theatre. The operation, as the surgeon, Dr Wiseman, had explained, would take a few hours. He couldn't say exactly how long as that would depend on what he discovered when he opened up Nick's back. In the meantime, Tiggy was welcome to wait in the relatives' room.

The waiting was the worst part. What if something went wrong? If Nick died on the table, how would she bear it?

But that wasn't going to happen. She had to believe that the operation would be a success.

She would wait, make sure he was all right. And

then? As she'd promised, as soon as the hospital was happy, she'd take him home until he was back on his feet. After that? She didn't know.

She heard a soft footstep and looked up to find her mother, father and two brothers standing in the doorway.

'Mum, Dad? Charlie, Alan? What are you doing here?'

They smiled down at her. 'Did you think for one moment we were going to let you do this on your own?' her mother asked. And then before she knew it she was in the safe cocoon of her family's arms.

It was several hours later before Luke came to tell her that the operation was over. Her family made a small half-circle around her as they waited for Luke to speak.

'It went better than we hoped,' he said. 'We managed to remove the shrapnel without too much difficulty. We won't know if there's residual nerve damage for a while, and your husband will be in ITU for a few hours before we transfer him to the ward, but...' he smiled at Tiggy '...I think it's safe to say that he's going to be fine.'

Relief made her feel dizzy. Nick was okay. That was all that really mattered.

'Can I see him?' Tiggy asked.

'Yes of course, although I'm afraid you're the only one allowed in at this stage.'

Tiggy said goodbye to her family, promising to phone them later, and hurried along to ITU. Steeling herself for what she'd find, she walked briskly towards him.

As she'd expected, there were lines everywhere and Nick looked pale. To her relief, he wasn't on a ventilator. She sat down next to the bed and studied him, noticing how the lines had deepened on his forehead and around his eyes.

Her heart tightened. He'd hate her to see him like this. That was part of the problem in their marriage. He'd never needed her—not in the way she'd needed him. And whatever had happened out there in Afghanistan, whatever had been eating at his soul, he hadn't been able to share that either. For the first time she realised that what her mother had said was true—she'd failed Nick as much as he'd failed her.

Could this be their second chance? She didn't know if the wounds they'd inflicted on each other were too deep to ever heal and she didn't even know if Nick could ever love her again, but what she did know was that she wasn't going to give up on him this time without a fight.

# CHAPTER THIRTEEN

WHEN TIGGY RETURNED that evening, she was delighted to find that Nick had been taken out of ITU and put in High Dependency instead. Luke was standing at the end of his bed, studying his chart.

'How is he?' Tiggy whispered.

'He's doing great. He's so fit I suspect he'll be back on his feet much sooner than we imagined.'

Tiggy smiled. 'I have no doubt of it.

Nick's eyes flickered open. 'Hi, Tigs,' he said drowsily. 'You look cute.' Then he fell asleep again.

'I'll leave you two alone,' Luke said. 'You know how to call for help if you need it.'

Tiggy remained by Nick's bed, unable to bring herself to leave him even to go for a coffee, until the nurses insisted that visiting was over.

The next morning she was told he'd continued to make such good progress that he'd been transferred onto the surgical ward. He was still on a saline drip but was conscious.

As she approached, he threw back the covers.

'Just what do you think you're doing?' Tiggy asked, pressing him back against the pillows.

'I need to pee.'

'Then you'll have to use a bottle. You're not allowed out of bed until tomorrow.'

'You expect me to pee in a bottle?' He couldn't have sounded more outraged had she suggested he rob a bank.

'I'll fetch one for you, shall I?' Now she knew he was going to be okay, Tiggy was beginning to enjoy herself.

He glared at her. 'If you think for one minute I'm about to lie here while you help me use a bottle, think again.'

'I'll get one of the nurses, then.'

Nick looked as if he was about to argue, but then sank back on the pillows. 'I suppose if I have to.'

'But the nurses are busy...' she smiled down at him '...so after you've finished with the bottle, I'll be giving you your bed bath.'

'You have got to be kidding!'

'Nope. 'Fraid not.'

Nick was prevented from saying anything in reply by the arrival of the nurse.

Tiggy fetched a basin of warm water and waited until the nurse had taken away the bottle before she popped behind the screens.

Nick studied her warily. 'You're not serious about this bed-bath stuff.'

'Perfectly serious.'

She plonked the basin on the locker. 'Now, we can do this the easy way or the hard way, as they say in the movies.' She was definitely beginning to enjoy herself.

'What's the easy way?'

'That's where you lie still and let me do what I need to.'

A slow smile crossed his face. 'I think I've heard you say that before.'

She bit back a smile. She wasn't about to admit that the night he was talking about was imprinted in her memory.

'And what's the hard way?'

'The hard way is when you resist—or try to help me.'

'Let's go for the easy way, then.'

She was beginning to have her doubts. It had seemed a good way of getting back at Nick, but she hadn't expected him to capitulate so quickly.

She unbuttoned his pyjama top. He'd never worn them, preferring to sleep naked.

Mustn't think of him naked.

The lower part of his torso was heavily bandaged. Tiggy's mouth dried. She dipped the facecloth in the water and wrung it out. She washed his face, feeling the rasp of his beard through the cloth.

'You could do with a shave,' she said mildly.

'Not sure I could trust you that far.' He grinned. He'd always used an open razor to shave.

'You'll do until tomorrow.'

She raised each arm in turn and soaped and rinsed. All the while he lay there, watching her with sleepy, amused brown eyes.

It turned into a game, both waiting to see just how far she'd go. She soaped his calves in turn, lifting them gently so as not to cause him any pain, but when it came to washing his upper thighs she couldn't resist glancing at him. His eyes were glinting and he had a half-smile on his lips. She rinsed the cloth and made to pull his pyjama trousers down. Suddenly his hand snaked out and grabbed hers. 'That's as far as you go, sweetheart,' he groaned.

She smiled down at him. 'Lost your nerve?' She covered him with the sheet again and tucked him in. 'At last, payback for the time you humiliated me at Camp Bastion. Remember? The press-ups?'

He looked at her through slitted eyes. 'I think we're quits, don't you?'

Grinning, Nick watched Tiggy stomp out of the room. God, he'd missed her. Missed her spark, missed the way she lifted her chin whenever she was mad, missed the feel of her hands on his body.

He'd missed everything about her.

And now?

He'd let her go in the first place because he'd wanted her to have the life she deserved. But she hadn't found someone else; hadn't had the children she desired. And why not? Had he hurt her so badly she had never let herself trust again? And he'd hurt her all over again by making love to her and walking away. So why the hell was she giving him the time of day? Pity? A sense of guilt for a failed marriage? Ridiculous—and yet what other explanation was there? That she still loved him?

Was it possible? A unfamiliar feeling spread through his chest, which he vaguely remembered as unadulterated happiness.

Was there a chance of a future for them?

Because, God help them both, he still loved her. He'd never stopped loving her. No one had ever come close to making him feel the way she had.

And the operation seemed to have been a success. He had his life back. But he didn't want his old life back. Not if it didn't include Tiggy.

# CHAPTER FOURTEEN

Nick stopped his wheelchair outside the front door and frowned.

He had insisted on wheeling himself. Tiggy wasn't even allowed to touch the wheelchair, never mind push him, but the doorway to the house had a small lip.

Nick gritted his teeth, reversed a metre or so down the path and, using his powerful arms, rushed the wheelchair at the door.

To no avail. As before, the wheelchair jammed against the doorway.

'For heaven's sake, Nick,' Tiggy said, exasperated. 'Let me at least get you inside.'

He turned and glared at her. As if it was her fault.

'I can manage,' he insisted.

'Suit yourself,' Tiggy responded mildly, squeezing herself past him and into the house. 'I'm going to make tea. When you get tired of flinging yourself at the immovable object that is the door, let me know.'

Receiving no response, apart from a not-too-well-hidden snarl, she set about doing as she'd said. She filled the kettle and lifted a couple of mugs from the kitchen cupboard.

The tea was made when a satisfied laugh came from

behind her. Nick was in the kitchen, grinning widely. 'Told you I could manage,' he said.

'Would have been easier if you'd allowed me to help.' She nodded at the table. 'Tea's there.'

'We've been through this, Tiggy. I'll have to be in this damn chair for a few days longer but, in the meantime, I will not be treated like—'

'A child?' Tiggy raised one eyebrow at him. 'Because you've been doing a good imitation of one since we left the hospital.'

Nick glared at her again and she glared back. 'Really, Nick, you might be wheelchair-bound but your behaviour over the last couple of hours has been inexcusable.'

To her surprise, the darkness left his eyes and he grinned.

'Trust you to say what you think, Tiggy. You're right. I have been behaving badly.'

No worse than you've behaved in the past, she added silently. Damn stubborn man.

'But don't you see? If I were one of my men, I would give no quarter and neither would they expect any. If they can come to terms with having to learn to walk all over again, so can I.'

'I'm quite sure they accept help when it's offered.'

'They accept help when they can't manage for themselves. I'll do no less.'

Tiggy shrugged, pretending a nonchalance she was far from feeling. 'Suit yourself.'

Nick's expression darkened. 'At least there's a good chance *I'll* get back on my feet,' he muttered.

'For God's sake, Nick, do you have to flay yourself alive every time you think of one of those poor men?

The war isn't your fault. What happened to them isn't your fault. You've spent the best part of your career doing your damnedest to keep them alive, to keep them from losing their limbs, to keep them whole.'

'I did have help, Tiggy,' he responded dryly.

'Then what about Luke? You saved his life. You saved his leg. If it hadn't been for you, God knows what would have happened to him.' She softened her voice. 'He told me you're the reason he became a doctor. Did you know that?'

'It seems to me that Luke tells you way too much.'

When they had finished their drinks Tiggy picked up the mugs and placed them in the sink.

'Do you want to lie down for a bit? You could use the sofa in the sitting room.'

'I thought we agreed you weren't going to treat me as a patient. If I want to lie down, I'll lie down.'

Tiggy whirled round. 'Okay. Suit yourself. You can rot in that chair for all I care. I'm going for a run.'

By the time she returned, she'd exercised away her irritation with Nick. The truth was she wasn't so much angry with him as unsure of how to be around him.

Nick was sitting in the armchair with his feet up on a stool, watching football.

'How was your run?' he asked with a smile.

Anyone would think she'd imagined the grumpy individual of earlier.

'It was good. Perhaps when you're up to it we can go together?'

Nick narrowed his eyes. 'Give me three weeks.'

'Three weeks! You're crazy to think you'll be running in three weeks.'

'Just watch me,' he said.

* * *

Over the next few days they settled into a routine. Tiggy prepared breakfast before she left for work and Nick always made it to the kitchen before it was on the table.

She suspected he set his alarm for six to give himself time to get dressed.

They would eat together then he would shoo her off to work, insisting she leave the breakfast dishes for him.

By the time she returned from the hospital he'd have a simple dinner ready or, more often, a take-away ordered, and they'd sit at the kitchen table and he would ask her about work. When she suggested she take him out in his wheelchair, he was aghast.

'No way is anyone going to see me in this contraption,' he protested. 'I'm not leaving this house until I can walk.'

'Then you'd better keep practising,' she said.

The first weekend she slept late and woke up to the smell of coffee. Nick was at the kitchen table, looking pleased with himself.

'Notice anything?' he asked.

'Yep. Seems you can finally make coffee.'

'You haven't tasted it yet.'

And, right enough, as soon as she took a sip she was transported back to the camp and the horrible coffee from the mess tent. She tipped hers down the sink and set about making another, decent pot.

Nick pretended to be offended. 'Hey, do you have any idea how long that took me to make?'

For the first time she noticed he wasn't in his wheelchair.

'You walked in here?' she asked incredulously.

'I wouldn't say walked exactly. More like stumbled.

But, yes, it won't be long before we can go running together.'

'Don't overdo it, Nick.'

He frowned at her. 'In my book, there's no such thing as overdoing it.'

She ignored him and went to sit at the table. 'In that case, have you made plans about what you're going to do when you're completely fit?'

'I have to appear before the medical board in a few weeks. They'll make a decision about my fitness to continue with the army then.'

Although his tone was nonchalant, a muscle twitched in his jaw, the way it always did when he was annoyed about something.

'What if they say no? What will you do then?'

He raised his eyes. 'They won't say no. I'll make sure of it.'

'You don't have to stay in the army. As I said before, someone of your experience could walk into a consultant post in any hospital in the UK.' She paused. 'Would it still be so terrible to be a civilian doctor?'

He shook his head. 'It's still tough out there. The men need me.'

'Don't you think you've done enough?'

He stared into the distance. 'Who can say what is enough? It never seems to be enough.' He leaned forward. 'Almost every week we're coming up with innovations that save more lives. You know they used to talk about the golden hour? Now they talk about the platinum ten minutes. If we can get the best medical care to the men within that time—assuming they're still alive—we can usually save them.'

'And it's people like you who have made it possible.'

He didn't seem to be listening to her. He seemed to have gone somewhere inside his head.

'When they stopped me going out on patrol with the men, I was furious. I knew that they needed the most experienced surgeon possible to be right there, alongside them. But once I got to consultant level the bloody command said I was too valuable to risk. Going out with the rapid response team was the next best thing.' He was speaking so softly she had to strain to hear him. 'It was bad enough when the injuries were shrapnel or bullet wounds but when they started using IEDs…' He shook his head. 'The injuries were more severe than anything we'd ever seen before.'

He was telling her more than he had in all the years they'd been married.

'But you saved them. Most of them.'

'Not all of them. Remember the soldier we lost when you were there?' When Tiggy nodded he continued. 'There was a young female army medic. She was one of the first women to go out on patrol with the men. She was only nineteen. I went out with the RRT when we got the call. We didn't know what to expect. You know how difficult it is to get the right information back at base. Anyway, by the time we got to her, it was too late. All I could do was hold her. She died in my arms. All the time she was dying I was thinking of you. Thinking of our lives back here. Knowing that you wanted me to give it up so we could have a normal life. I also knew I couldn't. As long as these men and women were out there, I had to be there too.'

'Why didn't you talk to me about it?'

'I didn't want to bring all that home. When I was with you I wanted to think of nothing but you. But I couldn't get the images out of my head. I couldn't rest at home, not when I knew I should be with them.'

'I thought you regretted marrying me,' she said sadly.

He raised his eyes again and she reeled back from the anguish she saw there.

'I did regret marrying you,' he said. 'I loved you, but I couldn't be with you. Why didn't you divorce me? My solicitor sent the papers.'

'Perhaps because for me marriage is forever,' she whispered. Although that wasn't the true reason. At least, not all of it. She knew now she'd never given up hope that one day he'd come back to her. That weekend, when she'd run away to her mother's, she'd been so sure he would come after her, tell her that he needed her more than the army, but he hadn't. When she'd returned home, determined to talk to him, to find a way to be together, he'd gone and had taken most of his belongings with him.

It had been then that she'd broken down. But she'd refused to call him or write. She wouldn't beg. If Nick no longer loved her, it was better that he'd left.

But it had taken years before she'd given up hope that he'd come back. All these years just one little sign from him would have been enough. But that sign had never come.

She turned away from him. 'You were the one who really left in the end, remember?'

'I thought it was best.'

'Best for whom?'

'You wanted a baby, Tiggy. I couldn't. Not then, perhaps not ever.'

'It wasn't a baby I wanted, Nick. I mean, of course I wanted our child, but only because I wanted something

that was part of both of us. Most of all I wanted us to
be a normal family. You, me, our child. Our children.
What was so wrong with that?'

He shook his head. 'It wasn't that I didn't want them
too. I did, but not when… It was crazy in Afghanistan
back then, Tiggy. I saw too many young men die, men
with young babies. Men leaving women to cope alone.
Just like my mother had to cope with me. I couldn't do
that to you.'

She pushed herself away from the table. 'As I said
before, it wasn't something for you to decide on your
own. You didn't have faith in us. You didn't have faith
in me. I was stronger than you gave me credit for. If
anything had happened to you it would have broken
me, of course it would, but I would have found a way
to go on. And if we'd had a child, at least I would have
had a part of you.'

He looked up at her. 'I know that now, Tigs. But I
thought I was doing the best thing for you.'

She shook her head. 'That's not good enough. If you
really loved me, Nick, nothing would have kept you
away.' She turned away. 'If you'll excuse me, I have
stuff I need to do.'

# CHAPTER FIFTEEN

TIGGY CAME BACK from work on Monday to the astonishing sight of Nick doing pirouettes in his wheelchair with both twins on his lap.

'Faster!' Chrissie squealed.

'Go round again,' Melody, the quieter twin, insisted.

'What on earth is going on? Where did you two come from?'

The twins, instead of leaping into her arms the way they usually did, stayed where they were, as if glued to Nick.

'Hi, sis.' Her brother Charlie appeared in the door of the sitting room. 'We were on our way back from doing some shopping in the city and thought we'd pop in. Mum said Nick was staying with you.'

He scooped up a twin in each arm and plonked them on the floor. 'That's enough, you two. Give Uncle Nick a break.'

'Uncle Nick?' Tiggy mouthed at her brother out of sight of Nick and the twins.

'I thought I would take Nick down to the pub for a pint if you don't mind keeping an eye on these two rascals. It's been a while.'

'I don't imagine Nick wants to go to the pub.' Behind Nick she shook her head.

'What you doing, Aunty Tiggy?' Chrissie asked. 'Why are you shaking your head at Daddy?'

'You never told us we had an Uncle Nick,' Melody complained. 'And he's got a wheelchair.'

'Tiggy thinks I can't be trusted in a pub, Charlie,' Nick said. He smiled ruefully. 'Had one too many a few nights ago.'

Charlie and Nick had always got along. They had rarely been on leave at the same time, but on the rare occasions they had met, they had always been relaxed in each other's company. Once they had even gone on a climbing trip together. Charlie had been shocked and annoyed with Tiggy when he'd heard that they'd separated, and had said so. After that, she'd refused to discuss the subject with him.

Nick was getting to his feet, having pulled his crutches towards him.

'A pint sounds great,' he said. 'It may take us a while to get there, though.'

'I'll give you a lift,' Tiggy offered.

Nick frowned at her. 'No,' he said. 'A walk sounds good to me.'

'If you're not back in an hour or two,' Tiggy warned, 'I'll be down to drag you both out of there.'

As soon as they'd left, Tiggy organised the children with some colouring pens and paper and set about making dinner.

When the men still hadn't returned an hour later she fed the twins. Then she telephoned her sister-in-law to let her know what was happening.

'Nick is back living with you?' Alice couldn't have sounded more aghast if Tiggy had said she was shacking up with Genghis Khan.

'It's a long story,' Tiggy said. 'I'll tell you all about it when I see you next.'

'But—'

'Sorry, I have to go.' Tiggy knew if she didn't get off the phone Alice would insist on a blow-by-blow account. On the other hand, the family had probably discussed it around the kitchen table ad nauseam.

'Can we play dressing-up?' Melody asked, interrupting her musings.

Tiggy smiled. 'Of course you can.'

When the girls had scuttled off to find the box of old clothes she kept for them to dress up in, she poured herself a glass of wine and wandered into the sitting room. Charlie was a traitor. But, then, she'd never talked about the break-up with her family.

When it had all started to go wrong she had been too embarrassed, too frightened to tell them she was losing Nick. There had also been her deep-rooted sense of loyalty to him and the conviction that whatever was wrong in their marriage had been between them and no one else. When Nick had moved out she'd avoided her family for weeks and had then simply told them that things hadn't worked out.

The door banged and the sounds of laughter drifted in on the night air.

'Where are you, sis?' Charlie called out.

She got to her feet. The two of them looked like naughty schoolboys.

'I presume you're ready for supper?' she said.

'How do I look?' a little voice piped up from the doorway. Tiggy spun around and for a moment she couldn't breathe. Melody was wearing her wedding dress. She had totally forgotten she had flung it in the box of dressing-up clothes. Chrissie was holding up the back like a bridesmaid and both girls were beaming from ear to ear.

She turned her head to find Nick's eyes on her.

Their wedding had been a small affair. They had decided to marry during Nick's leave. When he'd proposed, Tiggy hadn't been able to think of a single reason to delay. Her mother, on the other hand, had been doubtful.

'Isn't it a little soon, darling? You hardly know each other.'

'I know everything I need to, Mum,' Tiggy had replied. 'I love him, he loves me, we want to spend the rest of our lives together. What could be more simple?'

They had been in the kitchen of Tiggy's mother's house, finalizing the details of the wedding.

The crease between her mother's brows had deepened. 'Meeting someone under, let's just say, intense circumstances, can heighten feelings. Marriage can be hard work, darling. Not all men, particularly men like Nick, settle to it easily. Trust me, I know. Your dad was in the army when we met and he hadn't even been in a combat zone.'

'Come on, Mum. Charlie's marriage is fine. And he works in a combat zone!'

'But he knew Alice for several years before they married.'

Tiggy frowned. 'What are you saying, Mum? Don't you believe Nick loves me?'

To be honest, sometimes in the night when Nick hadn't been with her she'd wondered the same thing. Why had Nick fallen in love with her? She was ordinary, nothing special, not even particularly pretty—although Nick had told her repeatedly that he loved the way she looked. And as soon as she'd seen him again the demons of the night had subsided and all her doubts had vanished.

Her mother had sighed. 'I have no doubt he loves you. I just have to see the way he looks at you.'

'Right, then. That's all that matters.'

And their wedding day had been perfect. They'd chosen a country house hotel for the venue—actually, Tiggy had chosen it, as Nick had been back in Afghanistan at the time—and had had a simple ceremony followed by a dinner. Afterwards they had left for a cottage in Yorkshire where they had holed up for the rest of the week, staying in bed all day, only rising to go for walks or get something to eat. It had been the happiest week of Tiggy's life.

Nick was still looking at Melody with a strange look on his face.

'Will you marry me, Uncle Nick?' Melody asked. 'Daddy can be the best man.'

Nick turned his gaze on Tiggy and smiled. 'Sorry, honey. I'm afraid I'm already married.'

After they had eaten and everyone had gone, Tiggy took her wine into the sitting room. Nick was staring into the fire.

'How are you feeling?' Tiggy asked.

'I was thinking about our wedding. I thought I had never seen anyone more beautiful than you that day.'

'You didn't look too shabby yourself.' He'd been in full dress uniform and had looked as sexy as hell.

'What happened to us, Tiggy?'

She set her glass on the table and sat down next to him. 'I don't know, Nick. One minute we were so happy, as if nothing could ever touch us, and the next… I don't know…we were no longer living together.' She laced her hands together to stop them shaking. 'You were so distant that last year. I knew something was wrong, but I didn't know what. I knew even less how to fix it.'

'I don't think you could have.' He turned his dark brown eyes on her. 'It wasn't your fault, Tigs. You did nothing wrong. It was me.'

'Then tell me, Nick. Help me to understand. I always believed a man and wife who loved and trusted each other could share anything and everything—support one another through the bad times as well as the good. Yet you shut me out, Nick, and I couldn't understand it. I began to doubt your love for me and then I began to doubt myself and that the old adage was proving true: marry in haste, repent at leisure. And I felt you regretted our marriage.'

He leaned back on the sofa and studied the ceiling. 'I guess I thought by marrying you I could save myself,' he said after a moment. 'I thought that you would bring me peace, and for a while you did.'

'For a while?'

'The only time I felt truly alive was when I was in Afghanistan. Here with you, it didn't seem real. Nothing seemed real.'

'Oh!' She sucked in a breath as a sharp pain tore through her.

'I never meant to hurt you. It was the last thing I wanted.'

'But you did hurt me.'

'I know.'

'In that case I think you owe it to me to explain what you mean.' However much he didn't want to talk to her, she wasn't going to let him away with that. 'You could have tried talking to me, Nick. You never gave me a chance to try and understand.'

He pushed himself out of the sofa and onto his feet. 'I'm not sure I understood myself. Over the years we were married, things in Afghanistan got worse. It was like living in a capsule. The men, the staff, we were a unit, each relying completely on one another.'

'I know. Remember, I was out there. Did you fall in love with someone else, Nick? Is that what happened? The way you fell in love with me?'

He shook his head. 'No! Of course not. There's never been anyone else but you.'

'Then what?'

'When I was back here with you it was great for the first few days. But being around your family never seemed as real to me as being with the guys. And then after a few days I would get restless. I would wonder what was happening back at camp. Hell, Tiggy I felt guilty. I was with you, safe, and there were men and women out there who needed me.'

'*I* needed you.'

'Not in the way they did.'

She decided to let that pass.

'It hurt me to even think of you, Tiggy. When I was at the camp all I thought about was you—here, in this armchair with a book in your hand, in our bed, going about your day, your normal, peaceful day. And when I was back, it was as if I was infecting our home with the horror of Afghanistan. I wanted to keep it separate.

That's why I stopped telling you what was happening out there. It was to protect you.'

'Nick, I didn't need protecting—I was your wife. You shut me out. Don't you see, it was the worst thing you could have done to me? Couldn't you see that when you weren't telling me what was going on, what was happening inside my head was so much worse?'

Her breathing was ragged from the effort of saying the words that had been rattling around in her head for so long.

'You were different. You were happy with our life. I couldn't be. Trust me, Tigs, I tried. And you wanted children. I couldn't see how I could be a father, not while there was a chance I wouldn't be around to see him or her grow up.'

'So you signed up without telling me. Worse, you signed up for another tour after we'd agreed that you wouldn't. How did you think that made me feel?'

'I never expected the war to last for so long. I thought if I did one final tour, I could settle down. That it would be out of my system. That perhaps then we could have a family. That I could live like a normal person. I was wrong.'

Tiggy got to her feet. 'I suppose I should thank you for being so honest. But it's not the whole truth, is it, Nick? It wasn't just that you wanted to protect me—I could see you were desperate to get back.' She blinked. She wouldn't let him see her cry. 'I'm going to bed.'

He reached out a hand and touched her on the shoulder. 'I would give everything to change the past.' He smiled ruefully. 'But this is who I am, Tiggy. God help me, this is who I am.'

Her heart was a lump of ice. 'I suppose I should

thank you for being so honest. But I have to tell you, Nick, none of what you've told me makes me feel any better. You couldn't have loved me. Not really. In the end, I wasn't enough for you, was I?'

The next morning Tiggy stopped by Charlie's house on her way to work. One of the girls had left their favourite doll, and Tiggy knew that as soon as she discovered it was missing there would be tears.

Charlie was in the kitchen, wearing his commercial pilot's uniform. He'd left the army when the twins had been on the way and had joined one of the major airlines. Alice, he explained, had just left to fetch the girls from nursery school. Alan too had been decommissioned and was working with a large engineering firm in Sussex. After years of chasing anything in a skirt, he was engaged to a woman he adored.

Ironically, Tiggy was the only one who hadn't managed to find enduring love.

'Hey, Tiggy,' Charlie said as he straightened his tie. 'Mum's been on the phone, asking me about Nick, and Alice is determined to come and see you. The whole family is buzzing with the news of you and Nick getting back together. Why didn't you tell us?'

'Because we're not back together,' Tiggy said. 'And that's the reason I didn't tell you. I knew you'd all be discussing me.'

Charlie grinned. 'You know what this family's like, sis. One for all, all for one.'

He ruffled her hair. 'For what it's worth, I think it's great news. I always liked Nick.'

'Of course you did. You're both men's men and Nick was someone to go down the pub with, someone to climb bloody mountains with, or whatever else you two got up to.'

Charlie paused. 'I liked him because he was someone who understood what it was really like out there. I liked him because he loved you. But I admit, if he hadn't been on crutches last night I would have punched him for hurting you.'

'Would you?' She stood on tiptoe and kissed her brother on the cheek. 'I have to say he didn't look particularly chastened when you returned him last night.'

'I was going to give him a good ticking-off when I had him on his own, but somehow...' Charlie grinned sheepishly '...we got talking about Afghanistan and then before I knew it, it was time to get back.' He frowned. 'But if you like, when I get back from this trip, I can give him a good talking to.'

Tiggy had to laugh. 'And what are you going to say? Are you going to tell him that he should go down on his knees and apologise? A bit late for that.'

'What the hell went wrong between you two anyway? You never said.'

'I guess I didn't really know myself. Still don't. But tell me, what did you talk about?'

Charlie poured coffee into two mugs and handed one to Tiggy. 'What do you think we talked about? What we always talk about. I know you women talk about stuff like your innermost feelings and whatever, but men just aren't like that. Most of us prefer to talk about footie. That sort of thing. Or in Nick's and my case, what it was like being on active service. No one who hasn't been there can really understand.'

'I was there,' she reminded him quietly.

'I know. But it's not the same. It's not the same as

being there month after month. It's not the same as being fired at and wondering whether you'll be able to hold your nerve or whether you'll turn tail and run. It's not the same as knowing that men and women depend on you to protect them, or rescue them; that if you don't do your job, someone—someone's husband, father, brother sister, even mother—could die.'

'You never talked about it either!'

'No, I didn't, and Alice understood that. I told her some of it, but mostly I kept it to myself. It isn't something you want the people who love you to know. You want to protect them. It's natural.'

'I disagree. Charlie, we're not Victorian women and you're not Victorian men. Don't you see you do us a disservice by thinking like that?'

'I'm afraid you've yet to convince me, sis.' He folded his arms. 'Do you know Nick went to see the families of every man who died under his care? Do you know he visited each man he had operated on to see how they were coping?'

Tiggy sank into a chair. 'No, I didn't. Why didn't he tell me?'

Charlie raised an eyebrow. 'For all the reasons I have just told you. It was horrific out there. When we came back home it was to forget for a while.' He finished his coffee and glanced at his watch. 'Where's Mum? She's looking after the girls for Alice while she goes to the hairdresser. They'll be back any minute and I have to go. But you have to realise, Tiggy, it wasn't all bad out there. I know it's difficult for you to understand but in many ways it was the best time of my life. I have never felt so close to a group of men as I did to my fellow officers. In many ways, I miss it.'

'Sorry, sorry.' Their mother came in and plonked her bag on the table. 'The traffic was horrendous. Some accident, I suspect. Girls and Alice not back yet? Anyway, I'm here now, love, so you can get off. Oh, hello, Tiggy. What are you doing here? I've been wondering why you haven't been round to visit lately.' She peered behind Tiggy. 'And where is Nick?'

Charlie laughed, ruffled Tiggy's hair again and kissed their mother on the cheek. 'I'll leave you to answer the hundred and one questions, Tiggy, but I have to shoot.'

He picked up his captain's cap. His face grew serious. 'Don't give up on him, Tiggy. He's a good man and there aren't many of his sort about.'

# CHAPTER SIXTEEN

ALL THAT DAY and in the ones that followed, Tiggy could think of nothing but Nick and whether she should fight for him. Or at least tell him she still loved him. In the end she decided she just couldn't risk it. Not yet. At least, not until Nick gave her some indication that he still cared. She would rather let Nick walk out the door than face being rejected again.

They settled into a routine. She would go to work. While she was at work Nick, determined not to fail his medical, would do his exercises, probably three times as often as he needed to. Before supper they would go for a walk around the neighbourhood. Nick had discarded his crutches for a walking stick and hardly needed to use that any more.

Sometimes they would watch television, more often they would play Scrabble or do the crossword together. In many ways it was as if they were still married—except they weren't sleeping together.

One evening Nick suggested they play poker.

'Are you sure?' she teased. 'Remember, I always beat you.'

He smiled. 'I remember everything. You were so... so different from anyone I'd ever met.'

Instead of fetching the cards, Tiggy curled up in the

armchair. She took a deep breath. 'And you were so different from anyone I'd ever met before. I couldn't quite believe at first that you were in love with me, that you wanted to marry me.'

He came across to where she was sitting and took her hands in his. 'I can't believe you didn't know how amazing you are. It was impossible for me *not* to love you. I should have tried harder to keep away from you, but I couldn't.'

'But I wasn't enough for you in the end.'

A shadow crossed his face. 'It wasn't you. Tiggy, you were everything in my life that was good and pure and calm.'

The firelight flickered across his face. In his eyes she saw such terrible pain it almost took her breath away.

'Talk to me, Nick. Please. Charlie told me how you visited the dead men's families, and those you had treated too. Why didn't you tell me that's where you were going? I would have come with you.'

He shook his head.

'I'm not sure I have the answer to that. The last year of our marriage I don't know where my head was. All I knew was that I couldn't bear to be with you.'

It was as if he'd stuck a scalpel into her heart.

'I was aware of that,' she admitted. 'It really hurt.'

'I know,' he said softly. 'I regret that more than I can say. And you're right. I owe you more of an explanation. At first, I couldn't wait to come back to you. I dreamt of you most nights when I was away.' He smiled softly. 'Waking from those dreams and knowing you were hundreds of miles away was hell. But at least you were safe.' He was looking into the distance and not at her. 'Does any of this make sense?'

'I'm not sure. But go on.' Charlie had said much the same thing. Perhaps he was right and whatever the men and women experienced in Afghanistan couldn't be understood except by those who had shared it with them. She'd been there for such a short while and it had become so much worse over the years. She had to try and understand what had driven Nick away from her, even if it broke her heart.

'It was easier to work than think of you. When I was working I could forget everything. I couldn't let myself think of you. If I did I would have allowed your fear to infect me. I had to stay focused. I never knew when the firing would start and I would be needed. I never knew when I might have to go out to the men. I worried constantly about what would happen to you if I died. I was distracted just when I needed to be at my most focused. The men depended on me. It was my job to help bring as many men home as we could.'

A burning cinder from the logs fell on the floor and Nick paused to pick it up and throw it back on the fire. Outside the rain was beating against the windows.

'When they stopped sending me out with the men on patrol, I resented it, although I knew they were right to keep the most senior doctors based at camp.'

He shook his head again. It was almost as if he was talking to himself and had forgotten she was even there. She wanted to reach out to him, to run her hands across his face, to pull him towards her to take his pain into her, but she stayed still, almost scared to breathe lest she stop him talking.

'Then the Taliban started using IEDs. The injuries were horrific. Worse, far worse than anything we'd seen before. Sometimes there was nothing left to save.'

He glanced up at her. 'Are you sure you want to hear this?' he repeated.

Tiggy nodded.

'I had to shut down my mind to do what I needed to do. I stopped thinking that the war was just. I simply wanted us all to get the hell out of there and for the carnage to stop. But in the meantime I had to stay. I saw them, you know—the new recruits as they arrived. Some of them boys still.

'When I came home on leave I couldn't relax. I felt guilty every moment I was away from there. Every time I closed my eyes I would imagine a soldier being brought in, needing my help. And I wasn't there.'

'What about the other doctors and nurses—just as experienced and dedicated as you? It wasn't as if you were abandoning the men. And you needed time off.'

He smiled ruefully. 'I know, at least in my head I knew, but I didn't really believe it. I guess I had started to believe in my own myth. That if I was there, I could save more men.'

'They always did believe you were some kind of lucky talisman.'

'Rightly or wrongly, I began to resent every minute I wasn't at the camp. Being home, being with you, no longer felt real. It was as if I was playing a part in a kind of charade.'

'That's what our marriage was to you?'

'It wasn't you. It was never you. I realised I was causing you pain, I saw it in your eyes every time I looked at you. And when you started talking about babies and my leaving the army…' He rubbed his hand across his face. 'I couldn't do it. I knew you needed me but I believed the men needed me more. I had to choose.'

'You could have talked to me. Tried to explain. I loved you, Nick. I wouldn't have put you under more pressure.'

'You have to understand, Tiggy, none of this was clear in my head at that time. It was only later—after I was injured the first time—that I began to make some kind of sense of it. Even to myself.

'That's when I came looking for you. It had been four years since we'd separated, but I had to see you.'

'When you saw me with the twins?'

'Yes. I wanted to explain, apologise, I guess, for marrying you, letting you love me…' He shook his head again. 'I don't know what I expected. All I knew was that I needed to see you.'

'But you changed your mind and left?'

'After I rang the doorbell and there was no reply, I began to doubt you were even still living here, in which case I was planning to phone Charlie for your address. I was about to do that when you arrived. You were laughing as you got out of the car. You looked so beautiful, you took my breath away.'

'Go on,' she said quietly.

'I was watching you, drinking in the sight of you and cursing myself for letting you go. You went around to the boot and took out a pushchair. Then you reached out and took a baby from the back seat. And another one from the other side.'

'The twins,' Tiggy said.

'Yes. Melody and Chrissie. I know that now. But that day I thought they were yours. I thought you had found everything you'd ever wanted. Everything you deserved.' He rubbed a hand across his eyes.

'You looked so happy. I knew then I'd been hop-

ing that somehow, despite everything, you'd be waiting for me.'

'I shouldn't have left. I should have tried harder to get
you to talk to me. But when you told me you'd signed
up for another tour, I thought…' Her voice hitched. 'I
thought you'd fallen out of love with me. How could I
have believed otherwise?'

'I never fell out of love with you. But, yes, when you
left, it was almost a relief. It meant I could return to Afghanistan without feeling guilty.'

Tiggy uncurled herself and crossed over to him. She
sat on his lap and when he made to pull away from her
she wrapped her arms around his neck. 'I don't want to
talk any more. I don't want to think about the past—or
the future.' She tugged his head down towards hers. 'I
think it's time you kissed me.'

If sex had been good between them before, this time
it was mind-blowing. It was if all the pain and longing
Tiggy had felt over the years was poured into their love-
making. When they'd finished they lay in each other's
arms, not talking. What more was there to say? But for
the first time since Nick had left, Tiggy felt whole again.

After a while they made love once more, slowly
this time, savouring one another. Tiggy kissed every
scar, memorising the feel of his body that was at once
familiar but at the same time so very different. She
wasn't going to think about the past or the future. All
she wanted right at this moment was to be exactly where
she was.

The next morning Tiggy lay in bed, listening to the clat-
ter of Nick in the kitchen. He was whistling a tune she
didn't recognise but he sounded happy.

As was she. It didn't matter that there was still so much that was unresolved between them. She now knew in her heart that Nick had never stopped loving her. The future was uncertain; she wasn't even sure that they could find a way back together, and she'd be risking her heart all over again, but it was too late. She loved him, and he loved her. Surely that was the most important thing? And this time they would talk. There would be no more secrets.

Nick came into the room, carrying a tray. She smiled slowly when she saw that he was naked apart from the towel wrapped around his waist. She sat up, letting the sheet fall from her body. He placed the tray on the bedside table and grinned slowly. 'I guess coffee can wait, huh?'

The next few days were among the happiest Tiggy had known. They spent most of the time in bed, rediscovering each other's bodies. Neither of them talked about the future.

When they weren't in bed, they went for short runs together. This time it was Tiggy who ran backwards, teasing Nick about his inability to keep up. However, every day he was getting stronger. His limp had all but disappeared and his body was once more hard and muscled. In the evenings they took turns cooking and she showed Nick how to make omelettes and other simple dishes. Afterwards they would feed each other, prolonging the moment until they fell, laughing, into bed.

But of course it couldn't continue. This morning, the third time this week, she leaned over the sink hanging onto the edge for dear life before she was sick again. She could no longer even try to put it down to food poisoning. But that didn't mean she was pregnant.

She'd only had unprotected sex with Nick once, the first time, and since then they'd been careful to use contraception. Surely she couldn't have fallen pregnant?

Now, where had she heard that sort of denial before? Once was all it took. But her period could simply be late—stress and worry could do that, couldn't it?

She rinsed her face with cold water and sighed. Who was she trying to kid? Late periods were a pretty good indicator on their own, but put together with morning sickness…well, she'd have to have lost every ounce of common sense to deny the obvious. She was probably pregnant.

Pregnant. A tiny little baby was growing inside her. After thinking that motherhood might never be on the cards for her.

Nick's baby.

Nick, a father, whether he wanted to be or not.

Or not. Who was she kidding? Nick hadn't wanted to be a father six years ago. He had walked away from her then and she didn't know for sure that he'd wouldn't be walking away from her again. As soon as he was fit enough to pass his medical.

And although she loved him, although she would have given everything to have him around to be the father of her child, she wouldn't—couldn't—bear him to stay for the wrong reasons.

Which he would.

Tiggy washed her face and picked up her toothbrush. She almost didn't recognise the wild woman with burning eyes in the mirror. She smiled. Only a few weeks ago her life had been settled, a little bit boring perhaps but peaceful. Now she was reminded of those heady days in Afghanistan when she'd never felt more alive,

and however Nick felt about being a father wouldn't
change anything. She was going to have this baby.

But if she told him, would he feel trapped? Would
he stay out of some misplaced sense of duty, something
Nick did so well?

It wasn't as if she couldn't cope without him. Mum
would help and her job paid well enough.

But she was getting ahead of herself. First things
first. She had to know for sure if she was pregnant.

Then she would decide what, or if, to tell Nick.

# CHAPTER SEVENTEEN

FINALLY IT WAS time for Nick to return to the hospital for an appointment with the physio, followed by a check-up with the medical team. If they were happy with his progress he would go through a full army medical in a couple of weeks' time and a decision would be made on whether or not he was fit to remain in the army—and if he could continue in emergency medicine.

Tiggy had no doubt what the answer would be, but she refused to think about what would happen after that. Having had a week off, it was time for her to go back to work. Nick had insisted that he didn't need her to come with him to the hospital.

It was late afternoon and she'd just returned home after her early shift when the doorbell rang. At first Tiggy assumed that it was Nick, but when she opened the door it was to find a young, attractive woman she didn't recognise standing on the doorstep.

'Can I help?' she asked. Perhaps she was looking for directions?

The woman bit her lip.

'Does a Nick Casey still live here?' she asked.

Tiggy froze. All at once all the old insecurities returned. God in heaven, was this one of Nick's girl-friends? If so, she was so young—at least half his age.

A chill crept up her spine, to be replaced with an anger she hadn't known she was even capable of feeling.

'No,' Tiggy replied abruptly. 'Not for some time anyway.'

The rain was falling in a relentless sheet, soaking the woman. She didn't even seem to have an umbrella with her. Whoever she was, Tiggy couldn't leave her on the step. Besides, whatever the woman wanted with Nick, she had to know.

'Why don't you come in?'

'I don't want to disturb you.' The accent was American.

'Come in for a moment. At least to get dry.'

The woman hesitated for a few moments longer. Then she smiled. Instantly it lit up her face. She really was quite beautiful. 'If you're sure I'm not disturbing you?'

When her surprise guest was seated, Tiggy sat down opposite her. She decided to get straight to the point. 'How do you know Nick?'

'I don't really know him at all.'

'Oh?'

'He's my father.'

Tiggy was stunned. Whatever she'd expected, it hadn't been this. Nick had a daughter! A grown-up daughter. Why had he never said? Thoughts tumbled around her head. How could he have kept this from her?

'Nick is your father?' she said stupidly.

'Yes. At least, I think he is.' The girl took a photograph from her handbag and passed it to Tiggy. 'Is this him?'

It was definitely Nick. A much younger Nick but him nevertheless. She would have recognised those brown eyes and wide grin anywhere.

He wasn't alone in the photo. Next to him was a girl with brown hair and shining eyes, who was staring up at him lovingly.

'The woman?' Tiggy asked, her throat as dry as dust.

'My mother.'

Tiggy jumped to her feet. 'I'll just make some tea, shall I?' She needed a few moments alone to gather her thoughts. Nick had been seriously involved with someone before her, someone who had clearly adored him and with whom he'd had a child. How could he not have told her? What else had he kept from her? Was the woman in the photo, this girl, the real reason he'd left her six years ago? Had everything he'd told her been lies? She felt sick.

When she was satisfied she had her emotions under control, she returned to the sitting room. The girl leaped from the chair. 'I'm sorry. I haven't even told you my name. I'm Kate.'

'Hello, Kate. I'm Tiggy. Perhaps you should start from the beginning.'

For a second tears shimmered in Kate's eyes. Then she took a shuddering breath.

'I never knew my father. Mom would never talk about him. She died a month ago.'

Instinctively, Tiggy reached for her hand. 'I'm so sorry.'

'When I was going through her things I found that photo. I knew it had to be important to Mom. I asked around, but no one seemed to know who he was. All I could find out was that Mom had met a Brit when he was over on holiday, and by the time he'd left, she was pregnant.'

Nick was already a father. She couldn't get her head around what Kate was telling her.

'And now to get all the way here—to track him down to this address, only to find he's not here... I'll have to start looking for him all over again.'

Of course, Kate wouldn't have a clue that Nick had been in hospital.

Tiggy smiled grimly. Nick was going to get quite a shock. For whatever reason he'd kept his daughter a secret, there was no doubt he was going to come face to face with her.

'Your father is at the hospital. He's okay,' she added quickly, seeing the alarm in Kate's eyes. 'I mean, he's sort of okay. Look, I'd better tell you the whole story.'

By the time Tiggy had finished explaining it was almost dark.

'I need to see him,' Kate said.

'I'm bringing him back here tomorrow,' Tiggy said. 'Perhaps you should wait until then?'

But Kate was already gathering her bag, a determined look on her face. 'I've waited a long time to meet him. I don't want to wait any longer.'

'In that case, of course, I'll take you there.'

Tiggy left Kate at the hospital and sat in her car, watching the rain pour down the windscreen.

She was still reeling. Nick had a daughter and he was about to have another child. She couldn't begin to imagine how the news would affect a man who didn't want children.

She had been planning to tell him about the baby tonight, but now it would have to wait.

So she wouldn't tell him. At least not yet. Not until she had to.

# CHAPTER EIGHTEEN

WHEN THE DOORBELL rang, Tiggy opened the door to find Nick standing there. He looked as if he had been caught up in an earthquake.

The rain was still falling steadily, his hair was plastered to his head and his eyes were wild.

'Why haven't you been answering my phone calls?' he said, stepping into the hall. 'I was worried about you.'

She stood aside to let him pass. 'Come in. You don't have to worry about me—ever. And I'm sure the internet has a list of good hotels.'

'I thought I was staying here?' he said, shocked.

'I've decided that's not a good idea.'

Puzzled, he took her by the shoulders. 'What is it, Tiggy?'

'You didn't think you should have told me you had a daughter?'

'So that's why you haven't being taking my calls.' He shook the rain from his hair like a dog who'd been for a swim. 'Kate told me she'd been to see you. I realise it must have been a shock but I thought she'd explained...'

'Explained what, exactly?'

'Let's sit down and talk,' Nick said firmly, taking her by the hand and leading her into the sitting room.

'I'm all ears, Nick,' Tiggy said grimly. 'But, believe

me, this is going to take some explaining. You have a child and you didn't think I should know?'

'I didn't know myself.' Nick looked at her in astonishment. Could it be he'd really had no idea he was a father? 'You don't think I would have kept that from you? You don't think I would have had a daughter and deliberately excluded her from my life?'

'How would I know? You kept everything else from me.' She wasn't going to let him off the hook that easily. It was as if all the trust she'd being allowing herself to feel over the last week or so had been washed away like a pile of sticks in a flood.

'I swear to you I had no idea,' Nick said, sitting down next to her. He cupped her face in his hands and forced her to look at him. 'Her mother never told me she was pregnant. It was a brief fling—I was only eighteen.'

Could she believe him? She desperately wanted to. But he'd kept so much from her.

'So what are you going to do now?'

'I don't know.' Suddenly he smiled. 'She's quite a girl. I think I'm going to enjoy having her around. If I can persuade her to stay for a while, that is.' He reached out for her. 'I missed you.'

She pulled away. 'I'm sorry, Nick. I don't know what we've been doing these last weeks but it can't last. Too much has happened. We can't turn the clocks back and pretend that we don't have a past.'

'Forget the past. Isn't it time we started talking about the future? The doctors gave me the all-clear. As far as they're concerned I'm fit for work. Now everything's back to normal, we can start thinking about having a life together again.'

She turned away from him. 'I don't think that's possible. I don't think I can ever trust you again. I'll always be wondering what you're not telling me.'

'Then let's not think about the future. Let's take it one day at a time.'

'I can't. I'm sorry, Nick. I just can't.'

He looked at her for one slow moment. 'I'm not going to let you give up on me, Tiggy, and I'm sure as hell not going to give up on you. We've been apart for too long.'

She stumbled to her feet. 'You're fine now, Nick. I think it's time you left.'

'Left?'

'Yes. Go back to the hotel. Go to Kate. Do whatever the hell you want to, but stay out of my life.'

Nick paced up and down the hotel room. He'd made a mess of it. But, then, had he really expected that it would be easy to win Tiggy back? She was right. If he was going to convince her that they were meant to be together, he needed to convince her first that he'd changed.

But how the hell was he going to do that? A few weeks ago he'd had no one outside his work expecting anything from him. Now he had two women, both of whom were a handful. Kate he could do nothing about, except be there for her in a way he hadn't been able to when she'd been a child, a fact that burned him up, and wait for her to learn she could rely on him. But Tiggy? How could he put that right?

Then it came to him. Their marriage had broken down because he'd been unable to share his life with her, because he'd treated her as someone who'd needed to be protected. He'd thought he'd been doing the best for her, but hadn't she made it clear to him that that was the very thing she couldn't bear?

She wasn't the woman he'd married—she was so much more than that. She was strong, feisty and independent, and he loved her. And whatever she said, she loved him. But would she continue to love him when she knew everything there was to know about him?

There was only one way to find out. He picked up his mobile. It was time to call in a few favours.

Not for the first time Tiggy wondered if she was crazy. Nick had turned up at her door and insisted that she pack for a night away. When she'd tried to protest, he'd threatened to pack for her and to throw her in the back of the car along with her belongings.

'I've checked with the ward,' he said. 'You're not due on duty for a couple of days. I promise to have you back in plenty of time for your shift. Now, let me have your passport.'

Bewildered, Tiggy did as she was asked.

'Where are we going?' she asked as they headed north.

'I want to show you the place I spent my childhood.'

Tiggy was astounded. When they'd been married, she'd suggested several times that they visit Nick's old home in Ireland. But Nick had always refused, saying there was nothing in Ireland he cared to revisit. Eventually she'd stopped asking.

They took a flight to Dublin, where Nick had arranged for a hire car and from there they headed south.

'You should have asked Kate if she wanted to come,' Tiggy said. 'I'm sure she would have been interested.'

'Kate can come another time,' Nick said. 'Besides, she has plans for the next couple of days.'

The grim line of his mouth told Tiggy he wasn't pleased about something.

'You two haven't had a disagreement?'

'No, not exactly. It's just…'

'Just…?' Tiggy prompted.

'Oh, hell. It's Luke. My so-called doctor. I can't help but notice the way he's been looking at Kate. And I'd guess by the way she's behaving around him, she's not immune either.'

Tiggy hid a smile. Who would have thought? Nick acting the part of the concerned father. Except, judging by his expression, this was no act.

'So what's the problem? Luke's lovely, and Kate is clearly well able to take care of herself. She's not that much younger than I was when you went after me.'

'That was different,' Nick growled.

'And how exactly was it different?'

'Luke can't be taken seriously. I know stuff about his past I wish I didn't know—stuff that makes him a bad choice for Kate. And if that wasn't bad enough, he's a womaniser. You only have to see the way the nurses behave around him to know he has a reputation.'

This time Tiggy did laugh. 'And you were a saint when I met you? Do I need to tell you that I was warned off you the same way you want to warn off Kate? Trust me, Nick, don't even attempt it. Kate strikes me as a woman who can take care of herself. Just as I was,' she added softly.

'Sue was right, though, wasn't she? Perhaps you would have been better off if we'd never met.'

'Let's not go down that road again, Nick.' She gazed

out of the window at the lush rolling hills. 'I wouldn't change a second of the time we had together, not even if it meant not having the pain.'

Nick didn't reply but his hands tightened on the steering wheel.

Some time later Nick stopped the car at the top of a field just past a small village. The sun was sinking in the sky but at this time of year there were a couple of hours yet before it got dark.

'You lived in a field?' Tiggy asked with a smile. Without waiting for him to reply, she opened the door and stepped out of the car. The air was like liquid oxygen after London and she breathed deeply. In the distance smoke curled from a farmhouse chimney and in the fields nearby a flock of sheep grazed contentedly.

'That was where I was brought up.' Nick pointed to the farmhouse.

'But it's beautiful!' she said honestly. 'How can anyone not love it here?'

Nick shook his head. 'You see what you want to see : an idyllic-looking farmhouse that you imagine is filled with love and laughter. It wasn't like that for me.' He took her by the hand. 'Come with me.'

She let him lead her down a narrow track. 'We owned the farmhouse. When my father died, Mum and I tried to carry on. I was eight. It didn't matter at first that I couldn't really help as there were others to do the outside work—farmworkers my father employed. We could have managed—if my mother hadn't fallen to pieces.'

He stopped by a flat rock and without saying anything they sat down.

'What happened?' Tiggy asked.

'She started drinking. She became depressed. To be honest, I don't know which came first. All I know is that the mother I loved turned into someone I didn't recognise. I would come home from school to find that she hadn't shopped, let alone cooked. It was obvious that she'd spent most of the day in bed. I got to know the smell of mints pretty well.'

Tiggy closed her eyes. She could see Nick as a boy. Worse, she could feel that child's anger, bewilderment and hurt.

'I tried to look after her and the farm. Eventually the men who helped on the farm drifted away. I suspect Mum stopped paying them. One or two of their wives came to try and talk some sense into her but it was no use. I kept on trying. I cleaned and cooked as best I could—if you call tins of beans and bowls of cereal cooking. I milked the cows, cleaned out the barns, but it was no use. There was too much for a boy to do. I knew there wouldn't be enough hay to feed the cows in the winter but I also knew there was no money to buy any.

'I tried to speak to Mum. I begged her to get help. I pleaded, I shouted, I told her Dad would be ashamed to see the farm in such a state, but nothing got through to her.'

'Didn't the school try to help?'

'They tried to talk to me. I was falling behind with my schoolwork and falling asleep at my desk. But I wouldn't tell them about Mum. I was scared they would take me away. I kept on hoping that one day she would get up and be the mother she'd been before.'

He stared off into the distance and Tiggy reached for his hand.

'In the end we had to sell all the livestock. But still

we struggled on. Until finally the bank foreclosed. We had to sell. And at a knock-down price. I persuaded Mum to keep the barn—that building over there.' He pointed to a ramshackle building about a hundred metres from the farmhouse. 'There was just about enough left over from the sale to make it habitable.'

Tiggy blinked. The building he was pointing to was tiny. Surely it wasn't big enough for two people to live in it?

'I fixed it up as best I could and we managed. Somehow. Then, when I was sixteen, Mum died.'

He swallowed.

'Oh, Nick. Why didn't you tell me any of this?'

'Because I was ashamed. I couldn't save the farm and I couldn't save my mother. I began to wonder if there was anything I *could* do.'

'You were a child!'

'I didn't feel like a child. I felt I had let them down. Mum and Dad. Dad would have expected me to look after Mum.'

'What did you do then?' Tiggy asked.

'I could have gone into care, but I didn't want that and as I was sixteen they couldn't make me. I made up my mind I would be a doctor. Perhaps then I could do some good. My grades in school were rubbish but I had two years left to sit exams that would get me into university. When I wasn't at school I spent every spare minute at the library.'

He smiled. 'At least it was warm there. I managed to get a job at the local hospital as a night porter when I was seventeen, although I made myself a year older on my application. At nights when I wasn't working I was in the hospital library, learning anything and everything I could find in medical textbooks. One advantage: I learned to do without sleep. I passed my exams—all A stars—and applied to medical school. Edinburgh accepted me.

'It was still impossible financially so I joined the army as a cadet as a way of funding myself through medical school. Turned out it was the best decision of my life. I loved the army. After my chaotic upbringing I liked the order: the way meals were at certain times; the way there was a time and a place for everything. And years of working on the farm had left me strong and so I thrived on the physical challenges of being in the army.' He turned to look at her. 'I knew I had come home.'

It explained so much, but why hadn't he told her this before? She would never have given up on him had she known.

'Would you like to see the barn?' he asked.

'Won't the owners object?'

'I checked. They're away for a few days but they said to help myself. They use the barn as a self-catering rental during the summer.'

They walked hand in hand down the track until they came to the door of the house. Nick bent and retrieved the key from under a stone. He grinned and suddenly the sadness left his eyes. 'Exactly where I used to leave it.'

He unlocked the door and stepped aside to allow Tiggy to go in before him. The little house was dark, the only light coming from two small windows, and it took her eyes a few moments to adjust. There was an open fireplace in one thick wall with a couple of chairs in front of it, a small kitchen to the side and a double bed against the other wall, taking up most of the remainder of the space. Cosy for a weekend retreat, but for two people to live?

'There was a sofa where the chairs are now,' Nick said. 'It doubled up as my bed. Until Mum died. '

He glanced around the room. 'Mum had her bed where this one is now and I put up a curtain for her so she could have some privacy. As it was only a single, it left some space for my desk.'

He pointed to the fireplace. 'Mum did have her good days, especially in the beginning. Sometimes we used to toast marshmallows over the fire and she would tell me about her childhood. She came from Belfast. Sadly her parents wanted nothing to do with her when she married a man from the south.' He rubbed his hand across his forehead. 'I think that's enough reminiscing for a moment. How do you feel about staying here tonight? I could light a fire.'

'Can you bear to stay here with all its memories?'

He breathed deeply. 'You know, Tiggy, I'm glad I came. All my life I've been dreaming of this house, and those dreams haven't been pleasant. But it doesn't look anything like it used to.'

Tiggy couldn't bear it any longer. She crossed over to Nick and wound her arms around his neck.

'Come, my darling,' she said. 'I think we should lay these ghosts to rest for once and for all.'

Later, when they'd had their fill of one another and were lying in each other's arms, Tiggy looked up at Nick. Whatever she tried to tell herself, she knew she was where she needed to be.

The morning sun and the smell of frying bacon woke Tiggy to a new day.

Nick, wearing only a pair of jeans, was at the cooker,

fighting with the bacon, which appeared ready to go up in smoke. Tiggy leaped from the bed, rescued the bacon and retrieved the toast, which was threatening to go the same way. 'You know, for a man with a hero's reputation you're pretty useless in the kitchen. I'm surprised you didn't starve as a boy!'

Nick stood back. 'Give me complicated surgery any time.'

After breakfast they tidied the house and left the key under the stone. On their way back to the airport, Nick pulled up alongside a church on the outskirts of a village.

'This is where I was christened,' he said. 'And where my parents are buried.'

'Shall we see if we can find their graves?' Tiggy asked.

'I know exactly where they are.'

He led her through the gate and to the side of the church, before coming to stop in front of a simple stone engraved with the names and dates of Eleanor and Jack Casey.

'I couldn't afford a separate stone for my mother at the time,' Nick said softly.

Tiggy reached for his hand and squeezed it. 'You did everything you could for her. It wasn't within your power to save her.'

'I know. At least, I know that now.'

'Shall we go inside?'

Nick shrugged. 'If you like. There's not much to see.'

The church was small but had the most exquisite stained-glass windows. It was more beautiful to Tiggy than any cathedral. She sat in the front pew and let the peace wash over her.

Nick sat next to her. 'Maybe one day we can renew our vows here? Start over again?'

She imagined Nick as a baby, being christened at the altar, being brought up on the farm as happy as a pig in clover, then his life going so badly wrong. She could understand him now. She could even understand why their marriage hadn't survived. But a little piece of her still wondered if it was too late for them.

'With a baby?' she asked tentatively. 'In time?'

Nick took her by the hands. 'I'm not sure I can be the kind of father I want to be, and I still need to get my head around the fact I already have a daughter.' He folded his fingers around hers. 'But if it's what you want…'

His reply wasn't good enough. She needed him to want this baby as much as she did.

'Let's wait and see, Nick.'

# CHAPTER NINETEEN

A FEW DAYS after they returned to London, Tiggy received a phone call from Alice.

'Please, can you take them for the night?' she begged as soon as pleasantries were over. 'Charlie's on long haul and my mother's feeling poorly. I would take the twins with me but you know what a handful they can be. Your mother has something on she can't get out of and your dad finds it difficult to cope with them on his own. I wouldn't ask if I wasn't desperate. I know you have a lot on your plate, what with Nick and everything.' She dropped her voice. 'How's that going, by the way?'

'Of course I'll take the twins,' Tiggy reassured her, ignoring the question. The truth was she didn't know how she and Nick were doing. Since they'd returned from Ireland they'd resumed their earlier routine without returning to the topic of the future. 'I haven't seen Chrissie and Melody for ages. I've missed them.'

'You've probably forgotten what a handful they can be,' Alice replied dryly. 'But thanks, Tiggy. I owe you.'

They arranged that Alice would drop the girls off on her way to her mother's in an hour.

Nick wandered into the kitchen to wash his hands. He'd bought an old Harley-Davidson and was restoring it. He'd go mad, he'd said, if he didn't have something

to do. Although he'd passed his medical, he was still
on leave until he'd been assessed by the army doctors.
He looked so sexy in his T-shirt with the sleeves cut
off, his faded jeans and a smear of grease up one arm.

'You don't fancy holding the tools for me while I
work?' he asked.

'Sorry. No can do. Twin invasion on the horizon.'

'Perhaps they could hold the tools?'

Tiggy laughed. 'Nick, they're four years old!'

Nick wrapped his arms around her waist and nuz-
zled her neck. 'Do we have time to slip upstairs before
they arrive?'

'We most certainly do not.' But when Nick continued trailing kisses down her neck, her knees went weak.
'Perhaps if we're quick?'

They only just managed to shower and dress before
the twins arrived. The little girls ran into the house like
two miniature tornadoes. 'Aunty Tiggy! Uncle Nick! We
want to go to Hamleys. Mummy says if we ask nicely
you might take us. Please say yes!'

Tiggy sighed. A visit to the toy superstore wasn't her
first choice of a day out. But when the girls looked at
Nick with their butter-wouldn't-melt-in-my-mouth ex-
pressions, he immediately agreed.

'What is Hamleys anyway?' he asked Tiggy as the
girls did a victory dance around the kitchen.

'Looks like you're about to find out.'

Nick looked through the kitchen window, towards
his bike, which was waiting in the driveway. A tortured
look crossed his face. 'I guess the bike can wait. Lead
me to this place—whatever it is.'

'It's a toy store!' Nick said, sounding aghast as Tiggy
hurried inside after the excited twins. He whistled under

his breath. 'Good God, it's the size of a multi-storey car park.'

Melody and Chrissie were tugging at Tiggy's arms. 'Come on, Aunty Tiggy,' Melody pleaded. 'I want to see the doll's house.'

Chrissie's mouth settled into a line that didn't bode well. '*I* want to see the fairy-tale stuff.'

Tiggy turned to a still shell-shocked-looking Nick. 'I don't suppose…'

Nick sent her the ghost of a smile. 'I'll take one, you take the other.' He picked Chrissie up and tossed her into the air. She sent him a look that would have cowed lesser men. 'Please, put me down, Uncle Nick. I'm not a baby.'

'Okay.' Nick placed her back on the ground and raised his eyebrows at Tiggy, who suppressed a smile. She had no idea how he was going to cope with a couple of hours of Chrissie but she was looking forward to finding out.

After she and Melody had visited almost every department in the store and they still hadn't come across Nick and Chrissie, Tiggy was beginning to worry. But to her relief she spotted them eventually in the toy train department. Nick was sitting cross-legged with Chrissie on his lap as they watched the trains going around.

'So here you are,' Tiggy said.

Chrissie and Nick glanced at her before turning their attention back to the train set. 'Finished already?' Nick asked over his shoulder.

'It's been more than two hours, Nick. Aren't you and Chrissie hungry?'

Nick glanced at his watch. 'Two hours! No way. Anyway…' he ruffled Chrissie's curls, almost exactly the way he'd used to ruffle Tiggy's '…we've had a snack.'

When Chrissie did turn round Tiggy could see that they had indeed. Chrissie's mouth was covered in chocolate.

'We had chocolate milkshake *and* chocolate cake,' she said.

''S not fair,' Melody complained. 'Aunty Tiggy made me have yucky soup. She said I needed something proper for lunch.'

Nick removed Chrissie from his lap and stood up. 'Sorry, Tigs,' he said, looking sheepish. 'Guess I don't make a very good babysitter.'

Chrissie looked up at him adoringly. 'You're the best babysitter ever,' she said staunchly. 'Now, can we go back to our trains?'

# CHAPTER TWENTY

A COUPLE OF days later, when Nick returned from his army medical, he was grinning. Tiggy's heart sank. Although she was glad he'd passed, she couldn't bear to think he was going away again.

'You passed, then,' she said.

'Yes.'

'You'll be going back to Afghanistan?'

'Actually, I won't.' Nick looked at her. 'I've asked for a permanent post in the military hospital in Birmingham. Or, if you don't want to move, I'll resign from the army and look for a job in London.'

It was the last thing she'd expected.

'Why?' She needed him to spell it out.

'Because I don't want to leave you again. I want the life I had and thought I didn't want. I was wrong. I lost the woman I loved most in the world and I'm not going to lose her again.' He crouched by her chair. 'I've been such a fool, Tiggy. My life is nothing without you, never has been, never will be. I know it'll take time for you to learn to trust me again, but I can wait. I can, and will, wait forever.'

She closed her eyes. Could she believe him?

'I'm learning, Tigs. I'm learning that being a family means responsibility, but that it can be good too.

Kate and I have a lot of lost time to make up, but we're making progress. I'd like you to meet her properly. I want the two most important women in my life to get to know each other.'

'Looks like you've taken to being a father.' If he could be a decent father to Kate, perhaps he could be one to their child too?

'It still feels weird, but I'm learning family life can be fun. The other day, when we were at Hamleys with the girls, I realised that there are many ways to be a parent. I might not always get it right, but that doesn't matter. If there's enough love, like there is between you and your family, like Charlie and Alice have with their children, it can be good. Great even. Responsibility doesn't always have to feel bad.'

Something inside her chest shifted. It was what she'd been longing to hear. 'Your parents would have been proud of you. You do know that, don't you?'

'I did my best. It was all I could do. And you're right, the soldiers on the front line have the best medical personnel in the country to look after them. I don't want to look back any more. Life's too short.'

He pulled her to her feet and placed his hands on either side of her face. 'I know I have no right to ask you. I know I've hurt you badly. I would understand if you couldn't forgive me, but if I can't have you, I won't have anyone.'

She turned her face up to his. There were no guarantees in life, but she believed him when he said he loved her.

'Shut up and kiss me,' she demanded.

Of course they ended up in bed together.

Nick's hands were cupping her hips, sweeping like

feathers over her stomach sending ripples of liquid heat straight to her pelvis. Suddenly he paused and ran his hands over her abdomen again, before returning to her breasts. A look of wonder filled his eyes. 'Tiggy, are you pregnant?'

She gazed up at the man who, for better or for worse, she loved and would always love, no matter what pain he'd caused her, no matter if the future with him would always be like a roller-coaster. She would rather spend one minute in hell with him than a lifetime without him.

'Do you mind?'

He laughed and rolled over on his back, pulling her on top of him. 'Mind?' His hands caressed her bottom. 'It's perfect. You're perfect. Our whole bloody lives are going to be perfect.'

She smiled down at him. 'Maybe not perfect, at least not always, but pretty damn close.'

\* \* \* \* \*

# THE LONE WOLF'S CRAVING

BY
TINA BECKETT

First published in Great Britain 2013
by Mills & Boon, an imprint of Harlequin (UK) Limited.
Harlequin (UK) Limited, Eton House, 18-24 Paradise Road,
Richmond, Surrey TW9 1SR

© Tina Beckett 2013

ISBN: 978 0 263 89911 5

Harlequin (UK) policy is to use papers that are natural, renewable and recyclable products and made from wood grown in sustainable forests. The logging and manufacturing process conform to the legal environmental regulations of the country of origin.

Printed and bound in Spain
by Blackprint CPI, Barcelona

**Dear Reader**

Changes in life. We all go through them. Some of those changes make us stronger...and some of them have the power to bring us to our knees. The hero and heroine in THE LONE WOLF'S CRAVING, part two of the *Men of Honour* duet, are both going through such a change. They each struggle with the realisation that their lives will be forever altered as a result. They must make a choice: accept what the future holds and move forward, or rail against fate and remain trapped in a vicious cycle of anger and bitterness.

Thank you for joining Luke and Kate as they face the heartbreak that comes with change and search for the courage to overcome. Best of all—they find love along the way. I hope you enjoy reading about their journey as much as I enjoyed writing about it!

Much love

*Tina Beckett*

Born to a family that was always on the move, **Tina Beckett** learned to pack a suitcase almost before she knew how to tie her shoes. Fortunately she met a man who also loved to travel, and she snapped him right up. Married for over twenty years, Tina has three wonderful children and has lived in gorgeous places such as Portugal and Brazil.

Living where English reading material is difficult to find has its drawbacks, however. Tina had to come up with creative ways to satisfy her love for romance novels, so she picked up her pen and tried writing one. After her tenth book she realised she was hooked. She was officially a writer.

A three-times Golden Heart finalist, and fluent in Portuguese, Tina now divides her time between the United States and Brazil. She loves to use exotic locales as the backdrop for many of her stories. When she's not writing you can find her either on horseback or soldering stained-glass panels for her home.

Tina loves to hear from readers. You can contact her through her website or 'friend' her on Facebook.

**Recent titles by the same author:**

**These books are also available in eBook format from www.millsandboon.co.uk**

Dedication:

To those who have faced life-altering events.
May you always find the strength to face the future.

# CHAPTER ONE

HAD SHE FIGURED out who he was *before* or *after* she'd had sex with him?

Because Dr. Lucas Blackman sure as hell hadn't known the petite blonde American wandering around his emergency room was his wartime hero's long-lost daughter. Not when he'd pressed her against the wall in the supply closet and buried himself inside her. Not after it was over. In fact, she'd disappeared as quickly as she'd come.

He groaned at the unintended pun. And then again as memories of his actions yesterday washed over him: the snick of the lock; the fumbling with clothing; along with every second of pounding urgency that had happened afterward. Damn it if he wouldn't do it all over again, even knowing what he did now. That she'd probably used him to get what she'd wanted.

Not that he'd been the slightest bit hesitant at the time.

And that memory made his already sucky day even suckier. Walking to the physical therapy center to see how his friend was doing, and seeing the woman he'd had the best sex with—well, in a long damn time—standing beside him sent shock waves rolling through him that rooted him to the spot. Nick introducing her to one of the therapists as his daughter just made it that much worse.

He decided to back away while he still could.

Then her eyes met his and flitted away, making a painless getaway impossible. He could swear he saw a trace of guilt in the deep blue depths. At what? Their naughty rendezvous? At having coffee with him for the last two mornings, all the while being coy and secretive about her reasons for visiting the hospital?

Nick spied him, calling him over just as the therapist disappeared back into the rehabilitation center. His friend winced slightly as he rotated his upper body, his surgery site evidently still tender. "Come and meet Kate—er, Katherine." His friend glanced at her in question. "My daughter."

"Kate," she answered in the same low Southern drawl that had drawn him like a moth to a flame. First in the hospital cafeteria. Then in the tiny supply closet. He could still her soft moans as he'd taken her. Who knew a drawl during sex could be so damned hot. She'd reminded him of warm lazy summers by the lake, of county fairs and high school football games.

All things American.

He'd been homesick yesterday and devastated after losing a patient in the E.R., and there she'd been. As if sent just to ease his pain. And she had. She'd sent him right over the edge.

And she was his hero's daughter. The man who'd once saved his life. *His daughter!*

Hell, today had officially taken a nosedive.

He moved closer and held out his hand, forcing her to do the polite thing and take it. When she tried for a quick grip and release, he curled his fingers around hers and held on, his thumb gliding over her soft skin.

*Where do you think you're going, Miss Kate? No running away for you. Not this time.*

She'd taken off out of that supply closet like a bat out of hell. Before he'd even finished catching his breath. Just like Cinderella. Only she hadn't left a shoe behind. Just a pair of lacy panties, which he'd shoved into the pocket of his slacks before heading out the door. By then she had been long gone.

"Yes, Kate and I have already been…" he let his deliberate pause and raised brows get his message across, before completing the phrase "…thoroughly introduced."

Her soft gasp said his inference had hit its mark.

Nick glanced from one to the other. "You have? When?"

"Yesterday," she said, stretching the truth. Luke released her hand, watching as she took one step back, and then another. "I was looking for your room and he…helped me."

Helped her.

Oh, he'd helped her all right. Right up onto the scrub sink in the corner of the tiny closet. *After* he'd hiked her skirt up around her waist. He swallowed. What had happened after that was a blur.

One he'd never forget for as long as he lived.

A muscle in his jaw clenched as he stared at her and said, "I didn't know who you were at the time."

"I—I know. And I'm sorry. I should have said something."

So she *had* known he was Nick's doctor, and probably that they were friends, as well. A wave of disappointment washed over him. He should be used to it by now. The "being used" part, that was. His mother hadn't thought twice about using him to collect her monthly welfare checks, all the while earning a small fortune on the side by sleeping with other men. His father hadn't hesitated before sending him into a store to pick up a thing or two—without paying for it, of course.

And now Kate.

As cynical as Luke thought he was, he hadn't managed to see past those baby blues to the person beneath her melt-in-your-mouth sweetness.

And, damn, had she ever melted. The second his lips had met hers.

He hardened everything that wasn't already hard. "Yes. You should have."

She hadn't been in the cafeteria this morning, like she had the past couple of mornings, so he'd assumed he'd never see her again. Yet here she was. All twitchy and apologetic. And the only thing he wanted to do was yank her out of the room and find that closet all over again.

Not going to happen.

Nick stretched his back. "Well, I should probably head in to my physical therapy session."

That was his cue to leave. "And I have some patients to see so, if you'll excuse me, I'll head back."

"Wait! I want to…"

When he turned his head to look at her, Kate's teeth were digging into that delectable lower lip, as if trying to keep the rest of her sentence from coming out in a rush.

She glanced at Nick. "I'll come back when you're finished with therapy, if that's okay."

"Of course." The other man touched her arm. "It was good to finally meet you in person."

Well, Luke wasn't the only sucker, it would appear. She'd had his savior fooled, as well.

By the time he realized she meant to follow him down the hallway, it was too late to stop her. So as soon as they were a safe distance away, he turned to face her, propping one shoulder against the long narrow wall in the hallway to take some of the pressure off his now aching leg.

Pale silky hair, with just the slightest hint of a wave, fell over her shoulders, caressing her collarbone with every turn of her head. He remembered licking along that very spot.

He forced his gaze back to her eyes. "Yes?"

"I…I wanted explain." Her words tumbled over themselves. "I don't normally… I don't *ever*…" The flourish of a hand finished her thought.

She didn't normally sneak off and "do" her father's doctors?

"And you think I should know this because…?"

"I don't want you to think badly of me." Her hands caught each other, fingers twisting together.

She was nervous. Embarrassed by what they'd done. He stood upright before the realization could affect him. "I don't really even know you, so why does it matter?"

She flinched. "I guess it doesn't. But you're Ni—my father's doctor. I'd rather you didn't say anything to him about yesterday."

"I'm not."

"You're not going to tell him?"

"I'm not Nick's doctor. Not anymore."

Her breath hissed out. "So you *are* going to tell him…about us?"

And risk being shipped home to the States on the first available flight out of London? Not likely. He'd fought too hard to get this position. "No, I'm not going to tell him."

"Thank you." Her whole body went slack with relief. "I appreciate it. How's he doing, by the way? Was the surgery a success?"

That same feeling of unease washed over him. Surely she didn't think their time together had been a game-changer? "I'm afraid I can't give out that kind of information."

"But I'm his daughter."

"You're not listed as his next of kin."

"Because I've only just met the man."

And Luke had just barely met her. That hadn't stopped her from wrapping her legs around his waist. And it certainly wasn't keeping him from wanting to relive that moment…a whole lot slower this time. Definitely not something he wanted her to know.

"That's not my problem."

"Okay, I get it. You can't give me any details. But his life isn't in danger anymore, right?"

Luke made a *tsk* noise low in his throat, trying to keep his irritation from showing. The feeling of being used grew at her persistence. "Get him to add you to his list of relatives, and then we'll talk."

"You can't be serious."

"Oh, but I am." Despite his annoyance, his fingers itched to brush across that smooth, pale cheek and watch it come to life beneath his touch. Except he knew her skin wasn't the only thing that would come to life. Something else he didn't want her to realize.

"So, if he'll admit to being my father—in writing— you can tell me what's going on?"

He inclined his head. "It's a start. As long as he's okay with it." He held up a hand. "Which also has to be in writing."

Her lips thinned. "And if he refuses?"

"Then I can't tell you a blessed thing. Now, if you'll excuse me…"

She hesitated, her mouth opening as if ready to argue further, then she snapped it shut again, hitching her purse higher on her shoulder. "If that's the way you want it."

"I don't make the rules."

But he sure didn't mind breaking them. Hadn't he already proved that in the supply closet?

"Of course you don't."

He couldn't prevent the twitch of his lips at her waspish tone. She might be all peaches and cream on the surface, but underneath she had all the fire of a good Indian curry. You didn't notice it until the first three or four bites, but your tongue remembered the flavor long after you'd finished your meal.

Just like he'd remember the flavor of Kate's lips.

She blinked then swung away from him, preparing to walk back toward the physical therapy center.

For some reason he couldn't let her slip away without making her squirm one last time. "Oh, Kate, I almost forgot."

She turned back toward him. "Yes?"

He gave her a slow, wolfish smile. "I still have your panties."

He had her panties.

What had she expected her to do about it? Hold out her hand and demand he give them back to her right there at the hospital?

Kate ran her wrists under the cool stream of water in her hotel room, hoping to soothe her burning skin. It did no good.

God. What had she been thinking? Men like Dr. Luke Blackman were so far out of her league.

What did she do now? Call and make an appointment to pick up her errant piece of clothing? Or did he plan to keep them as a trophy?

And just where did he have them? At home? In his desk drawer? Above the deep sink with the words *Kate was nailed here* penned beneath them?

She held her wet hands to her cheeks and stared into the mirror, remembering the feel of his fingers on her skin as he'd yanked those very panties down her thighs…his eyes never leaving hers. Then he'd tossed them aside and reached for her hips…lifted her onto the sink.

A wave of heat rushed over her body. Kate had never in her life experienced anything so frighteningly sensual in her life. It had all been over in a matter of minutes. But she knew instinctively she'd never experience anything like that ever again.

She stared into the eyes reflected back at her.

She didn't look any different on the outside. Not a single scorch mark lingered on her skin, although she could still feel each and every place his lips had lingered.

Little had she known all those months ago that the picture and accompanying letter she'd found in a shoebox in her mother's closet—along with letters from scores of other men—would lead her to discover that the father she'd grown up with wasn't her biological father. Or that all her pent-up anger and frustration over the lies by those closest to her would build to the point that it had sought release—no matter what the source.

Luke had been the only person handy at the time.

She'd exploded all right. In a most delicious way.

And now she had to live with the consequences. At least, the emotional ones. Luke had taken care of the physical ones, muttering about the need for birth control, even though her mind hadn't exactly been up to the subject of unwanted pregnancies.

But thank heavens he'd taken precautions. Luke wouldn't need to disappear from his kid's life without a trace, like Nick had. And Kate wouldn't have to lie to her own child about his or her origins—about who its father was. Her eyes moistened. She wouldn't have to die—like her mother had—in order for her child to know the truth.

And most important of all, the only person in the entire world who'd have to live with the consequences of what she'd done in that supply closet…was herself.

# CHAPTER TWO

"She hates me."

Perched on one of the chairs that lined the glass wall of the therapy center, Nick's bald statement took him by surprise. Luke didn't have to ask who his friend was referring to.

"No, she doesn't. When she was here yesterday, she seemed…worried." That was as good a word as any.

His friend's jaw tightened. "I wish I could believe that. That's not the vibe she was giving off when I met her."

"It's a shock, I'm sure. You said she only learned about your existence a month ago, after she found a picture?"

"That's what she said." Nick scrubbed a hand over his head, making his hair stick up at odd angles. "I had a fling with a tourist just before I shipped out with my unit. She'd taken some pictures of us with her camera over the course of the evening. Large quantities of alcohol were involved, so I'm a bit fuzzy on all the details. Anyway, I left her a note the next day before I headed out. I had no idea the woman had got pregnant that night until much later."

"You've had contact with the woman?"

"Not since that day. Kate says she died six months ago." Something flashed through his eyes. Regret?

"And she's just now decided to find you?"

He gave a hard laugh. "She found the picture and my note stuffed in a shoebox. She got the bloke who raised her to admit he wasn't her real father." One shoulder went up. "She came looking for me at the house while I was in the hospital. Nearly ruined things for me and Tiggy in the process."

"Ouch." Kate did seem to have the ability to stir up trouble wherever she went. He hadn't slept much for the past two nights. "Things are okay between you and your wife now, though?"

Nick nodded, a smile curving his lips. "She's pregnant. I never thought I'd want kids, and now I find I have a grown daughter as well as a baby on the way."

"Congratulations!"

"I guess."

"Come on, Nick. What more could you ask for?"

"I could ask for my daughter to give me a chance."

"I'm sure she'll come round. She asked how you were doing. I couldn't tell her anything because of patient confidentiality." He paused. "Maybe I could talk to her. Tell her you're a regular hero."

Whoa, why the hell had he offered to do that? Being around Kate was not good for his equilibrium, especially now.

"I'm not a hero. Especially not in her eyes."

"She just doesn't know you yet. Maybe you should tell her what you did in the service. For men like me." Luke hated remembering his injury, how he'd had to fight his way back from the depths of despair when he'd realized his leg would never be right again. He knew he should be grateful it was still there. But on the days when it ached like nobody's business, he wished he'd just had it lopped off and been done with it.

"I was doing my job." His friend studied him for a moment. "If she asked you how I was doing, she must care. At least a little."

"Of course she does."

"What did you tell her?"

"That you had to sign off on her being your daughter first, giving the hospital permission before I could share any information."

"That could work…"

He frowned. "I'm not sure I follow."

"If I sign the papers, maybe you could be the one to talk to her for me, like you said. And the medical discussion could turn personal. You could feel her out."

Well, he'd already done that. It wasn't something he should do again if he wanted to maintain his sanity. And definitely not something he wanted to admit to Nick. The man who'd saved his leg could very well rip it back off with his bare hands if he found out what he'd done to his newfound daughter.

"You know," Luke said slowly, "I think it might be better coming from you."

"Didn't you just offer to talk to her for me a few minutes ago?"

Yes, and he'd already decided that was not a good idea. "I'm thinking a father-daughter discussion might be more direct. Just tell her that you shipped out right after you were with her mother and over your years of service you saved a lot of men's lives."

"It would be stronger coming from a friend." Nick cocked his head. "One of those very people I saved."

Wow. He'd never expected Nick to play the you-owe-me card. And, in all honesty, he probably wouldn't have now if *he* hadn't offered to talk to Kate, like a damned fool. His fingers went to his leg, a familiar ache reminding him of what could have been had Nick not been there.

"Not fair."

"I know." His friend's voice was low. "But I'm feeling desperate. She's due to leave for the States in a week or two, and I want to make sure things are okay between us before she goes."

"What do you expect me to do? Drop my pants and show her firsthand what a great job you did on my leg?"

He hadn't even done that in the supply closet. He'd simply unzipped and…

Oh, hell. This was not a good idea.

"No pants-dropping allowed. I may have just found out she's my daughter, but that doesn't mean I want you coming on to her. I've heard about your reputation from a couple of the nurses." His voice sharpened a bit. "You're still a hotshot, just like you were ten years ago."

Nick might be surprised. He wasn't guilty of half the stuff floating around the hospital grapevine. And his physical hotshot days were long gone. He might still have the use of his leg, but he'd never be a marathon runner. Or climb the Alps. Or even carry a woman across the threshold. He'd surprised himself by actually getting Kate up onto that sink—although he could lift things just fine, it was walking and lifting together that did him in.

Luckily, he wouldn't have to fess up to what had happened between him and Kate, because that was obviously not something Nick would be thrilled to hear. And Kate didn't want Nick knowing either, judging by her quiet plea in the hallway. "So you don't want me to charm her."

"I want you to talk to her." Nick's voice softened. "Tell her I'm not a bad-boy-love-'em-and-leave-'em type. Just an honest working man who made a mistake. One he regrets."

"So you want someone who you think is a Lothario to tell your daughter *you're* nothing like that."

Nick grinned. "Exactly."

Just then an attractive redhead dressed in scrubs came into the center and dropped a kiss on his friend's cheek. "I thought I'd check up on you. How are you feeling?"

"Better." He nodded at Luke. "Tiggy, you remember Dr. Blackman…Luke."

"Of course. He's the one who called and told me you were in the hospital." She smiled, her eyes crinkling at the corners. "Hello again. I don't know if I've ever thanked you properly for what you did. I'm very grateful."

"I'm glad Nick still had you listed as his next of kin."

"So am I." She laid her hand on her husband's shoulder. "Nick's told me a little about how you met."

Luke tensed, but forced himself to return her smile. "Nothing bad, I hope."

"No, just that you came across each other while in the service. I didn't even know that we did joint missions with the Americans." She took her husband's hand in hers.

So that's what Nick had told her.

No hint that she knew about Nick yanking him from the jaws of death. Or that he'd refused to saw his leg off on the spot, like one of the other medics had wanted to do.

Luke relaxed. He may have told his friend to come clean with Kate about what he'd done in the field, but

Luke himself told very few people about that day. Some of his buddies from his service days knew, but only because they'd been there when it had happened. Luke preferred it that way. Anyone who saw his scars and was brave enough to ask about them got a very watered-down version of what had actually gone down.

Hell. Nick was right. He owed the man a debt he could never repay.

Backing out of talking to Kate seemed pretty selfish in the face of it all. He made a quick decision. "About that favor you asked for. I can't promise anything, but I'll give it a shot. I'll need you to sign the paperwork, so I have an excuse to approach her."

His friend's eyes closed for a second and he took a deep breath before looking back at him. "Thank you. I owe you."

No. He didn't. And that was exactly the point.

Kate frowned as she took the envelope from the man at the front desk. It couldn't be from her father back in Memphis, he'd have simply emailed her if he couldn't reach her. And she didn't know anyone in London except Nick.

Oh, and one very enigmatic doctor.

And she didn't even know him. Just that he made her pulse explode...along with other things. Things she was trying very hard to forget.

Walking toward the twin elevators, she slid a thumb beneath the seal of the envelope and popped open the tab. A single sheet of paper was inside.

*Could you call me when you get in? I'm at*
*20-5555-6731*
*Thanks, Dr. Lucas Blackman*

A wave of panic went through her before she realized it probably wasn't anything related to Nick's health. If it were, he wouldn't have left a note. Then she gulped as she remembered his parting shot from yesterday. This couldn't be about her panties, could it? She'd prefer he just burn them and be done with it. It was just too humiliating to talk about over the phone. Or in person, for that matter.

But if she didn't call, she'd always wonder.

She wasn't sure what kept her from booking a flight out of London. She'd done what she'd come to do: looked her father in the eye and drawn her own conclusions. She'd expected that to be fairly quick and easy, but nothing had gone the way she'd planned.

Nick wasn't the type of person she'd braced herself to find. He hadn't denied being her father—which surprised her—but then again it was kind of hard to deny the obvious. But there was something in his face that made her want to take a step back and rethink her position. Especially in the face of all those other letters she'd found in the shoebox. Did the man who'd raised her even know about those other men?

She hardened her heart. If those closest to her hadn't thought twice about lying to her, why not the man who'd contributed nothing to her life other than his DNA?

Her mom had been trying to spare her feelings, she was sure. But surely with all her grandparents' money, her mother would have been able to track Nick down and tell him about the pregnancy. Or about the baby, once she'd been born. So why hadn't she?

Her mother wasn't here to answer any of those questions. Maybe she would have told her someday, but had never gotten the chance.

Or maybe she knew something about Nick that was

so terrible she hadn't wanted her daughter to have any contact with him. Maybe Nick had…forced her, or something.

She stepped off the elevator. No, she had found the note Nick had left the next morning. He wouldn't have done that if something bad had happened between him and her mother. And her mother certainly wouldn't have saved a picture of them together had that been the case.

Unlocking her door, she went into her room and dropped her purse on the bed. Her suitcase was still packed, sitting on the mahogany luggage rack. She could just shut the lid and leave with everything she'd come with.

Except answers. And, of course, one pair of panties.

Ugh. She smoothed out the note and traced her finger over the bold strokes of handwriting, smiling at the typical doctorlike scribbles. Luckily she'd had to decipher many notes like these during her physical therapy training, and later, with actual patients, to understand what their doctors wanted.

There was nothing for it but to call and find out what he wanted.

She punched the number that would allow her to reach an outside line and then dialed the rest of the digits listed on the note.

"Blackman here."

His voice sounded sharp, hurried. "Oh, I'm sorry. You left me a—"

"Kate?" His tone immediately changed. Softened. "I didn't expect you to call so soon."

She blinked and glanced at the note again. No time stamp. Was it possible he'd left it only a short time ago? "Oh, I…I just got in."

"Listen, I'm swamped right now. But basically your

father's listed you as next of kin and has given me permission to fill you in, if you've got some free time."

"I can be there in a half hour."

There was a pause. "Can we do it somewhere else? I have something of yours I need to return, and I'd rather it not be at the hospital."

If only he'd been that conscientious a couple of days ago.

And meeting him in her hotel room was out of the question. Not because she didn't trust him but because she didn't trust herself. If she'd have sex with him in a public hospital, what would stop her from peeling his clothes off in a private room?

"How about a restaurant?" *No, not a restaurant, dummy.* "I mean a coffee shop."

"A restaurant sounds great." He said something to someone with him then came back to her. "I've really got to go. I'll pick you up when I get off. Say around six this evening."

"Oh, um…"

"Say yes, Kate." His voice had gone all soft and gravelly, and she shivered. It was almost identical to the tone he'd used in the supply room. *Do you want this, Kate?*

She had. She'd said the word that had unleashed them both. And damn if she wasn't about to say it all over again.

"Yes."

# CHAPTER THREE

LUKE TURNED HIS car into the hotel, giving a soft whistle as he did. He'd heard of The Claymont—knew it was exclusive and pricey—but had never had any reason to visit before now.

Towering white columns framed an ornate cobblestone driveway, the swirling pattern in the black-and-white marble chips echoing the curve of the entryway. An intricate coat of arms placed in the middle reminded him of the X on a celebrity red carpet, giving vehicles a definite stopping point. The place oozed opulence—from the lion's-head fountain on a side wall, which splashed water into a rustic concrete trough, to the red-coated doorman who emerged from the interior of the hotel to greet him.

Kate had money. Lots of it.

Which might explain their encounter the other day. Maybe she was one of those cute socialites who got their kicks out of toying with danger.

And their time in that supply closet had definitely been dangerous. It had pushed the boundaries, even for him.

But he also remembered her hesitancy that first day at the entrance of the hospital. She hadn't acted like a spoiled little rich girl.

Maybe her mom had married into money. Nick said Kate's father knew she wasn't his biological daughter, so her mother hadn't used an unwanted pregnancy to trick anyone into marrying her.

She hadn't lied about it.

Except to Kate, evidently. It had to be rough having your world suddenly turned on its head.

He handed the keys of his little MGB to the valet.

"I won't be long," he said.

"Very good, sir."

The front entrance welcomed him, the double doors swishing open with a quiet hiss. What the hell would he do if she invited him up to her room?

It was a question he'd never thought he'd have to ask himself. But Nick was her father, so there would be no more supply closets…and definitely no hotel rooms in his future. He could keep his hands off her, really he could.

"May I help you, sir?"

The guy at the front desk was just as smooth and refined as he'd expected. "I'm here to see Kate Bradley."

"One moment." He tapped some buttons on his computer keyboard, but just as he was picking up the handset to dial her room, the elevator doors pinged and Kate herself emerged.

The air left his lungs, just as it had the first time he'd seen her. It wasn't so much the way she was dressed as the way she carried herself—although the dark jeans clung in all the right places and the dark green halter-top left her pale shoulders exposed, revealing a smattering of freckles.

"Sorry, I wasn't sure where we were going," she said when she reached him.

That soft drawl slid over his body like warm silk. Again.

He noticed the guy behind the desk just stood there, the phone still gripped in his hand. So Luke wasn't the only one who thought the whole damn package was irresistible. When he turned his eyes toward the other man and lifted his brows, the guy put the phone down with a quick click, his face turning red. "Can I get you anything, Ms. Bradley?"

*How about a fire extinguisher, so she can put you out?*

As if he himself was any better at containing that particular fire.

One side of his mouth quirked. Was Nick absolutely sure this was his kid? Because he just wasn't seeing the resemblance.

Kate smiled at the desk clerk, hiking the shiny metal links of her purse onto her shoulder. "I think I'm good. Thank you, though."

No thinking needed. She *was* good.

Giving himself an internal eye roll, he motioned toward the door. "Are you ready? I know a place a couple of miles from here."

Once in his little car and heading down the road, he noticed Kate flinching periodically as they passed other cars.

"It still seems so strange to be driving on the left. I keep thinking someone is going to honk at us. Or worse."

"You get used to it." Not that she was going to be here long enough for that. So exactly how was he supposed to shine up Nick's halo while avoiding tarnishing his own any further? By returning that little article of clothing she'd left behind a few days ago? "There's a paper bag in the glove box. You might want to take it with you."

She tugged on her seat belt as if needing a bit more breathing space and stared at the latch in front of her. "I think I'll wait until we get back to the hotel, if that's okay. My purse is pretty small."

She knew exactly what was in there. He'd had half a mind to take the easy way out and toss the panties into the garbage, but he hadn't. Luke had never been one to shy away from things that were uncomfortable, even when it had come to his folks' poverty…his dad's drunken anger. He'd just stood there and faced it down unblinking. "Don't forget them. I'd hate the wrong person to go digging through that glove box."

"Like your next conquest?"

Maybe she'd gotten wind of his reputation, as well. He really was going to have to appear a whole lot more boring at work. "I was thinking more along the lines of Nick—your father."

Kate's face drained of all color and she turned to stare at him. "You promised you wouldn't say anything about that."

Hell, the woman really didn't think much of him, did she? Luke rarely gave his word, but when he did, he moved hell and high water to keep it. He'd learned the hard way that most promises were quick on the tongue and easily broken. Not by him, though.

And yet he'd made two pretty big promises in the last couple of days. One to Nick and one to his daughter. "I already told you I'm not going to tell him."

He stopped for a red light, shifting down to first gear and glancing over at her. "What happened at the hospital stays between the two of us—no one's going to hear it from me."

Her eyes closed for a second, and she nodded. "Thank you. I couldn't bear it if anyone thought I was…"

"If anyone thought what?"

"It's not important."

If that soft sigh was anything to go by, it was important. At least, to her. But if she wanted to tell him, she would have. It was probably best to stick to neutral topics anyway, since the purpose of this outing was to discuss Nick's treatment, extol his virtues and then each go their merry way.

The light turned green, and Luke eased back into traffic. "Nick's going to make a full recovery, by the way. He had some shrapnel—leftover from an old wound—that shifted. It got a little too close to his spinal cord for comfort. He's just finishing up his course of physical therapy and then he'll be free to go about his business."

Kate twisted in her seat and stared at him. "That's wonderful. So he won't have any permanent damage?"

"No." Unlike himself, who carried a permanent reminder of his time in Afghanistan. "His physical therapy is taking a little longer than expected because of some nerve damage, but after that he should be good to go."

"Maybe I can help. I'm a physical therapist."

She was? Luke frowned. He'd been thinking along the lines of socialite, so the fact that she was a PT came as a complete surprise. "I don't know…"

"I'm licensed, specializing in LSVT."

Luke's head was still spinning at the revelation as he turned another corner. He'd known plenty of physical therapists, but Kate looked nothing like the professionals who'd hauled his ass out of bed after the injury that had nearly claimed his leg. Who'd propped him up-right and goaded him into taking his first shaky steps.

Although remembering the lean muscles beneath his hands as he'd lifted Kate onto that sink, he shouldn't be *that* surprised. And imagining those hands work-ing on his body…

Good God.

He swallowed. Nick would not be happy to know the thoughts racing through his mind right now. For the life of him, he couldn't think of anything to say, so he asked the obvious question. "LSVT?"

"It's a specialized voice therapy for Parkinson's pa-tients."

Ah, so she wasn't the brute-strength type of ther-apist after all. "Nick will need occupational therapy, not speech."

"Part of LSVT deals with the physical aspects of Parkinson's." Her chin tilted stubbornly.

He tried again. "Your father doesn't *have* Parkin-son's."

"Yes, he does, he's in the early…" She let out a soft sigh. "Oh. That's right. It's still hard for me to think of Nick as my father. I'm sure I could help him, though. I've already checked online, there are several hospitals here in England using LSVT. It could be useful, even though he doesn't have Parkinson's."

What had made her check on that? Was she thinking about staying in London? "I'm sure he's getting every-thing he needs at the hospital's PT center."

"But what about when he's not there? I could help him with some extra exercises…help his wife out with him. Maybe it would give me a chance to get to know him better."

Luke wasn't sure Tiggy would welcome the reminder

that Nick had fathered another child. Especially not in her condition. But it wasn't up to him. That was a decision the couple would have to make on their own.

He pulled into the parking lot of the Indian Palace Restaurant and set the handbrake. "Nick and Tiggy are under a lot of stress right now—with the surgery and everything. Now might not be a good time." Unhooking his seat belt, he waited for her to follow suit. "Listen, we'll eat, and I'll fill you in on his surgery and prognosis, and then you'll have a better grasp of his situation, okay?"

"Good. That'll give me more time to convince you."

Not good. He might not be the one she needed to convince, but all he could think was that it might be fun to let her try, anyway.

Kate took a quick gulp of water and then another, her mouth on fire. The smoldering sensation of swallowing hot coals continued as she sucked air in and out through pursed lips in a desperate effort to get some relief. "Oh, my God…" *Huff, huff.* "That's so good."

The man across from her gave her a quick grin. "Your face is pink. And your accent is really coming through."

"Because I'm on *f-i-ire.*"

She put every Southern bone she had into that last word. The food was just-this-side-of-pain spicy. And she loved it. It was hard to get good Indian food in the States, but Luke had assured her that Londoners loved it. And they were evidently not afraid of a little spice. Or a lot, in this case.

"Well, when you decide to go hot, you go all the way, don't you?"

Kate looked at him sharply, wondering if the amusement in his voice was in regard to the food or if he was talking about something else. She tossed her hair over her shoulder and reached for her napkin, using it to dab the still-burning corners of her mouth. The words had stung, but only because she'd let them.

Her mom had been a wonderful, loving mother, but she'd also been impulsive, throwing her whole being into whatever caught her interest. That had tended to change weekly—even daily. When she'd found Nick's note in that shoebox, it hadn't been the only "call me later" letter. There'd been others. Many of them. If not for the fact that her baby picture had been stapled onto a corner of one of the envelopes, which contained a picture of her mother with a much younger Nick, along with his note, she might never have wondered if the man she'd known as her father was actually her biological father.

Her mom's impulsiveness hadn't been restricted to hobbies and charities, it would seem. It had spilled into other areas. And she'd left a trail of broken hearts along the way. Her dad never seemed to indicate she'd strayed during their marriage. Or maybe he didn't know. Kate had never doubted his deep love for her mother, though. He'd been devoted to her. Her death had devastated them both. She was thankful *she'd* found that box and not her dad. She'd hidden everything except Nick's letter and her photo, which had been when her father had broken down and admitted he'd adopted her after he'd married her mother. She'd been two years old at the time.

All those men. Several of them had clearly not understood why her mother hadn't returned their calls. And she'd kept those letters. Why? As reminders?

God. The last thing she wanted to do was hurt anyone like that.

She glanced at Luke. He seemed well able to take care of himself. Their little fling in the storage closet probably hadn't left the slightest scratch.

Unlike she herself, who was still reeling from her actions. They'd been totally out of character for her.

Or were they? She didn't know anymore.

Dropping her napkin back in her lap, she feigned a sweet smile. "I always say if you're going to do something, you might as well make it worth your while."

He nodded at her plate. "Even if it stings."

"Maybe that's the goal."

His smile faded. "To do something that hurts you?"

"Better than hurting others, don't you think?"

He leaned back in his chair and regarded her for a few seconds, his expression grim. "Absolutely."

What was he thinking about? It didn't matter. The sooner she got this question-and-answer session over with, the better. The man had the ability to get under her skin, and she didn't like it. She'd never had casual sex before, and the last thing she wanted to do was look her mistake in the face repeatedly—no matter how handsome that face might be.

"So, you said Nick put me down on his list of relatives. What made him decide to do that?"

"That's something you'll have to ask him. But I assume it's because you're his daughter, and he's happy to have finally met you."

Something pricked at the back of her mind, raising her suspicions. "At the hospital, you said you weren't Nick's doctor anymore, so why are you the one filling me in on his condition? Why not his current doctor?"

"Because he asked me to."

"Why would he do that?" Her brain worked through the possibilities and came up with the most obvious choice. "You know him, don't you? Outside the hospital, I mean." It seemed like Nick knew everyone, except her.

"Yes."

She picked up her fork but didn't use it. She just stared at the gold-rimmed plate for a moment or two. "Did he know about me at all? Or did my mom never contact him again after their…time together?"

Did she want to know the answer to that? Not really, but she couldn't crawl back inside her shell and act like the past six months hadn't happened. Just like the tree of the knowledge of good and evil, what was known couldn't be *un*known ever again.

A warm hand reached over and covered hers. "I don't know," he said. "But I do know that Nick's a good man."

Really? She'd thought her mother had been a saint, too, until a couple of months ago.

"So you know everything about him, do you?" Nick hadn't seemed all that thrilled to find out he'd fathered a child after a one-night stand. And he'd never mentioned whether or not he'd been married to someone else at the time he'd slept with her mother. Please let it be no. She didn't want that hanging over her mother's memory, as well.

Everything inside her was so jumbled right now. She didn't know what to do or think. Her world had ceased making sense the moment she'd peeked inside that shoebox.

What was the big deal, anyway?

Nick had just had a one-night stand. Okay, well, she'd had a one-*day* stand. So who was she to judge anyone?

Luke's eyes hardened, and he let go of her hand. "No,

I don't know everything about him, but I can tell you he once saved a self-destructive dumbass from himself."

She tried to work through what he meant. Who…

Before she could finish her thought he dragged a hand through his hair and blew out a rough breath. "This dumbass owes him one. Big time."

Oh…*oh!*

She caught his hand, the same way he'd caught hers a few minutes earlier. "You're talking about yourself."

He wrapped his fingers around hers, holding her in place and sending crazy tingles skittering up her arm. And that slow, sexy smile was back full force. "Which word gave me away, Kate? *Self-destructive?* Or *dumbass?*"

"Neither." She was about to lay herself bare before him, and she had no idea why. "It was the talk about owing him. You're not the only one who does. I owe him, too. For my very life."

# CHAPTER FOUR

WHY THE HELL had he said anything?

Driving back to the hotel after their meal, he cursed himself for revealing so much. She'd already been warming up to the sparkly image of Nick he'd tried to paint, without needing any additional props. So why had he admitted to owing him?

The second he'd seen the confusion in her eyes, heard the raw vulnerability in her voice, he'd been lost. He'd kept up his crusty, uncaring shell through the rest of the meal, but his insides had turned into a gloppy, gooey mess. Like a marshmallow held a little too close to the fire.

Kate didn't owe Nick. Not the way he did. Yeah, his friend may have donated a few thousand sperm to the making of her, but that had been a rash, spur-of-the-moment act. What the man had done for *him* had been far different. Luke had been awake long enough after his injury to hear brief snatches of a heated argument between Nick—who'd been an army medic at the time—and someone else, their accents placing them as English.

*"He'll die, if we don't clamp those vessels right now..."*

*"...give me a few more minutes here."*

"...lose the leg, but save his life..."

"...get your bloody hands off my patient, and give me some room!"

"...Americans would rather have him back alive than in a body bag."

The second Luke's eyes had opened again, and he'd spied the familiar walls of a field hospital, his hands had gone straight to his leg. The sense of relief that had swept through him when his fingers had met thick wads of bandages—instead of empty air—had been enormous. Until he'd seen the actual damage and heard the grim prognosis.

He hadn't been out of the woods, and his leg, even if it could be saved in the long run, would never be the same.

Well, the appendage was still with him, but he wondered sometimes if the trade-off had been worth it.

Even as he thought it, his hand came off the stick shift of his car to massage the twisted muscles, but he stopped short. Kate didn't know exactly how Nick had saved his life. For all she knew, he'd simply kept him from doing anything stupid. No reason for her to know the literal truth.

She hadn't said much as she'd finished her meal and he'd paid the bill. They'd simply talked about Nick's original injury, about why it had flared up after all these years, and what had needed to happen during surgery to give him a shot at a normal life.

He turned a corner, heading toward her hotel. This was it. It was probably the last time he'd ever see her, if he was smart. He'd done what Nick had asked, there was no reason to prolong the inevitable. He glanced over at her and frowned. Her head was against the headrest, eyes closed.

Was she sleeping? He looked at the road, and then back at her. Her throat worked a couple times.

No, she wasn't asleep.

Oh, hell. Surely she wasn't fighting back tears. The sooner he got her back to…

A car from one of the lanes of oncoming traffic suddenly shifted for no apparent reason, its trajectory forming a weird serpentine shape as it drifted farther into their lane. It was coming right toward them!

"Hold on." Luke jerked the steering wheel hard to the left to avoid hitting it head on, the tires of his little car striking the curb hard and bumping up onto it. He braked, glancing into the rearview mirror just as the other vehicle passed them, creeping into the wrong lane yet again. If the idiot didn't gain control, he was going to…

The squeal of tires and the awful crunching sound that followed said the worst had indeed happened.

Luke swore and pushed a button to turn on his hazard lights. "Are you okay?"

"Fine, but… Oh, no!" Kate's eyes were now wide open, her head craning to look behind them.

Grabbing his cell phone from the clip on his belt, he dropped it in her lap. "Dial 999. Tell them we need an ambulance and that there's a doctor at the scene."

Not waiting for her reply, he leaped from the car and half skipped, half sprinted toward the accident scene, trying to override his pain threshold with gritted teeth. Damn it!

He tried to mentally separate the rubberneckers from those involved in the crash. Hell. Not good.

Three cars. No, four.

And there was smoke pouring from one of the vehicles, preventing him from getting a good look at its occupants. He headed toward that one first, seeing someone stagger from the driver's side and collapse onto the road a few feet away. If the smoke was obstructing the view of cars still coming toward them, the already bad accident could turn catastrophic.

He yelled to one of the bystanders, "Can you try signaling a warning to cars that are headed this way?"

He reached the victim who'd fallen, a young male, and crouched down, his leg screaming as the muscles contracted too quickly. He ignored the pain, noting the trickle of blood from the man's mouth was due to a busted lip and not from internal injuries.

Sour fumes hit his nostrils, drifting up his sinus passages.

Alcohol. Shit! This was the idiot who'd swerved into their lane. He wasn't hurt, just drunk.

"How can I help?" A man's voice came from over his shoulder. He glanced back beyond the man who had spoken and saw Kate running toward him, as well. He motioned her back, not needing a million bodies wandering around on a smoky roadway.

"Think you can drag him to the curb, in case his car goes up?" He hated that he had to ask for help, that he couldn't do it himself, but there were people in other cars who might be worse off.

But the man got beneath the drunk's arms and dutifully hauled him away from the smoking vehicle. Luke called out, "Don't let him go anywhere. The police will want to have a word or two with him."

Kate got to him just as he reached the second car. "I called it in. Help is on the way."

He glanced at her, before taking in the occupants of the next car, whose small red hood was now a crumpled mess. "I thought I told you to stay back."

"I know, but I'm strong. I can help."

The inference was plain. She'd seen him hobble down the road. Seen him pass off the first victim to someone else. No time to worry about that now.

He nodded at the backseat of the vehicle, the sudden sound of sirens bearing down on them a welcome relief.

"There's a car seat. Check it for me, will you? But if there's a child, don't move it."

Not waiting for an answer, he went around the front and yanked the driver's-side door open. The unconscious woman inside gasped, her mouth wide open as she sucked down air, the harsh unevenness of the sound sending an ominous chill through him. The edge of the steering wheel—despite the presence of an airbag—pressed against the right side of the woman's chest, which meant the force generated by the impact had traveled through the steering column and into her body.

He gulped, his heart rate spiking off the charts when he noted that with each inspiration the left side of the patient's chest rose in a normal fashion, but a significant portion of her right side collapsed inward instead of expanding—a clear sign that multiple ribs had broken free, preventing her diaphragm from doing its job.

Flail chest. Game-changer.

He needed to get her out of that car. Now.

A uniform appeared at his right, the man ducking his head to take a look. "You the doctor?"

"Yes. I have a critical patient here. Do we have an ETA on the ambulance?"

"One's about a minute out, another's on the way."

"She's first." He nodded at his patient, two fingers automatically going to her carotid artery to take her pulse, his gaze straying to the hand of his watch as he calculated the beats per minute.

"I'll see what I can do." The cop moved away.

"Tell them I need a backboard," he yelled after he'd gotten the count.

Rapid and thready, as he'd expected.

"Kate?" he called, remembering he'd asked her to check out the car seat. "What have you got back there? Anything?"

"Yes, there's a baby. I—I don't know how old she is. She's wrapped in a blanket, and she's breathing. I can't see blood anywhere, but she's unconscious."

"Okay, just stay with her for a few minutes and tell me if there are any changes."

He heard the telltale slam of a truck door nearby. *Thank God.* His mind followed the sound indicators.

*Swish. Click.* Wheels of a gurney being lowered and snapped into place.

*Rattle, rattle, rattle.* The stretcher being wheeled across the roadway toward him.

Another head appeared. "What have you got?"

"Probable rib fractures resulting in a flail chest. Pulse one-twenty and thready." He paused for a second before forcing the words out. "I'll need some help getting her out of here, though."

The paramedic blinked, his glance skipping over Luke's face for a second before nodding. "Right."

Luke limped back a pace or two to let the EMTs by, his hand going to his thigh and digging his fingers into the flesh to take his mind off the growing pain. It was nothing in comparison to the life-and-death battle going on inside that car. And she had a child. "There's a baby in the back," he said to the paramedics.

"My partner just had a look. Her vitals are strong. We'll tend to the baby next and bring her with us in the ambulance. Injuries in the other cars appear to be minimal."

"Good." At least he'd made the right call in staying with this particular patient. "Careful with her back and with the ribs on her right side. The steering wheel is still making contact there."

As soon as they'd secured the patient, he turned to Kate. "Do you have your international driver's permit?"

"Yes, why?"

"I need to ride with her in the ambulance, if possible. We're about a block away from the hotel. Just turn right at the next corner. And for heaven's sake, keep to the left. Think you can get there without killing yourself or anyone else?"

"Yes, but what about your car?"

"I'll pick it up later. I don't want to leave it here, and I need to go. Now."

Her glance went to his leg, where his fingers were still working to relieve the cramping. "Are you going to be all right?"

So she *had* noticed. Perfect.

He made his hand go slack, digging into his pocket for his car keys, instead. "I'll be fine."

One of the EMTs called over, "Ready to transport."

Kate reached over and plucked the keys from him. "Go. I'll take care of your car. Call me when you're done, okay?"

## CHAPTER FIVE

WHAT WAS WRONG with Luke's leg?

She'd been shocked by the way he'd hurried over to the scene of the accident. He'd had a kind of uneven, hobbling run that had done the job but certainly hadn't looked very comfortable. She'd never noticed him limp before. Had he twisted his ankle in his hurry to get over there?

Hmm…no, his hand had massaged his upper thigh, like he'd been working out a kink. A cramp? Maybe.

But the way he'd lowered his arm the second he'd seen her looking at it didn't fit that scenario, either. Kate put the keys to his car on the table in her hotel room and paced, the thick beige carpet beneath her feet deadening the sound. Glancing at her watch, she saw that it was just after eight. Already dark outside. Who knew how long he'd be at the hospital? He'd seemed to indicate he'd call, although he hadn't actually said the words.

Well, she did have his car. So he'd have to get in touch with her eventually.

Even as she thought it, the phone rang. Wow, that was fast.

She picked up the receiver. "I was wondering how long you'd be."

"Sorry?" The soft, clipped tones bore no resemblance to the low, intense murmur that had sent shivers over her in the supply closet. "Is this Kate, then?"

"Um…yes."

There was a pause. "You sound like her, you know."

Kate realized in a flash who it was and sat on the edge of the bed. "Nick?"

There was another pause, longer this time. "Yes."

She thought there might be a slight edge of hurt to his tone, but surely he didn't expect her to call him Dad. Only one man had earned that right. But the fact that Nick thought she sounded like her mother made a fresh wave of grief wash over her.

"I'm sorry. I didn't recognize your voice."

"That's to be expected, I suppose." He cleared his throat. "I'm actually calling on my wife's behalf. She wondered if you might like to have dinner at our house some time next week. I realize we haven't had much time together, and…well, she thought it was the right thing to do."

Surprise washed over her. "That's very kind. I'm sure none of this has been easy on her. Maybe it would have been better if I hadn't come to London."

"No. Absolutely not. I'm glad you did. I just wish I'd known that…well, that's neither here nor there. Could you come, do you think?"

"If she's sure."

"She is. She's had a rough go of it recently, but she'd like to get to know you. As would I." Another voice sounded in the background, and Nick answered before coming back on the line. "I'd invite Luke as well, of course."

Of course. She almost smiled. Maybe he and Tiggy thought they'd need Luke's help sorting out her Southern accent. Funny how she never thought of herself as having one. But then again, no one ever thought they did. "Will you be well enough to have company? I mean, with your surgery."

"I'm a bit sore still, but, well…I don't know how long you'll be here or when you'll be back."

Kate didn't know if she'd ever be back. It all depended on how everything went. And she *had* told Luke she wanted to get to know Nick better, and possibly help with his therapy in some way. "If you're sure."

"*We* are."

She couldn't help but smile at the emphasis he'd place on the word *we*. He sounded…happy.

He didn't want to pick up his car.

Oh, some perverse part of him did, but the realist in him wanted to just call her up and say, "Keep it." His flail chest patient, despite everyone's best efforts, hadn't made it. If that wasn't bad enough, she'd evidently been a single mom, and no one knew who the baby's father was.

So the child—a little girl—was now at the mercy of the system. At least until they could find someone to give them some answers about her relatives. A social worker had already come to the hospital and carried the baby away, saying she'd get her into foster care.

And his leg hurt like the devil. The stress of running—something he normally avoided—had done a number on it. And standing for another three hours as they'd feverishly fought to stabilize the patient hadn't helped, although he'd barely noticed the throbbing pain while they'd been in the thick of battle.

The thick of battle.

There's a term he hadn't used in a while. But it was true. Emergency medicine never knew what it might face on any given day. Some days were good. And some days were horrific. Like the day he'd taken Kate by storm after losing another patient.

A day very much like today. He leaned against the hallway wall just outside the break room to take the weight off his leg.

Only he couldn't afford to let his guard down like that again. There was that little promise he'd made to Nick to consider, but it was also ridiculous to think Kate would simply fall into bed with him whenever he lost a patient—for as long as she was here, anyway.

Not only that, but he had a feeling that she was going to ask questions as soon as he saw her. She'd already looked at him oddly at the accident site, and it was doubtful he'd be able to hide the limp that went along with overdoing it. The last thing he wanted to do was trudge through old, familiar territory.

Okay, so he could take a cab over to the hotel, meet her beside his car, jump in and take off. She'd be none the wiser, right?

Unless she asked him to come up.

He didn't see that happening.

But just in case… He straightened, exhaustion taking hold as he made his way to the nurses' station. Luckily, there was a familiar face behind the desk, her dyed hair just a shade shy of blue beneath the cool light of the tube fluorescents. Mimi Copeland. His favorite nurse.

He rested a hand on the desk and waited for her to glance up at him. When she did, she gave him a compassionate smile, deep wrinkles in her cheeks coming to life. "Well, hello, Dr. Blackman. Heard you had quite a night."

"You could say that. I have to pick my car up from a

visiting…friend. Could you do me a favor and call and let her know I'm on my way?"

"You mean could I *ring* her?"

He chuckled at her good-natured ribbing, trying to ignore the speculative gleam in her eyes. *Great*. He turned a pad of paper toward himself and scribbled down the number of the hotel. "If you could ask the front desk to give Kate Bradley a message, saying I'm on my way over and could she please meet me *downstairs*." There. He'd emphasized the word. Maybe that would keep the gossip to a minimum. He doubted it, but it was the best he could do on short notice.

"Sure thing, Doctor." As she started to dial, he slowly made his way to the entrance and hailed a cab. Thankfully he didn't have to hobble much farther than the hospital entrance to find one. He'd have to wait until he got home to down a muscle relaxant, as he didn't want to drive once he'd taken it.

All the way over to the hotel he rehearsed his words, needing to keep the conversation as short as possible.

He frowned when he got there. Kate was nowhere to be seen. Maybe she was waiting inside the lobby. He handed the driver a bill, telling him to keep the change, then climbed out of the taxi, stabilizing himself on the door for a minute when his leg complained at being roused.

"Are you all right?" the taxi driver asked.

"Yep." He slammed the door, pulled in a deep breath and started walking. Parking must be underground or around back, as he didn't see anything other than a car or two in the covered check-in lane. But there was a valet booth off to the side, so maybe Kate had just left the keys with him. He could hope, anyway.

He pulled even with the guy, shifting his weight to

his good leg. "Did a Katherine Bradley leave the keys to my car with you, by any chance?"

The man's dark mustache twitched as he leaned over to check a clipboard. "Not that I can see, sir. If you have her room number I can check if you'd like."

"That's all right. I'll ask at the front desk."

Fifty feet to get inside. Fifty feet to get back out. Then the valet would bring his car round. He gritted his teeth. Once upon a time he'd run training drills with huge packs on his back and come back ready for more. Those days were long gone. Right now he could barely walk the distance it took to get inside a hotel lobby.

He knew it wasn't fair to judge things by how he felt right now. By tomorrow morning he'd probably be fine. It was the afternoons and evenings, after he'd been on his feet all day, that gave him problems.

Having to run on it…well, that was never a good idea at any time of day. Not that he'd had a choice today.

And to have his patient die anyway…thanks to a drunken idiot who hadn't known when to quit.

Like him that day in Afghanistan? No, he hadn't been drinking and, yes, he'd been trying to save one of his buddy's lives, but rushing into an unknown area was never a good idea. He'd just made himself into a target.

He pushed away the memories and schooled his face to display cool disinterest. By the time he reached the young woman manning the front desk, he was back in control. She sent him a youthful megawatt smile, which just made him feel a million years old.

"Hello. How can I help you, sir?"

He braced his hands on the desk, hoping it didn't look like he was about to leap over it and attack her. Because he wasn't. He wasn't in any shape to do much of anything at the moment. "I'm trying to reach Kate… er…Katherine Bradley. She's staying here."

"And you would be…?" One perfectly groomed brow arched just a bit higher.

"Luke Blackman. Someone was supposed to leave a message that I was picking up my car."

Why the hell wasn't Kate stepping off that elevator?

"Oh, yes, I see it. I rang Ms. Bradley right afterward and let her know." She hesitated. "Would you like me to try again?"

"Please." Okay, so the word hadn't come out in the most gracious tone, so he tried again. "Thank you."

The receptionist waited, the phone pressed to her ear. "Ms. Bradley? A Mr. Blackman is here in the lobby. Will you be coming straight down?" She blinked a time or two then bit her lip. "Right. Yes, I'll tell him."

She set the phone down carefully. "She's having a bit of difficulty locating the key and wonders if you'd… um…give her a hand."

*What the…?*

He stood there for a moment, trying to figure out something that didn't involve walking, but came up empty.

"Lift?" he gritted. Why couldn't one thing go easily today?

"Just to your left, sir."

Luke swung away from the desk and did his best impression of a casual saunter, knowing it probably resembled more of a duck walk. How could someone misplace a set of keys in a hotel room? It's not like there were a million places it could be.

He made it to the elevator and pressed the button for the third floor, leaning against the nearest wall once he was inside. He should have gone with his first instinct and taken the taxi to his apartment and come back for the car tomorrow. But he had to ride right past the hotel, and had figured it would be just as easy to swing by on the way home. This was ridiculous.

When the doors opened again, he noted with relief that room 302 was just a few feet away. The door was ajar, but there was no sign of Kate. Which was good. At least she wouldn't stand there and watch him try to haul himself across the foyer. But if she expected him to be able to crawl around on his hands and knees and help search for the key, she'd be disappointed.

He knocked and the door swung open farther. "Kate?"

"Come on in. Sorry for the confusion."

When he pushed the door wider, he was shocked to find her seated in a chair, a glass of red wine in her hand, bare feet propped on the edge of the huge bed. Why was she just sitting there? Had she already located the key?

"I came to pick up my car."

"Oh, of course." She nodded at the table to her left, the slow drawl making it sound like she had all the time in the world. She was wearing some kind of stretchy pants and a loose T-shirt, like workout gear or something. "I've got the keys right here."

He drew a slow careful breath. "The receptionist said you couldn't find them."

Kate set the glass down and got to her feet, a spark of concern coming into her eyes. "Luke? How bad is it?"

He just stood there, trying to pretend he didn't hurt like a sonofabitch. He could do this. Stroll to that table, snatch the keys off it and walk back out. "I'm fine."

He took a step, forcing his leg to bear his full weight, and almost lost it. Sweat broke out on his forehead as he took a second and then a third step, his jaw working hard to contain the flurry of evil words that were swirling in his head.

"Stop it!" She grabbed the keys and moved in front of him. "I'm so sorry. I had no idea you'd be in this much pain."

"I don't know what you mean."

"I talked to Nick this evening, but I never imagined..."

His eyes closed. Of course she'd talked to him. He'd seen the way she'd looked at his leg at the accident scene. If she was truly a physical therapist, she could decode the signals, just like all the other therapists who'd worked on him. And none of them had done him a lick of good.

He knew that wasn't a fair assessment. They were the reason he was able to walk at all. But he wasn't walking. Not really. He was hobbling. He could put on a pretty good show for as long as it took him to get off work. But it cost him. Each and every damn day.

"Great. You talked to him. You know all my dirty little secrets." He held out his hand. "So give me the keys, and I'll get out of your hair."

"Sure. On one condition." She walked back to the side table, curvy hips bumping in a smooth, steady rhythm as she picked up a glass of water and two tablets sitting next to it. That didn't matter right now, though. Nothing did, except getting those keys, taking three steps out of the room and somehow reaching his car.

"The condition is that you tell me about how things went with your patient...while I work on your leg."

# CHAPTER SIX

SHE WAITED FOR the explosion she was sure would come, but there was none.

Instead, Luke pivoted on his good foot and sat on the edge of the bed. "I'm too tired to play this game with you right now, Kate. Please, just give me the keys."

"I'm not playing games. Nick said you'd been injured during your time in the service. Don't worry, he didn't give me all the gory details. But I can tell your leg hurts. It's been hurting ever since the accident, it's bothering you enough that you're having trouble walking across the room to pick up a set of keys. How safe is it for you to drive when it's like this?"

"Safe enough."

Okay, she probably should have met him downstairs like he'd asked, but she'd had no idea he'd be in such agony. And he wouldn't dream of coming out and admitting he was in pain. She'd had enough difficult patients to know when one was minimizing his problem, trying to keep it under wraps.

She set the glass, along with his keys and pills, on the dresser, then knelt next to the bed. "I have a heating pad, and I brought a few of my tools from home, in case I decided to…" She'd been about to say *"stay for a while,"* but it didn't seem appropriate to mention that right now. She didn't want there to be any kind of misunderstanding between them. She wasn't trying to start anything, but it had made her chest ache to see him try to hurry on that roadway today. He probably hadn't even realized she'd seen him.

"I just need to get some rest. It'll be fine by morning."

"I don't believe you."

He shut his eyes for a second, a muscle working in his jaw, before he fixed her with an angry glare. "No? Well, lady, I don't give a damn what you believe. I didn't seem to have any trouble lifting you onto that sink, did I? So give me my damn keys and let me get out of here."

Okay, that hurt. More than hurt. She clenched her jaw as angry words whisked up her airway and tumbled into her mouth, beating against the backs of her teeth in an effort to get out.

*This has nothing to do with you, Kate, and everything to do with Luke trying to protect himself.*

She'd had men like him cross her treatment table before. Military types who hated admitting weakness and hated it even worse when Kate focused all her attention on that weakness—which was what she had to do in order to help them. She was charged with manipulating the very spot, knowing the injury was as much a source of mental anguish as it was physical. And sometimes facing their own mortality day in and day out was more painful than anything else.

"No, you didn't have any trouble. But I should have noticed something was wrong even then."

"And if you had? Would it have made a difference?" The challenge was unmistakable.

Would she have still let him do what he had?

Definitely. It didn't make him any less attractive.

"No, it wouldn't have made any difference."

Admitting it made what they'd done seem that much worse, for some reason. Her patients were usually in a vulnerable place when she saw them. She would never dream of taking advantage of that.

But Luke *wasn't* her patient. She hadn't known about his injury at the time—he'd hidden it well. And he sure as hell hadn't been the picture of vulnerability. Then or now.

Because he was good at hiding his weakness.

But not nearly as good as her mother—who'd almost taken her secrets to the grave.

She pushed that thought aside. It had nothing to do with what would or wouldn't happen in this room. If Luke stood and demanded his keys, she'd give them to him and let him walk away. And she'd walk away, too. He'd talked about being too tired to play this game. Well, so was she. She was hurting inside, just like he was, even if it was for a completely different reason. And she wasn't sure if she could manage her pain *and* his right now.

All she wanted to do was ease a little of his hurt. Nothing more. And doing so would take her mind off her own problems. Off the fact that she still didn't know how she was going to deal with her newfound knowledge or what Nick's place would be in her life.

Or if she even wanted him to have a place.

She sucked in a deep breath and stood. "Come on, Luke. Surely it can't hurt to have me work on it a little bit. You can just think of it as getting a free massage."

A free massage.

Unfortunately that was not what he was thinking of at all, but he wasn't quite sure how he was going to get out of this room. His physical therapist had once told him he should use a cane, but he'd refused to go there. And most days he got along just fine without one.

It was only when he strained the damaged muscles beyond their limits that they gave him trouble. And when they rebelled, they went all out. The muscles were currently bunched in an angry ball at the top of his thigh. Forcing them to keep on working just made the knot tighten further.

A muscle relaxant would help, but it would take hours to take effect, and he'd still have a devil of a time getting to sleep tonight. And he was due at work first thing in the morning.

He wasn't sure he wanted Kate's hands on him right now, though. Not after what had happened between them before.

She hadn't bothered to wait for his response but was busy setting various items on the bed.

What could it hurt? If he embarrassed himself, it wasn't like she was going to be around to remind him of it. And he was dog tired. The last thing he wanted to do was stand up and somehow make his way back down to the car. His leg was going to fight him every step of the way.

"Where do you want me?"

Her fingers paused on a towel that she was rolling into a tight tube. "I'll lay a blanket on the floor. The bed is too soft."

She went to the closet, pulled a heavy brown blanket from the top shelf and folded it into a pallet, placing it at the foot of the bed. "Take your shoes and pants off, please."

Pants? Oh, hell, no.

"I'd rather keep them on, if it's all the same to you."

"Your shoes?"

He gave her a tight smile. "I think you know what I mean."

"I have to really knead those muscles, and to do that, I need to see what I'm working with."

His joking comment to Nick—asking if he wanted him to drop his pants and show Kate his handiwork—came back to taunt him. Yeah, well, he'd never expected to have to drop them…literally. And he wasn't all that thrilled with the idea of her seeing the ugly network of scars and divots where there should be a smooth layer of skin over muscle.

She stopped organizing stuff and looked up at him. "I'll put a towel over you. Besides, it's not like you'll be naked or anything."

He hadn't been naked that time in the supply closet either, but that hadn't stopped him from pulling her hips against him and sinking deep.

Yeah, something he'd better stop thinking about. Now.

Instead, he concentrated on the ache in his leg and the exhaustion that made him want to fall back onto the bed and ride out the pain with his eyes closed. He wouldn't be able to sleep, but he could at least stop thinking about things that didn't revolve around pain.

"How long will this take?"

"Around a half hour."

Surely he could survive that length of time.

"I want the towel first."

"Of course." She lifted a decent-sized bath towel. "I've got it right here."

Since the principal injury was at the top of his leg and hip—the explosion had damn near blown his balls off—that should cover the worst of his wound. She'd only need to see the scars that ran down the top of his thigh, where the shredded muscle fibers had been painstakingly stitched back together.

He was damned if he was going to undress in front of her, though. So he grabbed the towel from between her fingers and made his way—step by painful step—into the bathroom, where he proceeded to toe off his loafers and unzip his slacks. He didn't try to bend down and pull them off, he just let them slide down his legs, avoiding the mirror.

It seemed pretty stupid to worry about aesthetics in the face of everything else he had to worry about. But if he didn't look, he could avoid remembering the sudden searing pain that had ripped the breath from his lungs and the weakness that had stolen over him as his lifeblood had seeped from his body.

Flattening a hand on the vanity top, he supported part of his weight as he stepped out of the slacks. He then wrapped the towel tightly around his midsection and secured the loose end, thankful it hung almost to his knees.

There. That should do it.

He limped back into the room, the sound of elevator music coming from the television speakers.

Great. She was determined to really play this therapist thing to the hilt, wasn't she?

Kate patted the blanket, where she'd already laid out a pillow. "Let's put you on your back, head up here."

Holding the edges of the towel together with one hand and putting his other on the edge of the bed, he somehow managed to lower himself without falling. He stretched out, and just the act of being off that leg was heavenly. It still hurt, but now it was just a deep ache that went in through his skin and bored through all the layers before anchoring itself in his bone.

"Sit up for a second."

Once he did, she handed him a couple of pills and a glass of water.

He glanced at the pills. Ibuprofen. He lifted his brows. "Really?" He'd been planning on taking something a hell of a lot stronger when he got home.

"They'll help with the inflammation and at least take the edge off the pain. Hopefully by the time you're ready to leave."

"I know what they do."

"Oh." She colored. "Of course you do. Sorry. I don't have anything stronger."

He tossed the pills into his mouth and downed them with a long swig of icy water. He kept drinking until the glass was empty. "Thanks."

She took it from him. "You're welcome."

"You really don't have to do this."

"I know. But I want to." She nodded toward the pillow. "Lie back."

She slid the towel she'd rolled earlier beneath the knee of his injured leg to support it.

So far, so good.

The second she pushed the towel up, however, and he felt the first splash of warm oil hit his skin, Luke knew he'd made a terrible mistake.

# CHAPTER SEVEN

THE SCARS WERE everywhere. And she had a feeling she hadn't even seen the worst of them.

Kate swallowed back her horror as she smoothed the massage oil across his skin.

From beneath the towel a deep concave groove appeared, which branched into a spider web of smaller scars, the whole tangled mess stopping just before it reached his knee. Two square patches of skin appeared to have been slapped over a portion of his leg, one of them longer than the other, disappearing beneath the lower edge of the towel.

Skin grafts.

Where had they harvested them from?

Probably the back of his hip.

Luke's other leg was untouched. Smooth skin over strong muscles. His good leg had taken up the slack during the healing process, growing stronger even as the injured leg grew weaker. There was a size differential that was unmistakable.

When she glanced at his face, she saw his eyes were shut, long, curling lashes appearing at odds with the fierce lines of his cheekbones. He probably hated knowing she was looking at the damage—wondering if she was disgusted by the sight.

Not at all.

But she did feel a deep sadness at what had happened to him. She knew soldiers every day were struck down in the prime of their lives. Luke was lucky to be alive. And if she wasn't mistaken, he was very lucky to still have this leg. The damage had been extensive. Whoever had repaired it had done a good job. Nick? Not likely. It looked to be the work of more than one specialist. But he'd mentioned Nick saving his life, so he'd been involved somehow.

She pulled her mind back to the job at hand. "This is going to hurt at first, but it should start feeling better as things loosen up."

"I'll fine." Even as he said it, the muscles in his leg contracted as if undergoing an assault. And really it was. But it needed to be done.

She wouldn't dig in deep right away. She'd slowly work her way up to the hard stuff.

An unwilling smile tugged her lips.

Laying her hands on his leg, she started to massage, using long silky strokes that had little therapeutic value. It was really just a ploy to make his muscles think she wasn't going to go after them. As if by magic, the tension in his leg began to ease. She kept at it, discreetly edging the towel higher and higher, trying to do it without him noticing. Not because she wanted to sneak a peek, but because she had a feeling the worst of the damage was yet to come. She was right. More grafting. Furrows where skin should have overlaid muscle. It looked like he'd lost some actual muscle tissue. No wonder the leg was weak. It was a wonder he was walking as well as he was.

A low huff of air escaped his lungs, making her smile widen. He was determined to make her work for this, wasn't he? Well, he'd find she could be pretty stubborn herself. She wanted to get just one satisfied groan out of him.

She also needed to get her mind out of the gutter. She'd never had a patient affect her like this.

Because he *wasn't* her patient. And why did she feel the need to keep reminding herself of that fact? Maybe because she'd never worked on anyone she'd had sex with before.

Her strokes got firmer, but still not hard enough to make him wince. She stopped to pour a little more oil on her hands, letting it dribble onto his leg.

"The hotel's not going to be very happy if you get that stuff on their blanket," he said.

"It's water soluble. I'll take it down and ask them to clean it tomorrow. No biggie."

"Water soluble? As in…?"

Leave it to a doctor to understand the implications. "Don't worry, I'm not using *that* jelly on you."

His lips quirked, one eye opening to glance at her. "No need to, from what I remember."

*Egads.* Heat splashed hot and fast into her face. The man sure wasn't burdened by many inhibitions, was he?

Her best bet was to ignore that remark. "I want to get a couple of warm towels to put on your leg. Be right back."

She turned the hot tap on in the bathroom and reached to get a hand towel from the chrome fixture above the toilet. Her eyes met their reflection in the mirror, and she shook her head when she noted her face was as pink as she'd feared. If they were going to talk, she needed to direct the conversation and keep it in the shallow end of the pool.

Testing the water with her fingers, she refolded the

towel into a rectangle that would fit over the muscles just above his knee. The towel would help loosen those while she worked on the upper ones. She could reverse it later on.

She slid the towel beneath the flow of hot water and wet it enough to be effective, but not so much that it was dripping. She then switched on the heating rack on the wall and let it work on the bath towels already draped over it.

"Kate?"

"Coming." She hurried into the other room and knelt beside him again, sliding the towel into place and letting the moist heat soak deep into his muscles.

He groaned.

*Success!*

She worked for a few minutes, casting around for some innocuous topic of conversation. But Luke seemed pretty happy just to lie there for now, so maybe there was no need to talk. And judging from the twitch she'd just spotted behind that towel, he was struggling to keep his mind off how close she was getting to certain areas of his body.

Afraid he might leap up and demand to leave before she'd finished, she eased away and headed back down toward the center of his thigh.

A little more muscle went into the next wave of strokes as Kate tried to isolate muscle groups and loosen the thick adhesions caused by the scarring process. This was where things got serious, and in the same way her manipulation of his leg became more aggressive, so did Luke's demeanor. Not that he lashed out verbally, like he had earlier, but the bulge behind his towel subsided, and a muscle in his cheek began to pulse, letting her know he was struggling to deal with the discomfort. But he stayed put. It was probably a matter of pride more than anything else right now.

He may be a doctor by profession, but at his core he was still a tough military guy. Don't give quarter, don't show pain.

She stopped twice to replace the cooling towel with a fresh hot one, and shifted her attention to the lower section of his thigh, hoping to draw the pain down and out of his body. This area was less damaged than the upper portion and evidently less sensitive as well, because Luke relaxed the second she slid the warm towel up to cover the part on which she'd already worked. She sensed his relief that she was moving away from that area.

She reapplied the oil to her palms, noting they were pink from the work. But it felt good to be back in her element, helping someone who needed it. And it was helping her as well, keeping her mind off her current problems.

"Remember I told you about researching some of the UK hospitals that offer LSVT therapy?"

He grunted in response, and Kate wasn't sure that was an affirmation or not. So she kept going. "Your hospital offers it. Did you know that?"

She paused, glancing up to see his eyes had opened a bit and he was now regarding her with what looked like suspicion. Maybe he thought she was going to press him about helping with Nick. She'd still like to, if he needed it, but what she'd really love would be to observe how another therapy center operated. Maybe even work there for a bit while she was here, even if on a volunteer basis. Being cooped up in her hotel room day in and day out didn't appeal to her. And she didn't feel right inviting herself over to Nick and Tiggy's house.

Maybe Luke would be willing to put in a good word for her at the center.

"Anyway, I was thinking." She put her hands back on his leg and focused on massaging while she got to the point. "Maybe you could introduce me around and ask if I could observe their techniques."

No response. She sneaked another glance at his face. His eyes were closed again and that telltale muscle was working in his jaw. Surely she wasn't hurting him now. Her fingers were barely making any indentations in his skin.

"Luke, are you awake?"

"Oh, yeah. Wide awake."

His tone was odd, as well. She glanced at the towel, thinking maybe he was talking about what was behind it, but it was as still as death.

She swallowed, but forged ahead. "So what do you think?"

"Is that what this was all about?"

*This?* This what?

"I'm not sure what you mean."

"Were you trying to get an 'in' with the hospital in the same way you were trying to get an 'in' with Nick's treatment?"

"No, of course not." Outrage crowded her chest. She'd been trying to help him, and he was thinking she'd only done it to get something she wanted? "I miss my job, that's all. I was just sitting here thinking about how much I love doing this. How good it feels to watch your muscles relax as my hands slide over them. How good it feels to have…"

Oh, my. The towel wasn't so still anymore. In fact, it was—

"How good it feels to what, Kate?" His voice rumbled through her senses about the same time as he slowly lifted his body into a sitting position. Since she'd been kneeling over his leg, that put them nose to nose. A potent combination of anger and something even more powerful glittered in his eyes.

His hand slid around the back of her neck, keeping her from moving away.

"I—I was talking about work," she whispered, warm liquid anticipation beginning to flow through her veins, despite her words.

"Were you?" His thumb slid down her jaw until it hooked beneath her chin, tilting it up slightly. "I was talking about…this."

With that, his lips closed the narrow gap between them and slid over hers.

# CHAPTER EIGHT

HER HANDS WERE still on his leg.

Moisture from the towel draped over his upper thigh seeped through the dry one around his waist, but he didn't care. He'd done so well controlling his urges during that crazy massage. Well, during most of it, anyway. When that control had started to slip and his body had responded despite every effort he'd made to think of other things, Kate had seemed to know exactly what to do to help him regain it. She had clamped down on his leg and gone to town, drowning out any sensation other than acute discomfort. The pain had been welcome, though.

He waited for her to repeat the action and help him switch his body off again.

She didn't. Her hands just kept resting lightly on his thigh, even as her mouth began to return the pressure as it opened. Then her hands were off his leg and around his neck.

She'd had to go and ask that damn question. The one that had made him question her motives all over again. Because the second she had, he'd forgotten all about the pain. Or maybe that was the ibuprofen.

Right now he didn't care what had caused him to snap. Because kissing her lips had been all he'd thought about for the past three days. That and those sexy little sighs as he'd taken her.

Hell, he couldn't do this. Nick was counting on him to keep it in his pants.

Only his pants were long gone. And his leg was feeling better by the minute. Probably because every ounce of blood was rushing to the founding member of the do-something-stupid-now club.

But Nick…

Her fingers slid into his hair, sending shock waves rolling through his entire body.

Who cared what Nick thought, anyway? This woman had the ability to cut off all brain function that didn't involve getting her into a prone position as fast as possible.

No. Not fast. He'd already had the slam-bam experience with her, and it had rocked his world. So slow and easy would probably blow it to smithereens.

She whimpered and pressed closer, and he realized her mouth was still open, still inviting. Well, far be it for him to disappoint a lady. Wrapping one hand around her waist, he hauled her closer, swiveling her so her knees were beside his left hip.

The act tipped her sideways onto his chest, which was about as close as he dared get to pulling her onto his lap, which was where he really wanted her. He had enough sense, though, to know that was a recipe for disaster. And not just because of his leg.

Speaking of legs, still kissing her, he tossed the damp towel she'd used during the massage to the side and buried a hand in her hair, which was loose around her shoulders. God, it was so incredibly soft. Just like her mouth, which was drawing him deeper, urging him to take what he wanted.

And he would. Very soon.

Leaving her mouth, he pressed slow biting kisses inch by inch along her jaw, drawing a moan from her throat that went straight to his groin.

"I'm supposed to be taking care of your leg," she whispered.

He lifted his head, that drawl of hers singing through his head. "The leg's all better. Now it's my turn to take care of you."

"Oh."

He smiled. His hand skimmed beneath her T-shirt and found that skin he'd been craving, his fingers splaying over her back, thumb gliding in a back and forth arc over her hip. "How are your knees feeling?"

Her eyes widened. "M-my knees?"

Her skin turned deliciously pink and he lifted a hand, drawing his fingers along the line of her cheek. "You've been kneeling a while, and I thought it might be uncomfortable."

Kate wrinkled her nose and slid down until she was resting on her left hip. Her glance went to his towel, which appeared to be levitating. "I don't think you need to worry about your modesty anymore, do you?" Her fingers went to the tucked-in portion, and he moved to stop her before it was too late.

"Don't." The word was a harsh command, and she blinked up at him, surprise written across her face. He nodded toward the overhead light, forcing his voice to soften. "Can you turn that off?"

Kate tilted her head, her hands still gripping the edge of his towel. Turn off the light. Right now? She wouldn't be able to see him if she...

Oh. She got it. The towel had nothing to do with

modesty and everything to do with the condition of his leg. He didn't want her to see it. "Luke, I've already seen your leg. Touched it. It's okay. Really."

She leaned over and tasted his lips, nibbled across them, something inside of her aching over his request. Had he made all of his dates since the accident dim the lights before they were intimate?

At first she thought he was going to lean back and withdraw, or continue to insist that the lights go off, but then he grabbed her to him—fast enough that it took her breath away. His mouth slanted over hers, and if she thought he'd been kissing her before, she had been wrong. Hard lips held hers prisoner, forcing them apart and burying his tongue in the depths of her mouth.

He held her against him, her breasts flattening against his chest as he continued to take her mouth with long, hard strokes. A small sound exited her throat as she wound her arms around his head and held him close, trying to bind them together.

His head canted sideways as if needing to explore her from every angle, his mouth dragging across hers before settling back in and starting the sequence all over again.

This man was all muscle and sinew...and hot, heady need.

He drew back enough to whisper against her mouth. "There's a condom in my wallet in the bathroom."

"I'll get it." She knew exactly why he'd muttered it. He couldn't get up and walk to the bathroom. Not yet. Not with his leg the way it was. Oh, how that admission must have cost him. She'd just uncurled her legs and stood when a tug at her waistband stopped her. She turned back round, surprised when his fingers undid the button on her slacks and drew down the zipper.

She swallowed as he tugged her closer, still parting

the fabric and using the edges to slide them over her hips and down her calves.

"Step out of them."

She did as he asked, standing there in her white lace panties. Was he going to repeat his actions from the supply closet and yank them off her? No. Instead, he tunneled beneath the elastic of the legs, his hands curving up and over her butt. She expected him to squeeze her cheeks and feel her up—and she'd have been happy to let him but no. He used his grip to urge her toward him. When she hesitated, his mouth curved in that crazy half grin. "Come here, Kate."

She gulped, but allowed him to draw her closer until he was right there. *Right* there. Pressed against her. He opened his mouth and surrounded her, biting down with enough pressure to make her gasp. Then his tongue slid over her in one hot, wet swipe, the heat traveling right through the fabric. Her eyes shuddered closed, wanting more. Now. Just as her hips edged closer, he backed off, his hands sliding free of her panties. When she blinked down at him in confusion, he flashed another knowing smile. "My wallet is in the back pocket of my pants."

She stood paralyzed for a second or two, before her mind absorbed what he'd said. He wanted her to walk to the bathroom.

Lordy, he'd just set her body on fire, and the man knew it. She swiveled to the left, her legs a bit unsteady as they carried her toward the bathroom. With each step she felt his eyes on her, the place between her legs already pulsing with need. She'd been on the verge of exploding, and he'd barely even touched her.

And when he did?

She found his pants on the floor and picked them up, sliding her hand into the back pocket and retrieving his wallet. She flipped it open, and rummaged around before finding the compartment with the packet inside. Make that *two* packets. Hmm… Just in case, she removed both of them and headed back to the bedroom.

When she got there, the lights were off, and she squinted at the pallet, only to find it empty. For a second she thought he might have taken off, but then she remembered him asking her to turn out the lights. She'd refused, so he'd found a way to do it, anyway. So where was he? As if he'd read her thoughts, he called, "Over here."

Peering through the darkness, she could barely make out his form on the bed. Back leaning against the headboard, long legs stretched out in front of him.

She licked her lips. "Found them."

She knew why he'd asked her to get his wallet but why had he gotten on the bed while she'd been in the bathroom, instead of waiting for her to return?

He hadn't wanted her to see him struggle to walk, if his leg was still bothering him. So he'd done it quickly, while she'd been out of the room. Her heart cramped further. She ignored it. The last thing he'd want was for her to make a comment or try to reassure him.

Instead, she tossed the condoms onto the bed, hoping they landed somewhere near his left side. Then she crawled slowly toward him, her eyes beginning to adjust to the gloom. If she was on top, he wouldn't have to worry about his leg. When she reached him, she kissed his lips then put her plan into action, swinging her leg over his hips, straddling him— Oh…he was naked! And hard. Gloriously hard.

This was good.

Still pressing her mouth to his, her breasts flattened against his chest. The heat of his body burned against her most private place, making her squirm. *Mmm*. When he muttered something against her mouth, she wiggled again, feeling a definite response from him this time. So she repeated the act, sliding slowly along his naked length. There was definitely something to be said for being in charge of a man like this.

And men liked it, too, right? When the woman took the lead?

She leaned up onto her elbows and smoothed his hair back from his forehead.

"What do you think you're doing?" There was dark humor lacing his voice.

"Playing with your hair."

"No. I mean here." He pressed up with his hips, rubbing against her in a way that made her gasp. "What are you doing here?"

"I thought I'd be on top." She pressed a kiss to his throat then licked halfway to his chin. She was startled when all of a sudden she was flipped flat onto her back, where she landed with an *"Oomph."*

"You thought wrong." Her breath sawed in and out of her lungs at the dark, hungry look she could just make out in his eyes. "You think I can't do this?"

He pressed into her in a way that said, yes, he could, in fact. His voice lowered further. "I can. And I will. Very soon." His teeth grazed her cheek. "You can be on top next time."

All she heard were the words *very soon* and *next time*.

Then his mouth was on hers and he was kissing her until her head spun.

*Next time?* Oh, Lord, so he'd taken those two condoms at face value. They were going to have more than one session tonight. And next time she was going to be on top.

All she could think of was that maybe she should call the front desk and tell them to hold all her calls.

He sat up, straddling her hips in much the way she'd straddled his. Her hands went to his waist and started to slide lower, meaning to touch him. He stopped her. "Next time."

Not fair. But she wasn't about to argue.

Then his hands were on her shirt, and he tugged it up and over her head, letting it drop beside the bed. His palms curved over her breasts, molding them to his hands. Sweet desire pumped through her veins, and she arched into his touch. His fingers left their perch and glided from her collarbone, down over her breasts, grazing her nipples as they passed and then continued down her belly.

He swirled a lazy fingertip into her belly button, his thumb running along the elastic on her panties, then beneath it, traveling over the fine hairs until he'd reached her center. He moved lower, pushing inside, the same way his tongue had pushed inside her mouth a few minutes earlier.

She whimpered as the rest of his hand curved over that most sensitive part of her. He stroked in and out a couple of times, while she tried to lift her hips to meet him. He stilled.

"Rip open one of the condoms."

All she wanted to do was lie there and absorb the heady sensations caused by the continued intimate contact, but she dutifully fumbled her hand across the surface of the bed until she found the nearest condom.

It took several tries before she finally located the nick

in the side and tore the packaging. Luke rewarded her with a couple more easy glides of his thumb.

God, that felt good. Too good. Her fingers stopped what they were doing as her eyes fluttered shut. She needed to push against him. But couldn't because his weight was still on top of her.

"Take it out."

He had to be kidding. She could barely think, much less do anything requiring a co-ordinated plan of attack. "I—I…"

His thumb slowly withdrew, the pressure of the rest of his hand on her fading with each lost millimeter.

"Luke…" She squirmed. "Please."

"Take it out of the package, Kate."

Oh, that was mean. But her fingers somehow slid into the opening and found the condom, managing to wrestle it free.

As soon as she did, his hand was over hers, guiding her, before moving to grip himself by the base and letting her slowly unroll the condom over his length. Their fingers met in the middle. He joined her in finishing the process and the mingling of their hands on his flesh was heady.

He wrapped his hand around hers, using her fingers to slowly stroke himself over and over.

God. He was too much. She'd thought he'd been erotic in the supply closet. This was light years beyond that.

He finally released her and dragged his thumb across her lower lip, his other still lodged inside her body. "I don't think we're going to need any of your massage oil."

Her face heated as he withdrew his hand and slowly leaned over her, until his lips were at her ear. "I love it that you're so wet. So ready." He moved up over her hips, biting her earlobe. "Spread your legs for me, Kate."

She'd never had a man mutter words like this to her. Ever. And if he'd ordered her around in any other tone of voice, she'd have told him where to stick it. But his voice was low, mellow, rumbled directly against her ear and sent delicious shivers through her body. It was a complete turn-on and totally different from what she'd experienced in the past. He voiced his wishes and expected her to obey.

And hell if she didn't.

Her thighs parted, and Luke slid between them, his legs pressing against hers to hold them in place. She felt his fingers at the crotch of her panties, tugging them to one side, his penis finding her. He eased just inside, then withdrew, her moisture making each pass a little smoother. His breath shuddered against her cheek as he suddenly pushed completely inside her, stretching and filling her, and her muscles clenched around him in reaction.

"Holy hell."

She echoed that sentiment. Whew. He felt as good on a bed as he had on a sink. No, better, because there something incredibly intimate about having a man press you into a mattress.

She was glad she wasn't on top.

Sliding her palms down the smooth skin of his back, she tried to memorize the lusciousness of his warmth against her. She was still in her bra and panties, and there was no hint that he was in a hurry to remove either garment. That drove her crazy, as well. In fact, everything about this man did.

He withdrew only to thrust into her again, deeper this time, drawing a strangled moan from her as she strained upward, wanting to get closer. Keeping himself buried inside her, he lifted onto his elbows and kissed her lips, her collarbone, the top of her breast, before his mouth closed over the fabric-covered peak.

*Holy hell.* She didn't voice the words like he had, but they sang through her head over and over as he drew her nipple further into his mouth, the friction of the wet fabric over her sensitive flesh taking her higher. She wasn't far.

"Luke," she whispered, her shaking hands coming up to cradle his head against her as his tongue rubbed back and forth over her. The sensation went straight to her center, where her flesh tightened around his again.

*Move. Please.*

He did. Withdrawing just enough to put some space between them.

*No!*

When he kept tugging on her nipple, making no move to set up any kind of rhythm down below, she grew desperate. She lifted her hips in an effort to relieve some of the ache between her legs then backed away, rising to repeat the act as his breathing deepened, rattling against her chest.

She realized what he was doing. Holding still and forcing her to ride him as she might have done had she been on top. And so she did. Luke rewarded each strong pump of her hips with a long slow lap of his tongue before moving to the other breast, the agonizing vortex he was creating sucking her a little deeper with each stroke.

His knees were flat on the bed and so she hooked her feet around them in an effort to gain more leverage, pushing up hard, until the sensitive bead of flesh at the joint of her thighs finally connected with his pelvis.

*Oh! Yes. That.*

She mashed closer, holding herself high against him and rubbing in little circles, her legs shaking with exertion but needing this so very badly. She pressed her hands low on his back, using her arms to keep that precious line of connection.

*Please. Oh, God. Just a little bit more.*

Her legs started to fail her, and she lunged back up in desperation, forcing her body to slide against his over and over…

*Ahhhh!*

She went off, her body convulsing around him as she fell back to the bed. He followed her down, suddenly thrusting into her at a wild pace, releasing her breast and throwing his head back. The cords on his neck stood out and a growl erupted from his chest as he seated himself deep, deep within her, holding himself there for what seemed like forever.

When he settled back against her, his head dropped to her neck, breath gusting against her moist skin. An aftershock went through her, and her flesh clamped down on him again. He responded by pressing closer.

"Mmm." The contented sound came from somewhere down around her shoulder, punctuated with a small bite at the joint. The shot arced straight down her spinal cord, and she squeezed tight again. He paused, then repeated the act to the same effect. "I think somebody likes that."

She liked just about anything he did. She groaned, half amused, half embarrassed by what he made her body do.

He lifted his head and smiled down at her. "Look on the bright side, Kate. At least you didn't lose your panties this time."

# CHAPTER NINE

THE PHYSICAL THERAPIST *set aside her butcher's knife and pulled a protective silicone stump sleeve from a huge drawer filled with prosthetics of every imaginable size and shape—arms, legs, the bottom portion of a face—and held it up. "This looks to be the right size."*

*Luke glanced at the bed next to his where a young amputee had been brought in earlier today. It was now empty. So was the bed to his right. He frowned. Then who was the sleeve for?*

*Horror gripped him as he slowly dragged the sheet covering the lower half of his body away from his legs. The left one was fine. Strong. Whole. The right one...*

*The bloody bandages that had once covered his leg were now lying flat against the bed, still wound around and around, as if his leg had simply vanished into thin air, leaving behind the empty wrappings. And the therapist's face, observing him with a secretive smile, came into sudden focus as she leaned toward him.*

*Kate.*

*What had she done to him?*

*He screamed...*

"Luke." The sound came from beside him, along with a hand gripping his arm. Shaking him.

He jerked away from the touch, blinking as reality returned.

She leaned toward him just like before, only the smirk was gone. In its place was worry, her brows drawn together as she reached for him again.

"Luke? Are you okay?"

He fell back against the pillows, flexing his right leg. Still there. It was a dream.

Bloody hell, he was drenched with sweat. The last thing he wanted was for her to see him like this. He made to get up, only to have her stop him.

"Hey. What's going on?"

If he started suddenly yanking his clothes on, he had a feeling she'd follow him, pestering him with questions.

"Bad dream, I guess."

"I guess so. Are you okay?"

He dragged a hand through his hair, pushing it off his brow and ignoring her repeated question. "What time is it?"

"Just after eight in the morning. Sorry, I guess I fell asleep."

Kate was sitting with the sheet pulled up around her breasts—breasts that were now completely bare. Her blond hair was gloriously tousled, her eyes soft with sleep, but he couldn't banish the image of her tucking that huge knife out of sight. That strange, secretive smile. Maybe his subconscious couldn't separate the physical pain he'd endured last night from the pleasure she'd given him. She'd hurt him and then helped him. Just like in his dream.

"We both fell asleep." Maybe it was a good thing he'd had that dream. He needed something to knock some sense into his head. What he'd done last night had been crazy. And if Nick found out, he was going to kill him. "I need to get to work, though. My shift starts in a little over an hour."

"How's your leg?"

He jerked his glance to her face before he realized she wasn't talking about his dream but about the massage. He stretched it again, surprised that the muscles seemed to have recovered from the abuse he'd put them through at the accident scene. "All better. Thanks."

He put his feet over the side of the bed, keeping the sheet pulled over his thighs. He'd never thought to check last night to make sure the curtains were pulled all the way shut. They weren't, and daylight was pouring into the room through the gap between them.

"Um, Luke?"

He twisted to look at her, waiting for her to continue.

"Have you thought about what I asked? About the therapy center at the hospital?"

"No." All his misgivings from yesterday came rushing back. Along with all of his suspicions. "Have you talked to Nick about this?"

"Not yet. But I was planning on saying something soon."

"I think he's almost done with his physical therapy course. At least, that's what I understood. I'm supposed to meet him at the center when I get in today."

The hand Kate was using to hold the sheet curled until she was clenching it against herself. "Oh. I didn't realize he was almost finished with his treatment..."

Last night had been a mistake. The last thing he wanted to do was get involved in Nick's business. Especially since he couldn't seem to keep his hands off that "business."

"Like I said, you can talk to him about it."

"I'd still like to observe, even if Nick isn't there any more. I can learn so much from seeing other approaches."

Did he really want to have this discussion this morning? "I can't promise anything. But I'll check and see if they allow that kind of thing."

She leaned over and kissed him on the cheek. "Thank you."

He climbed out of bed, still feeling a little queasy from the dream he'd had. Maybe it really *was* his subconscious; maybe it was trying to give him a warning kick in the ass. He kept his leg angled where she couldn't see it. "Listen. This—" he motioned at the bed "—can't happen again."

Her eyes widened with hurt, and then her teeth came down on her lip. "Of course. I, um, feel the same way. I'm not going to be here for that long, anyway."

"Okay, then. As long as we're on the same page." He grabbed the rest of his clothes and headed for the bathroom. Why did he feel like such a schmuck? He'd just done what needed doing. Nick would not be happy about him spending the night here. Not that he planned on breathing a word of this to anyone. One slip-up was understandable—after all, Kate was a beautiful woman—but two? Not his usual style.

Especially not after displaying the kind of weakness he'd shown last night.

Hell, as erotic as it had been to make her set the pace, to force her to push up into him over and over, it had served a dual purpose. He'd been having a tough time getting the muscles in his weak leg to cooperate during the act. His pride had been stung when she'd climbed on top, and so he'd thought he'd show her that he was as good as the next guy.

Only he wasn't. He couldn't even make love to a woman without having to worry about his goddamned leg giving out in the middle of it.

He sat on the lid of the commode and dragged both his hands through his hair. Staring down at his leg and the mangled flesh and skin grafts that stretched from his right hip to his knee, he winced. He couldn't even stand to have a woman look at him. It was lights out, all the way.

Kate had undoubtedly seen quite a bit of the damage during the massage, but not all of it. And certainly not the stuff on the inside.

He stood and yanked on his briefs, letting the elastic waistband snap against his skin.

"Where'd you get the scar?" Her voice came from the other side of the door.

Was she kidding him? Scar…singular? He stepped into his slacks, zipping them up and fastening the button. "I already told you."

"No, not your leg. The one on your chest. Near your tattoo."

He glanced in the mirror at his other war wound. From a completely different war—and one that didn't bother him nearly as much. That one had been fought on the streets of Chicago in back of a bar—over a woman, of all things. He'd allowed himself to be goaded into going into the alley to fight, only to have the other guy pull a knife on him. He'd seen the metallic glint just as it had come toward him—too late to duck away.

The slice hadn't been terribly deep, but it had almost bisected his left nipple and stretched halfway down his stomach, where it was inches away from meeting up with his other wound. He'd been a drunken fool. Way too young to have gotten into a situation like that.

And it had sealed his decision to go into the military, as his father had basically disowned him that night. As soon as the stitches had come out, he'd gone to the nearest recruitment center and signed on the dotted line. The tattoo of an eagle on his left shoulder had come later, after he'd graduated from boot camp.

Funny how that scar didn't carry the same baggage as the other one. And he didn't mind anyone seeing that one. He rubbed his chest. "I got it in a bar fight."

There was silence for a second. Then her voice came back through. "Really? Was that before or after your leg injury?"

He doubted the outcome would have been quite the same if the fight had happened afterward. The other guy had wound up with a broken nose and a pair of black eyes once he'd kicked the knife out of his hand.

No kicking anything out of anyone's hand nowadays. "Before. I was young and stupid."

So what was his excuse now?

"Are you almost done? I need the bathroom."

He dragged his shirt on over his head and opened the door. "It's all yours. Listen, I'll see myself out."

"I hate to ask, but would you mind giving me a lift to the hospital, if you're headed that way? You mentioned Nick being there, and it would give me a chance to talk to him."

He wished he could say no and feel okay about it. But he couldn't. He'd spent the night and had had sex with her not once but twice. And if he now told her to find her own way to the hospital, it would make him seem like a jerk. At least in his own eyes.

"Sure." He'd planned on stopping home to shower and change, but he kept a spare set of clothes at the hospital for nights when he was on call. He could shower there, as well. No one would ever be the wiser. "Can you be ready in twenty?"

"Definitely." She closed the door. "Feel free to call down for room service if you want something to eat. They're pretty quick as long as you stick to the quick fare menu."

Room service. It figured.

"I can wait until I get to the hospital." He paused. "Do you want me to call down for something for you?"

"No, I'm not a big breakfast eater. I'll just grab some coffee at the hospital."

Thirty minutes later, they pulled up to the hospital and Luke parked his little car. As they walked through the entrance, a voice came from their left. "Kate?"

Luke glanced toward the sound.

Dammit. The very person he'd hoped to avoid this morning. Nick was walking down the hallway with Tiggy beside him.

Nick cocked his head, as if realizing for the first time that Luke was with her. "Hey, how lucky is this, to all run into each other at the same time?"

Luke held out his hand and shook Nick's. "Lucky indeed."

Unfortunately, out of the corner of his eye he noticed Kate's face go through a series of subtle color changes before it settled on pink. Bright pink.

She leaned up to give the other man a kiss on the cheek then smiled at Tiggy. "Luke was just telling me y'all might be here today."

He couldn't help but notice the typical southern expression, or Nick's smile, which signaled the other man had caught it as well.

"A few more minutes and you would have missed

us," Nick said, stretching his back. "Did you happen to ask Luke about next week?"

Next week? Now what had the woman gone and done?

"Oh, um. No. I thought you might like to do it yourself."

He reached a hand toward his wife, who took hold of it in both of hers. "We want you both to come and have dinner at our house next week."

Luke went very still. Kate knew about this and was supposed to tell him? And yet she'd said nothing?

She was unbelievable. First she wanted him to put in a good word for her at the rehab center, and now she was busy planning dinner engagements for him as if they were a frigging couple or something.

"And I take it Kate has already said yes."

"She has."

He sent her a sideways glare, noting her eyes were wide. With guilt? "She accepted for the both of us?"

"No, but I'm sure she'd be glad if you came."

"She would, would she?" Luke's eyes continued to zero in on her like laser scalpels, slicing his way to the truth.

As if realizing something was off between the two of them, Nick frowned, his glance skipping over him. Luke was well aware his clothes were wrinkled and he had a day's worth of stubble on his chin—things he'd hoped to remedy by the time he saw his friend.

"Are you just getting off work?" he said. "I thought you mentioned coming on duty about the time I finished with therapy."

Great. Now what?

Kate was no help. She was staring at the pattern in

the floor as if it had ancient Sanskrit writings hidden within it.

"No, I was out last night. Just getting in, in fact. I thought I'd shower here at the hospital."

Nick's attention turned to Kate, who, thank heavens, was much better groomed and who'd had a quick shower back at the hotel. "Well, I'm glad I caught you before I left."

Tiggy let go of his hand and dug around in her purse. "You already know where we live, but I wanted to give you our mobile numbers in case you need to get hold of us. We were thinking Tuesday evening. Could you come round at sixish? Would that work for both of you?"

Kate's head came up. "Fine with me."

It was too much to hope that he was on duty that night—but Luke didn't think he was. "I'll check my schedule and get back with you."

"I'm sure you'd love him to come, wouldn't you, Kate?"

Her eyes came up to meet his, and Luke swore he saw the barest hint of an apology in their blue depths. "Definitely. It wouldn't be the same without him."

# CHAPTER TEN

THE REHAB CENTER was modern and up-to-date, and Kate had been totally shocked when Luke called her that afternoon and said he'd arranged a tour—if she still wanted to see it. She did.

Laisse, one of the physical therapists, smiled at her. "Dr. Blackman tells me you're well versed in LSVT therapy."

Warmth spread through her chest. He'd actually remembered the name of it? "I'm a licensed physical therapist, but I also have my LSVT certification."

"Which tract? Big or Loud?"

"Both, but I've dealt more with the Big side of the spectrum as it deals with body movements, rather than the speech element. My father has Parkinson's—early stage—so I thought I might be able to help him with therapy. Turns out he's got a great therapist and hasn't needed me."

"So what brings you to London?"

This is where it got tricky, and for the first time she wished Luke was here to smooth the way for her. "I have a relative who was a patient here." Hopefully that would be enough of an explanation.

"Oh, I hope everything went well."

"It did. He's finishing up his treatment and should be fine."

Laisse stopped in front of an older woman, who was using an upper-body ergometer. The machine looked much like a bulky, gray stationary bike that had been turned on its head, and gave a steady whine as the woman pedaled with her hands, warming up her muscles before getting down to whatever therapies she would need. "How are we doing, Mrs. Wheaton?"

"It's a bit harder than I expected." Her breath rasped in and out as she struggled to keep pumping.

Laisse bent over and looked at the dial, twisting it to reduce the resistance level. "How's that? Better? I don't want to wear you out before our session."

"Yes, much easier, thank you."

"Do you think you can manage another two minutes?"

The woman nodded, her hands circling a bit faster.

They continued their tour. "Our LSVT therapist isn't here today, I'm sorry to say. She's due in tomorrow, if you'd like to come back."

"Would it be possible for me to observe her with a patient?"

"I'll check with the head therapist, but I don't think it will be a problem. We have relatives in quite a bit, watching as their loved ones have therapy. I'm sure Steffie wouldn't mind."

They stopped by the front desk and Laisse scribbled a note on a pad on the counter. "What was your last name again?"

"Bradley."

"Okay, Kate. I've got you down." She ran a finger down a black scheduling book. "Steffie's first appointment is at nine tomorrow. Let me check with her before

I say yes, but I don't expect there to be a problem. Why don't you come in at ten, if that's all right? She has several patients in a row."

"Wonderful." Kate pulled out her wallet and found one of her business cards. She wrote the hotel's phone number and her room number on the back. "This is where I'm staying. If there's a problem, would you mind giving me a call?"

"Of course." The whine of the ergometer slowed and then came to a halt. Laisse glanced over at the machine. "I need to get back to my patient, but I'll see you tomorrow, then."

"Yes. Thanks again for the tour. You have a beautiful facility."

Laisse looked around with pride. "Thank you. We're quite proud of it."

Shoving her wallet back in her purse, Kate glanced at the glass wall to her right, her fingers fumbling a bit when she spied Luke outside, looking in at her. What did he want? She assumed that once he'd dropped her off at the center, he'd wash his hands of her. Their last joint appearance would be at Nick's house for dinner and after that they'd each go their own way.

"Okay, I'll see you tomorrow. Thanks again."

"My pleasure." Laisse's voice lowered to almost a purr as she, too, noted who was on the other side of the viewing glass.

Kate squashed the urge to roll her eyes. "Do you know Dr. Blackman?"

"Not well. He introduced himself when he made your appointment. But I've heard quite a bit about him."

What did she mean? "Really?"

"He has quite a reputation with the nurses on the wards."

The image of all those letters in her mom's shoebox came back to haunt her, and she bit her lip. Luke certainly knew his way around a bedroom. A flush came over her as she remembered exactly the way he'd taken charge.

At the time she'd thought it was sensual beyond belief, but what if he was just like a male version of her mother? Someone who jumped from person to person, leaving behind a trail of broken hearts? She'd been worried about her own genetic traits after she'd leaped into bed with him, but maybe she wasn't the person she should be worried about.

Laisse turned away from the window with obvious reluctance and headed for her patient.

That settled it, then. Reputations didn't materialize out of thin air. And the other physical therapist certainly didn't seem opposed to having Luke come into the center. But no way did she want to watch Laisse fawn over him.

And Kate definitely didn't want to wind up as a letter in someone's shoebox. It was time to steer clear of him actively. It wouldn't be hard to do because she didn't work at the hospital and would be going home before too much longer.

She glanced at the window again, only to see him nod at her, his hands shoved into the pockets of his slacks. His white lab coat was nowhere to be seen. Great. Hopefully that didn't mean he was off duty.

Well, she was going to have to walk through that door some time, especially as Laisse was already working with her patient, although she'd seen the other woman peer in Luke's direction another time or two.

Making her way across the room, she reached the

glass door and pushed through it. Luke met her on the other side. "How did it go?" he asked.

"Pretty well. I'm going to come by and observe the LSVT therapist tomorrow morning."

"Good." He took her elbow and started to steer her away from the area. She frowned until she noted that Laisse was watching them.

Why did she get the feeling she was about to be added to the gossip swirling around Luke? She tugged her elbow out of his hold. "Did you need to see me about something?"

"I wanted to let you know that I'll be able to go to Nick's."

What did he expect her to say? That she was thrilled? Ecstatic? Horrified? She settled for none of the above. "Nick will be happy to hear that."

"I figured." He paused. "Listen, about what happened at your hotel room, I'd really prefer Nick not know."

She blinked in surprise and then let out a little laugh. "Oh, how the worm has turned. Wasn't it me who was worried about that very thing just a few days ago? I remember some doctor letting me stew in my own juices for a few moments before promising he wouldn't say anything."

Luke hooked his index finger under her chin, his thumb making a long slow pass over her lower lip. "So, are you going to make me stew in my own juices to get your revenge?"

No, because he'd probably have the last laugh. Somehow.

"Of course not. I'm not about to say anything to anyone. It's not something *I'm* likely to brag about."

His eyes narrowed just a bit. "Meaning?"

She glanced back at the viewing window, but Laisse was busy with her patient. At least, she appeared to be. "It's just that people around here appear to be inordinately interested in your...nocturnal activities."

His face cleared. "Ah, I see." His thumb still rested on her lower lip, and this time, instead of sliding across it, he tugged the center of it down, parting her lips for a heart-stopping second. Then he released her with a smile. "Nick seemed to be worried I might try to take advantage of you."

So even Nick had the idea that Luke slept around.

Wow. And now she'd been with him twice. No... three times, if you counted the two-in-one-night episode in her hotel room. Insisting on giving him that massage had been the dumbest idea she'd ever had.

"Well, good thing he was wrong. Isn't it? About you taking advantage of me, I mean."

"Definitely. Besides, I seem to remember it being the other way around."

Her eyes widened. Surely he didn't think...

"I didn't take advantage of anyone."

His smile widened. "No?" He moved in, lowering his head as if to keep their conversation private. "Let's see. I asked you to meet me down in the parking lot with my car keys. Instead, you invited me up to your hotel room. Hmm...actually *invited* is kind of a mild word. It might be closer to the truth to say you forced me to come up."

"I didn't force you to do anything." But she had, and she knew it. She'd said she lost the keys and then, when he'd come to her room to get them, she'd manipulated him into a massage.

But *Luke* was the one who'd initiated that devastating kiss.

And she'd responded like there was no tomorrow.

He was right. Looking at it from his perspective, the evidence did seem pretty damning.

"I was honestly trying to help, Luke. Things just kind of got out of hand."

"Hey, I was kidding. It was as much my fault as anyone's." He gave her hand a quick squeeze. "And all that talk around here? Don't believe everything you hear."

"So you haven't slept with anyone from the hospital?"

Why on earth had she asked that? It was none of her business who he did or didn't sleep with.

He hesitated, his smile fading. "Would you like me to give you names and dates?"

"No. I really wouldn't." She sucked in a quick breath, a shard of hurt burrowing deep. "Well, thanks for letting me know about dinner at Nick's. I'll let you get back to work."

"I'll walk you out."

"Oh, no need." All she wanted to do at the moment was get as far away from him as she could.

"At the risk of sounding like a broken record, you never did get that personal item out of my glove compartment."

Oh, heavens. With the chaos at the accident scene and having to drive his car back to the hotel afterward, she'd completely forgotten. Which meant her opportunity for a painless transition of bag to purse was long gone. Unlike her, he'd evidently remembered what was in there and had checked to see if she'd taken it with her. Time to put this little piece of history to bed.

She almost groaned aloud at that thought. "Let's get this over with."

He slanted her a glance that she couldn't read then

headed for the exit down the hallway. Kate followed him, the physical therapist within her taking over and looking for signs that his leg bothered him.

Right leg. Left leg. *Blip*. Right leg.

Yep, there it was. If you didn't know he had a problem, you'd miss it completely. The tiniest limp when his left leg lifted off the ground, transferring his full weight onto his right. He covered it well, but there was almost a forced look to his gait as if he'd learned to compensate. To make things appear normal when they really weren't.

Not wanting to show weakness.

Before they could make it to the door, a nurse came skidding around the corner and hurried toward them, her shoes squeaking on the polished flooring. "Dr. Blackman! Thank heavens I caught you before you left. Mindy Reynolds is asking to speak with you about her daughter. She's quite insistent."

Luke nodded and glanced at Kate. "She's a *patient*," he emphasized in low tones, as if remembering her question a few seconds ago.

"Oh, I never thought…" She swallowed the words, aware the nurse was still waiting there expectantly.

"I'll be there in just a minute." As the nurse walked away, he sighed. "Sorry, I have to go. I'll have to give you back that item we spoke of another time."

"Don't worry about them. Really." It was on the tip of her tongue to say she had plenty where that had come from, but it didn't seem appropriate.

"I'm not worried, Kate. I just don't believe in keeping things that don't belong to me."

As he turned and strolled in the direction the nurse had gone, his gait careful and even, she couldn't help

but think he was giving her a subtle warning with that
last line. He didn't keep things that didn't belong to
him…including her.

# CHAPTER ELEVEN

KATE TIGHTENED HER ponytail holder, slinging the towel around her neck as she switched off the treadmill in the hotel's exercise area, doing some quick calculations to convert kilometers into miles. The guy on the machine next to hers continued to jabber about his work problems—and his all-too-personal problems—seemingly oblivious that she was anxious to leave, despite only getting in two of her normal three miles.

Nothing was more charming than a man using his broken marriage to garner sympathy from other women—and hopefully getting laid in the process.

Kate wasn't buying a word of it. And she was more than anxious to make her getaway. "Well, have a good run."

To her irritation, he switched his machine off, as well. "I was just finishing." He shoved his surfer-blond hair out of his eyes with a muscular forearm. "Would you like to get a drink a little later in the bar?"

"I don't think your wife would exactly approve of that." She injected just enough irritation into her tone to show she wasn't interested in drinks, or anything else.

He swabbed down his face with the hotel towel. "Don't be like that. It's just a drink."

"I don't think so. I already have other plans." Like hell she did, but he didn't need to know that.

Kate headed for the door, the man hot on her heels—still trying to sweet-talk her. If this guy didn't buzz off pretty soon, those neglected body parts he'd mentioned were going to get some intimate attention—from the sharp edge of her knee.

He might be strong and reasonably attractive, but he made her feel nothing but revulsion. In a way it was a good sign. She really wouldn't leap into bed with any pretty face.

Just as she rounded the corner to the lobby she spied a familiar form speaking to the receptionist at the front desk.

Luke!

She had no idea what he was doing there, but she had never been so glad to see anyone in her life. He'd just slid a manila envelope across the counter top and turned to leave when his eyes found hers. She gave a wide, delighted smile. "Hey, there, stranger!"

The guy behind her stopped as well, settling in next to her.

Luke's brows lifted at her enthusiastic greeting then took in her workout gear, sliding up to her face before shifting to the jerk next to her. "Hi, yourself." He inclined his head toward the desk. "I was just dropping off your…belongings."

A peeved voice next to her said, "So your plans include this guy?"

She didn't turn her head to look but gave Luke a pleading glance. "As a matter of fact, they do. So, if you'll excuse me…"

Thankfully, Luke took the hint and made his way over to her. He gripped the ends of the towel around her neck and used them to draw her close, dropping a soft, lingering kiss on her lips that left her reeling. "Is this a workout buddy?" he murmured, keeping hold of the towel and giving the guy a level look.

Whatever silent communication passed between the two men seemed to work, because the weirdo edged a few steps to the side, putting some distance between them.

"Actually, I was just leaving." He nodded toward Kate. "Maybe I'll catch you in the exercise room tomorrow."

"I don't think so. I normally run at night." Which meant that if he tried to join her at night, she'd be free to run in the mornings again. Feeling strangely brave now that Luke was beside her, she glanced at the guy's zipper area. "Good luck with that little problem of yours."

The man's face flushed bright red and anger sizzled in his eyes before he glanced at Luke again. "Right. See you."

As soon as he'd stepped into the elevator, Kate sagged. "Sorry to put you in the middle of that. He wouldn't take no for an answer."

"Can't say I blame him." He let go of the towel. "Why didn't you just leave?"

"I did. I quit at two miles instead of three."

"You run three miles a day?"

Something in his voice made her look up at him. "Not every day, but most. Why?"

"No reason." He glanced in the direction of the elevators. "Do you normally wind up with a crew of men following you?"

Wondering if he thought she was being careless about safety, she said, "I used to run with my dad, until his Parkinson's diagnosis." She shrugged. "I haven't found another running partner yet but I don't purposely try to pick up guys. And since I was using the hotel's exercise room, I figured it was safe."

His fingers went to his leg, in an unconscious gesture that Kate found heart-wrenching.

She nodded at it. "How's it doing?"

"Fine." He drew in a determined breath. "Well, like I said, I left an envelope for you at the desk. The one from the glove compartment. Figured we needed to settle that account once and for all."

*I don't believe in keeping things that don't belong to me.*

And if someone *wanted* to belong to him?

What? She didn't! Not at all.

"Oh, okay. Well, thank you."

"I went ahead and washed them." His eyes held hers for several seconds as her face slowly ignited at the thought of her panties in with the rest of his clothes— mingling and touching parts of him. The slightest smile tipped the corners of his mouth as if he knew exactly what she was thinking. "I'll see you Tuesday evening, then."

At Nick's.

"I guess you will."

He hesitated, glancing at the elevators as if expecting the other guy to rematerialize at any second. "Would you like a ride? The hotel is right on my way."

Why did that offer make her heart sit up and blink? "That would be great, if you're sure."

"I am." He touched her cheek and then took a couple of steps back. "Be careful, Kate."

Be careful of the creepy workout buddy, not of him, right?

Then why did she feel like the warning was directed

at something much more personal than hotel exercise rooms?

And why did she feel the urge to take that warning and toss it to the wind?

# CHAPTER TWELVE

THE FRONT DOOR opened and Nick stood there in a pair of black track pants and a matching T-shirt. "Sorry for the casual attire, but comfortable clothing is easier on my back right now."

Luke shook hands with him and stepped aside to reveal Kate, who was standing behind him. "Kate's hotel is on the way here, so I picked her up."

"Thoughtful of you." Nick's eyes narrowed just a touch as he looked from one to the other. "Hello, Kate."

"Hi." She came around and kissed his cheek. "Thank you again for inviting me over."

A voice came from inside the house. "Don't leave them out on the porch, love. Invite them in."

He smiled and lifted his brows. "I'm just doing that now." He stood aside and gestured them inside. "Tiggy's just putting the finishing touches to the salad."

"I'll go see if I can help her."

Kate called out to the other woman, and Tiggy answered, leaving Luke alone in the entryway with Nick. The man's eyes were shrewder than he remembered.

"So how's it going with Kate?"

"Going?"

"With making me look good."

Luke's muscles relaxed. "I think she's basically there.

Not much more I can do, she just needs to get to know you over a period of time. How's Tiggy handling everything?"

"Surprisingly well." The other man led the way into a small, darkly paneled sitting area. "Would you like something to drink?"

"Whiskey, if you have it."

Nick took down two cut-glass tumblers from inside a cabinet and poured them each a drink. "Have a seat."

Why did he get the feeling he was about to be interrogated? Not that he blamed his friend, but he could ask Luke about Kate until he was blue in the face. He'd promised her he wouldn't say anything, and she'd promised to return the favor. He wouldn't be the one to crack under the pressure.

Besides, seeing her in that workout gear yesterday had driven home the differences between them. She was young and strong, able to do whatever she wanted physically. And when she'd talked about finding a running buddy, he'd realized he'd never be able to be that. For anyone.

Nick handed him the glass then sat in a chair across from his. "How did your dinner date go?"

How the hell did he know about that? He glanced at the door wondering if maybe Kate had—

"Relax. I'm not accusing you of doing anything. You'd mentioned taking her out to talk about my diagnosis. How is she dealing with finding out about me?" He took a sip of his drink. "I can see what's on the surface, but not what's going on underneath."

"I don't think she knows what to think. She doesn't have anything against you personally, it's just been a shock, from what I can gather." Luke took a healthy swallow of his drink. He'd have to be careful as he was driving Kate home tonight. And that was all he'd be doing.

His lecture to himself did as much good this time as it had last time. While his head knew he wasn't the right person for her, his body was in strong disagreement. It was telling him they were compatible in every way that mattered.

*Well, buddy, as hard as it is for you to comprehend, that's not all there is to life.*

"It's been a shock for all of us," Nick said.

"I can imagine. She did ask if she could see the physical therapy area at the hospital. So I took her over there."

"Was she looking for me? I was there on Saturday, but I think they've done about all they can for me." Nick sat with his back well away from the chair cushion, he noticed.

"How did things go?"

"It's been a damned hard road. But I'm determined to get back to where I was—for the baby's sake."

If only hard work was all it took to get there. Luke had worked his ass off and he was still nowhere near where he had once been. And he never would be. He'd never be able to chase a soccer ball across a field with his son. Never be able to swing his daughter round and round and listen to her squeal with happiness.

He shook away the thoughts. He'd accepted all of that years ago, so why was he suddenly torturing himself again?

He could still do his job, and that was all that mattered. He should be happy. Fulfilled. And he knew there were others who were a whole lot worse off than he was. So it was time to stop moping over stupid inconsequential things.

Such as not being able to run like other men.

As if some switch in his brain had been tripped into the "on" position, a vision of the muscle-bound hulk next to Kate came to life in his head, reviving yearnings he'd thought long dead. Stupid, unattainable desires of physical capability.

"Luke, are you all right?"

"What? I'm sorry, did you say something?" It was then that he realized it wasn't just Nick staring at him. Tiggy and Kate were now in the room as well—Tiggy propped on the arm of Nick's chair and Kate on the brown leather sofa across from them. All eyes were fastened firmly on him. Kate had a worried frown on her face as she stared at his groin area.

No, not his groin. Lower.

It was then he felt the pain of his fingers digging into the muscles of his right leg. Torturing it for failing him at every turn.

He released his hold, laying his palm flat on the fabric of his jeans. "Yeah, I'm fine. Sorry, had my mind on a case."

Kate's brows lifted a centimeter in question. She knew he was lying.

*Don't ask it. Not in front of them.*

Nick saved the day by turning to her instead. "I hear you were checking out the rehabilitation facilities over at the hospital."

"Yes, I wanted to see what they offered." She proceeded to talk about her LSVT training, answering questions as Tiggy or Nick voiced them, her face alive and animated, hands gesturing as she described different techniques. She loved her job as much as Luke loved his.

When the conversation inevitably rolled around to

her adoptive father back in Memphis, Kate grew hesitant, obviously not wanting to offend Nick or Tiggy. "He's been great about everything."

"How long are you planning on staying in London?" Nick draped his arm around Tiggy's waist. "We'd love to have you around for a while."

"I don't know." Again there was that strange hesitation. "Like I said, my dad has Parkinson's. I want to be available to help him however I can."

It had to be incredibly awkward for her to use the words *dad* and *father* when referring to the man who'd raised her. But then again, what else would she call him?

"Will you go back to your old job?"

"Possibly. They're holding it open for me, just in case. But they know my plans are kind of fluid right now."

So she wasn't just taking vacation time. He again wondered whether Kate was thinking about making a change, despite her father's Parkinson's diagnosis. If so, it would be a pretty drastic one.

Hadn't he done the same thing when he'd moved from Chicago to London? The difference was that Luke had nothing to hold him in the States. His mom and dad were divorced, and aside from the money he sent to his mother on a regular basis, she'd never shown any interest in having him come for a visit. And his dad… It would be better if Luke never saw him again.

Tiggy stood. "Well, I think everything is ready."

She hovered over her husband for a moment, as if making sure he was okay, before he shooed her away. "I'm fine."

They sat down at the dining room table and passed around roast beef and potatoes. Luke stretched his injured leg under the table, bumping Kate's foot by accident.

Her gaze jerked up, eyes widening, but she didn't move or say anything. Neither did he. In fact, he kept his foot right where it was—touching hers—in a game of chicken.

Who would move away first?

Everyone continued talking as if nothing was amiss, but that small area of contact burned through Luke, slowly traveling up his leg until it reached dangerous heights.

Kate blinked and stabbed a piece of meat with her fork, bringing it up to her mouth. On impulse, he slid his foot a little farther forward and hooked it around hers. She stopped chewing for a second or two.

He was playing a dangerous game, and he knew it. He'd basically promised Nick to refrain from any hankypanky, and here he was playing footsie with the man's daughter under his own table. But there was something reckless and dangerous about it, and he couldn't seem to make himself draw back.

Neither did she pull free, which just heightened the temptation to push things a little further, toying with forbidden fruit right under her father's nose.

What the hell was wrong with him? He wasn't a hormonal sixteen-year-old boy anymore, but here he was, behaving like one.

All he could think of was that while Kate had shunned that muscle-bound clod's advances, she was definitely not using her eyes to plead with Nick to rescue her like she had with him.

And that just sent another wave of heat spiking through him, making him want to up the ante. Just how far would she let him go?

He used the back of her foot to tip off his loafer, which he dragged back to his chair. The tablecloth was long enough that no one could see a thing. He then edged back toward her, using his socked toes to tug at the back of her left high heel. She grabbed her water glass and took a long sip as he casually answered something Nick had asked. When he turned his attention back to Kate, she surprised him by lifting her foot and allowing him to prise off her shoe.

Her look said, *Are you crazy?*

Probably. He had no idea why he was doing this. Was it the risk of discovery, like in the supply closet?

No, that encounter had had nothing to do with the taboo of public sex and everything to do with sheer need. He'd wanted her. And she'd apparently wanted him just as much.

He eased her shoe to the side and slid his foot up and over hers, while Kate carefully set down her water glass and wrapped her hands around her fork and knife. Probably wondering where to stab him first.

But, damn the woman, she wasn't scrabbling around for her shoe or trying to shove her foot back into it. Or trying to brush him off like she had The Persistent Hulk.

Luke wanted to see how far he could push her. Well, he might end up being the first to back down from this little encounter. Hmm. Time to send her running for the hills.

He gave her a slow smile. "So how does one decide to spend a lifetime trying various massage techniques on helpless patients?"

He was gratified to see color wash up her neck and settle in her cheeks. Not so gratified to see the scowl cross Nick's face.

A little too obvious?

Maybe. But he was feeling just a little bit desperate.

His toes edged up past the hem of her beige slacks, remembering exactly how the back pockets had hugged her delectable bottom. Her tongue moistened her lips as he ventured a bit higher.

"I wouldn't exactly call them helpless." She let go of her silverware and crossed her forearms on the edge of the table, leaning forward a bit. "Some of them are strong enough to heft, say, a hundred and twenty pounds, without batting an eyelid."

"Interesting number, that." He eyed her, his smile growing. She was skating on ice that was just as thin as his was.

Nick and Tiggy seemed oblivious to the suggestive comments winging back and forth across the table, but he was eventually going to have to call a halt to this particular game before things went too far.

"How about dessert?" Tiggy said, standing to clear plates.

When Kate started to join her, the other woman waved her away. "Stay there and enjoy yourself. I'll just be a minute."

"Thank you." Her leg suddenly pulled out of reach, and just as Luke thought he might emerge the victor, a weight settled on his good knee. Hell, she'd just propped her heel on him.

His smile widened. All the better.

Luke asked Nick about his work, making sure the question required a long-drawn-out answer, and then slipped his hand beneath the tablecloth, capturing Kate's foot before she had a chance to realize what he was doing and make her escape.

He heard her quick intake of breath as his fingers cupped her instep, his thumb massaging the curve of her arch. She squirmed and tried to pull away, but he held her fast. He couldn't tell if the sensation was just ticklish or if it was as heady to her as it was to him. Touching her skin to skin was suddenly bringing back a whole lot of memories. And bringing a lot of things to life that should be left napping.

Along with that came a terrible realization. He needed to have her again.

Kate's eyes were on Nick as he spoke, but her teeth came down on her lip as if trying to contain the sounds that might be bubbling up in her throat. And he wanted to hear them again. Each and every one.

Tiggy came back with a tray of coffee and pastries and served them each a generous portion.

If Kate thought she was finally going to be able to pull free, she was very much mistaken. He could cut and eat his dessert with just one hand without any problem. Because his other hand was occupied at the moment.

"So, do you have any plans over the next couple of days?" Tiggy asked Kate.

Luke spoke up. "I was planning on showing Kate some sights later on."

"How nice." Nick smiled, probably thinking Luke was looking for another opportunity to extol his virtues. "Big Ben is lovely at night."

"Yes, there is that. There are a few other things I'd like her to see, as well."

Kate shifted a bit, as if catching his drift. "I'm looking forward to it."

Little did Nick and Tiggy know they'd helped aid and abet the very thing Nick was worried about. Luke had just propositioned Kate right under their noses, and she'd accepted without batting an eyelid.

# CHAPTER THIRTEEN

THE SECOND THEY were back in Luke's car in the parking garage, his lips were on hers. As if the dam holding back all her pent-up desires had suddenly burst under the pressure, she moaned loudly, glad to finally let the sound out. Both hands went to the back of his neck, holding him close. The tiny hairs at his nape tickled, bringing home the reality that he really was here—kissing her like he couldn't get enough. She wanted to be closer. Wanted him right now.

"What the hell were you playing at back there?" The low words muttered against her mouth made her see stars.

She bit his lip then sucked it into her mouth, her breath coming in shallow gusts. "I didn't start that particular game. But I was certainly willing to finish it."

He swore softly. "So you're saying if I'd thrown you on top of that dining room table in front of Nick and Tiggy…"

"I'm saying I wouldn't have stopped you."

He moved in for another breath-stealing kiss. "Hell, woman, you're impossible. No wonder that guy back at the hotel didn't want to give up."

"He didn't have a chance."

His fingers tunneled in her hair. "And I do?"

"What do you think?"

"I think if this garage didn't have a whole slew of cameras…"

He'd actually thought of taking her right here? Oh, man. Damn those cameras, anyway!

"There's always my hotel room." She'd think about the repercussions later.

"No. I think I want you in *my* bed this time. Where I can do as I please."

Kate shivered in reaction. How on earth did he make everything sound like a sensual promise?

Because he himself was temptation incarnate.

"This time you're doing all the work, then." Not that she wanted him to. She just couldn't think of a single witty thing to say that was as bold as he was.

"Oh, Kate, I wouldn't have it any other way. You won't have to lift a finger. I promise."

She couldn't lift a finger.

Literally.

Luke had gone from holding her wrists over her head on the bed as he kissed her to pressing a finger to her lips and walking to his closet, coming back with a brown leather belt wrapped around his hand.

Uh, if he was into whipping or something, she was out of there.

"Wha—?"

"Shh. I'm not going to hurt you. It's my turn to do all the work, remember?"

He placed her hands on either side of a metal rung on the bed's headboard and then wrapped the flexible leather around her hands and the post, sliding the loop through the buckle, tightening it enough to hold her there, but not enough to cut off her circulation. He then repeated the act a couple of times until she had several layers around her wrists in a way that wouldn't come undone on their own. Her hands were now trapped.

She'd never been tied up before, and wasn't sure she'd like it, but his lips were on her cheek as he spoke softly to her. That, along with the feeling of helplessness, added another layer of sensuality. Luke had already proved he wouldn't hurt her. She was pretty sure if she started panicking, he'd release her immediately.

She didn't want to be released. Not yet. Maybe not ever.

Luke got off the bed and the lights clicked off, throwing the room into complete darkness. Kate frowned. She wanted to see him this time. "Luke, can't we—?"

"No. My turn to do all the work, remember? That means I make the decisions."

Great. She'd made that stupid comment and now she was going to have to suffer the consequences. Although *suffering* wasn't exactly the word she would use.

Warm lips touched her cheek again and slid over to her ear in a soft caress. "Unless you'd rather I blindfold you instead."

"I wouldn't be able to see you, either way." she groused.

"No, Kate, you wouldn't." His breath was warm, and she shivered again. "But I'd be able to see you."

She'd be lying there naked and exposed for his viewing pleasure while she was kept in utter darkness.

"Not fair." She forced a laugh, but it came out strangled.

"I never said I was going to play fair." The bed gave as he sat next to her. "So which will it be? Lights or blindfold?"

"Lights."

"Now, that's just a damn shame." He stroked her jaw, letting his hand trail down the line of her throat. When he reached the top button of her blouse, he flicked it open with nimble fingers. He moved on to the next one. "I like this shirt. I can unbutton it and spread it open…like this."

The front edges of her shirt were peeled apart and laid on the bed.

His hands glided across her abdomen, just his fingertips touching her. Goose bumps broke out over her flesh as he made his way up to her bra. He tapped the plastic fastener in the hollow of her breasts.

"I like this, as well."

He unclipped it and drew the edges sideways, forcing the fabric to slide slowly over her nipples as it went. They reacted instantly, and she pushed them upward almost against her will, the contact over far too quickly.

And Luke didn't seem in a hurry to replace the bra with his hands—or, better yet, his mouth.

Still sitting, he touched her imprisoned wrists, easing his fingers down the sensitive skin on the insides of her forearms, gliding past her elbows until he reached her shoulders.

He turned his hands over, his knuckles skimming the sides of her breasts, barely avoiding the nipple area, which was screaming for his touch. He repeated the gesture.

He wasn't into whipping. He was into torture instead.

On the third pass, with no relief in sight, she groaned. "Luke, please."

Sliding his hands under the back of her rib cage, his thumbs continued to stroke the sides of her breasts. Circling without touching the end zone. "What do you want, Kate?"

She swallowed. Was he going to make her say it?

"Tell me." His thumbs swept up the sides again, almost, almost grazing the right spot.

"I want you to touch me." The whispered words came out of their own accord.

His fingers paused in midstroke, just beyond reach. "Where?"

God, she wanted her hands free so she could show him instead.

She sucked down a couple of deep breaths, her body seething with need as she tried to screw up the courage. "M-my nipples."

"Your nipples. Mmm. Like this?" His thumbs gave a single sweet stroke across the sensitive buds and pure sensation streaked from her breasts straight down to her groin. A raw, tremulous sound erupted from her throat, and she strained against the leather belt holding her in place.

He didn't make her beg again but centered his attention right where she'd asked, murmuring his approval when she arched into his hands to increase the contact. He squeezed, his thumb and forefinger creating the most delicious mixture of pressure and friction imaginable, then leaned down and kissed her. Kate found herself trying to devour his mouth, her tongue seeking and finding his, rubbing against it like a needy cat. All the while he kept the main part of his attention centered on her breasts.

She wanted him inside her now. Needed him so badly. Dragging her mouth away, she squirmed and shifted, all the while trying to find the words inside her that would get her what she craved. "Luke, now. Please."

He immediately slowed, drawing his fingertips down

her stomach in long, soothing trails. "Not yet. Not for a while."

*What?* Surely he wasn't going to leave her hanging? Or, worse, leave her alone completely. They could go slow later. Or he could go as slow as he wanted to, she just needed…needed…

Release.

She squeezed her thighs together, her hips unconsciously rising and falling, seeking the kind of pressure she needed to get over the top of that mountain.

A knee wedged between hers. Thinking he was going to give her what she wanted, she quickly parted them wide for him. He moved onto the bed, kneeling between her legs before going down on his haunches, making no move to remove his clothing. Or to lie on top of her. All he did was continue to stroke her sensitized skin, avoiding all the important areas.

"Luke, what are you doing?"

She saw the glint of his teeth in the darkness. "I said not yet."

Too late, she realized he'd tricked her into separating her thighs, preventing her from using them to bring herself to completion. "No!"

"Yes." He leaned over and nipped her jaw. "You'll thank me later. I promise."

No, she wouldn't. Only someone with a sadistic sense of humor would say something like that.

Then his lips went to her nipple and pulled hard. The sudden wet heat chased away all thoughts of revenge, replacing them with a clawing need that took right up where it had left off. He leaned up and grabbed the fabric of his polo shirt, yanking it over his head.

Finally!

Kate found her eyes had grown accustomed to the

gloom, and she could barely make out the shadow of his tattoo and the diagonal trail of the old knife wound on his chest. But she still couldn't see clearly enough to satisfy her.

Her hands flexed on the bedpost, wanting to run her fingers down his chest and unsnap the button to his khakis. But she couldn't. He'd seen to that.

He did slide backward, however, and undo hers. Unlike the last time, he didn't leave her panties on. Instead, he peeled both garments down her legs, until they were gone.

Then his mouth was on her inner knee, licking his way slowly up. She swallowed, the urge to snap her legs together thwarted by the fact that he was still between them. Why did she get the feeling that had been his plan all along?

Oh, he was devious. Merciless. And she might just thank him later after all.

If only he'd hurry it up!

He bit her inner thigh, unexpectedly, causing her to jump and moving her thoughts firmly back to him.

His hands went to her hips, fingers curling around them, holding her in place as he made his way higher, inch by inch. He might be trying to keep her from squirming, but that was impossible at this point. Her body was following each and every movement his lips made and trying to anticipate where they might head next…to maximize the contact.

His palms went under her butt and lifted, as if serving her up for his pleasure. And his first bite made her cry out.

"I love hearing you whimper when I touch you." He took a slow swipe with his tongue, eliciting a pained moan this time, while he watched her. "It makes me so fucking hard."

Her, too. Her parts might be different but, God, he hit her right where it counted.

He continued to stare over the planes and hills of her body, his eyes boring into hers. He slid his hands out from beneath her, her butt dropping back to the surface of the bed, while he stayed exactly where he was.

*What? That was it?*

He gave her a slow smile. "Do you want me, Kate?"

"You know I do." Her heart was thundering in her chest, begging him to finish her off. All it would take was a few more seconds.

"Show me."

How? Her hands were tied. She couldn't touch him. Could barely move anything except her pelvis.

He nodded. "Do it. Show me what you want."

As if her body were on a different astral plane from that of her conscious self, she planted the soles of her feet flat on the bed, bent her knees and slowly pushed herself up to his waiting mouth. Held herself there as he tasted her, nibbled…the whisper of hot air touching her sensitive flesh. All the while his eyes remained just above the horizon, focused on her, watching each and every reaction. That's why he wanted her pelvis up. So he could see her slowly unravel. He was a terrible, sexy voyeur who had absolutely no shame. Absolutely no…

His lips zeroed in on the tiny erect nub of flesh and surrounded it, tongue gliding across it in a long exquisite stroke that seemed to go on forever while she pressed harder and harder against him, her insides winding impossibly tight. From a distance she heard herself panting his name, her voice sliding up an imaginary scale of notes, until her eyelids screwed down tight. And she screamed. Long and loud, the release of doing so incredible. All the while his mouth held her prisoner, his hands returning to support her butt when she would have collapsed. He kept her there for several seconds until every muscle in her body released at once, going totally boneless.

Still he kissed her, until he'd coaxed every last twitch from her body.

"God," she whispered. "Oh, God." She thought she might have kept saying those words over and over, but she wasn't sure. Then he was there, finally on top of her, finally sliding into her body, filling her.

Kissing her lips. Smoothing her hair away from her damp brow.

She'd never be the same again. Ever. She still couldn't bring herself to move, even when he withdrew and pushed forward again. Then words came from shaking lips. "Thank you."

She'd said it. And she didn't care.

He reached up and undid the belt, freeing her hands, still deep inside her. As she shut her eyes and pulled in a deep sigh, he cupped her face and kissed her again. "That was just the beginning."

For him, maybe. She was shot. But she was perfectly willing to entertain him after the orgasm he'd just given her.

As if he was a mind reader, he muttered, "Do you think you're done, Kate? Do you think your body is done?" He edged deeper and touched a spot inside that flickered back to life, despite herself. "It's not. It just doesn't know it yet."

## CHAPTER FOURTEEN

LUKE WAS DRESSED before she woke up. Just like he always was when he spent the night with someone.

It wasn't vanity. At least, he didn't think it was.

The fact that he didn't have a single full-length mirror in his house didn't mean a thing. He'd be the first to admit he couldn't stomach the sight of that atrophying, twisted lump of flesh he called a leg. The actual scars didn't faze him—he saw much worse on a daily basis at the hospital. It was what those scars represented that kept him from switching the lights on and making love like a normal person.

The sizzling scent of bacon brought his attention back to the skillet, and he adjusted the flame, turning the strips so they'd cook on the other side. The least he could do was feed her.

A slight smile tilted his lips as he remembered Kate's slim body writhing beneath his hands—pushing up toward his mouth. Yes, it was heady knowing he had the power to make her reach for her pleasure—to exercise a small amount of control over her. There was no denying it. But there was also method to his madness. He'd found the faster he got a woman to that plateau high above the easy petting and foreplay that went on in most relationships, the less likely she was to glance back toward earth and see him. The real him.

Then he could relax and enjoy her—enjoy the sex—without the elaborate maneuverings necessary to keep her attention off him. Once she was in the clouds, all he had to do was use his voice. Direct her. Keep her focused on her own body.

And the shorter the relationship was afterward, the less likely a woman was to want to cuddle on the couch. To start probing a little too deeply. Or insist the lights stay on.

Like Kate had tried to do.

He glanced down at his pants leg. No one would ever guess what was just below that fabric…and what lay deep beneath the skin, muscle and bone. Luke had become that leg. Obsessed with what its weakness had cost him.

Damn it!

Why was he slogging through all this again?

Because he knew his time with Kate needed to come to an end. Soon. Not just because of Nick—although not keeping his word on that front was eating at him—but also because that's the way it had to be. The way it had always been.

"Hey, why didn't you wake me up?"

Kate stood in the doorway, draped in one of his white dress shirts. She didn't have it buttoned up the front, just wrapped around her waist like a bathrobe. Her folded arms held it in place. Little did she know that doing so pulled the fabric taut against her breasts, the rosy outlines of her nipples clearly visible. Or maybe she did know.

Glancing at her face, he saw nothing but a puzzled question. She didn't understand why he hadn't woken her up, it was as simple as that. Nothing coy or cunning about her.

Unlike him, who'd manipulated her exactly where he'd wanted her.

He swallowed. Yep, he was as ugly inside as that damned leg. Maybe uglier.

"I thought you might like to sleep."

"Do you have to work?"

"Yes, in about an hour."

She pulled the shirt tighter. "Were you going to wake me at all?"

Of course he was. But not until the last minute, when she'd be forced to eat quickly so he could drive her back to the hotel.

Picking up a plate, he laid the bacon onto the paper towels covering it, choosing his words carefully. "I was going to let you sleep as long as possible, but, yes, I was going to wake you up."

She took a couple of steps closer, and he held the plate out, offering her some of the meat. She shook her head. "I need to go shower and get dressed."

"Your clothes are folded in the bathroom."

"Let me guess. You washed them."

There was an acid tinge to her voice that made him look at her a little closer. Should he not have washed them?

"Is something wrong?"

She shut her eyes and pulled in a deep breath. "No. Sorry. I just didn't mean to wind up here."

"At my house?"

"Among other things."

He set the plate down and moved toward her. "You seemed to enjoy it well enough."

She laughed. "Oh, I did. That's not the problem."

Strange. He was the one who normally went down this particular road. According to his mental GPS, it was called Regret Avenue, and he seemed to wind up there a lot.

"Hey, it's okay." He combed his fingers through her soft hair and let it fan out around her shoulders. "We're both consenting adults. We had a little fun. No one was injured. At least, I don't think anyone was." His thumb skimmed over her jaw. "I didn't hurt you, did I?"

"No, of course not. It's just that my mom…" She shook her head. "Never mind. You're right. It was fun. And now it's…"

She didn't finish the thought, but he could fill in the blank. *And now it's over.*

So why was he chafing at the thought? Because she was fun and honest and sexy, a combination he found lethal.

"Why don't you go get your shower and I'll make some toast and eggs to go along with this? How do you like yours?"

"I like them unbroken."

"Excuse me?" There was a wistfulness in her voice that made him squirm inside.

"Sorry. The eggs. I like them hard boiled."

Why did he think she was talking about something other than the eggs?

She was only in London for a little while, as was he. And even if they *had* been from the same geographical location in the States, it wasn't likely they could take things to the next level, even if he wanted to. Which he didn't. This was a vacation fling on her part, and a very pleasant encounter on his.

Nick came back to mind. His friend had slept with a tourist and had ended up fathering a child. Was she thinking that both her biological father and the man whose life he'd saved were both shallow bastards, happy with a quick roll in the hay?

He could see how it might look. But surely she knew Nick was not like that, even if *he* was.

He might not be able to reassure her about his own intentions, but he could at least defend Nick. "Your dad—Nick—is a good man. If he'd known your mom was pregnant, he'd have done his best to make it right."

"I know." She lifted one shoulder. "I'll go get that shower, if it's okay."

"Of course. The eggs should be done in around twenty minutes."

As she walked away, he wondered if he hadn't done such a good job at hiding after all. Because despite all the hard work he'd gone to last night, she seemed to know exactly who—and what—he was.

Kate was on her third day of observations. Laisse had gotten permission not only for her to explore their treatment methods but had handed her a form that would let her apply for an internship. It seemed her training in the States would be valid in the UK, with a bit of tweaking and the addition of a course or two. Nick had finished his therapy so she wouldn't get to help with it as she'd hoped, but they were getting to know each other a little better so she didn't need an excuse to see him.

As she watched the therapist direct a patient on the leg-press machine, she thought about where she and Nick would go from here.

Tiggy, after the initial awkwardness, had been wonderfully accepting of her. She and Nick were obviously deeply in love. She could see it in the way the other woman touched him repeatedly, and the way Nick's ruggedly handsome face softened whenever he looked at his wife. Although he received quite a few sideways looks from other women, he never gave them a second glance. He only had eyes for his wife.

What would it be like to have someone love you so completely that anyone else became invisible? Kate had had boyfriends and lovers, but none of them had scratched below the surface of her heart.

Her mind went to Luke, and she gave an internal headshake. Not in a million years would she go that route.

That man knew women. Intimately. It showed in the way he touched her, the way he could keep her on the cusp of an orgasm without actually letting her tumble over the edge. That only came with experience. Lots of it.

Was that why he seemed to get such pleasure out of watching her reactions? Was he sorting and categorizing her every whimper to have fresh material for whatever new woman crossed his path?

He oozed confidence—was the epitome of self-control. They both knew there would be another woman after her…and others after that.

Like her mother and her letters.

She swallowed. Her dad had loved her mom so very completely, would continue to love her memory no matter what he found out about her.

And as much as she loved him, she did not want to wind up like that. In love with someone who would leave her mourning his loss—even if that loss was emotional rather than physical. The loss that came when he inevitably moved on to the next girl in line.

Did Luke have some kind of secret addiction? She'd heard of there being such a thing, but wasn't sure if it was genuine or simply an excuse for bad behavior. Did Luke have a twisted need to go through woman after woman? Or was he just a shallow playboy?

She'd never gotten that impression from him. Not really. But then again, would her dad have married her mom knowing what was in her past? Knowing the fields of shattered hearts she'd left in her wake?

He might have. But *she* wouldn't. She couldn't.

Someone calling her name made her blink and look up with a start.

Tiggy frowned down at her. Judging from her nurse's uniform, she was working today. "So sorry. I didn't mean to frighten you."

"You didn't. I was just daydreaming."

The other woman smiled. "It's quite all right. I was on a break and decided to come by and see if you were here. Too bad Nick isn't still in therapy."

"Don't be. I'm glad he's fully recovered. He was very lucky, from what I understand. If he'd waited much longer to have the surgery…" She let her sentence trail away.

"Yes, he was lucky." Tiggy dropped into the chair next to hers. "And I'm a lucky woman to have him."

There it was again. The evidence of their love. Kate was happy for them but more certain than ever that what Tiggy and Nick had was rare.

"Did you and Luke know each other in the States?"

It was as if the other woman knew he'd been on her mind. "No. I met him here in London."

"He called me, you know, after Nick was admitted. He's part of the reason we're back together."

"I didn't know that." Kate touched her hand. "I know it's been awkward having me around…knowing I'm

Nick's daughter. I'm really sorry for showing up unannounced."

"We would have had to work through things eventually. You just hurried it along a bit." The corners of her eyes crinkled as she smiled and rubbed her abdomen. "I'm glad you're here. I want the baby to know his or her big sister."

Kate sucked in a quick breath, a wave of emotion rolling through her. The backs of her eyes prickled, and she blinked to keep the sensation from morphing into actual moisture. "Thank you so much. I expected you to want..." She tried to figure out what to say and finally settled for, "Thank you for including me. I'm so very grateful."

"You're a part of our lives now. Mine and Nick's."

Tiggy rose to her feet with another smile. "I should head back to work. But I'll see you later."

As Kate watched her walk away, a pang of envy went through her. She shook it off with a new sense of determination.

Someday. *Someday.* That was the kind of relationship she hoped to find with a man. Until then she wouldn't settle for less. She gave a rueful grin. Even if the sex was out of this world.

# CHAPTER FIFTEEN

"Is it broken?"

The child who sat cradling her right arm on the steel table in the exam room couldn't be older than four or five.

Luke glanced at the mother, who perched on a chair near the door, hands gripping the bottom of the seat. She looked like she might fly away at any second. She repeated her question. "Macy's arm? Is it broken?"

He tried to keep his mind on the situation at hand, but all he could hear was Kate's quiet request. *I'd like them unbroken.*

In trying to protect himself, he could end up hurting her badly, if he wasn't careful. And as soon as he got off tonight he was going to call her and let her know he wouldn't be bothering her anymore.

Thankful he wasn't dealing with a compound fracture—where the bone pushed through the skin—he laid a hand on the child's head to reassure her. "I'll need to get an X-ray, but I'd say there's a good possibility that this bone right here—" he ran his fingers along the outside of his own forearm "—the ulna, is broken. What happened?"

Her mother spoke up. "She was riding her bike and fell against a brick wall."

Had she answered a bit too quickly? He glanced down at the child and examined the skin around the injury. "That must have hurt." The area wasn't scraped, as he'd expect after contact with a wall, but there was quite a bit of bruising. "Do you hurt anywhere else?"

The child's glance went to her mother, and then she looked at her shoes—dingy white sneakers that dangled three feet off the floor. She shrugged a too-thin shoulder.

Something about this scenario stuck a familiar chord. Dread crowded his chest.

Luke frowned and took a closer look at the mother. Nervous. Shoulders slumped, a permanent curve to the back of her neck, as if she'd been beaten down her whole life. "Did she mention anything to you?"

"I didn't see her fall. She rode home and said her arm hurt."

"She got back on her bicycle after hurting her arm?" That didn't seem likely. The child was four. Where had the mother been?

"I think so. I didn't see it."

He forced a smile and looked back down at the girl. "I used to skin my knees or scrape my palms when I fell off my bike. Do your knees hurt?" The child's palms were as clean as a whistle. No abrasions from trying to stop her fall. The child said nothing, so he looked back at the mom, brows raised in question.

"She fell off her bike." The mother's hand went to her own cheek, in a kind of cupping motion that sent a chill down Luke's spine. His sense of foreboding grew.

The story didn't waver, no hint of asking her daughter for any kind of clarification. She was hiding something. About her daughter's accident…and behind her hand.

The woman's fingers stayed where they were, her

elbow resting on her knee in a casual gesture that was made to look like she was propping herself on it.

What was she hiding? And why the hell hadn't he looked at her more closely when he'd come into the room?

*Because you forgot. Grew complacent. And the urge to hide things never quite went away.*

He tried again, this time keeping an eye on the mother as he directed another question at Macy. "Did someone push you off your bike?" He gave her a reassuring smile that he hoped didn't look as scary as it felt. "Or hurt you in some other way?"

The mother was off her chair in a flash, just like he'd known she would be. And he got a better look at that cheek.

"I already told you, she fell off her bike."

He ignored the words, knowing they were a lie even as his eyes traveled over the woman's face. *Dammit.* Beneath a thick smear of beige makeup he caught a glimpse of purple skin. Her fingers were already back at the spot, moving back and forth as if scratching an itch that just wouldn't fade.

How many of those itches had she scratched over the years?

How many lights had she turned off so no one would see what she'd hidden from the world? Pretending normalcy where there was none?

He brushed away the thought before it took hold.

*This is not about you, Blackman. Get your head back in the game.*

"What happened to your cheek?" He knew better than try to pull her hand away and force her to admit the truth.

"M-my cheek? Nothing." She licked her lips, her

hand going back to cover the spot, no longer trying to make it appear casual. "It's just a rash. I get them sometimes."

*I bet you do.*

"Let me take a look. Maybe I can do something about it."

"No!" She moved away from him a pace or two before the backs of her knees hit the chair, and she went down with a plop. "It's eczema. I already have medicine for it."

How many lies did that make so far?

The last thing he wanted was for her to turn combative, though, and drag her daughter out of the room with a possible bone fracture. "It's okay. We'll just need to send Macy for an X-ray to see what's going on."

"I want to go with her."

"Of course you do." He picked up a phone. "Let me call and have them send someone down for her."

"O-okay." She twisted her hands in her lap. "I want to go with her."

The words were almost a whisper this time, and Luke wondered if it was a mother's silent plea not to be separated from her child.

Maybe so. But he couldn't dredge up much more sympathy for her than he'd had toward his own mother, who'd let her husband pound on her—and him—when he'd tried to step in between them. She'd never once tried to stop him from intervening.

Had little Macy done the same? Stepped in front of her father's fists, only to have him strike out at her instead? If she'd lifted a hand to ward off a blow, this was exactly the type of fracture that might have occurred.

He put in a call to Claire Mathers, the hospital administrator, who picked up right away.

"This is Dr. Blackman. I have a little girl down here around four years old with a possible fractured ulna. I need an X-ray and a consult." He said it with just enough emphasis that Claire would understand what he was saying.

It was one of the things he'd insisted on when he'd come to the hospital, that he have a way of reporting possible child abuse cases without raising alarms. He knew from experience that mothers did sometimes drag their children away from much-needed medical care if they feared they were about to be discovered. Claire had told him to call her, and she'd take it from there, alerting the authorities before the mother had a chance to take off.

"Just keep her there for a few minutes, and I'll send for someone."

"Thanks. Let us know when they're ready for her in X-Ray."

The mother settled back down in her chair, her chest rising in a sigh of relief. "It won't take long, will it?"

"Shouldn't be more than fifteen or twenty minutes." He wasn't leaving the room until Claire arrived. Glancing around the sterile white walls, hoping to find something to take the girl's mind off her pain, he came up empty. He'd have to go back to the old blow-up-the-surgical-glove trick. He drew one from a nearby dispenser, blew it up and handed it to the child, who gave her first tentative smile. He glanced at the mother again. "Is there anyone you'd like me to call? Macy's father, perhaps?"

She shook her head, settling deeper in her chair, her hand no longer covering her injury. "We're divorced."

"How about you? Do you want someone here with you while you wait? If Macy's arm is broken, it could be a while before they can set it. Your mother?" He paused, then said, "How about a boyfriend?"

A spot of color appeared along the woman's left cheekbone—the makeup and bruising hiding anything on the other side. "My boyfriend isn't home right now."

Otherwise she wouldn't be here with Macy. Another puzzle piece dropped into place.

"I see."

On impulse, he squatted beside her and looked into blue eyes that appeared just as washed out and hopeless as the rest of her. His mother had had that same look at times. That trapped, hopeless, beaten-down facade that hid a wealth of pain. He despised whoever had caused that. And yet by her silence she was resigning her child to the same sad existence.

He touched her hand. "Is there anything you'd like to talk about? We can step outside if you'd like."

A sound like the quick squeak of a child who couldn't see past the needle to the lifesaving vaccine came out of her throat. "No. Macy and I are fine. We're going to be just fine."

Hell. Why couldn't she just admit the truth? A small bead of anger coursed down his spine.

"Take a good look at your daughter, and tell me again how fine you are."

She met his eyes, the pain finally out in the open. "He loves us. He does."

How could she even say those words?

His mother had said the same thing. Over and over. He had never been sure if it had been a statement of fact or a prayer.

Luke had wanted no part of that particular cycle. He figured if he had some kind of genetic defect, he was going to turn it on himself and not someone else. He'd engaged in dangerous behaviors that had slowly escalated over the years. Going from merely reckless, to possibly deadly—as he'd found out during that knife fight.

Maybe his leg injury had been part of that quest to save others by harming himself. And just like this mother, he hid his scars from everyone. Even himself.

He stood to his feet, feeling defeated. She wasn't going to come out and admit the person she was with was an asshole, any more than his mother had.

Well, if she wouldn't do this the easy way then he hoped the authorities saw past the lies and took Macy out of that home before something much more valuable than her arm was broken. Maybe it would even shock the girl's mother into getting the help she seemed to desperately need.

"Will they be doing Macy's X-ray pretty soon?"

"I hope so."

*Come on, Claire. She's getting spooked.*

Just then there was a knock on the door and the administrator herself appeared, along with an orderly pushing a wheelchair.

"Hello, Dr. Blackman. Is this your patient?" Claire, her short dark hair dancing around an elfin face, glanced at him for confirmation. She smiled, looking as sweet as pie, but beneath the cheerful facade was a shark, one who wasn't afraid of taking a chunk out of anyone who deserved it.

He nodded. "Yes, this is Macy." He tweaked the child's hair. "Ms. Mathers is going to take you upstairs to get a picture of your arm."

"We'll just get her into the chair and be on our way."

Luke scribbled the word *Boyfriend* on a sheet of paper on the metal chart holder, handing it to Claire.

The other woman nodded that she understood. Then, before the orderly could move, Luke scooped the little girl into his arms and settled her into the wheelchair, making sure he didn't bump her arm in the process. "They'll get you all patched up."

At least physically. Who could say what kind of scars she'd carry on the inside? His palm scrubbed over his leg as he watched the group go out the door, the mother's frightened eyes glancing one last time at his face.

As soon as they were gone, he dropped into the chair the woman had vacated and dragged a hand through his hair. He felt awful about betraying her, but he'd had no choice. Not only was it the law to report suspected cases of child abuse, it was the right thing to do. He'd never have called Claire if he hadn't been very sure of the warning signs. From what he could see, Macy was being abused, and her mother wasn't able—or willing—to put a stop to it.

Instead, she'd hidden it, much like Luke's parents had hidden what had happened in their household.

All it would take was letting one person see the truth, and the spell would be broken forever. Macy's mom could then leap over the roadblock that kept her imprisoned. But she had to be willing. Once she took that first step it would get easier to take the next one…and the next.

He frowned. Wasn't he doing the same thing with his scars? He hid them even from himself. Why? Because if he didn't acknowledge they existed, he could pretend his life was normal.

Like Macy's mother did each and every day?

He'd been perfectly willing to stand there and lecture her, all the while knowing he was no better than she was.

Maybe he should follow his own diagnosis. Maybe it was time to let at least one person—besides his medical providers—in on his secret. But how on earth was he going to do that?

He could leave the lights on the next time he had a date, and just let the chips fall where they may.

Right. And if he did that with someone at work, he'd have to face them again day in and day out. No, he'd rather it be with someone outside the hospital. Someone he wasn't afraid would flinch away in disgust or coo with pity as soon as she got a good look at his reality.

Kate's image came to mind, the way she'd asked him to leave the lights on. And she'd already seen a good portion of his leg during that massage she'd given him.

*Take that first step. Just like you urged Macy's mother to do. You can do it.*

He took a steadying breath and tried to think. Kate had brushed away his arguments and hadn't made a single sound when she'd slid that towel up—not high enough to see the worst of the damage but enough that she had a pretty good idea what was there. And she had to have seen the difference in size between his legs.

And yet she'd slept with him, anyway. Had whimpered his name. Had wanted the lights on.

Even as he told himself it was crazy, he stood, wondering if Kate was still over in the physical therapy wing. They wouldn't have sex. He'd just take her to the nearest safe place and let her see the truth. Not for her sake but for his. He could—and would—expose who he really was once and for all.

# CHAPTER SIXTEEN

KATE PICKED UP her purse and headed for the door, waving at Laisse. The crew at the rehabilitation center had been wonderful. They were doing an excellent job with their patients. And it was interesting to see the different techniques used here.

"You're coming back tomorrow?" Laisse asked.

"If it's okay."

"Of course it is. Maybe we can have lunch together."

Kate nodded, giving the woman a smile. "I'd love that. Thanks again for everything."

"Anytime, love."

She smiled at the ready expression and pushed through the door, turning left to head toward the exit. A hand wrapped around her arm, halting her progress and ripping a squeaked sound of alarm from her throat.

"Hey, what the—?"

Whirling round, her breath caught when she saw Luke standing there. He'd made no attempt to see her for the past three days, and she'd assumed that was how he wanted it.

She took one look at his face and said, "Is everything okay?"

"Yes. Have you got a few minutes?"

"Of course. I was just headed back to the hotel. Do you want to come?"

He hesitated then shook his head. "Better if I don't."

She knew exactly why. It was dangerous. For both of them. At least Luke was honest enough to admit it. "Is your leg bothering you?"

"Yes. No." He scrubbed a hand down the back of his neck. "I'm not even sure why I'm here, other than I just had a rough case. It made me think."

"About?"

"About my past. About my current attitudes."

Kate wasn't sure what he was talking about, but he had a reason for seeking her out. She just needed to give him some space to get there. So she nodded. "How can I help?"

"Actually, I need to show you something."

"All right." She waited, figuring he was going to pull something out of his pocket or something, but he just stood there. She prodded him. "Do you want to show me here?"

He gave a quick laugh and glanced at the window, where Laisse was watching them with curious eyes. "I think that might get me arrested."

"Excuse me?" What on earth could he want to show her that was…? Well, she could think of one thing, but he'd already said he didn't want to go to her hotel room. She assumed that meant he didn't want to have sex with her. Which was fine by her.

His fingers were working his leg again, something he did regularly.

"Does it have to do with that?" She nodded at it.

He immediately shoved his hand into his pocket. "You asked about the lights several nights ago. And I wanted to show you why I didn't want them on."

"You want to show me your leg?"

"Yes."

Never in a million years would she have guessed that's what he wanted. "Can you tell me why?"

He dragged a hand through his hair. "I have no idea, really, except the case I mentioned a few minutes ago involved a child with a broken arm. I could tell her mother was hiding something. I think her boyfriend hit both of them and she's covering for him. All I could think about was that if she would just tell one person the truth, she could break the cycle."

"How awful. I'm sorry."

He waved away her sympathy. "Maybe I'm doing the same thing with my leg." A beat went by. "You're not going to be here much longer, and you've already seen part of it, so I thought… I want to see if I can get past this."

A sliver of hurt went through her. She was safe. Temporary. Of course she was the logical candidate. She was a physical therapist, used to seeing wounds of all shapes and sizes. She'd be leaving soon, and the implication was that he had no intention of trying to prolong their relationship once she got on that plane.

And she realized she'd actually harbored some kind of twisted hope that he *would* want to. That he might not be who she feared he was: a playboy, who hopped from one relationship to another.

She should put her plan of steering clear of him into action.

Except if she did so right now and refused his request, he was bound to take it the wrong way, maybe even think she was too disgusted by the thought to agree.

She already knew what she was going to say. Yes.

Just like she always did when it came to Luke. "Would you rather do it here than at your house? That's a long way to drive."

"I think you'd agree the supply closet doesn't have the best track record."

Neither did her hotel room. Or his apartment, for that matter. In fact, no place seemed to be safe.

As if aware of her thoughts, he said, "This isn't some ploy to get you back in bed." His quick grin looked pained. "I can think of better ways to do that."

Oh, he could, could he? "You seem pretty sure of yourself."

"Am I wrong?"

No, damn him. He wasn't wrong. And she was afraid that just by agreeing to go to his house, she was going to prove that once and for all. "What about your case?"

"I've handed it over to the hospital administrator. If she needs me to give a statement, she'll call me. I've already told her I might be out of the hospital for a while." He studied her for a few seconds, his lips thinning. "Listen, forget it. I'm sure you have other things to do. Like visit Nick."

Before she had a chance to open her mouth, he swung away, striding down the hall with that half swagger, half limp that tugged at her heartstrings. She couldn't bear him to think she was rejecting him, and she couldn't tell him the real reason…that she was terrified of her growing feelings.

She should just let him go. Instead, she hurried to catch up with him before he had a chance to disappear around the corner. She grabbed at his hand. "I want to."

He stopped but didn't look down at her. "You want to what?"

Kate swallowed. "Look at your leg. And anything else you might want me to do."

Luke gritted his teeth, forcing himself to stay put as Kate propped herself on her elbow, fingers trailing up the bare skin of his damaged leg. The curtains were wide open, and light invaded the room from all angles. There was a bed sheet within reach and habit made him want to yank it over himself, but he didn't.

She continued what she was doing, carefully following the ragged dips and grooves that marked where the explosive blasts had caught him, where the surgeons' scalpels had left their own distinctive marks as they'd done their best to make sense of the macerated muscle and sinew left behind.

And where they hadn't been able to find enough skin to cover the damage, they'd harvested pieces from the back of his uninjured hip. Kate had found each and every injury and had touched it. With her hands. With her mouth.

He'd been blown away. Sensations he couldn't even define had rocketed through him, tearing away what he *thought* he knew just as surely as the metal shrapnel had sliced through his leg and hip. What she'd done to him had created an amalgamation of lust and fear. Even now the urge to switch off the lights was almost overpowering.

But it was already too late. He'd let one person see the truth. And see him she had. She'd made love to him beneath the glare of the overhead lights—taking the lead this time. He couldn't remember the last time a woman had done that, although the fault for that lay entirely with him.

He was thoroughly sated—and yet there was a deep

well of need within him that wanted more. Wanted her. If the mind-over-matter school of thought really was true, Kate would be flat on her back again in a matter of seconds.

"Tell me about it." Her quiet voice broke through his thoughts, even as she continued to explore his leg. She was as naked as he was, and he drew a small measure of comfort from that. He could bet she'd remained that way on purpose, just to make him feel better.

And he did. He leaned over and pressed his lips to her bare shoulder, breathing in her scent. Their combined scents.

It was heady, and he didn't want to think about why that reached beneath his skin and touched something deep inside him.

He leaned back. "What do you want to know?"

"Everything." Her eyes met his. "How you were injured. What kinds of therapy you had."

Luke wasn't sure he wanted to relive those terrifying minutes leading up to his injury. In fact, a lot of the aftermath was fuzzy. But his purpose in dragging her back to his house had been to let someone see the truth. To know that he was capable of exposing it once and for all.

So he took a deep breath. "My commanding officer had received reports of insurgents, along with some possible injuries, so my company was sent on a reconnaissance mission. We were to meet up with British troops at the designated location. We weren't supposed to engage, just report our findings."

Her fingers paused and her palm curved over his thigh in an almost possessive gesture that made something twist inside him.

"Where was this?" she asked.

"In Afghanistan, ten years ago." He lay back against the pillows, threading his fingers behind his head. "We didn't know we were walking into a trap. I was hit, and Nick saved my life and my leg. That's about it."

Her brows went up. "You win the prize for the shortest explanation of an injury ever."

He laughed. "Just sticking to the facts, ma'am."

"Hmm." Her palm slid a few centimeters higher. And it seemed his brain actually did wield some power over his body because things shifted. "Did your surgery happen in the field?"

"No. They stabilized me and then shipped me off to Germany to do the biggest chunk of repairs, and then on to Walter Reed for the rest of it."

"You received a medical discharge."

She didn't even need to ask. His leg told her all that and more. "Yes."

"Were you a doctor in the military?"

"No, that came afterward." This subject was a little trickier. "After I heard about what Nick did, how he fought to save my leg, even when other people were telling him it was a lost cause, it made me want to do the same for others. The emergency room is basically a glorified triage unit."

"And you save lives."

"Not always." He remembered that accident victim he and Kate had encountered on their way back from the restaurant. That seemed like a lifetime ago. And he'd had no idea that agreeing to do Nick a favor would end up with Kate lying in his bed, hearing confessions he'd told no one.

"You helped that little girl today."

He'd filled Kate in on Macy and his suspicions about the boyfriend on the way to his house. "Who knows whether I made any difference at all? She might end up back at the emergency room with another injury in a couple of days. A couple of months."

Hell, he hoped not. Because he'd sure be tempted to take matters into his own hands at that point.

Although the guy could probably beat the living daylights out of him. Or send him toppling onto his ass with one good shove. But he'd be willing to give it a try. Surely he could get one or two good punches in before the other guy took him down. Then again, maybe the guy wouldn't bother sticking around. His dad had hightailed it out of the house at the first sign of police involvement. He had only been big and powerful around his wife and child, who'd lived in terror of his temper.

"If the mother knows the hospital is suspicious, maybe she'll make an effort or kick the guy out."

"Or maybe she's just the type of woman who jumps from loser to loser, as if she can't get enough." His breath came out in a rough snort. "I just don't understand not caring enough about your kid to find a good man and stick with him."

Kate's teeth came down on her lip, digging hard. A flicker of what looked like pain flashed through her eyes and was gone. But when her hand tried to withdraw from his thigh, he put his over it, holding it in place. "What is it?"

"Nothing." Even her voice sounded raw, as if he'd touched on something. But what? She'd been raised in a happy, stable home, from all appearances.

"Then why are you suddenly so fidgety?" He had the feeling she was about to run, and he didn't want her to.

"You said you were good at hiding things. You don't know the meaning of the word."

"I don't understand."

"I didn't know who my real father was until my mom died, remember?"

Damn. He hadn't even thought about that when he'd spouted off his little sob story. He rolled onto his side to face her. "I'm sorry, Kate. But at least Nick's a good man. So is your adoptive father, from what you've said. Your mom didn't go after losers."

"Really? I wouldn't know."

She'd totally lost him now. Was she saying Nick wasn't a good man? Or that her mother had indeed gone after losers?

"Was she with someone who hurt her?" The thought of someone lifting his hand and striking Kate made acid pour into his stomach, turning it sour.

"Again, I wouldn't know. There were so many of them."

"There were so many what? Men?" His fingers curled around hers, still afraid she was going to bolt at any second.

"Yes." She nodded, not quite meeting his eyes. "There were evidently lots of them. And I had no idea."

"But if they all happened before you were born, before she met your dad, I don't understand why you're—"

"I'm pretty sure they didn't just happen before she married my dad."

Her hand gripped his tightly, as if she needed some extra support.

"She saw other men while she was married?"

"Yes."

"You said you didn't find Nick's letter until after she died, so how do you know she did?" Could her father have accused her mother of something like that? If so, why?

"Because Nick's letter wasn't the only one I found

in that closet. There were lots of them. Maybe fifty, although I couldn't bring myself to count them." She paused for a long moment. "More than half of them were dated after Mom met my dad. And I'd bet every one of those men knew she was married. So, yes, I know exactly the type of woman who would sleep with loser after loser, even when she had a good man at home. Because that woman was my mother."

# CHAPTER SEVENTEEN

*YOU'RE NOT GOING to wind up like your mother.*

Luke's words—a reaction to her unintended revelation—still echoed in her head two days after their encounter. Oh, the irony of hearing them while sprawled on the bed of a man she barely knew. And to have them spoken by a man who'd slept with more than his share of women.

But he'd shown her his scars. Ones he'd hidden from everyone else, evidently. And he'd told her his story. The urge had been there to take him in her arms and kiss all that hurt away, but she'd had a sense that he wouldn't welcome the gesture.

And it was hearing him talk about his fight to regain the use of his leg that had made her realize something terrible. Something that could shatter everything she thought she knew about herself.

She loved him. And it was the last thing she'd ever intended to do. She was here in London for such a short time. Luke's job was here, while hers was back in Memphis. Along with her dad and the rest of her life. She couldn't just pick up and move to England, even if he suddenly asked her to.

Not that he ever would. He'd never given her any indication that he felt something more than simple physical attraction where she was concerned. Yes, their time together had been exciting and crazy, and he turned her on like no man ever had. That was nothing to build a whole life around, though.

*But he showed you his scars.*

The argument continued to run circles around anything she put forth to counter it. It refused to be swayed or moved by anything she threw at it. And, boy, did she have a whole arsenal up her sleeve.

She fingered a bouquet of white roses in a cut-glass vase. They had arrived yesterday morning, along with a little note.

*Thanks for last night.*
*L.B.*

L.B. Luke Blackman.

She wasn't exactly sure what he was thanking her for. Sex? For allowing him to drag her home and participate in a very revealing show-and-tell session? Well, the latter hadn't been much of a hardship. The man was pure chiseled muscle. Yes, his leg and hip were terribly scarred, but those scars didn't take away from his sizzling masculinity. They simply brought him back down to earth. Close enough that she could touch him. All of him.

And, boy, had she ever. There'd been something heady…almost taboo about the experience. Maybe because she knew not many women—if any—had ever got to experience that degree of intimacy with him. And in all honesty he'd come on so strong during their other lovemaking sessions that she hadn't been able to catch her breath long enough to care about what she had and hadn't seen.

She sat down in a chair and gazed at the petals of the flowers in front of her.

Perfect. Just like that night had been.

There had been something intensely personal about her mouth surrounding him. That he hadn't expected it was obvious. His quick gasp of surprise, followed by a hand shoving deep into her hair and closing around the loose strands—and those razor-edged seconds when she'd wondered if he might use his grip to pull her away—had been followed by a raw groan of acceptance…and need. That memory was seared in her brain.

He'd let her take him. Had handed over the reins and allowed her to pleasure him in whatever way she wanted. And she had. She'd done everything she'd ever dreamed of doing.

A shiver went over her, her nipples puckering when her mind flashed through several graphic images in quick succession, like a seductive slide show.

*Whew.* It had been like a fantasy come true.

But that's all it was. A fantasy. She would be leaving soon. She'd been putting off booking her return flight. She wasn't sure why, but she was eventually going to have to face the fact that the fairy-tale visit had come to an end. She'd go back into hibernation and forget what had happened here.

She hoped.

Nick had called that morning and asked her to come over and look at plans for their nursery. It was hard to believe she was going to be a half sister.

She'd called the physical therapy department at the hospital and told them she wouldn't be coming in today. Laisse seemed disappointed, especially when Kate mentioned she might be leaving soon. The other woman encouraged her to think it over. They were currently swamped and could use the extra hands—her boss had even mentioned hiring an extra therapist. Laisse had half hoped it might be Kate. They were already checking into the certification requirements.

It was sweet of her, but how uncomfortable would that be, working at the same hospital as Luke? She had to imagine things would be strained, especially if she saw him going out with another nurse—or any other woman, for that matter.

No, it was probably better to just head home and lick her wounds in private, not that Luke had led her on in any way. Besides, her father needed her now more than ever. She made a mental to call Luke after she got back from Nick's.

She stood and went over to her suitcase, looking for something to wear. As happy as she was for Nick and Tiggy, she found herself having to work up some genuine enthusiasm for the outing. Because what she wanted more than anything was to hear that phone ring and have it be Luke asking her out. Asking her to consider staying for a while longer. But other than the flowers and Nick, that phone had been totally silent. And so had she. Even Nick had noticed her disappointment when it had been him calling and not Luke. But she'd put on her happy voice and said she'd be thrilled to come over. He'd seemed to accept it. Then again, he was probably lost in his own world right now with the baby and everything else.

Finally deciding on a pair of beige slacks and a green wrap top, she tossed the clothes on the bed and went to take a quick shower. She wrapped herself in a towel and applied her makeup with a careful hand, trying to control the slight tremor of doom that seemed to have come out of nowhere. A half hour later, she was dressed, with her hair blow-dried to fall straight around her shoulders.

Just as she picked up her purse, ready to head to the lobby, the bedside phone rang. Her heart pounded in her chest as she picked it up, which was ridiculous. It was probably just Nick, asking if she was on her way.

"Hello?"

"Ms. Bradley?"

She sighed when she recognized the voice of the lady from the hotel reception desk. "Yes?"

"Mr. Blackman is downstairs. Do you want me to send him up?"

He was here? At the hotel? She couldn't hold back a huge smile. How much better was this than a phone call?

Okay, so did she let him come up?

Absolutely not. She might be a glutton for punishment but she hoped she hadn't reached the masochist stage yet. "Would you mind telling him I'll be right down?"

"Certainly."

She dropped the phone back on its cradle and took one more quick glance in the mirror, exhilaration giving way to nerves. Well, it was now or never.

The elevator doors opened and Luke swallowed when Kate walked out. Her normally wavy hair was now straight, with just the slightest hint of curve at the ends. The top she wore skimmed her breasts, some kind of tie wrapping just beneath them, which she'd knotted at the side. Man, did his fingers itch to pull one end of that string and see what happened.

He pushed away from the counter and went over to greet her, keeping his hands by his sides.

"Thank you for the flowers," she blurted when he got close. "But there was no need."

"I thought there was." He kept his voice low enough that only she could hear. He'd wanted to give them to her in person—as an excuse to see her again—but she hadn't been at the hospital. He'd resisted the urge to come over after work last night. Then he'd got Nick's call, mentioning that Kate was coming over to look at the nursery and asking if he wanted to, as well. It had given him the perfect excuse to come to the hotel.

She searched his face, as if looking for something and not finding it. "I was just getting ready to go to Nick's."

"I thought you might be. I stopped to see if you might want a ride."

"You know about…?" She slung her purse over her shoulder and crossed her arms. "You're going to his house as well, aren't you?"

"He called this morning and asked if I'd like to."

An expression of wariness passed through her eyes that made his muscles tense up. Did she think he was just trying to sleep with her every chance he got?

His glance went to the tie on her shirt again and he tightened his lips. Okay, so even *he* wasn't sure of his motives. Not good. "Since I'm here, we may as well ride together."

"I guess so."

His lips curved. If he'd expected her to lunge for him the second she saw him and wrap her arms around his neck, he could pretty much bet that wasn't going to happen. But that was good, right? Because he had to somehow get across that he planned on retreating to his customary fallback position—casual acquaintances, where he hoped they could remain until she left to go back to the States.

Waiting until she'd buckled herself into the car seat, he turned the ignition key and eased onto the street in front of the hotel. She sat stiffly with her hands folded in her lap, fingers twined.

He pulled his attention back to the road. "So what did you do today? I didn't see you at the hospital."

"No. I decided to stick close to the hotel. Went for a run. Caught up on the news."

He frowned, hands tightening on the wheel. "That's right. I forgot you're a runner. Have you had any more problems with your admirer from last week?"

"Who…? Oh, the surfer-type guy? I think he's already checked out. And he wasn't my admirer."

"No, just someone who wanted to be your new jogging buddy." He couldn't quite keep the bitter acid from rising in his throat and coloring his words.

She turned sideways. "Luke, is something wrong? I'm not really sure why you came to pick me up. Just because we slept together it doesn't mean you have to send flowers or take me places. I get it. This is a temporary fling, and we both know it. I'm not pushing for more, if that's what you're afraid of."

"That's definitely not what I'm afraid of."

"Then what is it?"

He wrapped his hand around the knob of the stick shift, letting the lever slide between his index and middle fingers as he put the car into third gear. The act gave him time to consider his answer. "After we leave Nick's, I'd like to talk to you. Maybe before we get back to the hotel."

Her eyes grew wary. "That's not necessary. I think I can guess what this is about."

She really couldn't. Because even he didn't know exactly what he meant to say. All he knew was that for the past two days he'd been at war with himself. Part of him said this girl was something special and he'd better hang on to her. And that part of him was spoiling for a fight. Because the other part of him, the part that said she needed someone who could fight for her—literally—said he needed to limp away from her as fast as he could.

He'd already done something he'd never done with a woman before: let her see him in all his battered, twisted glory. And he still had no idea why. Not really. It had been a reaction to his child abuse patient, but looking back at it he realized how utterly stupid that reasoning was. Yes, he was hiding something, but he wasn't hurting anyone in the process, except maybe himself. And he'd been able to deal with it for the past ten years.

Hadn't he?

He shook off the thoughts and tried to answer her. "I don't want you to the get the wrong idea."

"Believe me, I'm not."

Okay, he was messing this up big time. "That's why I wanted to wait until we left Nick's. So we could sit and talk like rational human beings."

"I think I'm being perfectly rational. I never thought we were an item. Not once. So don't worry about it."

Well, good. He could relax now. So why did his spine feel like it had been replaced by a length of cold, hard pipe?

There was nothing he could do about it now, though, because they were about a block away from Nick's place. And they somehow needed to get through that visit without Nick figuring out something was wrong.

"Look. Let's just visit Nick, ooh and ahh over his kid's new digs and then get out of there."

Her lips curved, her frown disappearing. "'His kid's new digs'? You make it sound like they're outfitting a bachelor pad or something. The baby might be a girl."

A daughter. He could picture what Kate's little girl might look like, if she ever had one. Creamy blond hair, big blue eyes, a smattering of freckles across her nose. And he would no more be able to dance with her than he would with her mother. No father-daughter dances. No camping trips. No soccer games.

But there was one thing he seemed to be really good at: throwing himself the biggest damn pity party known to man. He'd always thought he'd dealt with his disability pretty well.

Until Kate had come along.

He pulled into Nick's garage with a grim determination that things were about to change. He was going to hunt down his soul's AWOL Zen master and put him back on active duty. With a reminder that he still had another fifty or so years of service before he received his discharge papers. And then he'd get his life back on track.

# CHAPTER EIGHTEEN

"It's going to be beautiful," Kate said, standing inside the empty room in Nick and Tiggy's house. On the wall were color swatches and myriad fabrics taped beneath various pictures.

She saw Nick and Luke give each other The Look, and knew they had no idea how she could tell enough to even offer an opinion. But she could. Soft green walls and muted cream carpeting would provide a backdrop to various pieces of oak furniture: solid changing table with attached dresser, a carved crib with matching green linens and bumper pads, a cream wallpaper border with images of pastel animals, just above the height of the crib's top rail.

"Isn't it? I think it'll be brilliant."

Kate moved farther into the room and studied a magazine picture of the crib.

"It converts into a toddler bed once the baby's outgrown it."

A pang of envy went through her. She was still young, but the future suddenly stretched ahead of her like a barren wasteland. What if she never met anyone she wanted to share her life with? She wanted children someday. But she didn't want to do it the way her mother had.

Although Kate wouldn't trade her adoptive father for anything. He'd given her love and a safe haven. And now she had a second father figure. Nick may not have been there during her formative years but it was obvious he wanted to be a part of her life now, even though it had been her who'd sought him out. She'd been angry at the time—at him, at her mother, at everyone. But she saw now how silly her attitude had been. Nick had had no say in the matter. He hadn't even known she'd existed.

Kate forced herself to look more closely at the picture. "The railings convert into a headboard and footboard?"

"Exactly." Tiggy brushed her hands over her stomach, her whole demeanor glowing and happy. "It's quite a clever system, actually. You'll have to help me with the arranging once everything arrives in a couple of weeks."

"Oh, uh…" She hadn't thought about how to tell them she'd decided to head back to the States soon. It was doubtful she'd still be in London when the furniture got there. "I'm sure you've already got it set up in your mind." She kept the words vague, not wanting to get into this kind of discussion in front of Luke.

"Some of it, yes. But I don't know where the rocker should go. Or if the changing table should go on the wall beneath the window or next to the crib." She glanced at the wall in question. "Where would you put it if you were outfitting a room for your baby?"

Her baby?

Against her will, her eyes slid to Luke's and she noticed a strange heat in his gaze as he stared back—pupils darkening. She swallowed, her mind racing like crazy through all the possibilities. Then Nick broke the spell with the suggestion that the two of them go off for a drink in the den. Once they were gone she allowed herself to sag against the wall, trying her best to make it look casual, even though her legs were shaking. The look Luke had given her had been almost proprietorial, as if any child she might conceive would belong to him as well.

She drew in a slow, careful breath. "I think you're right. I'd want to see the furniture first before I made any firm decisions. Maybe once it arrives you'll know immediately where all of it should go.

"Which is why I want you here." Tiggy smiled. "I don't think Nick quite knows what to make of all this."

Kate tried to deflect Tiggy's attention from dates and turn it back onto the subject of her husband. "He seems really happy."

"We both are, I think." She stared at the door through which Nick had disappeared. "He didn't want children for a long time, you know." She gave Kate a quick hug. "I'm so happy he'll have two now."

"Nick has been really nice about all of this."

"That's the type of man he is. I'm quite partial to him."

Tears pricked Kate's eyelids. Did Tiggy realize how fortunate she was to have found someone like Nick? She thought she probably did.

"Let's go into the kitchen and I'll brew us some tea." She paused. "Or would you rather have coffee?"

"Tea would be wonderful."

"I have black, but I'm trying to stick to herbal during my pregnancy. I do miss my breakfast tea, though."

Once the water was hot, they sat at a small dinette table. Kate tipped milk from a little pitcher into a delicate china teacup, while Tiggy stirred a bit of sugar into her herbal variety. "So how are you enjoying London?" she asked.

"It's a beautiful city. And I love the hospital." And not just the hospital. But now was not the time to think about that. Afraid that Tiggy was going to ask about a date again, she decided to change the subject. "How long did you and Nick know each other before you started dating?"

Tiggy laughed. "Well, that's quite a story. We were attracted from almost the first moment we laid eyes on each other."

The words released a storm in Kate's heart as she remembered the flames that had licked along her veins the first time she'd seen Luke. It hadn't been long afterward they'd wound up in that infamous supply closet.

"How about you? Any boyfriends back home?"

"No, I haven't really had time for one." Which, if Kate really thought about it, was a lie. She just hadn't met someone who was more important than her work. Until now.

And that person had made it perfectly clear he was not the settling-down type. He was right about one thing, though. She was not her mother. She couldn't have a love affair with Luke and then move on to the next man within weeks. She wasn't built like that—even if Luke was. She believed in long-term commitments that endured through the good and bad, whereas Luke didn't even want one that lasted through the good times.

Tiggy touched her hand from across the table. "Someday someone special is going to come along… and you'll know."

"It's a nice thought. But in reality that's not always how it works."

"Not always," Tiggy acknowledged. "And even when it does, a lot of work still has to go into the relationship."

Exactly.

Almost as soon as they finished their tea, Nick and Luke wandered into the room. Nick kissed the top of Tiggy's head, while Luke stood a short distance away, leaning against a nearby wall. She wondered if he was trying to keep some space between them or if his leg was bothering him. When he saw her looking at him, he raised his brows in challenge and purposely shifted his weight onto his injured leg.

*Oh, Luke. Haven't you realized you don't have to prove yourself to the world?*

"What are you girls talking about?" Nick asked his wife, pulling up a chair and dropping down beside her. He motioned Luke to do the same, but Luke gave a wave of his hand, signifying he was fine where he was.

Heaven forbid he come over and sit by her.

"We were talking about love and how you know when it's real."

A flash of panic shot through Kate's chest. She didn't want Luke to think they'd been talking about the two of them. "Correction. We were talking about how the two of *you* fell in love."

Nick twirled a piece of Tiggy's hair. "We did, didn't we?"

The couple smiled at each other.

Tiggy leaned against her husband's shoulder. "And now we have Kate, as well."

Her eyes went funny for a second, and she had to blink to clear them. The woman who could have slammed the door in her face and told her to never bother them again had instead opened her heart to Kate, as well as her home. She smiled. "Thank you. You both have been so kind. I'm lucky to have not just one wonderful father but two."

Nick leaned back in his chair and scrubbed a hand across the side of his jaw. "Thank you for that. I never dreamed..." He sighed. "Luke said he'd be able to change your mind about me. I'm grateful he was right."

Luke didn't move, but he shot her a glance from his position by the wall. *Bingo.* He knew exactly what his friend was referring to. And that look was one of pure, unadulterated guilt.

"I didn't do anything," he insisted. Kate wasn't sure if the words were directed at Nick or her.

"I didn't know you were modest, too."

"Nick." There was a warning note to his voice now.

Kate's whole body went numb with shock when she realized the implications.

All that time they'd spent together... Had it all been part of some plan—an attempt to gain her trust and sympathy?

Nick nodded. "You're right. It doesn't matter why she's giving me a chance, just that she is."

*Please don't say anything else. Either of you.*

Her stomach rebelled as she remembered Luke dragging her to his house and showing her his scars. How he'd given her that sob story about how Nick had saved his life...his leg. What she'd done afterward.

Oh, God. She was a bigger fool than she'd thought.

Luke owed Nick his life...he'd said it himself. He'd do anything for the man. Including sleep with his daughter? Or had that been just a little side benefit?

Her cheeks burned red-hot as the horrible realization grew and took root. Luke had been charming her in his bad-boy way and she'd lapped it right up like a cat with a bowl of cream.

Had it all been an act? Had he lied about knowing who she was as they'd drunk coffee together those first few days? He'd acted like she'd tricked him—that she'd used him to get what she wanted. Maybe it was the other way around. Maybe *she* was the one who'd been tricked.

Luke was watching her closely.

She didn't care. Didn't care what he thought she was thinking about. Maybe he was hoping to score again tonight. No way. If she hadn't been stranded she'd have got the hell out of there and driven back to the hotel, where she'd have the biggest boo-hoo session known to womankind. Then tomorrow she was going to pick herself up and book a flight—the first available—out of London, leaving it far behind.

Along with Luke.

Furious and sick inside, she put on a brave but very fake smile and leaned over to kiss Nick's cheek. "I didn't need coaxing from anyone to see what a good man you are. And I'm incredibly fortunate to have found you. I need to get back to my job in the States so I'll be leaving soon—maybe even tomorrow." She gulped back a sob. "But I'll call you. And I'll expect you to keep me posted on the baby. I want pictures of that nursery when it's finished, and—"

Tiggy interrupted her speech. "I thought you were considering staying for a while longer? At least, I hoped you were."

"I'm sure I'll be back someday." But not until her heart had scabbed over. "Maybe after the baby is born." And after Luke has left London.

"We'd love you to stay with us. We have another bedroom."

"Thank you." She pushed back from the table. "I

really need to get back to the hotel, so I'll get out of your hair."

"Are you sure?" Tiggy's voice sounded uneasy. Leave it to a woman to sense when something was wrong. Really wrong. "Can't you stay a while longer?"

Not unless they all wanted to see what a human fire hose looked like. Because she was going to lose it soon.

"No, I'm sorry. I can take a cab."

Luke took a step toward the table. "I'll take you. I have to go back that way, anyway."

The last thing she wanted to do was sit next to him in that tiny car and listen to him try to explain away Nick's words. But maybe he wouldn't even try.

As soon as he dropped her off, though, she was never going to see Luke Blackman again.

# CHAPTER NINETEEN

LUKE CURSED TO himself as he shifted the car into Reverse and backed out of the driveway.

He'd seen the moment her face had closed in on itself, her smile fading as she'd realized what Nick had been saying. It was true. He *had* offered to try to portray his friend in a good light—it's why he'd invited her to dinner that first time. But from that point on, what they'd done together had had nothing to do with Nick.

The need to set her straight burned in his chest, along with an explanation that hung on the tip of his tongue. She'd been horrified by Nick's words—humiliated that *he* might have become involved with her for that reason alone. It was why she'd suddenly decided to pick up and leave London tomorrow, he was sure of it. And that fact burned like bile in the back of his throat.

So why wasn't he turning to her and pleading for her to believe him when he said that sleeping with her had had nothing to do with any promise he'd made to Nick?

And yet he held himself still and kept it all inside him. Even as she gripped her hands tightly in her lap and stared out the windshield as if she was barely holding it together.

Wasn't it better this way? The only reason he'd shown her his scars had been because he'd known she was leaving. How much easier did it make things that she was flying out sooner than expected? And that she'd have no thoughts of coming back to pick up where they'd left off?

*Easier?* That wasn't the right word, because he wanted her to stay and he had no idea why.

Oh, he had an idea. A good one. But he wasn't about to admit it to himself or anyone else, because he couldn't do anything about it.

Seeing that muscular man standing next to Kate in the lobby of the hotel and seeing the healthy glow in her cheeks had been a game-changer for him. Much like the moment he'd realized that car-accident victim had been suffering from flail chest.

The terrain shifted along with his normal response reflexes.

With every other woman there'd been a gradual period of backing off. He'd slept with them a couple of times then he had suddenly been busier at work, offering to take on longer shifts. Not because he'd been an ass who hadn't been able to stick with any one woman but because he hadn't wanted to deal with the ramifications involved with being in a relationship. Or how his physical limitations might affect any children they might have. His lifestyle was something he'd come to accept, even if it wasn't something he'd label as ideal.

Anyway, his method of easing out of any potential relationships had worked until now. The woman in question either got tired of waiting—thinking his sudden lack of availability meant he was a workaholic who'd be the worst kind of husband imaginable—or she got the hint that he wasn't looking for anything lasting.

He was having a harder time selling that line to his heart right now. But deep inside he knew that allowing things to end right here was what he should do. Kate could have any guy in the world. *Any guy.* Why would she want to be with one who regularly tortured himself with thoughts of what he couldn't do?

Even if by some strange twist she did, the last thing Luke wanted was to be her pet project. To feel like every time he gave the slightest twinge of discomfort she was going to pull out all her tools and go to work on him. He wanted to be her equal, not another patient in a long line of patients. Because he'd end up hiding his pain, which would make him resentful of having to do just that. When he got home, all he wanted to do was relax and let his leg recover from the day's work.

The last thing he'd wanted to do, though, was hurt her. "Are you okay?"

She gave a soft laugh that was so devoid of humor it made him wince. "I will be once I get back in my own environment."

"About what Nick said…" He swallowed hard. "I'm sorry."

There. He'd done it. His apology wasn't meant to confirm Nick's assertion, but he knew Kate would take it that way. And he was going to let it stand.

"Don't be. I knew the score from the very beginning." They pulled up in front of her hotel. "I just never thought you were capable of stooping to that level."

"Kate—"

"Don't." She clicked her door open and stepped out onto the polished cobblestones. Giving him one last hard look, she said, "Goodbye, Luke."

The door slammed, and then she was walking away toward the entrance of the hotel. He shifted into Neutral and stepped on the parking brake, his chest tight and his body poised to get out of the car. Closing his eyes, he took a deep breath. And then another. Before he could change his mind he released the brake, put the car into gear and pulled out of the hotel entrance, knowing it was the last time he would ever see Kate Bradley. The pain was worse than anything he'd experienced with his leg. And there was absolutely nothing he could do to fix it.

Kate got off the plane in Memphis and found her dad there to meet her. The tears she'd banished for the past twenty-four hours suddenly resurfaced, and before she knew it she found her face buried against his familiar chest, his arms coming round her. The slight tremor from his Parkinson's just made her tears fall faster.

"Hey, kiddo. What's wrong?" The alarm in his voice was unmistakable.

She scrubbed her eyes with her forearm. "Just missed you, that's all."

Her dad cupped her chin and tipped it up, looking into her face. "You sure?"

"Yes." She pulled in a deep breath. It was time to leave what had happened in England behind her and get on with her life.

Had her mother's insides cramped each time she'd said goodbye to someone? Or had she just smiled and gone on her way?

Kate would never know the reasons she'd done what she had, but she knew her mother had loved her...just as she'd loved Tim Bradley.

She looped her arm around her dad's waist as she drew him away from the gate and toward the baggage claim area. Banishing the last of her tears, she said, "So how have you been? Have you kept up with your therapy?"

"I have. My doctor is going to try a new treatment regimen."

"That's wonderful. What is it?"

The next hour or so was spent giving her an update on his doctors' appointments and the medication he'd be taking in the near future. Kate forced her mind to absorb every word her father said, knowing that it would keep her from dwelling on things she couldn't change.

She'd half hoped she'd get to Heathrow airport to find Luke waiting for her, telling her she'd been all wrong about him. But his tight apology still rang in her ears, an indictment that had said he was indeed guilty of toying with her in order to plead Nick's case.

"Do you want to go out for dinner, or do you want to go straight home?"

She smiled. Her dad was one of the most selfless people she'd ever known, and she loved him dearly. "Can we do both? I need to shower and change, but I'd love to go out and hear all the news."

"Sure thing, pumpkin. And you can tell me how things went in London."

She'd tell him some of it, but not everything. She'd leave out the broken heart she was currently sporting. Neither would they discuss her mother and that shoebox.

He hadn't mentioned it. Maybe he—like Kate—realized it would do no good to dredge up the past and try to figure out what had gone on in her mother's mind. Her mom had indeed carried some secrets to the grave. Or had tried to. She had a feeling Luke would, as well. Would he ever show his scars to another woman?

Her stomach twisted. Did it matter?

If she was honest with herself, she'd say yes because, despite how much his deception had hurt, she really did wish him well. That meant being honest with himself and whoever he was involved with in the future. He needed to face his past and come to terms with it in order to have a shot at a normal life.

Just like she'd have to come to terms with him. And somehow...*somehow* figure out how to put him—and everything that had gone on between them—in the past, once and for all.

If one more person asked him where Kate was, he was going to blow a gasket.

Why would anyone assume he knew?

Maybe because he did?

He alone had seen the look on Kate's face. Knew what had run through her mind. He was the only one who knew what they'd done together.

And for that he would burn. No need to add any earthly voices to the damning mix.

He turned toward his latest inquisitor—Laisse from the physical therapy center—and pasted on a smile. One that hid the ache in his leg, which had grown over the course of the day. One week and counting, since she'd left. "From what I understood, she had to get back home to her job."

"I'm really disappointed she didn't at least come in to say goodbye. We'd talked about her staying at the center. I even thought she was considering it. She would have been a great addition."

She'd seriously thought about working in London? That dark pit in his heart grew a little larger. At least Nick had no idea what had happened, and he intended to keep it that way.

"I don't know anything about that." He knew his tone was short, not inviting her to share anything else about Kate's plans.

"Did you know she was leaving so soon? It's only been a couple of weeks."

The other woman fell into step beside him, and he forced a sigh of exasperation back down his throat. It had been a killer week, with three drug overdoses and a couple of kids who'd taken the family car for a joyride and ended up wrapping it around a streetlight. He didn't think he could handle much more. "She might have mentioned it."

In actuality, she hadn't mentioned much of anything during that car ride back to the hotel. He'd picked up the phone the next afternoon and dialed her number, out of morbid curiosity, but she'd already checked out.

Laisse wasn't the only who hadn't received a goodbye.

He brushed the woman off the best he could and made his way to the front entrance. Hell, why was he suddenly getting that homesick feeling again?

It had nothing to do with missing the United States, though, and everything to do with missing a certain throaty drawl that went straight to his gut.

Yeah, he missed her. So what? He'd missed plenty of women after they'd parted ways.

Hadn't he?

Or was it just Kate?

He stopped outside the double doors of the hospital and leaned against one of the brick entry columns, trying to gather his thoughts. Tonight just might be a drinking night.

That was one way to relieve the ache that went far beyond his mangled limb.

As he pushed off to make his way to his car, a silver coupé pulled up next to him. The passenger window powered down and there inside was the last person he wanted to see.

Nick.

"Thought you might feel like heading to a pub for a drink. Unless you have plans."

Plans. Not likely. He couldn't stomach the thought of going on a date—or anything else—with anyone other than Kate. And she was long gone.

"No plans."

"Great. Get in."

Luke opened the passenger door and slid inside the vehicle, stretching his sore leg out in front of him with a sigh. Felt good to get off it.

"Leg bothering you?"

"Not much. How about your back?"

"Hanging in there." He shifted the car into Drive with a laugh. "Will you look at us? Battered and bruised and neither willing to admit we're any different than we once were."

Luke grunted, but didn't answer. He'd admitted it all right. Each and every day. It was why he'd let Kate walk away, when what he'd really wanted to do was tell her that he...

No use thinking thoughts like that. So he changed the topic. "How's Tiggy doing?"

"Great. I'm one lucky SOB." He glanced over at him. "I heard from Kate a couple of days ago. Thought you might like to know."

The hand farthest from Nick slowly tightened into a fist as he tried to stop himself from demanding to know how she was doing...how she'd sounded over the phone...if she missed him at all. Instead, he said, "Oh?"

"Yep. She sounded kind of off."

"Off? In what way?" He forced his voice to remain

casual. He'd hoped against hope she'd get home and forget about him. Blow him off as some jerk who didn't deserve a second thought—just like the guy from the hotel. "Is her father okay? She said he was in the early stages of Parkinson's."

"Seems so strange to hear someone else being called her father, even though I know I don't have the right to think she might one day call me that."

"I got the idea the whole situation was kind of confusing."

"Her mother had other letters in that shoebox, did you know that?"

"Yes." Which made him feel like even more of a dick in not trying to explain that he'd been genuinely attracted to her. That the time they'd spent together had had nothing to do with any favor for Nick. "She told me."

Nick pulled over to the side of the road in front of a pub called The Grill. As Luke stepped on his leg, he realized he probably should have headed straight home. The car ride over had made the muscles stiff, and they were now protesting at being made to go back to work.

"Why aren't you using a cane?"

He tightened his jaw and forced his gait to steady back out. "Don't need one. Besides, patients aren't thrilled about seeing their doctor hobble around the E.R. with a walker."

It was Friday night and the place was hopping. Only these voices sounded animated and hopeful, not those of the beaten-down drunks he'd hoped to find. The last thing he wanted to do was find himself surrounded by revelers.

Because he had nothing to celebrate.

They ventured into the dim recesses of the place and

found a table right away, by some miracle. Luke looked at the drinks menu. He needed something strong. He could always leave his car at the hospital and take a cab back to his apartment.

"I'll have a whiskey, straight."

Nick went to the bar, returning with Luke's whiskey and a Perrier and a glass of ice for himself. When Luke frowned at him, he said, "Someone has to be the designated driver."

Suspicion flared in the back of his mind. What the hell? He'd thought his friend had been looking for a drinking partner.

"Tough day?" Nick leaned back in his seat. "Tiggy said you've been looking a little worse for the wear the last few days."

That's right. He'd noticed her pop by his wing a couple of times. She'd given a little wave and then she'd been off again. Nick's wife seemed pretty shrewd—had she figured something out? Like the fact that he and Kate had been a little more friendly than he'd tried to portray?

Luke tossed back his whiskey and swallowed, welcoming the heat as it burned its way down his esophagus and hit the floor of his stomach. "Now, what's this all about?"

Nick poured his water over the glass of ice and took a drink. "I wanted to ask you a question."

That's what he was afraid of. "Shoot."

"Okay. That night you and Kate came over to dinner I could have sworn there was something cozy going on between you."

"*Cozy.* That's a hell of a word."

"Better than the one that originally came to mind."

Yeah, it probably was. "She's an attractive woman. It'd be hard for any man not to notice."

"I'm assuming this went beyond 'noticing.'"

"Are you asking if I slept with her?"

The other man's jaw tightened. "I'm asking if you care about her."

The shot hit him right between the eyes. He could have fended off a question about his sex life, but this was his friend. Kate's father. A man who'd saved his life. He deserved the truth.

He took a second sip of his whiskey and tried to formulate words. "Yes, I cared about her. A little more than I probably should have."

"How so?"

"I let things go further than I should have, let's just put it that way."

"But not so far that she felt the need to stay."

Luke smiled. "She thinks it was all a set-up, remember? That I did it to beef up your image."

"Damn. That's what I was afraid of." Nick propped his arms on the table in front of him. "I'll call her and set her straight."

"No. Don't. It's better this way."

"You said you cared about her." Nick's eyes zeroed in on his face.

"That doesn't mean I want her to come back over here expecting something I can't give her."

"Like what?"

"A ring. A chance for a normal life." That's exactly what he wanted to do. But it was impossible.

"Normal meaning..."

Luke pushed back in his seat with a rough laugh. "Meaning a guy who can keep up with her." He paused, not sure exactly how to make Nick understand. "She runs for fun, Nick. She's young and healthy. Strong."

"And you aren't all those things?"

"I can barely walk at times, much less run. I don't want Kate—or anyone—having to deal with me on one of my bad days. Don't want her sitting home because I can't run or hike…or even friggin' dance with her."

He slugged back the rest of his drink and thumped the glass onto the table. "We came on a car accident after we went out to dinner one night, and I couldn't even drag one of the victims out of the car. I had to ask for help. What if that victim had been Kate?"

Nick's face tightened, his brows coming together. "You know, before I had my surgery, I felt the same way. Didn't want Tiggy saddled with me if things took a turn for the worse and I ended up in a wheelchair."

"But you didn't wind up in one."

"No, but I almost ruined my life by coming up with all kinds of depressing outcomes—none of which were based on reality."

"That's where you and I are different, Nick. Because my depressing outcome is very real. This leg is never going to get any better."

"And yet you're a doctor. A damn good one, from what I've seen. Your patients don't need you to jump hurdles or play hopscotch. And neither does Kate. At least, not the Kate that I got to know over the last couple of weeks. She cares about you, too. I could see it. Saw the way you smiled each other. Tiggy noticed it, as well."

Great, it seemed like the whole world knew his secret, including Laisse and some of the others at the hospital. Maybe it was time to own up to it. At least to himself.

He loved the woman. He had no idea when it had happened or why. But he did. It's why he'd had to let her go.

"She's gone. So there's your answer."

"I think she left *because* she cared. I didn't even realize it until you two were at the house and she got this funny look on her face when I mentioned our little agreement." His hand wrapped around his glass in a fist. "I've kicked myself so many times for saying that in front of her. But it just came out, and once it was said, there was no way to take it back."

"You didn't mess anything up. I just couldn't see any future for us."

"Because you're a damn fool. Just like I almost was." Nick leaned forward. "If you don't try to make this right, I think you'll regret it."

Maybe.

His friend sighed. "Don't make me regret fighting to save your leg that day. There were other men who weren't so lucky. You think they don't deserve a shot at happiness? You think the married ones should leave their wives and go off and live in a cave somewhere?"

Anger flared in his chest. "Of course not, but this is not the same."

"You're right. It's not." Nick slid his glass to the side and got as close to being in Luke's face as he could with a table between them. "You're a whole lot better off than some of the men I worked on. So maybe it's time you stopped feeling so damned sorry for yourself and started living your life…before it's too late. Before you lose a whole lot more than a chunk of your leg."

Luke's anger morphed into fury. "Back off, Nick. This is none of your business."

"Like hell it's not. Kate is my daughter." He leaned

back with a sigh and dug out his wallet, tossing a couple of bills onto the table. "I can't tell you what to do. But I'm asking you to think about it. Don't throw away something good—someone you care about—just because you're afraid of what the future might hold. You never know, Luke. It might just hold something pretty damn terrific."

# CHAPTER TWENTY

*IN THROUGH THE NOSE, out through the mouth.*

The incline on the hill was a killer, but Kate forced herself to power through—she was now past the three-mile mark. She pulled deep breaths in and blew them out in a rhythmic cycle that could hold the world at bay just a little while longer. A classic rock band pumped through her ear buds and kept her company, the lead singer whining about being done wrong by a lover.

Been there. Done that.

She'd constantly wanted to call Luke over the past two weeks. And tell him what? That she was coming back to England? That she'd take him any way she could get him?

No, she respected herself more than that. Nick had called a few days ago, saying he hoped she hadn't gotten the wrong idea about what he'd said on her last night in London.

Nope, she hadn't. In fact, he'd saved her from making a fool of herself. If Luke had wanted her, he'd have said something to try to make her stay. Instead, that car had been filled with silence. And it had spoken loudly enough to get his point across.

*In through the nose. Out through the mouth.*

Her normal jogging route was busy today, full of

businesspeople all hoping to burn off a few extra calories before the start of a new week. Kate's reasons for running had nothing to do with calories and everything to do with pain management.

She cleared the ridge of the hill and shortened her strides as she started down the other side.

Up ahead, along the left-hand side of the trail, she spied someone on one of the benches dotted along the running path. A cane was propped against the seat next to the man and his right leg was stretched out in front of him.

Strange.

Although the trail was paved with a fresh coat of asphalt, the five-mile track didn't usually attract anyone other than power walkers and joggers because it ran next to a canal and was flanked by woods on both sides. Her eyes clipped to the left as she passed the bench, and the air stuttered from her lungs. She ran a couple more steps before she faltered, her mind whirling. She stopped and swiped at a trickle of sweat on her temple, struggling to make sense of what she'd just seen.

That couldn't have been…

No. It couldn't.

She geared herself up to take off again, forcing herself not to look back, not to invite the crush of disappointment that would surely follow.

And then she heard her name.

Low. Familiar.

Unmistakable.

She turned round slowly, swallowing when she saw the man was on his feet, cane in hand.

Luke.

But how? Why?

She tried to say something but could think of nothing

that would explain his sudden appearance in Memphis. On *her* jogging trail.

And Luke didn't use a cane.

Or he hadn't. Had something happened?

She closed the space between them, still trying to catch her breath. "What's wrong? Your leg, is it—?"

"It's fine."

She plopped down on the bench, her muscles suddenly too shaky to support her weight. Luke eased down beside her, resting the cane between his legs.

Maybe she was suffering from oxygen deprivation or something. "You're supposed to be in London."

"I'm taking some time off."

Okay. That explained why he was in the States but not why he was *here*.

"Are you originally from Memphis?" She felt totally lost. Totally out of her element.

"Nope. Chicago." He flashed her a smile that made her insides warm.

He wasn't here to return her panties, because those had been given back ages ago. "You're going to have to help me out a little here, Luke. I'm not sure… Why are you in Memphis?"

"I came to find you."

He had? "But why?"

"To tell you Nick was wrong." His fingertips gripped the cane, turning it slightly before his eyes came up to meet hers. "I did agree to talk to you for him, but that had nothing to do with what went on between you and me."

"It—it didn't?" This was exactly what she'd wanted him to say that last night. And yet he hadn't. So why now?

"I should have said something as soon as we got

into the car, but it just seemed easier to let you think the worst of me."

"Because you didn't want to give me any reason to stay." The truth stole the air from her lungs, much like that proverbial wall that runners hit halfway through a marathon. And it hurt. Lord, how it hurt.

"No. I didn't want you to stay." He shifted in his seat until he actually faced her, his gaze trailing over her face. "It was stupid and cowardly. And I'm not proud of letting you leave like that. I want to try to set things straight."

He'd come an awful long way just to do that.

"Okay. But I—"

"I'm not quite finished." His chest rose as he took a deep breath. "I also want to ask you to give me another chance. To come back to London with me."

Her mouth popped open and she stared at him. She slicked some loose strands of hair back from her face, suddenly very aware that her green T-shirt was sweat-soaked and she was a mess. "What?"

"Nick seems to think you might care about me. And I know I care about you." He dragged a hand through his hair. "Hell, that's not what I want to say. I *love* you, dammit. I want you with me."

Despite the shock rolling through her system, his rough words made her smile. They were about as far from the cool, seductive lover she'd known in London as they could get. As was the cane.

She sidestepped his shocking statement, needing time to think. "Why are you using a cane, if your leg is okay?"

"Because I've finally accepted that I need it. I don't use it at work, but it takes some of the strain off at home." He smiled. "And it's a big help when walking up crazy hills along a jogging path."

That's right. She was at the three-mile mark, which meant Luke had walked almost two miles to get where he was.

As if reading her mind, he nodded. "I was going to keep walking until I found you but realized my leg wasn't going to make it any further." His smile faded. "That's another thing. Even if you agree to give me another chance, you need to know my leg will never be any better than it is right now."

"I'm not sure why that's even…" Her heart flipped in her chest, her eyes filling with tears. "You think I care about your leg?"

"I can't run with you, Kate. And I want to. More than anything." His voice turned gravelly in a way that tore at her insides.

"I never wanted you for a running partner. Never." She cupped his face and leaned in so he could see the truth in her eyes. "I love you. I do. Everything about you. Including your leg."

Luke dragged her to him, his mouth covering hers in an instant. His long fiery kiss had none of his usual smoothness. It was rough and raw—just like his words had been—and she couldn't get enough. Because *this* was Luke. The real Luke, full of insecurities and despair…and capable of happiness, just like any other human being. He was just a man.

She vaguely heard his cane clattering to the ground, but she wrapped her arms around his neck and held him to her, afraid that if she let him go, she'd find he wasn't here at all. The breath she'd just finished catching was off and running all over again, but this time she didn't care. All she wanted was this man...this crazy mixed-up—

"Get a room!" The half-amused yell came from the trail next to them, and she pulled her head back slightly, while keeping her arms around Luke's neck. A young man had just run by them, his long strides carrying him on down the trail and out of sight as he turned a corner.

"I think he wants us to get a room," she whispered, as she turned back toward Luke

He grinned. "And what about you, Kate? Is that what you want?" She heard the question loud and clear, and her heart sang in her chest.

She leaned forward and kissed him again. "I don't want just a room. I want the whole house."

His breath left his lips on a sigh. "You've got it. Anything you want."

"In that case, I'll call my dad and let him know I'll be out for a while."

"Your dad already knows, I think. I called him and explained the situation. He told me where I could find you."

"In that case, I know a little place we can be alone."

Luke picked up his cane and climbed to his feet. "We'd better get started, then. It'll take me a while to get back down the path."

"There's no hurry." She took his free hand in hers. "We've got all the time in the world."

# EPILOGUE

"She's beautiful." Kate's voice held a note of awe as she gazed down at the newborn in her arms, daring to stroke a tiny hand.

Luke perched on the arm of the chair his fiancée currently occupied. "Yes, she is." He dropped a kiss on her head. "You're going to have to give her back, though."

"I know. I can hardly believe I have a little sister."

That was easy for Luke to believe. What was harder was that the smart, beautiful woman next to him had actually agreed to marry him—on his first proposal, even though he'd been prepared to ask her over and over again, if necessary. As long as it took to convince her that he loved her.

He'd offered to practice medicine back in the States but Kate had wanted to come back with him so he could finish out his year at the hospital in London. And as a side benefit he got to see her any time he wanted to as she was working in the physical therapy center.

They'd both been asked to stay on at the hospital when his term ended, and Luke wasn't sure what they were going to do. He would leave that up to Kate. She had her father's Parkinson's to think of. The new regimen of medicine had slowed the progress of the disease but until a cure could be found, it was always there—waiting in the wings.

Luke didn't care where they ended up, as long as they were together.

He eyed the cane propped on the chair next to him with a rueful smile. Who would have guessed that, instead of making his leg weaker, it had made it more tolerant of work? He got through his day without it for the most part, but it allowed his remaining muscles to recuperate between shifts. Kate—putting on her PT hat—had said it was similar to a runner sitting out a day or two in order to let the stressed muscle fibers regenerate. The strategies that worked for her worked for him, as well.

Although he didn't run with her, he did go to the park and sit on a bench, enjoying the sight of her lithe frame as she powered past him and blew him a kiss. And sometimes there was a special reward for him when they got back home to his apartment—when she'd let him slowly peel off her sweaty workout gear and join her in the shower.

Something he'd better not think about right now. Especially not with a baby in the room.

The door to the restroom opened and Nick and Tiggy came out, the new mother wheeling her IV stand along with her. She looked good, a lot better than twelve hours ago, when the obstetrician—a worried frown between his brows—had ordered an emergency C-section, saying the baby's heart rate was slowing down too much. It had been a good call because the cord had been wrapped around the infant's neck, each contraction tightening it and reducing the baby's blood flow.

Tiggy glanced over at them, bent slightly at the waist

to keep pressure off her sutures. "Ugh. That was not fun. Thanks for holding her for me."

"I told you we needed to wait for a nurse," Nick chided softly.

"I *am* a nurse. Besides, there are two doctors right here in the room."

Nick helped her settle back in her bed with an amused sigh. "The longer they keep you, the better."

"Oh, no. I'm ready to leave. I have a wedding to plan."

Kate stood and carried the baby over to her, gently placing the child in her arms. "The wedding is still four months away. You'll be exhausted for the next couple of months so you need to take it easy."

"She's going to be a good baby, aren't you, love?" She gazed down at the baby with adoration. They'd named her Poppy, in honor of fallen soldiers everywhere.

"Well, we'd better let you get some rest." Kate stood and held her hand out for Luke, who ignored it, wrapping his left arm around her waist instead and tugging her close.

Nick grinned. "Thank you for coming. It means a lot to both of us."

"I wouldn't have missed it. Besides, this is where I belong." She wrapped her arms around Luke's waist and returned his squeeze with a smile.

Picking up his cane, he put it to the floor and took a step toward the door. Kate matched his pace perfectly, trying neither to push him forward nor slow him down. His hand relished the warm, solid feel of the wood beneath his hand. Kate had bought him a fancy carved cane in the States with a secret engraving beneath the handle that no one knew about but them: *Luke ♥s Kate*.

Truer words had never been written.

Who would have thought what he'd deemed a sign of weakness had actually become a symbol of strength? Because it was only after he'd accepted his limitations that he'd been able to open himself up to true and lasting happiness. And been free to embrace it.

With a woman who was strong and courageous enough for both of them.

* * * * *

# She's loved and lost — will she ever learn to open her heart again?

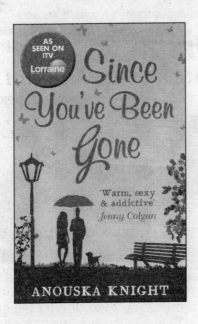

From the winner of ITV Lorraine's Racy Reads, Anouska Knight, comes a heart-warming tale of love, loss and confectionery.

**'The perfect summer read — warm, sexy and addictive!'**
—Jenny Colgan

For exclusive content visit:
**www.millsandboon.co.uk/anouskaknight**

  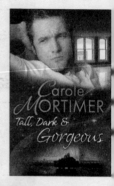